Moses

A Lost Egyptian Account of the Exodus

Book Two of the Moses Trilogy

by

Mechiel Pentz

A historical novel informed by the Biblical Lunar-Solar
Chronology

Confirmation

What if the man who once ruled Egypt never surrendered its divine authority?

In this gripping second volume of the *Moses* trilogy, the discovery of Menkheperre's hidden chamber shakes the foundations of accepted history. As Egyptologist Arthur Maddison races to preserve what remains, he finds evidence of a deeper struggle—one not just for power, but for the royal *Ka*, the sacred essence of kingship believed to pass from Pharaoh to Pharaoh.

Menkheperre, son of Thutmose III, claimed the *Ka* was never his to inherit. Instead, he believed it had passed to one man: the exiled Moses. But Moses never declared it. He never needed to.

Now, as plagues descend and power shifts, the line between prophet and king begins to blur.

Moses - A Lost Egyptian Account of the Exodus continues the thrilling journey through lost history, spiritual conflict, and a legacy that could rewrite the fate of empires.

Moses - A Lost Egyptian Account of the Exodus

(A historical novel informed by the Biblical Lunar-Solar Chronology)

© 2025 Mechiel Pentz

This is a work of historical fiction. While based on real historical and biblical events, many conversations, emotions, and interpretations have been fictionalized for narrative depth.

All ancient Egyptian rulers and Old Testament figures mentioned are historical persons, and their names are used deliberately in line with the historical record.

Any modern-day characters, locations, or events depicted in the story are entirely fictional. Any resemblance to real persons, living or dead, is purely coincidental or creatively imagined.

First Edition

ISBN: (Paperback): 978-1-7641625-7-9

Cover design by Mechiel Pentz

To contact the author or learn more, email:
mapenprojects@gmail.com

Table of Content

"To the oppressed who remembered their name, and the kings who feared it."

— M.P.

Then the LORD said to Moses, "See, I have made you like God to Pharaoh, and your brother Aaron will be your prophet.

— Exodus 7:1

Preface

There are truths too dangerous for kings to record—and too powerful for time to erase.

When I stepped into the sealed chamber beneath the monastery in Luxor, I believed I had found a historical anomaly. Instead, I uncovered a legacy that whispers of forgotten heirs, a royal secret, and a spiritual inheritance unlike anything I had studied before.

An obscure prince, Menkheperre, believed the royal *Ka*—the essence of divine kingship—passed from one man to another. But even he questioned the one who may have carried it.

This is not just a story of Egypt's past. It is the story of a question that refuses to stay buried.

Arthur Maddison

Chapter 1 - Missing in Egypt

2011: Trapped in Luxor

Professor Arthur Maddison paced the confines of the small flat in central Luxor, each measured step wearing a path in the threadbare Persian carpet. The four walls seemed to close in with each passing hour, the ceiling fan stirring the hot air without cooling it. Outside, beyond these suffocating confines, the ancient city burned with revolutionary fury.

The acrid smell of smoke seeped through the closed windows despite his best efforts to seal them with damp towels. It carried with it the unmistakable scent of burning rubber, melting plastic, and something else—the pungent odor of a civilization in violent transition. February in Egypt was supposed to be pleasant—mild and dry—but the heat from the fires raging across the city made the small apartment stifling.

Sweat trickled down Maddison's spine, dampening his once-crisp Oxford shirt that now clung to his lean frame. At sixty-two, his body remained wiry and strong from decades of archaeological fieldwork, though his face had weathered into a map of fine lines that deepened with his current anxiety. His silver hair, usually neatly combed, now stood in disarray from his habit of running agitated fingers through it.

He moved to the window, carefully peeling back the edge of the heavy damask curtain. The streets below were chaos—angry mobs surging like floodwaters through narrow alleys, burning vehicles sending plumes of black smoke into the twilight sky, occasional bursts of gunfire that made his heart lurch painfully against his ribs.

The monastery where he and Bishop Farouk had made their extraordinary discovery was in one of the hardest-hit areas, visible only as a distant silhouette against the orange glow of flames. Was it still standing? Had the hidden chamber survived? All those inscriptions—potentially world-changing evidence—lost to the flames of revolution.

"Three thousand years of history," he whispered to the empty room, "and we might be the first to truly understand it... if it survives this madness."

Three days trapped in this flat, with dwindling supplies and no word from Farouk since their desperate escape. The bishop had promised to return when it was safe, his dark eyes intense with a mixture of fear and exhilaration as they'd parted. "Trust no one until I return, Arthur," Farouk had said, gripping his shoulder with surprising strength. "What we've found will rewrite history—or be buried forever if the wrong people learn of it first."

A sudden explosion nearby rattled the windows. Maddison flinched violently, his elbow knocking over a glass of water that spread across his meticulously annotated papers. He scrambled to save them, blotting the pages with his handkerchief.

The Victorian elevator—a relic of 19th-century exploration—leading to that untouched chamber that had somehow remained sealed despite centuries of tomb robbers and archaeological expeditions. The inscriptions that contradicted everything historians believed about that period, the artifacts arranged with deliberate symbolic purpose. If he could just get back there, document everything properly...

The Call to London

In the fading light, he stared at the satellite phone—the only reliable means of communication with the outside world. His fingers hovered over it momentarily before he picked it up with sudden resolve.

"Harrington-Price Associates, this is Emma speaking."

The crisp, professional voice of his secretary was like a lifeline from another world. Maddison closed his eyes briefly, imagining the orderly calm of his London office—the smell of old books and leather chairs, the gentle patter of rain against leaded windows. "Emma, it's Professor Maddison."

The sharp intake of breath told him everything about her state of mind. Emma Harrington was not given to displays of emotion; her

Yorkshire upbringing having instilled in her a stoicism that matched his own reserved nature.

"Professor! Thank God! We've been trying to reach you for days. The department is in an uproar. Are you alright? Where are you?"

Maddison hesitated, his gaze drifting to the window where the orange glow of fires cast dancing shadows. The fewer people who knew his exact whereabouts, the better.

"I'm quite alright, Emma. Just experiencing some... technical difficulties with communications."

"Professor, we've seen the news. Egypt is in chaos. There are riots, fires—people are being killed! Please tell me you're not still there."

"I'm perfectly safe, I assure you," he said, sidestepping her question. "Just checking in to let you know there's no need for concern. I expect to be back in London within two weeks."

"But where exactly are you, Professor? The department's been asking questions. Your lectures have been reassigned. Dr. Reynolds has been calling hourly for updates."

"Has he now?" Maddison's tone cooled several degrees. Reynolds had always been too interested in his research, always hovering at the edges of his discoveries like a vulture. "Well, you can tell Reynolds that I'm continuing my research and will provide a full report upon my return."

The long silence spoke volumes about her dissatisfaction with his answer.

"Your laptop was found, Professor," she said finally. "In Alexandria. The police contacted the university yesterday."

Maddison felt a flicker of concern, though the laptop contained nothing about his recent discovery—just routine research notes and correspondence. Still, it could be used to trace his movements.

"I see. Well, these things happen. Just routine academic work on it anyway."

"Professor, there's something you should know about Dr. Reynolds. He's been—"

But Maddison had already ended the call. If they'd found his laptop in Alexandria, they could trace his movements to Luxor—which might actually prove helpful if he needed rescue later. And if Reynolds was asking questions...

Embassy Inquiries

Emma Harrington replaced the receiver with a trembling hand. She looked across the office to where James Porter, the department's administrative assistant, was watching her with undisguised concern.

"That was him?" James asked, moving to perch on the edge of her desk.

Emma nodded, her brow furrowed. "He wouldn't say where he is. Something's wrong, James. I can hear it in his voice."

After navigating a labyrinth of bureaucratic transfers, Emma was connected to the British Embassy in Cairo.

"My name is Emma Harrington. I'm calling about Professor Arthur Maddison of King's College London. We believe he may be in danger somewhere in Egypt."

The embassy official sounded weary, his voice carrying the strain of someone dealing with dozens of similar calls as British nationals sought evacuation from the unrest.

"When was your last contact with Professor Maddison, Ms. Harrington?"

"Just this morning. But he refused to disclose his location and seemed... not himself. This is completely out of character for him." Emma's fingers tightened around the receiver. "There's also the matter of his stolen laptop."

"I see Professor Maddison entered Egypt three weeks ago. His last known location was Alexandria, according to hotel records."

"Yes, that's where his laptop was found. He was supposed to be conducting research in the Bibliotheca Alexandrina, then returning to London."

"Thank you for this information, Ms. Harrington. We've recovered Professor Maddison's computer from local authorities in Alexandria. We'll look into Professor Maddison's whereabouts as a matter of priority.

Alexandria Investigation

In Alexandria, British Embassy security officer Richard Blackwood sat across from Hosni Nassar, the thin, nervous man who had turned in the laptop. Blackwood had the weathered look of someone who had spent too many years in harsh climates—skin tanned like old leather, blue eyes sharp beneath sandy brows.

"Thank you for agreeing to speak with me, Mr. Nassar," Blackwood said in fluent Arabic. "I understand you're the one who turned in the laptop belonging to Professor Maddison."

Nassar nodded quickly, his eyes darting nervously. "I found it. On the street."

Blackwood smiled thinly. "Mr. Nassar, we both know that's not true. The hotel's security cameras show you entering the professor's room disguised as housekeeping staff."

Nassar's shoulders slumped. "I did not hurt the professor. I swear it by Allah. He was not even there when I took the computer."

"Where was he?"

"I don't know. Out. The room was empty."

Hotel Villa Jolie

At the Hotel Villa Jolie, Blackwood and his Egyptian liaison, Amara Khalil, spoke with the elderly doorman who remembered Professor Maddison's departure.

"Yes, I remember the English professor," the doorman said. "He left very early in the morning. There was another man with him. Egyptian, but dressed like a foreigner—Western clothes, expensive watch. A religious man."

"How do you know he was religious?"

The doorman tapped his own collar. "He wore the collar of a Christian priest, but not Catholic. Coptic, I think. He spoke to the professor in English, but I heard him give directions to the taxi driver in perfect Arabic—Upper Egypt. Luxor or Aswan, perhaps."

"Did you overhear anything?"

The doorman closed his eyes, searching through decades of memories. "He said, 'We found it in Thebes.' The professor looked at him sharply when he said this, like he should not have spoken of it. Then they got into a taxi and left."

"Thebes," Blackwood repeated, exchanging a glance with Amara. The ancient name for Luxor.

"In my fifty years at this hotel, I have seen many archaeologists come and go," the doorman continued. "Most are like children, eager to show their new toys. This one—he was different. He had the look of a man who has found something he almost wishes he hadn't."

As they left the hotel, Blackwood's satellite phone rang.

"Rich, we've got a problem," came his superior's tense voice. "The Times just ran a story online about Professor Maddison. It's already being picked up by other outlets."

Blackwood opened the message to find a screenshot: FAMOUS EGYPTOLOGIST ARTHUR MADDISON DISAPPEARS IN EGYPT.

"How did this leak?"

"The university press office received inquiries from reporters after Maddison missed a scheduled lecture series."

"This complicates things," Blackwood said, showing the screen to Amara. "If he's in hiding, this will flush him out. If he's been kidnapped..."

"The price just went up," Amara finished grimly.

Return to the Chamber

The knock at Maddison's door came at exactly nine that evening—three sharp raps he recognized as Farouk's signature. He opened the door to find the bishop looking haggard but alert, his normally immaculate beard untrimmed, dark circles beneath his eyes, dressed in civilian clothes.

"Quickly," Farouk said, his voice barely above a whisper. "There is a curfew. We must move fast."

Maddison shouldered his bag and followed Farouk down the building's back stairs to where a dusty sedan waited, engine idling.

"Your injury?" Maddison asked, noting the bishop's slight limp as they slipped into the car.

"Nothing serious," Farouk replied dismissively, putting the car in gear. "A souvenir from our escape. What matters is what we have discovered."

They drove through darkened streets, a city transformed by violence. Buildings that had once been bustling shops were now burnt-out shells, their windows gaping like empty eye sockets. Farouk navigated around military checkpoints through back streets and alleys.

"I feared you might not return," Maddison said finally.

Farouk's hands tightened on the steering wheel. "There were... complications. The monastery suffered damage, but not as extensive as I feared. The chamber remains untouched, as far as we can tell."

"There have been inquiries about you," Farouk continued. "Men asking questions in the markets, at hotels. Europeans, but not tourists. They carry themselves like soldiers, though they wear no uniforms."

"Embassy personnel, perhaps," Maddison suggested.

"Perhaps. But they seemed particularly interested in what you might have found, not just your whereabouts. They asked about ancient texts, about hidden chambers."

They arrived at the monastery at ten that night—the same time Blackwood arrived at Maddison's abandoned flat, their paths crossing like ships in the night. The monastery rose from the darkness like a fortress, its ancient stone walls scarred but standing.

Farouk led Maddison through a side entrance and down familiar corridors to the guesthouse. The room was untouched by fire, though dust covered everything like a shroud.

"The brothers focused their efforts on saving the chapel and ancient manuscripts," Farouk explained. "This area was... less of a priority."

Maddison moved to the passage door that opened to the Victorian elevator shaft, his hands caressing the mechanism with the tenderness of a lover. The descent was slower than before, the mechanism occasionally making alarming grinding noises, but eventually the elevator settled at the bottom.

Inside, the main chamber was exactly as they had left it—a vast rectangular space with walls covered in hieroglyphs that seemed to move in the lantern light, the elaborate relief carving that had so captivated Maddison.

"Let's begin where we left off," Maddison said, moving purposefully toward the relief. His exhaustion had vanished, replaced by the singular focus that had driven him across continents and decades of scholarly pursuit.

Hours passed in focused work, the outside world temporarily forgotten in the timeless space beneath the desert. Maddison felt fully alive again, immersed in the puzzle that had drawn him to Egypt—the mysterious connection between pharaonic Egypt and the early Hebrews.

"Look at this," he called to Farouk, pointing to a series of hieroglyphs below Hatshepsut's cartouche. "The date Hatshepsut became king and the decree she made against the Israelites."

"The implications are... significant," Farouk said, his voice neutral but his eyes blazing. "Many will resist such evidence. It threatens too many established positions."

But resistance didn't matter now. The truth was here, carved in stone that had survived empires and revolutions alike. And he, Arthur Maddison, would be the one to reveal this to the world, to bridge the gap between faiths and histories that had seemed irreconcilable. If he survived the night, if they escaped the violence above, his name would echo through the corridors of academia forever.

Chapter 2 - The Coronation

1473 BC–Thebes, The Ceremony

The Great Hall of Amun-Ra blazed with the light of a thousand oil lamps, their golden flames dancing like restless spirits across walls that had stood since the dawn of Egyptian civilization. The hieroglyphs carved into the massive sandstone blocks seemed to undulate in the flickering light—ancient words recording the deeds of dynasties of pharaohs, all men, all born to rule by divine right. Now those silent witnesses would record something unprecedented: the coronation of a woman who dared to claim not the title of Queen, but of King.

Four hundred of Egypt's elite pressed against the polished limestone walls, a living tapestry of power and privilege. Nobles from the fertile Delta to the First Cataract stood in precise formation according to rank, their elaborate wigs freshly dressed, bodies gleaming with scented oils that had traveled thousands of miles along trade routes Hatshepsut herself had reopened. Priests of every major cult—their shaven heads reflecting the lamplight like polished ivory—gathered in solemn clusters, whispering prayers or perhaps plotting alliances, depending on which gods they served, and which mortals paid their temple tributes. The air hung heavy with competing scents: blue lotus blooms floated in alabaster bowls, releasing their narcotic fragrance; kyphi incense smoldered in golden censers, its sacred smoke spiraling toward the heavens carrying prayers to the gods; and beneath it all, the earthy musk of bodies anointed with moringa oil and perfumes distilled from lilies cultivated in temple gardens.

Hatshepsut herself had spent hours in preparation, sequestered in her chambers as attendants transformed the daughter of Thutmose I into a living incarnation of Horus. Her slender body had been scrubbed with natron and honey, then rubbed with oils until her copper skin gleamed like polished bronze. Kohl darkened her eyes, malachite powder shadowed her lids, and red ochre stained her lips—not the cosmetics of seduction, but the sacred markings of divine kingship.

Now she waited in an antechamber, breathing deeply as she had been taught by her childhood tutor—a technique to master fear, to project the unshakable confidence expected of one born to rule. The false beard that would mark her as king felt alien against her skin, but she had practiced wearing it for months in secret, until it became merely another element of the elaborate costume of power.

"It is time, Great One," whispered a eunuch attendant, his eyes downcast in deference.

Hatshepsut nodded once, sharply. She had waited for this moment through years of careful manipulation, strategic marriages, and ruthless elimination of obstacles. She would not show hesitation now.

In the Great Hall, Hapuseneb, the High Priest of Amun, raised his arms toward the vaulted ceiling in a gesture that commanded immediate silence. He was a man of imposing stature, with shoulders broad enough to suggest the strength of his peasant ancestors, though his hands had grown soft with decades of temple luxury. The magnificent pectoral adorning his chest—forty pounds of gold and lapis lazuli—caught the lamplight like a fragment of starry sky torn from the heavens. Its weight would have crippled a lesser man, but Hapuseneb wore it with practiced dignity, understanding that such displays were the tangible symbols of power that common people understood.

"The moment of manifestation is upon us!" His voice boomed across the vast chamber, trained through decades of temple rituals to reach the farthest worshipper. "Today, Egypt witnesses what the gods have ordained since the foundation stones of creation were laid in the primordial waters!"

The assembly stilled. In the sudden silence, the distant cry of a hawk—sacred to Horus—echoed through a high window, a coincidence that Hapuseneb silently thanked the gods for providing.

"Since the time of Menes, the Two Lands have been united under the Double Crown," he continued. "Through flood and drought, through invasion and victory, through plenty and famine, the unbroken line of divine kings has guided Egypt along the path of Ma'at—truth, justice, and cosmic order!"

A murmur of assent rippled through the gathering. Even those who opposed what was about to happen could not deny the sacred truth of these words.

"But the gods are not bound by the expectations of mortals, "Hapuseneb voice dropped to a theatrical near-whisper that somehow carried to every corner of the hall. "Their wisdom transcends our understanding; their plans unfold across centuries while we see only moments."

The massive cedar doors at the far end of the hall—imported at staggering expense from the forests of Lebanon—swung open with ceremonial slowness. The hinges had been oiled with sacred fat mixed with myrrh, ensuring they opened in perfect silence, creating the illusion that they moved by divine will rather than the straining muscles of unseen servants.

"BEHOLD!" thundered Hapuseneb, his voice rising to a fever pitch that sent several small birds roosting in the high beams fluttering in panic. "Behold the daughter of Amun-Ra himself, conceived when the great god took the form of Thutmose I and visited Queen Ahmose in her chamber! The divine scent filled her bedchamber as the god's seed filled her womb! This is no mere woman who stands before you but the living Horus upon the earth!"

A collective intake of breath rippled through the assembly as Hatshepsut strode forward with deliberate steps. She had practiced this walk for months—not the delicate glide of a queen or royal wife, but the powerful stride of a warrior-king. Her muscular frame, honed through years of ritual dancing and careful exercise rather than battlefield combat, was clothed not in the diaphanous gowns of a queen but in the traditional shendyt kilt of pharaoh. The ceremonial false beard—symbol of divine kingship since time immemorial—jutted from her chin, and her eyes blazed with the certainty of one who had been born to rule. The Double Crown of Upper and Lower Egypt sat upon her head—the white cone of Upper Egypt nestled within the red crown of Lower Egypt, symbolizing the ancient unification that was the foundation of pharaonic power. Its weight was tremendous, both physically and metaphorically, but Hatshepsut bore it with a straight neck and proud carriage that dared anyone to question her right to its burden.

From his position near the back of the hall, Senenmut watched with carefully controlled features that betrayed none of the fierce pride and terror warring within his breast. Unlike the nobles surrounding him who had been born to privilege, he had risen from the dust of common birth through intellect, loyalty, and the alchemy of ambition tempered with patience. Once a simple scribe, he had proven himself an administrative genius, slowly accumulating titles and responsibilities until he became indispensable to the royal household—and particularly to the woman who now claimed its highest position.

His eyes missed nothing as they scanned the crowd, noting every raised eyebrow, every whispered comment, every gesture of disapproval or support. The fate of their grand gamble—for it was as much his as hers—would be determined in the next few moments. All their careful planning, the years of cultivating allies, the strategic placement of loyal officials in key positions, the calculated generosity toward influential temples—all would either bear fruit today or collapse into ruin that would destroy them both.

Hatshepsut ascended the dais where the throne of Egypt awaited, each step measured and inevitable as the rising of the Nile. She turned to face her subjects, her gaze briefly falling on young Thutmose III, her nephew and stepson—the child whose birthright she was arguably usurping, though she preferred to think of it as safeguarding until he reached true maturity.

The boy stood in rigid silence beside his tutor, his narrow shoulders already showing the promise of the warrior he would become. Unlike other children his age who might have fidgeted or shown discomfort during such lengthy ceremonies, Thutmose remained perfectly still, his dark eyes—so like his father's—revealing nothing of his thoughts. But Hatshepsut was not deceived by this composure. In the subtle tightening of his jaw, the almost imperceptible narrowing of his gaze, she recognized something dangerous: patience paired with resentment, a combination that would one day threaten everything she built. That day was far off—

he was still just a boy of nine summers—but she made a mental note to watch him more carefully as he grew into manhood.

"I claim the Double Crown not through mere ambition," Hatshepsut declared, her voice trained through countless secret rehearsals to project masculine authority, "but through divine ordination and necessity. Egypt requires strength now, not the promise of it years hence when a boy becomes a man."

Her gaze swept across the assembly, lingering momentarily on those nobles she knew harbored the deepest reservations. "Look to our borders—the Nubians press from the south, the Bedouin from the east. The granaries require careful management, the temples demand proper reverence, and the people deserve prosperity and security. Can a child provide these things? Or does Egypt need one who already understands the weight of rule?"

Near the middle of the hall, Vizier Useramen muttered to his companion, his voice barely audible above the ceremonial chants that had begun again. He was a man of advanced years whose family had served the royal house for seven generations—a lineage of impeccable loyalty now tested by this unprecedented claim to power.

"A woman as Pharaoh?" he hissed through clenched teeth that still showed white and strong despite his sixty years. "This perversion of Ma'at cannot stand. The cosmic order itself will reject it."

"Yet the priests support her," replied the other, a wealthy nomarch from the Delta whose shrewd management had transformed his province into one of Egypt's most productive regions. His warehouses had doubled in value since Hatshepsut had reopened the trade routes to Punt during her regency, and the practical matters of prosperity often outweighed concerns of tradition in his worldview.

"Hapuseneb supports her because she has granted his temple more land and gold than the previous three pharaohs combined, "Vizier Useramen scoffed. "And this tale of divine conception—convenient, is it not, that Amun-Ra himself should father a daughter who now requires his priesthood to validate her rule?"

"Lower your voice, old friend," warned the nomarch, noticing the sharp gaze of a nearby royal guard whose hand had drifted casually toward the dagger at his belt. "The walls of the palace have ears, and those ears belong to her now. Whatever our private thoughts, today she becomes Pharaoh—and pharaohs have long memories for those who oppose them."

As Hatshepsut completed the ancient rituals of coronation—accepting the crook and flail, symbols of royal authority; receiving the blessings of the priests of each major deity; offering sacrifices to her divine ancestors; and finally taking her seat upon the throne of Horus—the atmosphere in the Great Hall shifted subtly from solemn ceremony to celebration. Servants appeared as if conjured by magic, bearing trays laden with vessels of the finest wines from the royal vineyards at Thebes and imported delicacies from across the known world.

The Celebration

The hall transformed over the hours from temple to banquet house, solemn ritual giving way to increasingly uninhibited revelry. Dancers with lithe bodies and jingling golden ankle bracelets moved sinuously between groups of increasingly intoxicated nobles, while musicians coaxed hypnotic melodies from their harps, flutes, and sistrum rattles. The scent of roasted meats and exotic spices mingled with the heavier perfumes of incense and bodies warmed by wine and excitement.

Hatshepsut observed it all from her elevated position, sipping sparingly from her own golden cup, watching as inhibitions dissolved and tongues loosened with each passing hour. This, too, was part of her carefully orchestrated strategy—let them drink, let them talk, let her spies learn who truly supported her ascension and who merely posed as allies while harboring treacherous thoughts.

As the night deepened, the celebration grew more raucous. Several minor nobles had already drunk themselves into undignified stupors, their servants discreetly removing them before they could embarrass themselves further. Others engaged in increasingly bold displays of affection with dancers or fellow guests, the inhibitions of rank and propriety dissolved by wine and the peculiar license that great celebrations sometimes grant.

Hatshepsut watched it all with the detached interest of a falcon surveying potential prey, cataloguing behaviors and weakness for future reference. When the moon reached its zenith, she rose from her throne—a signal that the official portion of the festivities had concluded. The most senior nobles who remained sufficiently sober bowed deeply as she departed, while those too intoxicated to notice her exit continued their revels, now overseen by Hapuseneb who would ensure the celebrations continued until dawn as tradition demanded.

Private Chambers

The royal residence lay quiet under the silver light of Khonsu's moon when Hatshepsut finally escaped the remnants of the court who had followed her from the Great Hall, still seeking favors or assurances or simply the reflected glory of the new pharaoh's attention. She dismissed her attendants with a single authoritative gesture as she entered her private chambers—rooms that had once belonged to her father, and briefly to her husband, before she claimed them as her own.

Only one figure awaited her in the spacious apartment, standing motionless beside a window that overlooked the palace gardens, his tall frame silhouetted against the star-scattered sky.

"I wondered if you would come," she said, breaking the silence.

Senenmut turned, his eyes bright with triumph and something more primal, more dangerous. He had removed his ceremonial wig, revealing a closely-shaven scalp that emphasized the strong angles of his face—a face not conventionally handsome by Egyptian standards, yet compelling in its intelligence and intensity.

"Did you doubt it, Great One?" he asked, using her formal title even in this most private moment.

"I doubt everything and everyone," she replied, removing the heavy crown with a sigh of profound relief. "It is how I have survived to see this day."

When the door closed behind him, Hatshepsut turned back to Senenmut, her eyes no longer those of Pharaoh but of a woman who had carried an impossible burden for too long. With deliberate movements, she removed the false beard that symbolized her masculine authority, then raised a hand to her ornate headdress.

"Help me with this," she commanded softly. "It has been digging into my scalp since midday."

Senenmut moved forward, his hands—calloused from years of overseeing royal construction projects despite his elevated status—working with surprising gentleness to remove the complicated arrangement of fabric and jewelery. As the headdress came away, revealing her natural hair cropped short for practical purposes, Hatshepsut closed her eyes momentarily, the relief evident in the softening of her features.

"You have done it," he said, his voice a reverent whisper in the stillness. "All of Egypt now bows before you."

"Not all," she replied, opening her eyes to fix him with a penetrating stare. "There are still those who doubt, those who scheme, those who wait for me to falter."

"They will learn, as others have," Senenmut promised. He set the headdress carefully on a cedar table inlaid with ivory and lapis. "The people already speak of omens and portents—a double rainbow appeared over the Eastern desert this morning. The priests are calling it a sign of Amun-Ra's approval."

"Hapuseneb's doing, no doubt," Hatshepsut said with a knowing smile. "He has always understood the value of a well-timed miracle."

"Does it matter if it sways the common people to your cause?"

"I suppose not," she conceded, moving to a divan covered in leopard skin—another symbol of royalty, as only pharaoh was permitted to hunt the sacred beast. She sank onto it with a grace that belied her exhaustion. "Pour wine, Senenmut. The finest Canaanite vintage—we have earned it today."

He complied, filling two golden cups with the deep red liquid that had traveled hundreds of miles to reach this moment. As he handed her a cup, their fingers brushed briefly—a seemingly accidental touch that sent visible tension through both their bodies.

"To Egypt's newest king," he toasted, raising his cup.

"To those who made her reign possible," she countered, holding his gaze over the rim of her cup as she drank. "Even Moses."

"Moses could never have given you what you truly desired," he said carefully, knowing he treads on dangerous ground. "His god demanded his complete devotion."

"As Egypt demands mine," she replied with a brittle edge to her voice. "He could have ruled beside me, Senenmut. Could have shared in creating an empire greater than any the world has seen. Instead..." Her fingers tightened around her golden cup until her knuckles showed white against her copper skin. "Instead, he chose his slave heritage over Egypt's throne. Over me."

Her laugh was as dry and bitter as natron. "Let him wander the desert with his invisible god while I rule the greatest civilization on earth. And let his people learn that their chosen leader's rejection has consequences for them all."

Senenmut studied her face, noting the flicker of old pain beneath the veneer of contempt. "He wounded you deeply."

"He taught me a valuable lesson," she corrected sharply. "Never to place personal desire above political necessity. Moses could have been useful to me—a figurehead to placate the Hebrews while I consolidated power. Instead, he chose self-righteous exile." She drained her cup in one defiant swallow. "His loss, not mine."

Senenmut refilled her cup without being asked, then set the wine jar aside and moved to stand before her. With slow deliberation, he knelt at her feet—not in the full prostration of a subject before pharaoh, but in the more intimate posture of a man before the woman he desired.

"Egypt has had many kings," he said, his voice low and intent, "but none like you. You have rewritten what is possible, Hatshepsut. You have bent history itself to your will."

"And what is my will now, Senenmut?" she asked, a dangerous edge to her voice. "Now that I have taken what was denied me by birth?"

"Only you can answer that, Great One." His hand moved to rest lightly on her ankle, a touch that would have earned another man immediate execution. "But whatever you desire next, I am here to help you claim it."

Hatshepsut regarded him through half-lidded eyes, the wine and exhaustion and triumph of the day combining to lower barriers she normally maintained with vigilant care. "The crown is heavier than it appears," she said softly, an admission she would make to no other living soul.

"Then let me help you bear its weight, if only for tonight," he replied, his hand moving upward along her calf with deliberate slowness.

In the privacy of her chamber, she was neither king nor queen but simply Hatshepsut—a woman of flesh and blood and long-denied desire. Her hand reached out to trace the strong line of his jaw, the gesture both permission and command.

"They whisper that I am unnatural," she murmured as he rose to sit beside her on the divan. "That a woman cannot truly rule without a man to guide her hand."

"Let them whisper," Senenmut said, his breath warm against her ear as he leaned closer. "You have never been merely a woman, and I have never been merely a man. We are something more together—vision and execution, mind and hand, the perfect joining of complementary forces."

She pulled back slightly to look into his eyes, finding there the unwavering loyalty that had made him indispensable to her rise. But there was something else too—a hunger that matched her own, carefully controlled through years of necessary discretion but now, in this moment of triumph, demanding acknowledgment.

"And tonight?" she asked, her voice barely above a whisper.

"Tonight," he said, one hand moving to the elaborate collar that still adorned her throat, beginning to unfasten it with practiced case, "we are simply two souls celebrating a victory thirty centuries in the making."

Under the watchful eyes of painted gods on her chamber ceiling, Pharaoh Hatshepsut surrendered her divine persona and reclaimed, for a few precious hours, the humanity that the throne demanded she transcend. Her body—trained for endurance rather than pleasure through years of ritual dancing and ceremonial duties—remembered other, more primal rhythms as Senenmut's hands and lips awakened sensations long suppressed beneath the weight of ambition.

Tomorrow would bring new challenges: nobles to reward or punish, borders to secure, monuments to commission that would ensure her name lived for eternity. There would be whispers to silence, alliances to strengthen, and a young stepson to mold into a tool rather than a threat. But tonight belonged to the woman behind the crown, and the man who loved both her incarnations with equal devotion.

For one night, the woman who would be king allowed herself to forget the price of her ambition. Come morning, the false beard would be replaced, the royal regalia donned once more, and Hatshepsut would again become the living Horus, ruler of the Two Lands. But in these dark hours between triumph and responsibility, she permitted herself the luxury of being simply—gloriously—human.

Chapter 3 - The Journey to Avaris

1473 BC - City of Thebes

The royal decree arrived with the formality of a funeral procession, slicing through the market day's clamor like a bronze blade. A herald clads in the pristine white linen of court officials stood in the dust-choked marketplace of Thebes, his skin burnished copper in the merciless Egyptian sun. Unfurling a papyrus scroll bearing the crimson seal of Hatshepsut, he waited as silence rippled outward like water disturbed by a fallen stone. The crowd parted before him—Egyptians with curiosity, Israelites with dread. "*By decree of Her Divine Majesty, Hatshepsut, Lord of the Two Lands, Beloved of Amun,*" the herald proclaimed, his voice carrying across the square with practiced authority, his eyes sweeping over the gathered Israelites with the cold indifference of a hawk surveying field mice. "*All persons of Israelite lineage are hereby commanded to journey to the city of Avaris to establish residence among their kin. This resettlement is by royal command and serves the interests of both crown and kingdom.*"

The herald paused, allowing the weight of his next words to settle like a granite block upon the shoulders of those who listened. "Any Israelite caught from Thebes to Bubastis after ninety days have expired will be executed as a spy." His pronouncement hung in the air like the promise of a storm, terrible in its finality.

Nun stood among the crowd, his weathered hand resting protectively on his son Joshua's shoulder, feeling the boy's slight frame tremble beneath his calloused palm. At eight years old, the child had known only Thebes as his home, born here beneath the shadow of great pylons and obelisks in this sprawling city of temples and monuments. Yet Nun had always known their days had been as numbered as grains in an hourglass.

The Night Before Departure

That night, as they packed their meager belongings by the guttering light of an oil lamp, Joshua clutched a wooden cat figure—a toy of cedar and ebony, lovingly polished by small hands, given to him by an Egyptian playmate whose father now looked away when they passed in the street.

"Must we leave everything behind, Father?" the boy asked, his voice small yet steady, his eyes wide with the uncertainty that only children can fully express, caught between trust in their elders and the bewildering cruelty of an adult world.

Nun paused in his work, the sinews in his forearms relaxing as he studied his son's face. The flickering oil lamp cast dancing shadows across the mud-brick walls of their humble dwelling—a shelter for nine years, but never truly theirs. The walls held memories: Joshua's birth cries, whispered prayers, furtive celebrations of forbidden festivals.

"Not everything," Nun replied, his voice rough as desert sandstone yet warm with emotion that belied his stern features. "Our most precious possessions travel with us." He tapped Joshua's chest, above his heart, feeling the rapid pulse beneath his fingertip. "Our faith. Our history. These cannot be packed in bundles or carried on donkeys, yet they weigh more than Pharaoh's gold."

Joshua nodded solemnly, though Nun could see he did not fully comprehend. How could he? The boy had been born in captivity, had never known the freedom his ancestors once enjoyed, had never tasted the sweet water of liberty that Nun himself knew only through the stories passed down from father to son like precious heirlooms.

"I remember when Moses held you as a babe," Nun said, carefully wrapping their clay dishes in linen worn thin from years of washing. "Even then, dressed in royal finery with gold at his throat and wrists, there was something in his eyes—a recognition, perhaps. As if the blood of Abraham called to him through the veil of his Egyptian upbringing, whispering truths his ears had never heard but his soul somehow remembered."

"The prince who died?" Joshua asked, running his fingers along the wooden cat's arched back.

Nun shook his head, a ghost of bitterness passing across his face like a cloud shadow. "Not died, disappeared. Eleazar and I taught him our language in secret, our customs when no Egyptian eyes watched. He learned of his true heritage in the shadows between palace pillars. And then he disappeared—some say after killing an Egyptian who was beating one of our people until the sand drank deep of Hebrew blood."

He did not share with Joshua his deeper disappointment—that for a brief, shining moment, he had believed Moses might be their deliverer, the one prophesied to lead them from bondage. That hope had flared like a torch in darkness only to be extinguished when the prince vanished into the eastern wilderness, taking with him Eleazar and Nun's desperate hopes.

The Journey Commences

Dawn found them joining a stream of fellow Israelites flowing from the city like water from a broken vessel, their footfalls leaving faint impressions in the dew-dampened earth. Twenty-five souls at first—neighbors, distant kin, those who had formed their small community within the great city of Thebes. By the time they reached the outskirts, their numbers had swelled to over a hundred, a procession of the displaced marked by quiet dignity in the face of exile.

Nun cast one final glance at the city's magnificent temples rising above the feathered crowns of palm trees, their limestone facades gleaming gold in the morning sun like false promises. For all its splendor, Thebes had never truly been home. Perhaps nowhere in Egypt ever would be—this land that had devoured their labor and crushed their spirits beneath monuments to foreign gods.

The March North

The journey northward transformed their small band into an army of the displaced, a living river of humanity flowing along the ancient lifeline of the Nile. At each settlement along the great river, more Israelites joined their ranks—families with crying children whose tears left clean tracks on dust-coated faces, elders whose bones ached with each step yet refused to be carried, young men whose eyes burned with silent rage at their uprooting, flames of defiance carefully banked beneath downcast gazes.

By the time Memphis came into view, its white walls shimmering in the distance like a mirage born of exhaustion and hope, they numbered over two thousand souls. Their procession stretched back along the river road like a great serpent, attended by bleating goats and sheep whose ribs showed through matted wool, oxen straining against yokes as they pulled carts laden with household goods, and the occasional donkey carrying the elderly or infirm whose pride had finally yielded to necessity.

That evening, as they made camp in the lengthening shadow of Memphis, Nun sat with Joshua beneath a canopy of stars that seemed to Nun like divine eyes watching their suffering with eternal patience. The boy had walked bravely all day, never complaining despite feet blistered raw and legs trembling with exhaustion.

"Tomorrow, we continue into the delta," Nun said, breaking off a piece of flatbread baked three days before and passing it to his son. The bread was hard now, but their hunger was harder still. "The land there is different—wetter, greener. The soil is black as a moonless night and rich as a king's treasury. It is where our ancestor Joseph once ruled as vizier, his dreams and wisdom saving two nations."

Joshua's eyes widened, fatigue momentarily forgotten. "The one who interpreted Pharaoh's dreams? Who saw the seven fat cows and seven thin?"

"The very same," Nun nodded, pleased that his teachings had taken root in fertile ground despite the barren circumstances of their lives. "When famine ravaged the land like a devouring beast, Joseph's wisdom saved not only Egypt but our entire family. Pharaoh gave him authority second only to the throne itself—a foreigner with a shepherd's past wearing the gold collar of royal favor."

"Then why are we treated as slaves now?" Joshua asked, his young face troubled by the injustice, shadows deepening the hollows beneath his eyes making him appear older than his years.

Nun sighed deeply, a sound like desert wind through abandoned dwellings. "For more than a hundred years, we lived in peace with the Hyksos kings who ruled Lower Egypt. They were foreigners like us, desert people who understood our ways. They respected Joseph, who had saved Egypt from famine, and they honored his descendants."

Nun spat into the dust, his contempt palpable.

"Then came Ahmose with his armies out of Thebes. Like a desert storm he swept down upon the Delta, his chariots thundering across the land. The Hyksos, who had grown soft in their century of rule, could not stand against him. He drove them back across the eastern deserts, slaughtering those who could not flee fast enough."

His fingers tightened on Joshua's shoulder, the pressure a testament to his barely contained fury.

"And we, the children of Jacob, the father of Joseph, what became of us? Ahmose looked upon us and saw only friends of his enemies. 'These Hebrews are no different from the Hyksos,' he declared. 'They shall build the monuments to my glory.'"

"Remember this, my son. Remember who we were before the lash. For one day, this too shall pass. The mighty fall, kingdoms crumble into dust, but our people—our people endure."

The boy was quiet for a long moment, absorbing this bitter truth. Around them, thousands of fellow Israelites prepared for sleep under the open sky, the murmur of prayers and soft weeping creating a sorrowful lullaby carried on the night breeze that still held the day's heat.

"Will we ever be free again, Father?" Joshua finally asked, his small voice steady despite the enormity of the question.

Nun gazed up at the stars—the same stars Abraham had been promised would number his descendants, countless as sand grains on the shore of an endless sea.

"The God of our fathers has not forgotten His covenant," he answered softly, his faith a stubborn flame that years of bondage had failed to extinguish. "This I believe with all my heart."

Through Goshen

As they approached Bubastis, their number had swelled to over four thousand, a veritable tide of humanity flowing north like the annual inundation of the life-giving Nile. The temple of Bastet loomed on the horizon, its cat-headed goddess carved in granite seemingly watching their procession with ancient, indifferent eyes that had witnessed the rise and fall of dynasties.

Beyond Bubastis, the landscape changed dramatically. After days of travel through dusty lands where their feet raised clouds that clung to sweat-slicked skin and parched throats, they crested a gentle rise and beheld a sight that made Nun halt mid-stride, his breath catching in his chest.

"Look there, Joshua," he said, pointing ahead with a hand that trembled slightly.

Spread before them like an emerald set in gold lay the region of Goshen. Fields of barley and wheat swayed in the gentle breeze like a verdant sea. Orchards heavy with fruit lined irrigation canals that glinted silver in the afternoon sun, water bringing life to a land blessed by divine favor. Sheep and cattle grazed on lush pastureland, their coats clean and sleek, tended by shepherds who, even at this distance, were recognizably Hebrew by their garments and bearing.

"It's so green," Joshua whispered in awe, his eyes wide as saucers, reflecting the abundance before them like mirrors.

"This was our homeland in Egypt," Nun explained, his voice thick with emotion that constricted his throat. "When Jacob brought our people here during the great famine, his silver hair already proclaiming his advanced years, Pharaoh gave Goshen to us as a gift worthy of the man who had saved his kingdom. For generations, our people thrived here, tending flocks and fields as our fathers had done since time immemorial."

The group halted abruptly as a dark mass appeared on the distant horizon, spreading across the terrain like an advancing shadow. As it drew nearer, the magnitude became clear —a vast column of men, perhaps four thousand strong, marching toward Thebes. Though unchained, their status as slaves was unmistakable in their hollow-eyed stares and the watchful Egyptian overseers flanking the column with whips coiled at their sides. The men walked with the mechanical rhythm of those who had learned that resistance meant death, their bodies moving forward while their spirits remained trapped in the lands from which they had been torn.

"Fresh slaves for the quarries," said Nun, his weathered face hardening as he watched the procession approach. "They march them without chains now —they've learned that men who have nowhere to flee will walk to their own doom without the weight of iron." He placed a protective hand on his son's shoulder. Joshua stood rigid beside his father, his young warrior's frame tensed as though ready to spring into action despite the futility of any such gesture. The passing slaves represented what any Hebrew might become if the Pharaoh's appetite for construction grew more ravenous —not the familiar bondage they had adapted to over generations, but the crushing labor that consumed men entirely, leaving nothing but dust.

As the two groups passed each other on the road, an Egyptian taskmaster shouted harsh commands, forcing the Hebrew travelers to step aside into the ditches to make way. Soon they disappeared over the horizon.

As Nun and the group skirted the edges of Goshen, some of their kinsmen came out to greet them, offering water in clay jars and food in woven baskets to the travelers. But Nun noted the relief in their eyes—gratitude that they, at least, had been permitted to remain in this pocket of abundance while others marched toward uncertainty.

"Will they be forced to leave too?" Joshua asked, watching as the villagers returned to their homes, casting anxious glances over their shoulders.

"Eventually," Nun replied grimly. "This new policy is like a net, drawing us all together for some purpose that only Pharaoh and his advisors fully comprehend."

Arrival at Avaris

The next day past Goshen, the fertile lands gave way to harder ground where only scrub and thorns flourished. The air grew heavier, laden with unfamiliar scents—smoke from countless kilns, wet clay awaiting the potter's hand, human sweat from bodies pressed too closely together. And then, carried on the evening breeze like a harbinger of their future, came an odor that made Joshua wrinkle his nose in disgust.

"What is that smell, Father?" he asked, covering his face with the edge of his garment.

"Avaris," he replied grimly. "Our destination." Nun's fingers unconsciously traced the worn edges of the sacred texts hidden beneath his cloak; texts he had used to teach Moses the language and customs of the Hebrew people during those intense two years in Thebes. What had begun as a scholarly mission—appointed by the elders to ensure the Egyptian-raised prince understood his true heritage—had stretched into eight years away from home.

The following morning revealed the city in all its grim reality, sprawled before them as they topped a final rise. Where Thebes rose in monumental splendor and Memphis sat in elegant dignity, Avaris sprawled like a festering wound across the landscape, a city born of necessity rather than divine planning. Smoke from kilns and foundries hung in a perpetual pall above the eastern quarter like a curse made visible. The canals that should have brought fresh water were choked with refuse, their surfaces slick with rainbow-hued oils and floating detritus. And everywhere—people. Thousands upon thousands, packed into quarters that might reasonably house hundreds, moving like ants across a disturbed hill.

Joshua pressed closer to his father's side as they approached one of the entry points, his small body seeking protection against this assault on all senses. "This is to be our home?" he asked, his voice barely audible above the cacophony of shouts, animal cries, and the constant thud of construction that formed Avaris's heartbeat.

Before them lay the Israelite quarter—rows of hastily constructed dwellings packed so tightly together that one could scarcely pass between them without turning sideways. Nothing like the spacious settlements of Goshen with their courtyards and gardens, nothing like even their modest home in Thebes. These were not dwellings built for families to grow and thrive; they were barracks built for laborers whose only value lay in the strength of their backs and the skill of their hands.

Nun knelt before his son, grasping his shoulders firmly with hands that bore the callouses of a lifetime of servitude. "Listen to me, Joshua," he said, his voice urgent yet controlled, his eyes boring into his son's as if to imprint his words directly upon the boy's soul. "Whatever happens here, remember who you are. You are Joshua, son of Nun, of the tribe of Ephraim, descended from Jacob who once saved this very land."

Where is our home?" the boy asked, his young face solemn yet unafraid, a warrior's heart already beating in a child's chest.

"For now, our home is with each other," he replied, brushing a lock of sweat-dampened hair from his son's forehead. "But someday, we will return to the land promised to our fathers." He brushed the dust from his son's hair with a calloused hand that knew both tenderness and toil. "And you, my Joshua, may live to see that day."

Finding Their Place

As they moved past the entry point, Nun could see the four thousand souls who had traveled with them now dispersing like tributaries from a great river, each seeking their own tribal connections in this sea of humanity. The twelve tribes of Israel—descended from the twelve sons of Jacob—had maintained their separate identities even through generations of bondage. Now they flowed like water finding its own level, each stream seeking its proper channel in the delta of exile.

"Come, Joshua," Nun said, guiding his son through the crowd with the confidence of a man who knew exactly where he was going even in unfamiliar territory. "Our family awaits us."

They made their way through the dusty lanes of the Israelite quarter, moving westward toward the muddy waters of the Nile branch that flowed past Avaris like a resigned witness to human suffering. This area, though still cramped and overcrowded with humanity packed tighter than reeds in a marsh, had the slight advantage of fresh water nearby and occasional breezes off the river that dispersed some of the city's oppressive heat and stench.

"Is it true that Moses' brother lives here?" Joshua asked, struggling to keep pace with his father's determined stride, his small legs working twice as hard to cover the same ground.

"Yes," Nun replied in a lowered voice that would not carry to unfriendly ears. "Aaron has remained faithful to our ways, though his brother was raised in Pharaoh's household eating from golden plates while we ate dust. He serves as a priest among our people, keeping alive the flame of faith when storms of oppression threaten to extinguish it."

They passed groups of Levites performing ritual washing in a secluded area, their movements deliberate and reverent despite the squalor surrounding them, and clusters of men from the tribe of Judah deep in discussion whose voices fell silent as Egyptians passed. As they approached the western section, where rickety dwellings pressed close to the marshy riverbank like beggars seeking alms, a familiar voice called out above the general clamor.

"Nun! At last, you have arrived! The God of Abraham be praised!"

An elderly man with kind eyes that had not lost their spark despite decades of witnessing injustice pushed through the crowd with surprising vigor, arms outstretched in welcome. "Nephew! The God of our fathers be praised for your safe passage!"

Nun embraced his uncle Kemuel tightly, feeling the old man's ribs beneath his thin garment, testament to the scarcity that had become their daily bread. "We are here, as commanded," he said simply.

"And this must be Joshua," Kemuel said, bending to look the boy in the eyes with genuine interest rather than the cursory glance of an elder acknowledging a child's existence.

That night, crowded into their assigned dwelling with fifteen other Ephraimites whose bodies provided the only warmth against the desert's cooling breath, Nun finally allowed himself to feel the full weight of their situation. Around them, four thousand four hundred souls had been absorbed into the mass of Israelites already inhabiting Avaris—each finding their place among their own clan, each preparing for the harsh reality of their new existence in this city of mud and misery.

And somewhere—perhaps closer than any dared hope—events were unfolding that would shake the very foundations of Egypt itself, sending cracks through Pharaoh's certainty like fissures in a poorly fired vessel.

The time of waiting was ending, the hour of deliverance approaching on sandaled feet that had once walked palace corridors but now knew the harsh embrace of wilderness stone.

Chapter 4 - History Wiped Out

1472 BC Hatshepsut visits to Pi-Ramesses

The royal barge cut through the waters of the Nile like a spear through flesh, its gilded prow rising high above the muddy waters. Forty oarsmen propelled the vessel northward, their bare backs gleaming with sweat under the merciless sun, their movements synchronized by the rhythmic beat of a drummer seated in the stern. Hatshepsut stood at the prow, regal and immovable as the statues she had commissioned throughout the land. The desert wind whipped at her ceremonial garments, the linen snapping like the wings of a great falcon. The White Palace of Pi-Ramesses rose before her, its walls gleaming in the harsh sunlight.

The sun beat down mercilessly on the western quarter of Avaris, where the Israelites had made their homes over generations. The area bustled with activity as women ground grain for the evening meal and craftsmen worked diligently at their trades. Children darted between mud-brick dwellings, their laughter mingling with the sounds of daily life.

Ephres, a young messenger who was fishing in the river, came running through the narrow streets, his breath coming in ragged gasps. "Aaron! Elder Aaron!" he called out, stumbling to a halt when he spotted the tall, dignified figure inspecting the construction of a new dwelling.

Aaron turned, recognizing the urgency in the boy's voice. "What is it, Ephres?"

"The royal barge," Ephres panted, pointing toward the river. "It approaches from the south! The father says it's the Pharaoh herself!"

A murmur rippled through the gathering crowd. Pharaoh coming to Avaris was rare enough, but the word "herself" caught everyone's attention.

"Are you certain?" Aaron asked, his brow furrowing.

"Yes, Elder. The royal standard flies at the mast."

As Ephres darted away, Aaron made his way toward the Nile, his mind racing. A royal visit could mean anything—new decrees, higher tributes, or worse, new labor demands for their people who had already suffered generations of servitude.

When Aaron reached the riverbank, a crowd has assembled and he found Nun already waiting, his nine-year-old son Joshua standing close beside him.

"Ephres says the Pharaoh comes," Aaron said, clasping Nun's forearm in greeting.

Nun nodded, his expression thoughtful. "So, I've heard. I thought it prudent we see for ourselves."

"Your time at the royal court may prove valuable today," Aaron said.

"My time as Moses' Hebrew tutor taught me much about Egyptian ways," Nun agreed, placing a protective hand on Joshua's shoulder. "The royal household holds few secrets from those who know where to look."

Young Joshua, tall for his nine years, stood on his tiptoes, straining to see the approaching vessel. "Father, there!" he pointed. "Is that it?"

All three turned to watch as the magnificent barge glided into view, its golden decorations gleaming blindingly in the afternoon sun.

Nun stepped forward, shielding his eyes with one hand. He studied the distant figures with the practiced precision of one who had spent years observing court protocol. After a long moment, his breath caught.

"By the God of Abraham," he whispered.

"What is it?" Aaron asked, concerned by the shock in Nun's voice.

"When we left Thebes last year, Princess Hatshepsut was merely regent for young Thutmose III," Nun explained, his voice low so only Aaron and Joshua could hear. "But that is not a regent on that barge. She wears the royal regalia of a ruling Pharaoh."

Aaron's eyes widened. "A woman as Pharaoh? Not merely as regent?"

"The double crown, the false beard, the crook and flail—all symbols reserved only for Pharaoh," Nun confirmed, disbelief evident in his voice.

"Somehow, in the time since we departed Thebes, Hatshepsut has claimed the throne of Egypt for herself."

Young Joshua tugged at his father's robe, his dark eyes serious. "Is that allowed, Father? Can a woman be Pharaoh?"

Nun rested his hand on his son's head. "In all of Egypt's long history, never happened."

"What does this mean for our people?" Aaron asked, watching the approaching vessel with growing concern.

Nun's expression was grave. "I cannot say. Hatshepsut was always shrewd, calculating. During my time in the palace, I observed her closely as I tutored Moses in our language and ways. She is not needlessly cruel, but she is ruthlessly determined. No one who takes such a bold step will allow anything—or anyone—to stand in her way."

They stood in silence as the royal barge drew closer. From their vantage point, they could now clearly see Hatshepsut's profile, sharp against the sky, her posture unbending, radiating authority.

"Look," Aaron pointed. "She stands at the prow like a living statue. And beside her—"

"Senenmut," Nun finished. "Her chief architect and closest advisor. He had already risen high when we left Thebes. It seems his star continues to ascend alongside hers."

Joshua watched wide-eyed as the vessel passed before them, the rhythmic drumbeat guiding the oarsmen echoing across the water.

Barge approach the Palace

"Fifty years," she murmured to Senenmut, who stood a respectful distance behind her, his own eyes fixed on the approaching city. "Over fifty years since the exodus of the Hyksos, and still the stench of foreign gods lingers in this place."

Senenmut moved slightly closer, close enough to speak without being overheard by the attendants who hovered like shadows at the edges of the royal canopy. Tall and lean, his body hardened not by noble combat training but by the real work of building and creating, he carried himself with a quiet dignity that many born to nobility never achieved.

"The Hyksos, yes," Senenmut replied carefully, his deep-set eyes scanning the shoreline where crowds were gathering to witness the royal arrival. "Though most who remain are the Israelites who served them."

A cold smile played across Hatshepsut's lips, her teeth flashing briefly white against the ochre paint that stained them red. "The distinction matters little. It was not the Hyksos who betrayed Egypt's trust. It was not the Hyksos who killed Moses."

The lie had served her well. The pharaoh Moses, mysteriously murdered by Israelite rebels—it had given her the regency, and eventually the crown. That his actual crime had been killing an Egyptian who had beaten an Israelite slave was an irony not lost on her. Moses, the adopted son of the previous pharaoh's daughter, raised to rule, had thrown it all away for these people. Had thrown her away, when she had offered him power through her.

The royal barge glided to a halt alongside the alabaster quay of the palace, where a delegation of nobles and priests awaited with bowed heads. Senenmut disembarked first, ensuring all was in order before extending his hand to assist Hatshepsut, though she accepted it only as a formality. The court officials prostrated themselves on either side, their foreheads touching the ground, not daring to look upon her directly. Inside the grand reception hall, servants rushed forward with cool drinks, fragrant oils, and fresh linens, while musicians played softly in the background.

"Tomorrow we shall see what remains of this city that once harbored Egypt's enemies."

The royal inspection of Avaris was methodical and thorough. Hatshepsut descended from her litter at key points throughout the city, her face betraying nothing as she surveyed what had once been the capital of the hated Hyksos kings. Servants hurried to spread embroidered cloths before her golden sandals touched the earth. She moved with purpose through the granaries where wheat poured into storage for the coming year, past construction sites where limestone blocks rose slowly into new temples, and along the muddy canals where workers sweated under the midday sun.

On the fifth night of her stay, Hatshepsut called her council to the audience chamber. She had spent the day walking through the Israelite quarter, and the experience had left her in a dangerous mood. The officials could sense it as they filed in and took their positions, standing stiffly before the cedar throne where she sat, fingers drumming against the armrest.

"This city remains polluted," she announced without preamble. "I have searched five days for proper reverence to our gods and found only token gestures. The temples stand half-attended while the Israelites' numbers grow unchecked."

Senenmut stood slightly apart from the other officials, his eyes fixed on Hatshepsut's face. He alone could read the deeper currents beneath her anger.

"Divine One," ventured the high priest, "the northern temples have always been—"

"Neglected," she cut him off. "Yes. That ends now." She rose from her seat and walked to a table where maps and scrolls lay open. "These Hebrews worship no proper god, make no offerings to those who protect Egypt. Their stubborn devotion to their invisible deity mocks everything we hold sacred."

She unrolled a fresh papyrus and dipped a reed pen in ink. Her pen scratched across the surface, outlining her decree. "But the record begins tonight. Every mention of these Hebrews' supposed greatness is to be erased. This Joseph who allegedly saved Egypt during the famine— remove his name from the archives. Jacob and his sons—strike them from every monument."

The officials exchanged glances, but none dared question her. Pharaoh's word was divine law.

"These people are an abomination," Hatshepsut continued, setting down her pen. Outside, the sounds of evening prayers rose from the Egyptian quarter, but from the Israelite section of the city came only the normal noises of a people preparing for sleep. "They live among us yet remain apart. They use our water, farm our land, yet reject our gods."

She turned to the military commander, who straightened under her gaze. "Increase their labors until no man remains standing. I will wipe them all out."

"Divine Majesty," Senenmut spoke for the first time, his deep voice measured and calm, "the Israelites provide skilled labor that would be difficult to replace. Their stonemasons are among our finest."

Hatshepsut's eyes locked with his. Those watching could not decipher the silent exchange that passed between them, but after a moment, she gave a slight nod.

"They will not be destroyed," she conceded, "but they will be broken—broken until they abandon their foreign ways. Egypt has tolerated their presence for too long without demanding their souls in return."

As her barge pulled away from the shores of Pi-Ramesses in the gathering dusk, Hatshepsut gazed back at the city. The setting sun painted the white walls blood-red, a sight that pleased her sense of poetic justice. Moses had walked these streets once, had chosen these people over her, over Egypt. For that alone, they would pay. The weight of the double crown was heavy on her brow, but no heavier than the weight of betrayal she had carried since Moses fled.

"He should have stayed," she thought, watching as the city receded in the distance. "Together, we could have ruled an empire greater than any before. Instead, he chose slaves over me."

The thought hardened something inside her that had once been soft, completing a transformation that had begun seven years ago. She was no longer the woman Moses had rejected. She was Pharaoh.

She turned away from the railing as darkness fell, calling for wine. Tomorrow they would reach a more pleasant part of her kingdom, away from this place with its bitter memories and foreign stench. Thebes awaited her return—pure, devoted Thebes, where her monuments rose daily toward the sky, proclaiming her glory to eternity.

Chapter 5 - The Female King

1471 BC - The Land of Punt

The docks at Sayn Aknu bustled with activity as Hatshepsut's royal procession arrived, the clatter of wooden cranes and the shouts of the dockworkers creating a cacophony that assaulted the ears after the relative quiet of the river journey. The sea breeze carried the scent of salt and exotic spices, mingling with the pungent aroma of fresh pitch being applied to the ships' hulls. Gulls wheeled overhead, their cries plaintive against the cloudless blue sky.

"Magnificent," she breathed, surveying the four vessels that had once belonged to Nubian raiders. Now transformed under Egyptian craftsmanship, they were sleeker, stronger, designed for a journey never undertaken by an Egyptian ruler. Their cedar hulls gleamed with fresh pitch, their ropes and sails new and strong. Each prow bore a carved head of Hathor, goddess of distant lands, their eyes painted with protective kohl to guide the way through unknown waters.

A tall Nubian man stepped forward from the crowd of workers and sailors, his ebony skin gleaming with sweat, his massive shoulders broader than any Egyptian's. He prostrated himself before her, pressing his forehead to the wooden dock that had been hurriedly swept clean for the royal visit.

"Rise," Hatshepsut commanded, her interest piqued by the foreigner who moved with such confidence among her people. "You are Nehesi, are you not? The navigator who knows the southern waters?"

"I am, Great One," he confirmed, rising to his full impressive height but keeping his eyes respectfully lowered. His voice was deep and accented, but his Egyptian was flawless. A golden earring glinted in one ear—a sign of his status among his own people.

Hatshepsut's eyes gleamed with anticipation, the excitement of a child given a new toy breaking briefly through her royal composure. "And now you will sail there for Egypt's first female Pharaoh. Tell me of your preparations."

As Nehesi detailed the expedition plans, Hatshepsut walked the length of the largest vessel, her hand trailing along its railing. The wood was smooth beneath her fingers, polished by countless hands before hers. The Nubian ships had been captured a decade ago during Moses' campaign against the southern rebels. She remembered him returning from that campaign, bronzed by the sun, his eyes alight with victory and tales of exotic lands beyond Egypt's borders. Now these ships would serve a grander purpose—to restore Egypt's trade routes and bring back treasures' unseen since before the Hyksos occupation.

"The journey will take many weeks, Great One," Nehesi explained, following her at a respectful distance. "We must follow the coast, stopping at friendly ports to replenish supplies. The Land of Punt lies beyond the Southern Gate, where the great green sea narrows between lands."

Hatshepsut nodded, her mind already envisioning the glory this expedition would bring. Not merely the treasure, though that would be substantial, but the legacy. No female ruler—no, she corrected herself— no king in generations had undertaken such a journey. "You will bring back myrrh trees—living ones that can be planted in the soil of Egypt," she said, her voice taking on a dreamy quality as she envisioned the terraced gardens she would create. "Gold, ebony, ivory, exotic animals— all the treasures Punt can offer."

Senenmut approached cautiously, waiting until the Nubian had withdrawn before speaking. The afternoon sun cast his shadow long across the dock, merging with hers in a way that seemed somehow significant. "This expedition will cost the royal treasury dearly."

"And it will return that cost tenfold," Hatshepsut countered, turning to face him. "More importantly, it will show Egypt and the world that under my rule, we have truly recovered from the chaos of foreign rule. That we can once again reach beyond our borders and claim the wealth that is rightfully ours."

She turned to face the sea, her expression hardening as she gazed out over the water that stretched endlessly to the horizon. "I will restore Egypt's greatness. And when the ships return laden with treasure, not even the priests who whisper 'woman' behind my back will question my right to rule."

The voyage from Sayn Aknu to Punt tested the mettle of even the most seasoned sailors. For forty days and nights, Hatshepsut's fleet navigated treacherous waters, the Pharaoh herself standing resolute at the prow of the lead vessel, her ceremonial beard steadfast against the salt-laden winds that filled their billowing linen sails. Unlike her predecessors who merely dispatched envoys, Hatshepsut had determined to witness the fabled land with her own eyes—a decision that had shocked the court but earned boundless respect from her crew who watched their female king endure each hardship without complaint.

When at last the verdant shores of Punt emerged from the morning mist, Hatshepsut's breath caught in her throat. Paradise revealed itself in lush green hillsides cascading to pristine beaches, where elegant stilt houses perched above crystalline waters. The Puntite queen, heavy-limbed and adorned with gold, received Hatshepsut with curious reverence, their delegations exchanging formalities beneath the shade of aromatic trees.

Days stretched into weeks as Hatshepsut walked among fragrant gardens, selecting the finest myrrh saplings to transplant to Egyptian soil. Her scribes recorded every detail as trade flourished—Egyptian grain and crafts exchanged for heaps of frankincense, ebony, cinnamon bark, and exotic spices that perfumed the air with promises of wealth. Leopards and baboons were corralled for the journey home, while elephant tusks and gold dust were carefully stored in the ships' holds.

"This bounty will silence those who whisper that a woman cannot rule," Senenmut observed quietly as they prepared for departure, the Puntite royalty loading one final gift—a small chest of rare healing herbs known only to their people.

Hatshepsut nodded, her eyes reflecting the setting sun over foreign waters. "They question not the gender of prosperity," she replied, "only its absence."

When her fleet returned to Egypt, laden with treasures that seemed plucked from dreams, the very priests who had once questioned her claim to the throne now bowed deeply before her. The expedition to Punt had accomplished what no decree could—legitimacy bought with frankincense and myrrh, with gold and exotic animals that now processed behind her through the Temple of Karnak, living testaments to a female Pharaoh's undeniable success.

The Temple of Karnak echoed with triumphant chants and the rhythmic beating of drums, the sounds reverberating off the massive stone columns that soared toward the heavens like the trunks of petrified palms. Incense smoke coiled in thick clouds beneath the painted ceilings, weaving through shafts of sunlight that slanted down from high windows. Hatshepsut stood before her people, resplendent in the regalia of kingship. Her false beard jutted proudly from her chin, her crown combining the red of Lower Egypt and the white of Upper Egypt in perfect union. The golden cobra at her brow gleamed in the torchlight, its jeweled eyes seeming to move as she turned her head.

Behind her, a procession of servants carried treasures that seemed drawn from the realm of dreams: living myrrh trees in baskets of earth, their aromatic leaves rustling softly; elephant tusks taller than a man, polished to a gleaming ivory; sacks of gold dust and aromatic resins that perfumed the air with exotic scents; and exotic animals that caused the crowd to gasp in wonder—baboons with intelligent eyes, slender cats with spotted coats, and birds whose plumage rivalled the painted ceilings in brilliance.

Nehesi walked proudly at the head of the returning sailors, his dark skin contrasting with the white linen of his new Egyptian garments—a gift from his pharaoh for the successful voyage. Behind him came his crew, sunburned and weary but standing tall, men who had seen wonders and returned to tell the tale.

The nobles and priests who had once questioned her legitimacy now bowed deeply, their objections silenced by success. Gold spoke louder than tradition, and the expedition to Punt had yielded gold in abundance. Young Thutmose stood nearby, his eyes dark and unreadable, following the procession of treasures with keen interest. Hatshepsut noted with satisfaction that there was respect in his gaze as it turned to her—grudging, perhaps, but real.

Later, in the quiet of her private chambers, Hatshepsut dismissed her attendants, keeping only Senenmut by her side. She removed the heavy crown and false beard, allowing herself a moment of vulnerability seen by few.

"They accept me now," she said softly, watching the play of lamplight on the golden artifacts from Punt. A small monkey, a gift from the ruler of Punt, chattered softly from its perch near the window. "Not as woman ruling in a man's place, but as Pharaoh."

Senenmut smiled, daring to step closer than protocol permitted. "They have no choice but to accept what is before their eyes. You have achieved what no king before you have done in generations."

She turned to him, her expression softening momentarily. "And what of the boy? Does Thutmose still chafe under my rule?"

"He learns the arts of war and governance as you commanded," Senenmut replied, his eyes meeting hers directly. "Though he watches you with keen eyes."

Hatshepsut laughed, the sound both bitter and satisfied. "Let him watch and learn. He will have his time—when I decide it should come."

She walked to the balcony overlooking the great temple complex she had commissioned, its massive columns piercing the night sky like spears thrust upward by giants. The moon bathed the limestone in silver light, transforming the earthly structure into something otherworldly, eternal. In the distance, construction continued on her mortuary temple, where the story of the Punt expedition was already being carved in eternal stone.

"Moses thought to rule through me," she mused, her hands resting on the cool stone balustrade. "Then he abandoned his throne for the sake of slaves. His people labor under my command, his legacy erased from our monuments, and I reign supreme."

As darkness fell over Thebes, the ancient capital that had seen pharaohs come and go for a thousand years, Hatshepsut surveyed her kingdom with cold satisfaction. She had transformed herself from regent to king, from woman to living god. The revenge she had enacted against those who had betrayed or doubted her was complete. As Pharaoh Maatkare Hatshepsut, daughter of Amun, King of Upper and Lower Egypt, she had written her name in stone and gold, ensuring that it would endure for all eternity.

1459 BC - The Weight of the Double Crown

Twelve years had passed since the triumphant return from Punt, twelve years that had added weight to Hatshepsut's frame and lines to her face, but also depth to her achievements. The sun god Ra blessed the western banks of the Nile with a spectacular display of gold and crimson as his celestial barge sailed toward the underworld, painting the limestone cliffs with fire and blood. Queen Hatshepsut stood atop the uppermost terrace of Djeser-Djeseru, her magnificent mortuary temple at Deir el-Bahari, her hand resting on the cool limestone balustrade, fingers tracing the hieroglyphs that proclaimed her divinity. Her kohl-rimmed eyes, still sharp despite the years, swept across the monuments of her twenty-one-year reign, pride swelling in her chest even as her breath came heavier than it once had.

"Is it to your satisfaction, Divine One?" asked Nebrut, her loyal steward who had replaced the irreplaceable Senenmut after his death the year before. The man's voice carried the proper reverence, but lacked the warmth, the intimate understanding that Senenmut had possessed—a void as vast as the western desert that no amount of obsequious service could fill. Hatshepsut nodded slowly, the false beard affixed to her chin feeling particularly heavy this evening. "It is... magnificent," she said, her voice deeper than most women's but no longer carrying the commanding resonance it once had.

At fifty-one, the woman who had dared to claim the throne of Egypt as king rather than queen consort had changed from the lithe, determined daughter of Thutmose I. Where once stood a slender-waisted warrior princess now stood a woman whose flesh hung in folds beneath her royal robes, whose face had grown round with years of palace feasts and ceremonial beer. The linen of her pleated robe strained across her girth, and although the kohl rimming her eyes remained as perfect as ever, no cosmetic could disguise the deep lines etched by time and responsibility.

Below her sprawled the temple that would tell her story for eternity—the immense colonnaded halls where limestone pillars soared upward like reeds of primordial creation, the garden terraces planted with exotic myrrh trees from Punt, their fragrant gum scenting the evening air with promises of rebirth, and the magnificent reliefs depicting her greatest achievement: the trading expedition to the fabled Land of Punt, where every chisel stroke had been guided by Senenmut's exacting vision. She had commissioned those reliefs herself, insisting that every detail be perfect, right down to the obese Queen of Punt whose image had once amused her. Now, with bitter irony, Hatshepsut recognized something of herself in that foreign queen's form, time's cruel mirror held up to royal vanity.

"You should see it now, old friend," she murmured to the empty air, words meant for ears long stopped with natron and resin. "The temple is finished. Just as you designed it." She could almost feel Senenmut beside her, tall and proud, eyes gleaming with intelligence and something more, something only she had been privileged to see in their private moments.

The wind carried no reply, only the distant call of ibis returning to roost and the eternal murmur of the Nile. Senenmut's absence remained a hollow cavern in her heart that no monument, however grand, could fill. A sudden, sharp pain lanced through her jaw, catching her off guard, white-hot as a blacksmith's iron. Hatshepsut staggered, clutching at her face, a most unpharaonic gesture that would have horrified her courtiers had any been present to witness this moment of frailty. The pain receded to a dull throb centered in an upper tooth on the left side, pulsing in time with her heart. Her royal physician had examined it, offering honeyed plasters and incantations to Sekhmet for healing. Neither remedy had helped, the pain returning like a stubborn enemy at Egypt's borders.

She probed the offending tooth with her tongue, feeling the deep cavity that had formed there, rough-edged and sensitive. Another reminder that she was mortal; despite the divine office she held. Pain cared nothing for royal decrees.

The journey back across the Nile to the palace at Thebes was mercifully brief, though each small wave that slapped against the hull sent tremors of pain through her jaw. Seated beneath a canopy on the royal vessel, Hatshepsut watched the shoreline glide past. On the eastern bank rose the great temple of Karnak, where she had erected obelisks taller than any pharaoh before her, their gold-capped peaks catching the last rays of the setting sun, flaring like distant beacons.

By the time she reached her private chambers, the pain had intensified, radiating from her jaw up to her temple like poison spreading through the body. Her body servant, an aging Nubian woman who had been with her since girlhood, helped her remove the heavy ceremonial regalia—the false beard that chafed her skin raw by day's end, the double crown of Upper and Lower Egypt with its weight of history and expectation.

Alone again, she lowered her bulk onto a cedar chair inlaid with ivory, its legs creaking slightly under her weight. She caught sight of herself in a polished bronze mirror—a distorted reflection, but clear enough to see what she had become. Her face, once delicately formed with high cheekbones and almond eyes, had grown jowly, the skin hanging in loose folds despite the finest unguents and oils.

"The council awaits, Divine One," came Nebrut's voice from beyond the door. "Thutmose has brought reports from the northern border. There are rumors of Mitanni movements."

The council chamber was lit by dozens of oil lamps, their light reflecting off the golden accents decorating the walls and columns. As Hatshepsut entered, moving with deliberate grace that disguised the effort each step cost her, the assembled ministers and priests rose and prostrated themselves. Only one figure remained standing—Thutmose III, dressed in the regalia of a general, golden arm bands gleaming against skin bronzed by campaigns in the field, but wearing also the uraeus serpent that marked him as co-ruler.

"You are late, Mother of Egypt," he said, using the formal address that always seemed to carry a hint of mockery. His eyes, dark as Nubian ebony, assessed her with the calculating gaze of a man measuring the remaining sand in an hourglass.

"A king is never late," Hatshepsut replied evenly, lowering herself onto her throne with practiced dignity. "The world simply awaits the king's pleasure."

Thutmose's lips tightened, but he said nothing more as he took his seat at her right hand. He had grown into a handsome man, lean and hard muscled from years of military training, ambition burning in eyes she had once looked into as they gazed up from a child's face.

The council meeting dragged on interminably, reports of granary levels and tax collections punctuated by priests droning about proper observances.

Throughout it all, the pain in Hatshepsut's tooth grew steadily worse until she could taste blood where she had bitten the inside of her cheek.

"And what of these Mitanni movements?" she asked when she could bear the tedium no longer.

Thutmose straightened, clearly eager to discuss military matters. "Our spies report unusual activity along the northern frontier. They gather forces at Kadesh. They may be testing our resolve."

"Do you recommend action?"

"A show of force, at least. I could lead a contingent northward—" his eyes gleamed with barely suppressed eagerness.

"To what end?" Hatshepsut interrupted. "To provoke a conflict, we do not need. Egypt prospers in peace, nephew. Remember that."

"Egypt grows soft in peace," Thutmose countered, a challenging edge to his voice. "Our neighbors mistake patience for weakness. The army grows restless, and the young nobles speak of glory denied them."

Around the council table, ministers exchanged uneasy glances. Such open disagreement between the co-rulers was rare, a crack in the facade of divine harmony that ruled the Two Lands.

When at last the ministers had been dismissed, only Hatshepsut and Thutmose remained, facing each other across the polished cedarwood table.

"You undermine me," she said without preamble, too weary for elaborate protocol.

"I seek only to protect Egypt's interests," he replied, his eyes never leaving hers. "As is my duty as pharaoh."

"I am King," she corrected sharply.

Thutmose leaned forward. "For how much longer, Majesty? The priests whisper that your health fails. The people see that you no longer appear in public as often as you once did. They remember when Hatshepsut led processions through Thebes, straight-backed as a cedar of Lebanon."

A fresh stab of pain shot through Hatshepsut's jaw, as if to emphasize his point. She fought to keep her expression neutral, drawing on reserves of will be forged through decades of ruling men who thought a woman had no right to power.

"I am in perfect health," she lied. "And I will remain King of Upper and Lower Egypt until Osiris calls me to the Field of Reeds."

"Of course," Thutmose said, inclining his head with exaggerated deference. "I merely thought... with Senenmut gone this past year, and your daughter Neferura also deceased... perhaps you might wish to... ease your burdens."

The mention of Senenmut was like a dagger to her heart, slipping past royal defenses to pierce the woman beneath the crown. Had Thutmose known of their closeness? Had everyone at court seen what she had thought so carefully concealed?

"My burdens are mine to bear," she said coldly. "You are dismissed."

After Thutmose had gone, his straight-backed stride that of a man confident in his future, Hatshepsut remained seated at the council table, her hand pressed against her aching jaw, feeling the unnatural heat there. The pain seemed to have doubled since the mention of Senenmut's name, as if grief and physical suffering had twined together like the twin serpents of her uraeus crown.

Rising with effort that she concealed even from herself, she made her way back to her private chambers, each step measured and deliberate. The night stretched before her, long and lonely, filled with pain both physical and spiritual. Tomorrow she would visit her mortuary temple again, to ensure that the artisans had carved her name deeply enough that it could never be erased, never be forgotten when she had joined the gods.

The stars of Nut's body glittered coldly overhead as she gazed from her balcony toward the western cliffs where she would one day rest. One tooth, one year, one lifetime in the endless flow of the Nile's waters. Soon, she would join the gods, take her place among the imperishable stars. But not tonight. Tonight, she was still pharaoh, still king, still Hatshepsut.

Even as the pain in her jaw promised darker days to come, she stood tall, her shadow cast long across the palace floor—the shadow of a woman who had made herself king.

Chapter 6 - The Crown Passes

1458 BC - Thebes

The merciless Egyptian sun blazed from a cloudless azure sky, casting pools of shimmering heat across the royal training grounds. Young warriors moved with the lethal precision of desert predators, their oiled bronze skin glistening as they thrust and parried in perfect formation. Their weapons flashed like captured lightning, the clash of bronze against bronze ringing out in rhythmic symphony. At their center, commanding the space with exceptional grace and barely contained power, stood Thutmose III, nephew and reluctant co-ruler to the woman who had dominated Egypt with an iron will for two relentless decades.

Sweat carved glistening rivulets down his muscled torso, mapping the contours of a body honed by years of martial discipline. His movements held the fluid economy of a hunting leopard; each thrust of his khopesh blade cutting through the superheated air with deadly precision. At twenty-four, he was the embodiment of a warrior in his prime—a man born to command yet still forced to dwell in the elongated shadow of his aunt's formidable rule. His eyes, sharp and predatory as a desert falcon's, tracked every movement of his men, cataloging their strengths and weaknesses with a general's meticulous precision.

"Again!" he commanded, his voice carrying across the training ground with the authority that was his birthright. "The Mitanni will not pause while you fumble with your grip or catch your breath! They will slice open your belly and leave your entrails for the jackals!"

His captain, Ahmose, approached through the dust cloud raised by stamping feet. The grizzled veteran's face bore the scars of a dozen campaigns, his respect evident as he bowed slightly. "My lord, perhaps enough for today? The men have trained since dawn, and the heat saps even the strongest warrior's strength."

Thutmose wiped the stinging sweat from his brow with the back of his hand, his expression softening almost imperceptibly at his trusted captain's counsel. "The enemies of Egypt do not rest, Ahmose. Their spears grow no duller while we seek shade." Nevertheless, he nodded, recognizing the wisdom in the older man's words.

Leaning closer to Ahmose, he lowered his voice to a murmur meant only for the captain's ears. "Select the most promising fifty from this cohort. Send them at night to the barracks at Pi-Ramesses. I want them trained in all aspects of warfare—not just spearmen, but bowmen, charioteers, drivers, even support roles—armorers, cooks, physicians. Have them scattered among different regiments, with only their immediate commanders knowing they answer to me." His eyes darted toward the palace before continuing. "The Mitanni threat grows while she concerns herself with monuments and trade. Egypt must be ready, even if Hatshepsut refuses to see the danger. This remains between us, old friend. If she learns I am building my own loyal force..." He left the consequence unspoken, placing a firm hand on Ahmose's shoulder, who nodded with grim understanding of both the command and the risk.

As his men dispersed like particles of sand in the wind, Thutmose stood alone, his gaze drawn inexorably toward the royal palace. Its magnificent limestone walls gleamed like polished bone against the relentless blue sky, the ornate golden capstones catching fire in the afternoon light. Somewhere within those labyrinthine corridors and chambers, behind walls adorned with the finest art in the Two Lands, the woman who had denied him his rightful throne for sixteen long years was waning like the moon before dawn's inevitable approach.

"She weakens," Ahmose said quietly, following his master's gaze. "The physicians say the Female King will not see another new moon."

The Dying Queen

In her opulent royal chamber, Hatshepsut reclined upon a couch of cedarwood inlaid with ivory and gold, surrounded by the trappings of power she had seized and held with uncompromising determination. The heady scent of myrrh and frankincense wafted through the air from copper braziers, their smoke curling in lazy spirals toward the painted ceiling, but even these precious aromatics could not entirely mask the sickly-sweet smell of decay that surrounded her like an invisible shroud.

The abscess in her tooth had spread with insidious determination, poisoning her blood over weeks despite the desperate ministrations of Egypt's finest physicians. Her face, once beautiful enough to capture the desire of two pharaohs and the respect of an entire kingdom, was now grotesquely distorted, swollen on one side like an overripe fruit ready to burst.

Senefer, the royal physician, knelt beside her, his aged hands trembling slightly as he prepared another poultice of honey, natron and rare herbs brought at great expense from lands far beyond Egypt's borders. His eyes, rheumy with age and heavy with the knowledge of impending failure, avoided meeting hers directly.

"My king," he said softly, using the male title she had insisted upon throughout her unprecedented reign. "This will ease the pain somewhat, but I fear—"

"Speak plainly, Senefer," she commanded, her voice weaker than the day before but still carrying the unmistakable authority that had cowed the priests and nobles of Egypt for decades. "I am dying. The shadows gather at the edges of my vision, and Anubis whispers my name in the silence between heartbeats."

The physician lowered his eyes in respect and resignation. "The infection spreads like Nile flood waters, my king. It resists all remedies. The gods may yet—"

"The gods gave me twenty-one years as ruler of the Two Lands," she interrupted, a flash of her old imperious manner briefly illuminating her ravaged features. "More than they granted my father or my brother." She turned her head with effort to look out the window, where she could see the top of her magnificent temple at Deir el-Bahari, its perfect proportions a testament to her vision. "I have built monuments that will speak my name when all who knew me are dust. That is immortality enough. Now leave me."

When the physician had backed away in obeisance and gone, Hatshepsut closed her eyes against the pulsing pain that had become her constant companion. Senenmut was gone—her friend, architect, advisor, perhaps lover—dead these past two years. She was alone now, as perhaps she had always truly been, surrounded by courtiers but isolated by the unique burden of her position.

The massive cedar doors opened again with barely a whisper against the polished floor, and she did not need to look to know who entered. The footsteps were measured, military—deliberate as a heartbeat—her nephew and co-regent, whom she had kept from power for two decades while she ruled in male regalia and false beard.

"Queen of Egypt," Thutmose said, his deep voice carefully neutral as he approached her couch, the scent of the training grounds—sweat, leather, and bronze—cutting through the cloying sweetness of her sickroom.

Hatshepsut opened her eyes, the effort visible. "Nephew." She studied him with the practiced assessment of a lifetime spent measuring men's strength and intentions—the broad shoulders beneath his simple linen kilt, the stern face with its high cheekbones that reminded her so much of his grandfather, the first Thutmose, whose name meant "Born of Thoth," god of wisdom. "You look well. The sun has burnished you like copper."

"You do not," he replied bluntly, without cruelty but with the soldier's directness that was his nature.

A laugh escaped her, a sound like dried papyrus tearing, quickly turning to a grimace of pain that she could no longer disguise. "No. I do not." She gestured weakly to a stool beside her, inlaid with scenes of hunting in the marshes. "Sit. Let us not waste precious breath on pretense when the Western Horizon beckons me."

Thutmose sat, his back straight as a spear shaft, his hands resting on his knees with a warrior's readiness. "The physician says—"

"The physician knows nothing that I do not already feel in my bones," she interrupted, her voice momentarily stronger. "My journey to the afterlife approaches, and my ka grows restless to begin its crossing." She looked at him directly, her gaze still penetrating despite the fever that glazed her eyes. "Are you pleased, Nephew? Does the prospect of my death fill your heart with lightness?"

"No," he answered, surprising her with his evident sincerity. "You were always good to me.

"And the usurper who took your throne when you were but a child," she added, watching him closely for the resentment she had always sensed simmering beneath his carefully composed exterior.

Thutmose was silent for a moment, his eyes drifting to the window where her temple was visible. "You did what you believed was necessary for Egypt," he finally said, each word measured. "As will I when the Double Crown rests solely upon my brow."

She nodded slightly, a queen's approval that seemed to come from ancient habit. "You have learned patience, at least. The virtue I least expected from you as a hot-blooded youth. That restraint will serve you well when you sit alone upon the Horus Throne." She shifted uncomfortably, trying to find relief where none existed. "Tell me of your plans. Let an old woman glimpse the future she will not live to see."

"I have no plans beyond seeing Egypt prosper," he said diplomatically, but his eyes betrayed the careful calculation behind the words.

"You are a poor liar, nephew. That, at least, has not changed since boyhood." A ghost of a smile touched her swollen lips. "Your men train daily for war, not harvest festivals. The scouts you've sent to Syria return with maps of fortifications, not trading contracts." She attempted a full smile through her pain. "The warrior-king strains against his leash, eager to run free across the battlefield."

Thutmose leaned forward, dropping pretense like a discarded cloak. "Egypt has been too long at peace," he said, his voice low and intense. "Our enemies grow bold while we build monuments. The Mitanni push at our borders in the north. They think us weak, ripe for plucking like overripe dates."

"Because a woman ruled?" she challenged, old fire briefly rekindling in her sunken eyes.

"Because we have not shown our strength beyond our borders for a generation," he countered, rising to pace the chamber like a caged lion.

"When I was a boy, I heard tales of my grandfather crossing the Euphrates, striking terror into the hearts of our enemies. Entire kingdoms trembled at the mere rumor of Egyptian chariots on the horizon. Egypt was feared then."

"Fear is a poor foundation for lasting rule," she said softly, watching him with new interest. "It crumbles when the sword arm weakens."

"And you would make it feared again." It was not a question.

"I would make it respected again," he corrected, stopping his pacing to face her directly. "Trade flourishes when disruption is costly. Tribute flows when backed by the threat of force. Diplomacy works best when both parties know what waits behind the smile. This is how empires endure beyond the reign of a single pharaoh, be they man or woman."

Hatshepsut watched him, truly seeing for the first time the king he would soon become. The boy she had sidelined had grown into a man of purpose and vision, different from her own but no less potent. "And what of my legacy?" she asked, her voice barely above a whisper now. "Will you tear down my monuments as I am accused of doing to your father's? Will you chisel my name from the stones and replace it with your own?"

Thutmose stopped his pacing, his expression softening almost imperceptibly. "Your achievements cannot be denied, even by those who resented your rule. The expedition to Punt, the temples you built, the years of abundance..." He met her gaze directly. "I will not destroy what strengthens Egypt. Your monuments tell of Egypt's greatness, not merely your own."

"A diplomatic answer," she said with a weak smile. "Perhaps you learned something from me after all, besides how to wait in silence."

"I learned to watch," he replied, a shadow crossing his face. "Twenty years of watching and waiting while others ruled in my name."

Hatshepsut closed her eyes briefly, the pain becoming too much to bear while maintaining her royal composure. "Then you will not wait much longer," she whispered. "The gods call me to account for my deeds."

Thutmose moved closer, surprising her by taking her hand—once elegant and commanding, now thin and spotted with age. It was perhaps the first gentle touch between them in years, bridging the vast gulf that had separated aunt from nephew, usurper from rightful heir. "Rest now, aunt. Egypt has not forgotten what you built, and neither shall I."

She looked up at him, this nephew who had waited so long in her shadow, suddenly seeing not the boy she had displaced but the man who would soon command the mightiest army in the known world. "Go," she whispered. "Return to your soldiers. They will need you more than I do now. Egypt will need you."

He bowed, a gesture of genuine respect rather than mere formality, and left her chamber without another word, his footsteps receding like the tide.

Alone again, Hatshepsut turned her gaze to the window, where the last light of day painted her great monuments in shimmering gold. She had ruled not as queen but as king, donning the false beard and male regalia to command a world that respected only masculine power. She had built what no woman before her had built, reached heights no female had dared to contemplate. Let the gods judge her as they would. She had seized her moment in the great span of Egypt's endless history.

The New King

The next day Thutmose walked the palace corridors which seemed longer than usual as he made his way to his aunt's chambers, passing beneath towering columns painted with scenes of royal triumph spanning three dynasties. Guards stepped aside, their eyes lowered in deference. Priests murmured prayers as he passed, the scent of sacred incense hanging in the air like an invisible fog.

He paused at the intricately carved doors to her chamber, steeling himself for what lay beyond, then entered without announcement, as was his right as co-regent and heir.

The room was unnaturally still, silent in a way that only death's presence can impose. Hatshepsut lay on her royal couch, her body already prepared with the first anointments of the embalmers, her face peaceful for the first time in weeks. The swelling had subsided somewhat in death, returning to her some shadow of the beauty and dignity she had possessed in life. Around her, attendants stood motionless as statues, waiting for his command, their eyes carefully averted from his face to allow the new king his private moment with the dead.

Thutmose approached slowly, his sandaled feet making no sound on the polished floor. He studied the face of the woman who had ruled Egypt in his place, searching his heart for the hatred he had nursed for so many years. To his surprise, he found only a quiet acceptance of what had been and what would now be. Perhaps, he thought, there was wisdom in the priests' teachings that hatred burned only the vessel that contained it.

"She died alone," a priestess of Isis said softly from the shadows, her shaved head covered with a leopard skin denoting her high rank. "As she lived, despite the crowds that surrounded her."

Thutmose reached out, gently closing his aunt's eyes with his fingertips, completing the ritual that would begin her journey to the afterlife. "No," he said, his voice carrying the certainty of his new authority. "She lived surrounded by Egypt. And Egypt will remember her, in stone and story alike."

He straightened, feeling the weight of the Two Lands settling fully on his shoulders for the first time, like a physical burden and blessing combined. For twenty years he had waited, trained, prepared for this moment. Now, with the Mitanni approaching from the north like storm clouds, there was no time for the extended mourning period that tradition demanded.

"Begin the preparations," he ordered the waiting priests and officials. "The seventy days of mourning will commence immediately. Her body shall be prepared as befits a king of Egypt." He turned to his chamberlain. "But first, summon the royal council. There are decisions regarding our northern borders that cannot wait, even for death."

As he turned to leave, his eye caught sight of his reflection in a polished copper mirror mounted on one wall. For a moment, startled, he thought he saw his aunt's determination reflected in his own features—

the same set of jaw, the same unwavering gaze that looked beyond immediate concerns to the horizon of history.

"You wondered if I would tear down your monuments," he said softly to the still form behind him, words meant for her ka alone. "Watch from the Field of Reeds, aunt. I will build Egypt higher than even you dreamed possible, and your works shall stand beside mine in the eyes of eternity."

Chapter 7 - A Warrior Arises

1457 BC-The Royal Approach

Pharaoh Thutmose III's royal barge sliced through the Nile's sacred waters like a ceremonial dagger's blade. Its cedar hull blazed with inlaid gold that caught the merciless Egyptian sun, flashing signals of divine authority to all who beheld it. Forty oarsmen, their dark skin gleaming with sweat and oil, drove the vessel forward in perfect rhythm, their movements synchronized as the cosmic dance of stars that guided Egypt's destiny.

At the prow stood Thutmose III himself, barely twenty-two years old yet already marked by the gods for greatness. His was not the soft frame of a palace-dweller but the hardened body of one who had prepared for war since boyhood. The muscles of his shoulders and back rippled beneath skin burnished copper by the sun, and though he wore the ceremonial uraeus serpent upon his brow—the cobra goddess Wadjet who protected the pharaoh—it was his eyes that commanded attention. They were a hunter's eyes, a falcon searching the horizon for prey.

Three weeks had passed since Queen Hatshepsut had drawn her final breath, ending two decades of her iron-fisted rule. Fifty days of mourning still lay ahead for Egypt, but the young pharaoh's thoughts had already turned from death to the preservation of empire.

Shadows of the Past

As the royal vessel approached Avaris in the late afternoon, the muddy shoreline came alive with movement. Hundreds of Israelites had gathered, their simple linen garments fluttering in the hot breeze that swept across the delta.

Aaron stood at the riverbank, the weight of fifteen years pressing upon his shoulders as heavily as the Egyptian sun. At sixty-five, his beard was now streaked with gray, his eyes creased at the corners from decades of squinting against the harsh desert light. Beside him stood Joshua, no longer the curious nine-year-old boy but a formidable man of twenty-three, tall and broad-shouldered, with the quiet confidence that comes from surviving under oppression.

Aaron shielded his eyes against the glare. "It's happening again. Though much has changed since Hatshepsut made her bold entrance."

Joshua nodded, his expression somber. "I remember that day clearly. I stood barely reaching your elbow, father clutching my shoulder."

"Nun would be proud to see the man you've become," Aaron said, his voice heavy with memory. Nun had passed three seasons prior, leaving Joshua to carry his wisdom and legacy.

The familiar drumbeat reached them first—the rhythmic pounding that signaled the approach of royal power. Unlike fifteen years ago, no excited messenger had run through the streets. The Israelites had grown wary of royal visits, each one seemingly bringing new burdens.

The royal barge came into view, its grandeur unmistakable even at a distance. Where Hatshepsut's vessel had shone with gold, Thutmose III's barge bore symbols of war and conquest—painted scenes of battle and tribute from foreign lands.

"He stands differently than she did," Joshua noted. "Hatshepsut posed like a statue, immovable, making a statement. He paces the deck like a caged lion."

As the barge drew closer, they could see Thutmose more clearly. Unlike the slender, composed figure of Hatshepsut, he was stocky and muscular, his movements sharp and decisive. The double crown sat upon his head, and the ceremonial beard extended from his chin, but he wore them with casual familiarity rather than as revolutionary symbols. This was a man born to rule, who had simply reclaimed what he considered rightfully his after years of waiting.

The royal barge slowed as it approached the designated landing. Unlike Hatshepsut's carefully choreographed arrival fifteen years earlier, this approach carried the urgency of impending war.

The War Council

By the time the royal barge docked at Pi-Ramesses, evening was approaching. The palace complex loomed against the darkening sky; its walls and columns painted in vibrant colors that celebrated the might of Egypt. Servants rushed forward to assist the royal party, their heads bowed, their movements practiced to the point of invisibility.

Thutmose dismissed his retinue with a gesture. "Prepare my war council chamber. I will join the generals within the hour."

The vast chamber of polished limestone that served as Thutmose's war room was illuminated by dozens of oil lamps. Their flames cast dancing shadows across walls adorned with battle scenes of past pharaonic victories. Maps of papyrus and leather were spread across tables of cedarwood imported at great expense from Lebanon. The air was thick with tension and the heady scent of incense that partially masked the smell of sweat from men who had spent the day in armor, awaiting their king.

General Djehuti stood rigid beside his officers, his face cross-hatched with battle scars earned in service to Thutmose's father. The missing two fingers on his left hand were not hidden but displayed proudly— testimony to his willingness to sacrifice for Egypt. His armor, polished to a high sheen for the royal audience, nevertheless bore the dents and scratches of campaigns that had expanded Egypt's borders under the previous pharaoh.

The double doors swung open without announcement. Thutmose entered, having changed from his ceremonial regalia into a simpler kilt and pectoral that emphasized the warrior rather than the god-king. The royal uraeus still blazed upon his brow, but now he looked every inch the military commander his grandfather had been.

"I come not as divine king but as war-leader, Djehuti," he stated, dispensing with the formal greetings that usually consumed the first hour of any royal audience. "Address me as you would have my father before battle."

Djehuti straightened, something like relief crossing his weathered features. Like many military men, he preferred direct speech to the flowery language of the court.

"As you command, Lord of the Two Lands," he responded, his voice like gravel underfoot.

The general moved to the largest map, jabbing a scarred finger at a region north of Egypt's borders where the troublesome kingdom of Mitanni had been expanding its influence for a generation.

"Our web of informants confirms what we feared," Djehuti reported. "The Mitanni forces have established a forward camp here, in the valley between these ridges. Protected, with good water access—they've chosen their position well."

Nakht, the chief of military intelligence whose shrewd eyes belied his deceptively placid face, stepped forward. His was the dangerous work of gathering information deep in enemy territory, and his reports had saved Egypt from surprise attack more than once during Hatshepsut's reign.

"They have perhaps fifteen hundred men now, Son of Ra," Nakht elaborated. "But our agents report at least two more divisions marching to join them. When assembled, they will number four thousand spears, six hundred chariots."

Rekhmire frowned, fingering his golden pectoral nervously. Unlike the battle-hardened men around him, the chief advisor's experience was in administration rather than warfare, and the numbers troubled him.

"A formidable force," he observed. "And during our time of holy mourning, when they know our attention is divided."

Djehuti's battle-worn face hardened. "Their timing is no coincidence. They perceive Egypt as weakened in this time of change. Our intelligence suggests they will be ready to advance within twenty days, when the moon is full."

Thutmose circled the table slowly, studying the terrain with the eye of a hunter assessing his prey's escape routes. His finger traced potential battle lines, the movement precise and deliberate. The room fell silent, every man watching their young king's reaction, measuring his response against what his father might have done, or what Hatshepsut would have commanded.

"And our preparedness for war?" Thutmose finally asked, his tone neutral.

Djehuti exchanged glances with his officers, a flicker of pride crossing his scarred face. He had spent the years of Hatshepsut's peaceful reign preparing for this moment, knowing that no peace lasts forever in a world of ambitious men.

"We are Egypt, Great House," he stated with simple pride. "Our chariots are lighter, faster than the Mitanni's heavy vehicles. Our composite bows outrange theirs. Our men train daily while theirs grow fat in their camps."

Horemheb, the commander of chariots whose muscled arms bore the ritual scars of his rank, stepped forward. At thirty, he represented the new generation of Egyptian military leadership—men who had come of age during Hatshepsut's reign of trade rather than conquest, but who had never forgotten Egypt's martial traditions.

"The chariot divisions stand ready, Divine One," Horemheb reported. "Five hundred vehicles, each with driver and archer. The finest the Two Lands has ever produced. The horses are Arabian stock, bred for speed and endurance."

Thutmose's eyes narrowed as he assessed the man's confidence. Was this mere boasting, or the justified pride of a commander who knew his forces' capabilities?

"Fine words," the young pharaoh said. "I would see this readiness with my own eyes, not merely hear of it from courtiers' lips."

He placed both hands flat on the map, leaning forward, his gaze challenging each man in turn. None looked away—a good sign, he noted. These were not men who would shrink in battle.

"Tomorrow at dawn, I will inspect every division," Thutmose declared. "Every chariot, every archer, every spearman. I will see their drills, their formations, their discipline."

The generals exchanged surprised glances. This was not the ceremonial inspection they expected from a young pharaoh who had spent his life in the shadow of a woman regarded as one of Egypt's greatest rulers. They had anticipated a brief appearance, perhaps a blessing of the troops before retiring to the luxury of the palace.

"As you command, Son of Ra," Djehuti replied, new respect evident in his tone. "All will be prepared."

Thutmose straightened, his eyes burning with a fire that reminded the oldest officers of his grandfather, the great Thutmose I who had extended Egypt's borders further than any pharaoh before him.

"The Mitanni believe they face a novice ruler, a boy who has lived in a woman's shadow," he stated, his voice low but carrying to every corner of the chamber. "By the holy name of Amun-Ra, I swear they shall discover their error written in their own blood."

A murmur of approval rippled through the assembly. Useramen, watching from the doorway, allowed himself a small, satisfied smile. He had known from the boy's early years that beneath the obligatory deference to his stepmother-aunt lay the heart of a conqueror. Now, at last, Egypt would see the true heir of Thutmose II.

Dawn of the Warrior King

The eastern horizon was just beginning to lighten with the promise of Ra's return when Thutmose emerged from his chambers the next morning. He had slept little; his mind filled with the strategic possibilities presented by the maps. Now, dressed not in the finery of a god-king but in the practical armor of a war leader, he strode through the palace corridors with purpose.

"My chariot," he commanded the startled attendants. "Not the ceremonial vehicle, but my war chariot."

By the time the sun broke over the distant hills, painting the training grounds of Pi-Ramesses in hues of gold and crimson, Thutmose was already approaching the assembled troops. The vast plain stretched to the horizon, transformed into a sea of ordered military formations that testified to Djehuti's organizational skills.

Five thousand Egyptian soldiers stood in perfect ranks—spearmen, archers, and elite guards, their weapons shining in the early light. On the right flank, hundreds of war chariots were arranged in precise lines, the horses stamping and snorting, eager for movement after hours of stillness.

The assembled officers gaped in astonishment as their pharaoh arrived not in a litter carried by servants but astride his own war chariot, taking the reins himself with the skill of a practiced charioteer. He wore battle armor rather than ceremonial attire, the only mark of his royal status the uraeus serpent on his simple leather helmet.

General Djehuti, mounted in his own chariot, rode to meet his king. Surprise and approval warred on his scarred face as he realized the young ruler intended a true military review, not a symbolic appearance.

"Your father would be proud to see you thus, Great House," the old general observed, genuine emotion roughening his already graveled voice. "He too preferred the chariot to the litter on days of inspection."

Thutmose's hands were sure on the reins, controlling the spirited horses with the skill of one who had practiced far more than court protocol demanded.

"What use is a pharaoh who cannot lead his men into battle, General?" the young ruler responded. "Hatshepsut ruled through administrators and architects. I shall rule through the point of a spear."

He drew the chariot to a halt before the assembled officers, who stood straighter under his assessing gaze.

"I will see everything," Thutmose announced, his voice carrying across the morning air. "No ceremonial parades, no rehearsed displays. Show me how these men will fight when the Mitanni come."

Trial by Sun

Throughout the blistering day, as Ra's fiery eye crossed the vault of heaven, Thutmose moved among the troops with tireless energy. He watched chariot formations execute complex maneuvers at full gallop, wheels spraying sand as they turned in perfect coordination, archers losing volleys while the vehicles swerved and pivoted at breakneck speed.

"Faster!" he called to one squadron. "The Mitanni will not stand still for your arrows! Again!"

He stood during infantry formations as they demonstrated the shield-wall, feeling the ground shake as they advanced in disciplined ranks, spears bristling like the spines of some great beast. He nodded with approval as each man maintained his position, shields overlapping to create an impenetrable barrier.

"Good," he told the infantry commander. "But can they hold formation when charging downhill? Show me."

The archers particularly impressed him, their Egyptian composite bows—technological marvels of wood, horn, and sinew—delivering arrows with a force and accuracy that no other nation could match. He watched as they struck targets at extreme ranges, nodding with satisfaction as an officer explained the new arrow designs that would penetrate Mitanni armor.

As the sun began its descent toward the western horizon, Thutmose had seen every division, spoken with dozens of officers, even tested the weight and balance of the weapons himself. His skin was darkened further by the sun, streaked with dust, but his eyes burned with a satisfaction that none of his courtiers had ever witnessed.

The senior officers gathered as Thutmose returned to his chariot for the final time. They awaited his judgment, this young king who had surprised them all with his knowledge and endurance. Not once had he retreated to the shade pavilion erected for his comfort; not once had he called for wine or refreshment.

"I have seen enough," Thutmose announced, his voice carrying to all nearby.

He removed his helmet, revealing sweat-soaked hair and a face transformed by newfound certainty. This was no longer the prince who had stood in Hatshepsut's shadow, but a warrior-king coming into his inheritance.

"The army of Egypt is ready," he declared. "When the Mitanni come, we shall not merely defend—we shall destroy."

The Golden Promise

He turned to face the assembled divisions, raising his war mace high above his head. The bronze head caught the light of the setting sun, blazing like the eye of Horus himself. His voice rose, carrying across the training ground to the most distant ranks.

"Men of Egypt! For years I have waited, watched, and learned while others ruled in my name. That time is ended! The blood of conquerors flows in my veins! When we march against the Mitanni, it will not be as the army of Hatshepsut, but as the spear of Thutmose!"

A roar went up from thousands of throats, a sound like the breaking of a great wave upon the shore. Spears and bows were thrust skyward in salute. Even the most battle-hardened veterans found themselves caught in the young pharaoh's sudden, magnetic authority.

Thutmose raised his hand, and the roar of the soldiers gradually subsided. His eyes, outlined in kohl that made them appear both divine and dangerous, swept across the assembly of warriors before him.

"Hear me, men of Egypt! For every enemy you vanquish, for every right hand you bring before me as proof of your valor, I shall reward you with a golden butterfly—crafted by the finest artisans of our realm, bearing the blessed cartouche of my name. These tokens will not merely signify your bravery on the battlefield; they shall be your gateway to glory and prosperity in this life and the next. The more butterflies you earn, the higher your standing shall be among your brothers-in-arms and in my royal court. Let these golden wings remind you that death is but a transformation, and that through your courage, you shall transcend ordinary existence and take flight toward immortality, just as the soul rises to join the gods!"

The declaration ignited the assembled warriors like flame to dried papyrus. A thunderous cheer erupted across the ranks, men stamping their feet and clashing weapons against shields in rhythmic fervor. Young soldiers yet untested in battle envisioned their necks adorned with golden butterflies, their future glory already taking shape in their minds. The sound rolled across the training grounds and echoed against the distant temples, carrying the promise of blood, gold, and the rebirth of Egypt's martial might under their true pharaoh.

Pharaoh Ascendant

General Djehuti approached, bowing deeply for the first time with genuine reverence rather than mere protocol. In twenty years of service, he had never bent his knee with such conviction. "And so, begins your legacy, Lord of the Two Lands," the old warrior said, voice rough with emotion.

Thutmose watched the sun setting behind the ranks of his army, casting long shadows across the land he had been born to rule. His expression hardened with resolve, the last light of day sculpting his features into a living monument.

"No, General," he replied. "Today marks the beginning of Egypt's greatest glory. What my grandfather began, what my father continued— I shall complete. The world beyond our borders will tremble at the mention of Egypt's name."

The last rays of the setting sun caught the gold of his uraeus, making the cobra seem to come alive with fire as darkness descended upon the Two Lands. In the gathering twilight, his silhouette stood sharp against the horizon—no longer a king in waiting, but a pharaoh ascendant.

"The gods have prepared me for this moment," Thutmose said, his voice barely above a whisper yet somehow heard by all who needed to hear it." Twenty years in shadow have forged not a king, but a weapon. And now, I shall be unleashed."

As torches were lit around the training ground, illuminating the vast army in flickering light, Thutmose remained motionless, already seeing in his mind's eye the victories to come and the empire he would build.

Under the ancient stars of Egypt, a new constellation was forming—the warrior pharaoh and his destiny, written not in the heavens but in the blood of his enemies and the glory of the empire he would forge.

Chapter 8 - Battle of Megiddo

1457 BC – Which Route to Megiddo

Three weeks later, Thutmose stood at the narrow mountain pass leading to Megiddo, the dust of travel coating his skin like a second layer, the smell of men and horses thick in the still air. His officers gathered around him in tense silence, sweat beading on their brows despite the cooling evening breeze. Before them lay three potential routes: two wider paths that curved around the mountains to approach Megiddo from the north and south, and a treacherous central pass—the Aruna Pass—that cut directly through the mountains. It was barely wide enough for two men to walk abreast, let alone for chariots to pass.

The tension in the air was palpable as the generals eyed the narrow defile with obvious apprehension. They had followed their Pharaoh this far without question, but this... this was madness.

"The enemy expects us to take the northern or southern route," said Djehuty, gesturing to the map spread before them on a portable wooden table. His gnarled finger traced the wider paths. "They have positioned scouts on both paths. Our own scouts have observed their movements."

Thutmose studied the narrow central path, his mind calculating risks against advantages with the precision of a mathematician. His grandfather would have taken the bold path, he knew. And he was his grandfather's true heir, whatever the nobles might whisper about his legitimacy.

"And the Aruna Pass?" His voice betrayed nothing of his inner thoughts.

"Unguarded, my lord," replied the scout, a wiry Nubian whose dark skin bore the tattoos of his tribe alongside the scars of Egyptian battles. "But for good reason. It is nearly impassable for an army. The chariots would have to be dismantled and carried piece by piece. In places, the rock walls close in so tightly a man must turn sideways to pass. If the enemy discovered us halfway through..."

His voice trailed off, the implications clear to all present. They would be trapped like fish in a barrel, unable to fight effectively, unable to retreat.

A heavy silence fell over the war council as the setting sun cast long shadows across their faces. To choose the direct path was to risk the entire army in a narrow defile where they would be vulnerable to ambush. Yet to take either of the safer routes would sacrifice the element of surprise. Thutmose felt the weight of their stares, the silent questioning of his judgment.

He had waited too long for this moment to choose caution now.

"What say you, my generals?" Thutmose asked, though his mind was already made. The blood of conquerors ran in his veins, and he would not disappoint his ancestors now.

The oldest of his commanders spoke first, his beard gray with age and wisdom. "The northern route is safest, my Pharaoh. We would lose no men to the terrain, and our chariots could deploy in formation."

"And arrive exactly where they expect us," Thutmose countered, his tone sharpening. He turned to the others. "And you?"

One by one, they counselled caution—all except Djehuty, who alone met his gaze directly. The old general's eyes held a spark of the same fire that burned in Thutmose's heart.

"The Aruna Pass, my lord," Djehuty said firmly, silencing the murmurs of the other officers. "The enemy believes no army would be foolish enough to attempt it. That is precisely why we must. The unexpected path often leads to the greatest victory."

Thutmose smiled, a predatory flash of teeth. "My thoughts exactly." He turned back to the council, and now his voice carried the unmistakable weight of command. "We take the Aruna Pass. Single file. The chariots will be dismantled and carried by hand if necessary."

"My Pharaoh," protested one of the older generals, his face flushed with either heat or insubordination, "it will take days to move the entire army through such a narrow pass. If the enemy discovers us halfway through—"

"Then we will fight halfway through," Thutmose replied sharply, cutting him off with a gesture as final as an executioner's blade. "I will lead the vanguard myself. If I, your Pharaoh, am willing to risk the pass, can my warriors do less?"

He let his gaze pass over each man in turn, a silent challenge in his eyes. No one dared argue further. The decision was made.

"Prepare the men," he ordered. "We move before dawn."

As the council dispersed, Djehuty remained behind, his weathered face thoughtful in the gathering darkness.

"This is the moment that will define your reign," the old general said quietly. "Twenty years you have waited while Hatshepsut ruled. Now all will see whether the son of Thutmose II is truly his father's heir."

Thutmose nodded, his face betraying nothing of the fierce anticipation that coursed through his veins like fire. "Not just my father's heir, Djehuty. By the time this campaign is done, they will speak my name alongside the greatest kings of our history."

In the distance, beyond the mountains, the enemy camped in ignorant bliss, unaware that death approached by the path no sane commander would choose.

1457 BC – Aruna Pass, Megiddo

Dawn had not yet broken when the army began its perilous journey. The stars still glittered overhead like the jewels in Pharaoh's crown as the first troops entered the narrow confines of the Aruna pass. Thutmose, true to his word, led the vanguard, his chariot disassembled and carried by his most trusted guards. Behind him stretched the long snake of Egypt's army, moving in silence through the treacherous pass.

The walls of rock rose steep on either side, cutting off the sky to a narrow ribbon of blue above. In some places, the men had to turn sideways to squeeze through, their weapons scraping against the unforgiving stone. The clatter of equipment echoed softly, each sound amplified by the close confines until it seemed that the mountains themselves whispered of their passage.

The wooden frames of the war chariots, their wheels removed and carried separately, passed from hand to hand along the line. The horses, blind folded to prevent them from panicking in the narrow space, were led carefully, their handlers murmuring soothing words into twitching ears.

By midday, the heat in the narrow pass had become oppressive, the sun beating down directly into the confined space, turning it into a stone oven. Men sweated and strained, their breath coming in harsh gasps as they climbed the steeper sections. The smell of dust and sweat mingled with the sharp tang of horse urine and the metallic scent of bronze weapons. Yet no one complained. Their Pharaoh led them, his lean figure visible ahead, his determination a tangible force driving them forward.

Thutmose himself felt the strain, his muscles aching from the difficult terrain, but he allowed no sign of weakness to show. His face remained impassive, his steps steady. From time to time, he would speak words of encouragement to the men nearest him, calling them by name when he recognized a face. A Pharaoh was a god, but a commander must be a man among men, his father had taught him.

As dusk approached on that second grueling day, Thutmose reached the far end of the pass, emerging onto a small plateau that overlooked the plains of Megiddo. The evening air felt cool against his skin after the stifling heat of the narrow gorge, and he drew in a deep breath, savoring the taste of freedom after the claustrophobic journey.

Far below, he could see the campfires of the enemy, the Mitanni and their allies, spread across the valley floor like stars fallen to earth. They faced north and south, expecting the Egyptian army to appear from either direction. Their sentries patrolled the obvious approaches with predictable regularity.

They did not look to the narrow pass directly behind them. Not once did a sentry turn to scan the heights where death gathered like a storm cloud.

A fierce satisfaction filled Thutmose's chest. His gamble—or rather, his strategic brilliance—was about to pay dividends in blood and victory. He turned to watch as more of his men emerged from the pass, their faces painted orange and gold by the setting sun. They moved with the silent discipline that made Egypt's armies feared throughout the known world.

Through the night and the following day, the Egyptian army continued to emerge from the Aruna pass, reassembling chariots and forming battle lines in strict silence. Fires were forbidden, food consumed cold, voices kept to whispers. By the second dawn, Thutmose's entire force was arrayed on the heights above Megiddo, undetected by the enemy below.

The Battle commences

Thutmose stood before his chariot, now reassembled and gleaming in the morning light. His armor had been polished to remove the dust of travel, the golden vulture emblem on his breastplate catching the sun's rays. His charioteer, a Syrian prince taken as hostage in a previous generation and raised to serve Egypt, held the reins of the two magnificent horses that stamped impatiently, sensing the coming battle.

The Pharaoh surveyed his assembled force with pride. They had accomplished the impossible already. Now came the reward.

"Our enemy sleeps," Thutmose said to his assembled commanders, his voice pitched low but carrying clearly in the still morning air. "They believe themselves safe for now, expecting us days from now on the northern or southern approach." He pointed to the sprawling camp below, where figures could be seen moving about their morning routines, unaware of the doom that hung over them. "By midday, they will know the wrath of Egypt."

He climbed into his chariot, taking the reins himself—a gesture that did not go unnoticed by his men. A Pharaoh who drove his own chariot into battle was a Pharaoh worth dying for.

"For Egypt!" he cried, and the war cry was taken up by thousands of throats as the Egyptian army surged down the slope toward the unsuspecting enemy. The sound rolled ahead of them like thunder, a divine announcement of the storm about to break.

The surprise was total and devastating. Thutmose's chariot led the charge, his horses snorting clouds of dust as they thundered down the slope, their hooves striking sparks from the stony ground. The Pharaoh himself stood tall and terrible, his bow already drawn, his face set in the ritual expression of divine wrath that generations of Egyptian artists had portrayed on temple walls.

Behind him, the Egyptian chariots formed a deadly spearhead, followed by ranks of infantry with spears levelled, their formations precise despite the downhill charge. The morning sun glinted off bronze spearheads and painted shields, making the attacking force seem to shimmer like a mirage—a nightmare made manifest.

The enemy camp erupted in chaos. Men scrambled for weapons, horses reared in panic, and commanders shouted contradictory orders that went unheard in the tumult. Some warriors fell to their knees in prayer, believing the gods themselves had descended upon them. Others fled without even attempting to arm themselves. The Mitanni coalition had expected days to prepare for the Egyptian approach. Instead, death descended upon them from the mountains themselves.

Thutmose's chariot smashed through the first line of hastily assembled defenders, men who had not even had time to don armor properly. His bow sang, arrows finding targets with unerring precision as his charioteer guided the horses through the chaos. The Syrian prince had been trained since childhood for this role, and his hands were steady on the reins despite the carnage around them. Around them, the Pharaoh's chariot warriors cut bloody swathes through the panicked enemy forces.

"Forward!" he bellowed above the din of battle, his voice carrying the authority of the divine. "Give them no time to form ranks!"

The Egyptian chariots ploughed through the enemy like scythes through wheat, while the infantry followed, finishing off the wounded and securing the ground already taken. The discipline that had seen them through the treacherous pass now manifested as deadly efficiency on the battlefield.

The Mitanni forces broke before the Egyptian onslaught, fleeing toward the walled city of Megiddo in desperate retreat. What had begun as a battle quickly became a rout, a slaughter so one-sided that even some of the Egyptian veterans looked disturbed by the ease of their killing.

But then discipline faltered. Egyptian soldiers, seeing the enemy forces scattered and dying across the battlefield, began to break ranks. Men who moments before had fought as a single coordinated force now dropped to their knees beside fallen Mitanni warriors, drawing knives to claim their grisly trophies. The promise of golden butterflies proved too powerful a lure, as soldier after soldier severed right hands from their vanquished foes, collecting them in sacks and cloth bundles with fevered intensity.

"No!" Thutmose raged, seeing his men dispersing across the field to harvest their rewards rather than pressing their advantage. His voice, powerful as it was, could not compete with the promise of wealth he himself had made. "To the city! Take Megiddo now, before they can seal the gates! The dead will remain dead, but our victory slips away with every moment wasted!"

But his words were lost in the chaos of victory. Before his eyes, the fleeing enemy reached the safety of Megiddo's walls. The great gates swung closed with a distant boom that seemed to echo the slamming shut of opportunity. The coalition forces were trapped inside the city, but they had denied the Egyptians their complete victory.

Thutmose pulled his chariot to a halt, his face dark with fury and disappointment. His charioteer wisely said nothing, keeping his eyes fixed on the horses as the Pharaoh surveyed the scene with mounting anger. What should have been the crushing defeat of his enemies would now become a protracted siege.

"Secure the camp," he ordered his commanders, his voice dangerously quiet. "Establish a perimeter around Megiddo. No one enters or leaves the city."

As his men rushed to obey, chastened by the cold anger in their ruler's voice, Thutmose gazed at the walled city that had snatched complete victory from his grasp. His first battle as Pharaoh had been a success—but not the decisive triumph he had sought.

His general Djehuty approached, blood splattered across his armor. The old warrior's face was grim but satisfied as he bowed before his king.

"My Pharaoh, the enemy commander's tent has been found intact. His battle plans reveal allies approaching from the north. They expected to join forces here at Megiddo within the week."

Thutmose nodded grimly. "Then we will be here to greet them as well." He dismounted from his chariot, planting his feet firmly on enemy soil. The ground beneath him had been Syrian land when the sun rose. Now it was Egyptian. "Megiddo will fall. And when it does, all of Syria will know that Egypt has returned to the field of battle."

He looked toward the horizon, where dust clouds might soon announce the approach of enemy reinforcements. Let them come. The son of Thutmose was ready.

Seven Months Later

Seven grueling months later, each morning, Menkheperre rose before the sun to offer prayers to Amun and Ra. Each evening, he stood at the war council, his authority absolute. His presence became legend among his troops—never faltering, never yielding.

When the city finally opened its gates, it was not with banners but with broken spears and bare hands. The rebel kings prostrated themselves before the Pharaoh. Menkheperre descended from his chariot with divine calm, arms outstretched to the sky.

"Amun has spoken through patience and steel! Egypt stands eternal!"

The priests accompanying him recorded the campaign with fervor, chronicling divine omens witnessed throughout the siege: a falcon circling the camp on the first day, the full moon rising red the night before the surrender, and a rainstorm breaking a months-long drought after Menkheperre's personal prayer.

To the Pharaoh, these were not chance. They were divine endorsements.

That night, as he poured a libation before a golden statue of Ra within his war pavilion, Menkheperre spoke aloud with unshakable conviction.

"You have stretched my days and tested my will. And I prevailed. Let the world know I hold the royal Ka."

His generals toasted him not merely as Pharaoh—but as the embodiment of the divine.

In his heart, Menkheperre believed no force, no prophecy, no forgotten prince, could rival the favor that Megiddo had proven.

But the gods would soon be silent.

Chapter 9 - Mitanni Revenge

1439 BC - Eighteen Years Later

Eighteen blood-soaked years had passed since Thutmose's first campaign, and with each savage triumph, his faith in the gods had grown stronger than the granite foundations of Karnak itself, deeper than the sacred wells that tapped the primordial waters of creation. Fifteen glorious campaigns had followed that initial baptism of fire and bronze, each one a blood-drunk testament to divine favor, each conquest carved in enemy flesh and written in the smoke of burning cities. The trembling boy who had once cowered in Hatshepsut's perfumed shadow now strode across corpse-littered battlefields like Horus incarnate, his name whispered in terror and reverence from the fever-misted swamps at the Nile's source to the salt-crusted mouths of the delta.

Egypt's empire stretched like a ravenous beast across the known world, its appetite fed by rivers of enemy blood and mountains of plundered gold. Tribute flowed from conquered kingdoms in endless, glittering processions—Nubian gold still warm from virgin mines, silver from the mountain kingdoms that caught the first kiss of dawn, precious stones that held captured starlight in their crystalline hearts. The double crown of the Two Lands had never drunk deeper of power, never tasted such intoxicating dominion over the affairs of mortal men.

Each dawn, as the sacred ibis called across the Nile's mist-shrouded waters, Thutmose III knelt naked before the golden statue of Amun-Ra, his muscled body gleaming with oils of frankincense and myrrh, offering prayers of gratitude that rose like incense smoke to the throne of heaven. The god's painted eyes seemed to burn with approval, blessing this mortal vessel who had carried divine will to the furthest corners of the earth.

"The gods have made me their instrument," he often declared to his priests, his voice rich with conviction. "Through divine will, Egypt shall rule all lands beneath the sun."

But the gods, as Thutmose would learn, were as changeable as the desert winds.

Beyond the Euphrates

The Euphrates writhed like a serpent of molten silver beneath the pitiless sun, its ancient waters thick with the silt of a thousand buried kingdoms, whispering secrets that only the dead could understand. The merciless heat struck Thutmose's bronzed flesh like hammer blows from Ptah's forge, sending rivers of sweat coursing down the iron-hard muscles of his shoulders, disappearing beneath the royal collar of gold and lapis lazuli that blazed like captured lightning against his throat. Beyond those sacred waters, shimmering in waves of desert heat like a fever dream, lay the throbbing heart of Mitanni power—his seventeenth campaign, destined to be carved in letters of fire across the scroll of eternity.

The very air thrummed with divine promise, heavy with the musk of destiny.

Or so the gods had promised in his dreams.

"The signs are favorable, Great One," his high priest had assured him before departure, reading omens in the smoke of sacred incense. "Ra's falcon soars high, and Ptah has blessed your weapons with victory."

Now, standing on the threshold of conquest, Thutmose felt that familiar surge of divine confidence coursing through his veins like liquid gold. This would be the campaign that eclipsed even his grandfather's legendary achievements, the final proof of his divine nature.

"Great One, the crossing point is secured," announced Ahmose, his battle-scarred commander whose loyalty had been forged in the fires of countless victories. The veteran warrior's eyes held the same confidence that blazed in his pharaoh's heart.

Thutmose nodded, his falcon-sharp gaze fixed on the far shore where destiny awaited. "We cross before dawn. Tomorrow, the gods shall witness our greatest triumph."

As darkness wrapped the landscape in velvet shadows, ten thousand Egyptian soldiers prepared for what they believed would be another glorious victory. Their pharaoh moved among them like a living deity, his presence alone worth a thousand reinforcements. These men had never known defeat under his command—how could they? The gods themselves fought beside them.

"My father planted his stele on this bank," Thutmose told his generals around the shielded fire. "Tomorrow, I shall place mine deeper in enemy territory than any Egyptian has dared venture. The gods have ordained it."

Dawn came like a gift from Ra himself, painting the sky in shades of gold and crimson as the Egyptian army crossed the Euphrates. Thutmose stood proudly in the lead vessel, his golden pectoral catching the first rays of sunlight and sending flashes of divine radiance across the water. Surely this was Ra's blessing made manifest.

By midday, with the sun blazing overhead like the eye of Horus, the entire force had crossed. Thutmose raised his war scepter high, his voice carrying the authority of the gods themselves.

"Burn their cities! Destroy their temples! Let them know that Egypt has arrived, and with it, divine judgment!"

The Mitanni Response

Saushtatar of Mitanni received news of the Egyptian invasion like a man struck by lightning. For too long, this pharaoh had carved through kingdoms like a scythe through wheat, claiming divine mandate for his endless conquests. Now the Egyptian dared to cross the sacred Euphrates, to violate lands that Mitanni blood had claimed through generations of warfare.

"Twenty thousand warriors," Saushtatar commanded his generals, his voice sharp as a blade forged in celestial fire. "Every chariot, every horse, every man who can hold a spear. This Egyptian god-king shall learn that the horse lords of Mitanni bow to no foreign deity." Within days, the greatest chariot forces the world had ever seen gathered like storm clouds on the horizon. Five thousand war chariots, each drawn by horses bred for speed and power, their bronze-shod wheels ready to crush Egyptian ambitions beneath their weight. The thunder of their approach echoed across the plains like the voice of an angry god.

Clash of Empires

When Thutmose first beheld the Mitanni host, it was as though the very gates of the underworld had vomited forth an army of the damned. A cold serpent of premonition slithered down his spine despite the furnace heat of the desert, its icy coils tightening around his heart with each thunderous hoofbeat that shook the earth beneath his feet. His scouts had babbled warnings of their numbers, voices cracking with barely contained terror, but nothing—not the fevered nightmares of dying men, not the apocalyptic visions of mad prophets—could have prepared him for this sight of damnation made manifest.

A sea of bronze and horsehair plumes stretched beyond the horizon's bleeding edge; a metallic forest of death that made his own army seem like children clutching toy spears. War chariots by the thousand, their wheels shod with bronze that caught the sun like the eyes of demons, their horses snorting steam like the breath of Set's own hellhounds. The thunder of their approach rolled across the desert like the voice of an enraged god, promising annihilation to all who dared stand before it.

For the first time in nineteen years of warfare, doubt crept into the pharaoh's heart like poison into a wound.

"Form ranks!" he commanded, masking his uncertainty behind royal authority. "The gods fight beside us! Stand firm!"

The battle joined with the fury of cosmic forces colliding, a symphony of destruction that would have made the gods themselves weep tears of blood. Mitanni chariots crashed against Egyptian lines like tsunami waves against granite cliffs, their bronze-shod wheels grinding flesh to crimson paste, their horses screaming with voices that sounded almost human in their agony. The air became thick as honey with the copper-sweet stench of spilled blood, the acrid smoke of burning chariots, and the bowel-loosening reek of men dying in terror and pain.

Thutmose fought from his golden chariot like a man possessed by all the demons of the desert, his composite bow—a masterwork of horn and sinew that had drunk the blood of a thousand enemies—singing its death song as arrow after arrow found beating hearts with the precision of divine judgment. His Nubian driver, muscles corded like ship's rope beneath skin black as polished obsidian, wove through the chaos with supernatural skill, the horses' flanks white with foam and painted crimson with spatters of enemy blood.

Yet even as he fought with the savage fury of Set unleashed, even as his arrows carved paths of destruction through enemy ranks like the finger of an avenging god, Thutmose could taste the bitter poison of defeat creeping across his tongue like the kiss of a cobra. The Mitanni numbers were a plague of locusts darkening the sky, their horses fresh while his own mounts stumbled with exhaustion, their chariots heavier and more numerous than the stars in heaven's vault.

Where were the gods now? Where was the divine favor that had carried him through sixteen triumphant campaigns?

The Price of Divine Abandonment

"Sound the retreat," Thutmose ordered at last, the words tasting like grave dust in his mouth. Never had he spoken such words. Never had the gods allowed such humiliation to befall their chosen son.

As the Egyptians began their fighting withdrawal, Thutmose remained at the rear, covering his men's retreat with arrows that flew true as eagles to their prey. It was then that catastrophe struck like a serpent from the shadows. A Mitanni spear, hurled by a warrior whose face bore the ritual scars of their war cult, found the gap in his armor where bronze plates joined at his side.

Pain exploded through him like molten copper as the spearhead lodged deep in his flesh. Through sheer divine will—or perhaps the last flickering of divine favor—he dispatched his attacker with a shaft through the throat, then gripped the protruding spear and snapped it off with a roar that would have made Sekhmet proud.

Blood darkened his royal kilt, but his face betrayed nothing of the agony that clawed at his soul.

"Retreat! Back to Egypt!" he commanded. "The day is lost..."

The words hung in the air like a curse. For the first time in his reign, Thutmose III had tasted defeat.

The Wounded God-King

The retreat across the lands they had so recently conquered was a nightmare of pain and bitter reflection. As fever clawed at his mind with talons of fire and the infection spread through his wound like liquid poison coursing through his royal veins, Thutmose found himself drowning in questions that tasted of blasphemy and damnation. The wound throbbed with each heartbeat like a second heart, a corrupt organ that pumped liquid agony instead of life-giving blood through his god-king's body.

Had he somehow offended the gods? Had his pride grown too great, his confidence too absolute? The spearhead lodged in his side throbbed with each heartbeat, a constant reminder of mortality, of weakness, of... humanity.

When they finally reached Egyptian soil and the safety of the border fortresses, Saushtatar's army established camp just beyond the frontier, their watch fires visible from the Egyptian walls like malevolent stars. They were waiting—waiting to see if Egypt's god-king would live or die.

"They know I am wounded," Thutmose confided to his physician in the flickering lamplight of his tent. The elderly healer's face was grave as he examined the festering wound. "They wait to see if the gods will claim their pharaoh."

But it was not just the Mitanni who waited. Throughout the camp, whispered conversations died when officers approached. Thutmose caught fragments—worried murmurs about divine displeasure, hushed speculation about what sins might have brought this catastrophe upon them.

And something else. Something that chilled his fever-wracked body more than any winter wind.

"Moses..." he heard one soldier whisper to another. "They say the Hebrew still lives... that he has cursed Egypt from beyond the grave..."

Thutmose closed his eyes, feeling the royal ka—that divine essence that made him pharaoh—flickering within him like a dying flame. For eighteen years, he had been certain of his divinity, unshakeable in his conviction that the gods had chosen him to rule the world.

Now, as poison spread through his veins and defeat bitter as gall coated his tongue, he wondered if perhaps the gods had found him wanting after all.

Waiting in the Shadows

The journey back to Pi-Ramesses was a fever-dream odyssey through the valley of shadows, each mile measured in drops of royal blood that stained the sand beneath his chariot's wheels. When Thutmose finally collapsed in his palace chambers—carried like a broken doll by servants whose faces were wet with tears of terror and grief—he knew with the terrible clarity that comes only to the dying that this battle, the one raging like wildfire through his poisoned veins, was one that could not be won with strategy or strength of arms or divine favor.

The golden walls of his chamber seemed to pulse and breathe around him like the throat of some monstrous beast, and in the dancing, shadows cast by oil lamps, he saw the shapes of vultures circling, patient as eternity itself.

In the shadows beyond Egypt's borders, Saushtatar's army waited like vultures for news that would reshape the ancient world. And in the depths of his own soul, Thutmose III—conqueror of nations, beloved of the gods, the mighty pharaoh who had never known defeat—waited to learn whether the divine favor that had defined his reign had truly abandoned him at last.

The gods, it seemed, were no longer listening to their chosen son.

Chapter 10 - The Deception

March 1439 BC The Death Chamber

The morning sun cast long shadows across the palace corridors as Prince Menkheperre, son of Thutmose III—owner of the sacred chamber whose mysterious hieroglyphs had confounded temple scribes for years—strode toward the royal apartments, his sandals slapping against the polished limestone floor with military precision. His bronzed face, carved with the same noble lines as his adoptive father's, betrayed nothing of the turmoil that gripped his heart, a mask of royal dignity concealing the fear that threatened to overwhelm him like the annual flood waters of the Nile. At twenty years old, the son that his mother Merytre-Hatshepsut had brought into Thutmose's household six years ago had grown into a formidable warrior, yet sweat beaded beneath his golden collar despite the morning's coolness, the weight of impending catastrophe pressing down upon his broad shoulders—shoulders that would soon bear the divine mantle of pharaoh in ways no heir had ever imagined possible.

Behind him walked Rekhmire, the Vizier of Upper Egypt, a man whose wisdom was as legendary as his loyalty, his lean frame hardened by five decades under Egypt's merciless sun moving with the quiet grace of a desert panther. Beside them glided Merytre-Hatshepsut, the Great Royal Wife whose composed exterior masked a mother's fierce determination and a queen's calculating mind. Her regal bearing, adorned with the sacred uraeus serpent upon her brow that seemed to writhe with golden life in the flickering torchlight, commanded respect even in this moment of crisis. The woman who had brought Menkheperre into Thutmose's household as a fourteen-year-old boy now walked beside him as an equal partner in the most audacious deception in Egypt's four-thousand-year history.

"Has word spread beyond these walls?" Menkheperre asked without turning, his voice low and taut as a drawn bowstring, each word weighted with the gravity of empire hanging in the balance.

"No, my prince," Rekhmire replied, his words measured as carefully as grain during famine. "The royal physicians speak to no one. The servants have been confined to their quarters with orders that carry the penalty of death if broken. Even their whispers die before reaching the outer chambers."

"I have personally ensured absolute silence among my household staff," Merytre-Hatshepsut added, her voice steady as the eternal Nile, smooth as polished obsidian yet hard as the granite of Aswan. "The loyal ones remain; the questionable ones have been... reassigned to duties that require no speech. But we cannot maintain this illusion indefinitely, my son. The Mitanni wait beyond our borders like jackals in the night, their yellow eyes gleaming with hunger for Egyptian gold, and if they discover the truth..."

They reached the massive cedar doors of the royal apartments, imported at vast expense from the forests of Lebanon, their surfaces carved with scenes of the pharaoh's victories over Asiatic princes and Nubian kings. Two Medjay guards stood motionless as statues of black granite, their ebony skin glistening with scented oils, their eyes forward, their faces impassive beneath their leopard-skin headpieces. Yet even these warriors, trained from childhood to show no emotion, could not completely mask the fear that hung in the air like the scent of incense, palpable as the heat rising from desert stones at noon.

Inside, the chamber was dim as a tomb, heavy curtains of Babylonian silk drawn against the morning light that would have revealed too much of death's handiwork. The air was thick with the smell of natron and medicinal herbs—myrrh from the land of Punt, frankincense from Arabia Felix, and the bitter aroma of henbane—and beneath it all, the unmistakable odor of death's corruption beginning its inexorable work despite the priests' best efforts.

Upon the royal bed, carved from a single block of alabaster and adorned with gold leaf that caught what little light penetrated the chamber like trapped sunbeams, lay Thutmose III, Mighty Bull, Lord of the Two Lands, Beloved of Ra. His once powerful body, which had led cavalry charges against the chariots of Mitanni and climbed the walls of besieged cities with sword in hand, already grew cold and rigid as the granite monuments he had erected to proclaim his glory. The royal physicians stood back respectfully as the family approached, their shaven heads bowed like wheat before the desert wind, their faces downcast behind linen masks soaked in protective oils that could ward off disease but not the finality of death.

"When?" Menkheperre asked simply, his throat constricting around the word as though it were a poisoned dart.

"As the moon reached its zenith, my prince," answered the chief physician, his voice barely above a whisper, as though death might claim him too if he spoke louder. "The wound had festered beyond our skill to heal, the poison spreading through his blood like Nile crocodiles through river reeds, consuming all in its path."

Menkheperre gazed down at the man who had not only ruled Egypt for forty-one years but had taken him as a son when his mother became Great Royal Wife, seeing past humble origins to recognize the fierce spirit that burned within. Merytre-Hatshepsut moved to the opposite side of the bed, her jeweled fingers—rings of lapis lazuli and carnelian that had adorned queens for a thousand years—reaching out to touch her husband's marble-cold forehead with the tenderness of a mother soothing a sleeping child. In death, Thutmose's face had relaxed, the lines of command and worry smoothed away like footprints in sand after a desert wind, the fierce eyes that had stared down kings and generals now closed forever, the mouth that had issued commands obeyed by millions now silent as the tombs in the Valley of Kings.

"May your journey through the underworld be swift, beloved husband," Merytre-Hatshepsut whispered, her voice carrying the weight of genuine grief mixed with the steel of royal duty. "May Osiris welcome you among the gods, and may your name live forever in the mouths of men and in the hearts of your sons."

"Father," Menkheperre added, his voice steady despite the storm of grief and fear raging within like a khamsin wind, "your work is not finished. Your spirit shall continue through me, as the sacred texts foretold."

The Council of Deception

The council chamber fell silent as a tomb as Rekhmire outlined his strategy, his words filling the vast space like incense smoke, intoxicating and dangerous. Around the massive table of acacia wood imported from the forests beyond the Third Cataract, polished to a mirror sheen by generations of servants until it gleamed like dark water under starlight, sat the highest officials of Egypt: the High Priest of Amun, corpulent and adorned with enough gold to ransom a kingdom, his multiple chins quivering like disturbed pond water; the General of the Armies, his face a living map of scars from battles fought across three continents; the Chief Scribe, thin as a papyrus reed and just as flexible in his loyalties; and the royal architects, whose skilled hands shaped monuments meant to outlast the stars themselves.

"The prince must become Thutmose III—in body, in voice, in spirit," Rekhmire declared, his obsidian eyes glinting with the same dangerous intelligence that had served two pharaohs across decades of court intrigue. "The king must not die, for Egypt's sake. For the sake of the true heir who must one day claim his birthright."

"Impossible," muttered the High Priest, his heavy gold collar gleaming like captured sunlight as his jowls trembled with indignation. "Such deceit would offend the gods themselves. The divine ka cannot be counterfeited like common jewelery hammered by coppersmiths in the bazaars. The rituals of succession are sacred, immutable as the flooding of the Nile, established by the gods when the world was young."

"This is not deceit," Merytre-Hatshepsut spoke for the first time, rising from her throne-like chair with the fluid grace of a desert cat, her voice cutting through the chamber like a blade forged in the sacred fires of Ptah. The golden uraeus upon her brow seemed to sway hypnotically as she moved, the sacred serpent's ruby eyes glowing like drops of divine blood. "This is the fulfilment of the ancient texts, mysteries known only to the highest priestesses of Isis, secrets passed down through the sacred bloodline from the time of the god-kings who ruled before the pyramids cast their shadows across the sand."

She moved to stand beside Menkheperre, her hand resting on his shoulder in a gesture that spoke of both maternal love and royal authority. "I have spent these past months studying the Texts of Continuity, scrolls so ancient that their papyrus crumbles at a touch, their hieroglyphs written in ink mixed with the blood of sacred bulls. The Ritual of Continuity speaks of times when the royal ka may flow from father to son like water from one sacred vessel to another, when Egypt's need transcends the ordinary laws of succession."

The High Priest's small eyes widened like a hippo surfacing from murky water. "You speak of texts known only to..."

"I am Wife of Amun," she replied with quiet authority that made the chamber's massive stone columns seem to lean inward to catch her words. "I am she who walks between the worlds of gods and men, keeper of mysteries that predate the building of Memphis. These sacred truths are mine to interpret, mine to implement when the very survival of the Two Lands hangs in the balance like a sword suspended by a hair." She gestured toward the painted walls where scenes of Egypt's glorious past glowed in the lamplight—pharaohs receiving tribute from Nubian princes, Egyptian chariots crushing Asiatic armies, the gods themselves blessing the eternal kingdom with prosperity and power. "The signs have been manifested for those with eyes to see—the sacred ibis nesting atop Menkheperre's chamber for seven consecutive nights, the five planets aligning during the last full moon like celestial sentinels guarding Egypt's destiny, the dreams that have visited me wherein Thutmose himself spoke of the great deception that would preserve his empire."

The General leaned forward, his weathered hands—scarred by sword-grips and marked by the burns of Greek fire—folded before him on the polished table. "Even if the gods smile upon this... transformation," he said carefully, choosing his words like a man walking through a field of hidden cobras, "the prince must become his father in every detail—voice, mannerisms, knowledge of military tactics and the names of every officer who has sworn the blood oath. Thutmose III was a warrior king who fought alongside his men, who could identify a captain's horse from a hundred paces and remember the name of every soldier's eldest son. His men knew him by sight, by the way he held a khopesh sword, by the timbre of his war cry that could be heard above the clash of bronze on bronze."

"A monumental challenge," Rekhmire acknowledged, inclining his grizzled head slightly, "but not insurmountable for one who carries his father's fire in his veins. Many of the soldiers who accompanied Thutmose to the northern campaigns have seen Prince Menkheperre in battle, cutting down Mitanni charioteers with the same deadly grace, the same berserker fury that made his adoptive father a legend whispered in fear around enemy campfires from the Euphrates to the borders of Punt."

Merytre-Hatshepsut moved to the great map of Egypt painted on the chamber's eastern wall, her finger tracing the sacred course of the Nile from its mysterious source beyond the Cataracts to its fertile delta where it embraced the Great Green Sea. "The ritual must be completed at Karnak, before the sacred wall where your father's annals will be inscribed for eternity in hieroglyphs that will proclaim his victories when the present becomes dust and legend. Your wife Meritamun awaits there, heavy with your first child—a child who must be born not to an uncertain prince, but to Thutmose III reincarnate, blessed by the gods and destined to rule."

All eyes turned to Menkheperre, evaluating, measuring, weighing his worth like precious metal assayed by master craftsmen. Though barely into his third decade, his broad shoulders already bore the invisible weight of command, his dark eyes reflecting the same calculating intelligence that had made Thutmose III the terror of his enemies and the beloved protector of his people.

"And my brother Amenhotep?" he asked, his voice carrying new depths of authority, new harmonics of command that seemed to resonate with the very stones of the palace.

"He will remain in Memphis under my protection," Merytre-Hatshepsut declared with the finality of divine decree, her voice ringing with the absolute certainty of a mother defending her young. "Hidden from the daggers of court assassins and the poison of ambitious nobles, protected like the most precious jewel in Pharaoh's treasury until he comes of age. I will return there immediately after we complete the transformation ritual at Thebes, resuming my role as guardian and teacher until the wheel of fate turns full circle."

The Mitanni Deception

The rumor spread through the Mitanni camp like wildfire consuming dry grass in the season of Shemu, carried on the desert wind by merchants and spies, camp followers and captured Egyptian slaves desperate to curry favor with their captors. Thutmose III lives! The whispers raced from tent to tent, growing in the telling until they took on the weight of divine pronouncement. The Egyptian pharaoh, that lion of the battlefield whose very name struck terror into the hearts of kings from Babylon to the cataracts of Nubia, had survived his mortal wounds through the intervention of his patron gods, his recovery as miraculous as his legendary prowess in battle.

In his ornate command tent, hung with tapestries looted from the palaces of a dozen conquered kingdoms—silk from distant Serica, wool dyed with Tyrian purple, cotton soft as cloud-shadows from the mysterious lands beyond the sources of the Nile—Saushtatar received the intelligence with the skepticism of a man who had built his reputation on the bones of those who had underestimated him. His powerful frame, hardened by three decades of warfare that had taken him from the shores of the Caspian Sea to the walls of Memphis, tensed like a lion sensing the approach of hunters as he paced across carpets thick enough to muffle the sound of his mounting rage.

"Impossible," he growled, his voice rumbling like distant thunder rolling across the Mesopotamian plains before a summer storm. The jeweled hilt of his curved sword, a masterwork of Damascus steel blessed by the fire-priests of Ahura Mazda, caught the lamplight as he gesticulated in frustrated disbelief. "I saw the Egyptian spear pierce his side myself, watched the bronze point emerge from between his shoulder blades slick with royal blood, saw him fall from his chariot like a felled cedar. No man survives such a wound, not even one who fancies himself a living god walking among mere mortals."

"Nevertheless, my king," replied his most trusted general, a battle-scarred veteran whose loyalty had been purchased with gold and sealed with blood oaths sworn before the altar of Mitra, "our most reliable spies—men who have served us faithfully for a decade, who know the difference between rumor and reality—report seeing him with their own eyes at the palace in Pi-Ramesses. They describe him walking the corridors issuing orders to his commanders, meeting with his council of advisors, reviewing reports from the border fortresses. They say he moves with a slight limp from his wound, favoring his left side as a man might who had felt the kiss of bronze, but his eyes..." The general paused, choosing his words carefully. "His eyes burn with the same fire as before, the same terrible intensity that made strong men tremble when they spoke of war."

Preparations for the Sacred Journey

In Pi-Ramesses, preparations began with the frantic urgency of men racing against the desert wind. Merytre-Hatshepsut took personal command of the complex logistics, her mind—trained in the intricacies of palace administration and temple ritual—working with the precision of a master craftsman setting precious stones into a golden collar. The Great Royal Wife had not achieved her exalted position through beauty alone, though the gods had blessed her with features that could launch a thousand ships or topple kingdoms; her intelligence was as sharp as obsidian, her will as unbreakable as Egyptian granite.

"The borders must be secured, but with minimal forces," she advised, standing before the great map of Egypt's territories that covered an entire wall of the planning chamber, the sacred river painted in lapis lazuli blue winding through the golden desert like the serpent of life itself. Her finger traced the vulnerable points along the eastern delta where foreign invaders had breached Egypt's defenses in ages past, where the bones of Hyksos charioteers still bleached beneath the sand.

"We need our remaining troops dispersed throughout the Two Lands—close enough to be recalled if the Mitanni probe our defenses, yet spread thin enough to create the illusion of a strength we do not possess. Let them rebuild the fortifications damaged in recent conflicts, train new recruits from among the peasantry whose sons dream of glory and Egyptian gold."

"The deception must be layered like the finest bronze," Rekhmire added, his ancient eyes glinting with admiration for the queen's strategic mind. "Supply trains must move day and night between Memphis and the frontier, heavily guarded but deliberately visible to enemy scouts. Let the Mitanni spies count wagons loaded with grain and weapons, see fresh horses being driven to the cavalry camps, observe the dust clouds that speak of armies on the march."

"How soon can we depart for Thebes?" Menkheperre asked, his voice already carrying the deeper resonance he was learning to cultivate, the subtle shift in tone and cadence that would transform him from prince to pharaoh in the eyes and ears of those who served Egypt.

"Three days," Merytre-Hatshepsut calculated with the precision of a master astronomer plotting the course of celestial bodies. "The royal barge must be prepared—not merely the vessel itself, but the entire flotilla that befits a pharaoh's progress up the sacred river. Twenty ships at minimum, carrying guards and servants, priests and scribes, the portable treasures that proclaim divine majesty to every mud-brick village and limestone temple that lines the Nile's banks."

She turned to face her son, her dark eyes reflecting the weight of the burden they would share. "The journey upriver will take nearly twenty days—twenty precious days we will use to perfect your transformation, to practice the subtle arts of voice and gesture that will convince even those who knew Thutmose III from boyhood that his ka has indeed found new habitation in your flesh."

The Sacred Burden

As Ra's golden chariot rolled toward the western horizon, painting the sky in shades of carnelian and gold that rivalled the treasures buried with the ancient kings, Menkheperre stood upon his private balcony overlooking the royal gardens. The evening air was heavy with the perfume of exotic blooms imported at staggering expense from the mysterious lands beyond the reach of Egyptian armies—jasmine from the Indies, roses from the mountains of Persia, lotus blossoms the size of dinner platters floating in reflecting pools that mirrored the first stars emerging in the darkening sky like diamonds scattered across black silk.

Yet his thoughts were not on the beauty surrounding him, but on journeys yet to come and destinies waiting to unfold like papyrus scrolls in the hands of fate. In distant Thebes, Meritamun waited, her belly swollen with their first child, unaware that her husband had died and been reborn in the body of another. Would she recognize the ka of her beloved when it gazed at her through different eyes? The ancient texts spoke of recognition that transcended physical form, of souls calling to souls across the barriers of flesh and bone, but doubt gnawed at his heart like carrion beetles working at sun-dried meat.

Merytre-Hatshepsut joined him on the balcony, her presence a comfort and strength in the overwhelming weight of the deception they had undertaken. The night breeze stirred the golden ornaments in her elaborately braided hair, creating a soft music like wind chimes in a temple courtyard, while the sacred uraeus upon her brow seemed to watch the world with ruby eyes that missed nothing.

"You question yourself," she observed quietly, her voice carrying the maternal wisdom that had guided him through the trials of adolescence and the challenges of young manhood. "I can see it in the set of your shoulders, hear it in the rhythm of your breathing. Doubt is a luxury we cannot afford, my son."

"I doubt everything," he admitted, his hands gripping the balcony's stone railing with enough force to whiten his knuckles. "Will Meritamun recognize me when I arrive not as her husband but as her husband's reincarnated ka inhabiting another man's flesh? Will our child be born under a blessing or a curse? Will the gods strike me down for this ultimate blasphemy, or will they smile upon the deception that preserves Egypt from the chaos that follows a weak succession?"

The Great Royal Wife placed her hand over his, her touch warm with understanding and strong with unwavering resolve. "The texts speak of recognition that flows deeper than sight or touch, my beloved son. Your wife will know her husband's ka, for love recognizes love regardless of the vessel that contains it. Your child will be born to a reincarnated pharaoh, blessed by the gods and destined for greatness. As for divine wrath..." She smiled with the serene confidence of one who had walked between the worlds of men and gods for decades. "The gods favor those who preserve Egypt above those who preserve themselves. They honor sacrifice made for the greater good, cunning employed in service of justice, deception wielded as a weapon against chaos."

As the last light faded from the western sky and the eternal stars emerged to begin their nightly journey across the heavens, a strange peace settled over Menkheperre like a mantle of authority woven from starlight and divine purpose. Tomorrow would bring new challenges, new tests of will and wit, but tonight he could rest in the knowledge that he had chosen the path of duty over personal desire, the welfare of the kingdom over the comfort of truth.

Soon they would journey to Thebes, to the great temple complex of Karnak where the ritual of transformation would be completed among columns that had witnessed the coronation of pharaohs for a thousand years. There, before the sacred wall where his adoptive father's annals would be inscribed in hieroglyphs destined to outlast the pyramids themselves, he would complete his metamorphosis from prince to pharaoh, from Menkheperre to Thutmose III reborn.

And when the ritual was complete, when the ancient words had been spoken and the sacred oils applied, Merytre-Hatshepsut would return to Memphis like a lioness to her hidden den, there to guard and guide young Amenhotep—to protect the bloodline in case something should befall Menkheperre.

Chapter 11 - Rise Again Thutmose III

April 1439 BC The Return to Thebes

The great war barge swept around the final bend of the eternal Nile like a golden hawk stooping upon its prey, and there before them lay Thebes—magnificent, terrible, glorious Thebes! The city rose from the mud-black earth of the eastern bank in a symphony of white limestone and red granite, her temples and palaces catching the fierce Egyptian sun and hurling it back in blinding sheets of reflected glory.

Menkheperre stood at the gilded prow like a bronze statue come to life, the sacred crook and flail of his murdered father gripped in hands that no longer trembled. Twenty days upon the sacred river had burned away the last traces of the frightened prince who had fled Memphis in terror. The merciless sun had darkened his olive skin to match the deeper bronze of the man whose identity he had stolen, whose very soul he now claimed as his own.

By all the gods of Egypt, he looked the part! Every gesture studied and perfected, every mannerism copied until it had become second nature. The way Thutmose had held his shoulders, the precise angle of his royal chin, the measured cadence of his speech—all of it now flowed through Menkheperre's veins like the sacred blood of Ra himself.

Beside him, the vizier Rekhmire stood with the patience of a crocodile awaiting the perfect moment to strike. The old fox had orchestrated this magnificent deception with the skill of a master sculptor, chiseling away at Menkheperre's identity until only Thutmose remained.

"The people have gathered like flies to honey," Rekhmire observed, his voice barely above a whisper. "Word has traveled faster than our swiftest courier."

Sweet Isis! The riverbanks swarmed with humanity—nobles draped in their finest linen and gold, priests gleaming like white ibises in the sun, and the common rabble pressed together in a great sea of sweating, shouting, weeping flesh. They had come to witness the impossible: the return from death of their beloved god-king.

"My father always said his heart beat strongest when he gazed upon Thebes," Menkheperre murmured, his voice pitched to the deeper register that had become as natural as breathing. "Now I understand the passion that consumed him."

A flicker of something—approval? warning? — crossed Rekhmire's weathered features. "Remember, my lord. You speak now as Thutmose himself."

"I am Thutmose III!" The words came without thought, driven by a conviction that burned in his very bones. "The ka-transfer is complete. I feel his divine essence flowing through my mortal flesh."

The old vizier nodded, satisfied as a cat with cream. "The Ritual of Continuity has worked its ancient magic. Your father's immortal spirit lives again in you."

But even as the words left his lips, a cold serpent of realization coiled in Menkheperre's belly. In years to come, when young Amenhotep took the throne, the scribes would record only that Thutmose III had ruled Egypt with wisdom and strength.

The name Menkheperre would vanish from the chronicles as if it had never existed. He would become a ghost, a whisper, a man who had never drawn breath upon this sacred earth.

The thought struck him like a physical blow. To save Egypt, he was not merely assuming his father's identity—he was murdering his own, burying Prince Menkheperre as surely as if he had wrapped the corpse in linen and lowered it into a tomb.

The Royal Procession

The procession to the palace unfolded like a great ceremony to the gods themselves. The streets of Thebes had become a river of humanity, pressing forward with desperate hunger to glimpse their miraculously returned pharaoh. Menkheperre moved through them with the measured dignity of a lion stalking through tall grass, occasionally raising his hand in the royal blessing that sent the crowd into paroxysms of joy.

At his side, the Second Prophet of Amun muttered prayers in the ancient tongue, his voice weaving a web of sanctity around the supposed miracle.

"The people wept for three days when word came of your death, Divine One," the priest confided, his words barely audible above the roar of the crowd. "Your return is being proclaimed as the greatest miracle since the gods first raised Egypt from the primordial waters."

"Amun-Ra has shown his divine favor," Menkheperre replied, employing the formal cadences that rolled off his tongue like sacred incantations. "The Great God reached into the very heart of the underworld to retrieve his beloved son."

The priest's eyes shone with fanatic fervor. "The High Priest awaits your coming at Karnak. He has prepared the final rituals that will complete your resurrection."

"Tomorrow," Rekhmire interjected smoothly. "Today, the Divine One must rest and be reunited with his royal household." As the palace gates loomed before them—those massive portals of cedar and bronze that had witnessed the comings and goings of gods and kings— Menkheperre felt his heart hammering against his ribs like a caged bird. Beyond those doors waited Meritamun, his beloved wife, heavy with his child. She who alone could destroy everything with a single glance, a single word, a single moment of doubt.

The palace guards prostrated themselves as one man as the gates swung wide. Within the great columned hall, the entire royal household had assembled in glittering array. Stewards and scribes, fan-bearers and musicians, all pressed their foreheads to the cool marble floor in submission to their returned god-king.

And there, at the far end of the hall beneath a canopy of gold and precious stones, stood Meritamun.

By all the gods, she was magnificent! Even heavy with child, she carried herself like a queen born to rule empires. But she had not prostrated herself as protocol demanded. Instead, she stood like a statue carved from amber and ivory, one slender hand resting upon the pronounced curve of her belly, tears streaming down her face like liquid silver.

The great hall fell silent as the tomb of Osiris as Menkheperre approached her, each footstep echoing like the beating of his own heart. When he reached her, Meritamun's dark eyes searched his transformed features with the intensity of a scribe reading sacred texts.

"My lord," she whispered, her voice breaking like waves upon stone. "They told me you had returned from the dead."

Menkheperre reached out with hands that trembled despite all his training, taking her fingers in his own. "I have returned, beloved," he said in his father's voice. "Amun-Ra has granted me passage back from the Western Shore of eternity."

Her gaze intensified until he felt it might burn through to his very soul. For one terrible moment he was certain she would denounce him, tear away the sacred lies and expose him as the pretender he was. But then, like the sunrise after the darkest night, her eyes softened with something that might have been acceptance—or the most loving deception of all.

"The child stirred within me when I heard the news," she said, her voice carrying clearly through the hushed hall. "As if he recognized his father's voice calling from beyond death itself."

Relief flooded through him like the Nile in flood season. Whether she truly believed in the divine ka-transfer or had simply chosen to accept this magnificent lie for the sake of Egypt, she was with them.

The Sacred Ritual

The Great Temple of Karnak throbbed with power like the beating heart of Egypt herself. Incense smoke hung in blue-gray clouds among the forest of massive columns that stretched toward the heavens like the pillars supporting the sky itself. In the holy of holies, where only the highest priests and the divine pharaoh might tread, the golden statue of Amun-Ra waited in terrible splendor.

Menkheperre stood before the god like a mortal man facing judgment before the throne of eternity itself. The weight of the Double Crown pressed upon his brow like the hand of destiny. The High Priest of Amun raised his ceremonial staff, and the very air seemed to crackle with sacred power.

"Behold the infinite mercy of Amun-Ra!" the High Priest's voice boomed through the sanctuary like thunder rolling across the desert. "The Great God has reached into the very heart of the underworld to retrieve his beloved son!"

What followed was a ceremony of such ancient power that it seemed to reach back to the very dawn of Egyptian civilization. Menkheperre was anointed with seven sacred oils, each one representing a different aspect of divine kingship. Prayers were chanted in the old tongue, words so archaic that their meaning had been lost in the mists of time, yet their power remained undiminished.

Then came the moment that would make or break everything—the consultation with the oracle of Amun.

The massive golden statue of the god would be asked the ultimate question. Its movement—forward for divine approval, backward for condemnation—would reveal the will of the gods themselves. Menkheperre knew that gold had already changed hands to ensure the right outcome, but still his heart hammered like war drums as the ritual began.

"Great Amun-Ra, Lord of Thrones of the Two Lands, does the divine Thutmose stand before you this day, returned by your mighty hand from the Western Shore of eternity?"

The temple fell silent as the tomb of the first pharaoh. For one terrible, eternal moment, the golden statue remained as still as death itself. Then, with a slight tremor that might have been divine intervention or merely the carefully coordinated efforts of well-paid priests, the statue began to move. Forward it came, advancing toward Menkheperre in unmistakable divine approval.

The reaction was explosive. Gasps of wonder swept through the sanctuary like wildfire, followed by cries of joy and religious ecstasy.

"The god has spoken!" the High Priest proclaimed, his voice cracking with emotion. "Thutmose lives! The ka-transfer is complete! Amun-Ra has worked a miracle that will be remembered until the end of days!"

The remainder of the coronation ceremony unfolded with all the ancient majesty of Egypt's most sacred traditions. The crook and flail were placed in Menkheperre's hands while hymns of praise echoed from the temple walls. Finally came the recitation of the royal titulary—those five great names by which he would be known throughout the kingdom and for all eternity.

When at last the ceremonies reached their conclusion, the newly confirmed pharaoh processed from Karnak Temple to his waiting barge while the people of Thebes lined the sacred avenue. They threw flowers and precious oils, crying out praises to their miraculously returned ruler.

"They truly believe," Rekhmire murmured at his side, satisfaction evident in every line of his weathered face. "The gods themselves have blessed our great work."

"The gods have permitted it," Menkheperre corrected quietly, feeling the weight of divine judgment upon his shoulders. "Whether they truly bless it remains to be seen."

The New Queen's Test

The royal apartments blazed with luxury that would have made Midas himself weep with envy. Incense burners released fragrant clouds of myrrh and frankincense, while the walls glowed with fresh paintings depicting the pharaoh in communion with the gods. Only when the massive doors sealed them in privacy did Meritamun's carefully maintained composure finally crack like a dam bursting under flood waters.

"What madness is this?" she hissed, yanking her hands free from his grasp with the fury of a wildcat. "Do you truly expect me to believe that my husband has crawled back from the realm of the dead?"

"Not from death," Rekhmire corrected with maddening calm. "The Divine One never crossed the threshold into Osiris's kingdom. His sacred ka was preserved through the ancient Ritual of Continuity, allowing it to inhabit a new and worthy vessel."

Meritamun turned upon the vizier with eyes that blazed like stars. "Do not recite temple mysteries to me as if I were some village girl who believes in ghost stories, Rekhmire! I know the sacred rituals as well as any priest who ever shaved his skull." She whirled back to face Menkheperre. "And you—my beloved husband—how could you agree to this blasphemous charade?"

For a heartbeat, Menkheperre hesitated between the man he had been and the god he had become. Then the truth burst from his lips like blood from a spear wound.

"Because Egypt bleeds!" he said, using his own voice for the first time since entering Thebes. "Because without a strong pharaoh on the throne, the kingdom will tear itself apart like jackals fighting over carrion."

Her eyes widened at the sound of his true voice. "Menkheperre," she breathed, and in that single word lay a world of recognition and heartbreak.

"I am both Menkheperre and Thutmose now," he said, stepping toward her like a man walking through fire. "I have studied my father's ways until they became my own, learned to think his thoughts and dream his dreams. In time, even I will forget where Thutmose ends and Menkheperre begins."

"The child I carry is yours," she said fiercely, her hand protecting her belly like a shield. "Not his!"

When Rekhmire left them alone, Meritamun approached him slowly, studying his transformed features with careful attention.

"They have done their work well," she admitted, reaching up to trace the line of his jaw. "Your face has become his face. Even your eyes seem darker, older."

"But why?" The question escaped her like a cry of pain. "Why not rule as regent as was planned? Why this... transformation?"

"My father's dying wish. He saw civil war coming like a sandstorm on the horizon. The nomarchs of the south grow fat and arrogant on their wealth. They would never bow to a boy-king, not even with a regent to guide him."

"And what of me?" The question came out like the hiss of an angry cobra. "Am I to share my bed with my father's son and call him by my father's name? Am I to bear a child and pretend its father is a dead man?"

The brutal honesty of her words hit him like a physical blow. "The marriage bond is part of the royal continuity," he said awkwardly. "But I would never presume... your chambers will remain your own, beloved."

A smile touched her lips, sad as a funeral song. "And what becomes of us, Menkheperre? What of the love we shared before you chose to die and be reborn as your father?"

"That love must be buried with Prince Menkheperre," he said, each word feeling like another nail in his coffin. "For Egypt's sake, for our child's sake, for the sake of all who depend upon the throne's stability."

Meritamun stepped back, composing herself with the iron discipline of a queen. "Very well. Before the court and the people, I will acknowledge you as Thutmose returned from death. But know this—I do it not for you, nor for Rekhmire's elaborate schemes, but for the child I carry. This babe deserves to be born into a stable kingdom."

The Hidden Chamber

That night, in the sacred privacy of the royal bedchamber, Menkheperre slowly removed the heavy regalia of divine kingship. With each item removed, he felt a strange sensation, as if he were shedding not merely the trappings of power but fragments of his very soul. The man who had been Prince Menkheperre was dying by degrees, being consumed from within by the divine persona of Thutmose III. Meritamun entered like a goddess descending from the stars, having exchanged her ceremonial robes for a simple dress of finest linen.

"You performed magnificently today," she said. "Even I found myself believing the miracle."

They stood together on the balcony, gazing out at moonlit Thebes. The conversation turned to their unborn child, and the terrible question of what he would be told of his true parentage.

"The child will know me as Thutmose," Menkheperre said slowly, the words tasting like poison. "For the stability of Egypt, for the security of the dynasty, that is how it must be."

"And when he is grown to manhood? Will he never learn the truth about his real father?"

Menkheperre crossed to join her, the cool night air a blessed relief. Far below, the Nile flowed like liquid silver in the moonlight, eternal and unchanging.

"There must be some record," he said at last. "Some testament to the truth, hidden but preserved for all time."

"A secret chamber beneath Karnak?" Meritamun suggested.

"No," Menkheperre shook his head with sudden certainty. "Not Karnak. The priesthood has too much power there already. It must be somewhere else... somewhere that will endure long after we have all returned to dust."

Then inspiration blazed in his eyes like divine fire.

"I will build it myself!" he declared with the fervor of a prophet receiving revelation. "A hidden chamber within a monument of my own creation—Thutmose's creation. A place where the truth will be recorded in stone and gold, imperishable as the pyramids themselves. So that one day, even if thousands of years pass and Egypt herself crumbles to dust, someone will discover it and know that Prince Menkheperre once lived and breathed and loved upon this earth."

Meritamun studied him with new respect. "Not just for our child, then. But for history itself."

"History belongs to those who write it," Menkheperre said, feeling the weight and truth of the words. "The scribes will record that Thutmose III ruled Egypt with wisdom and strength. But I will write my own history in secret places, hidden from all eyes but meant for all time."

May 1439 BC Birth of an Heir

The cry of a newborn infant echoed through the royal apartments like the voice of destiny itself. Menkheperre, who had spent the endless night pacing his adjacent chamber like a caged leopard, froze mid-stride as if struck by divine lightning.

The cedar doors swung wide, and the royal midwife emerged like a priestess bearing sacred offerings. In her arms lay a small bundle wrapped in linen finer than spider silk.

"A son, Divine One!" she announced, dropping to her knees. "Strong as Horus the Avenger and blessed with the mark of Ra himself!"

With hands that suddenly seemed too large and clumsy, Menkheperre took his son, his and Meritamun's child, though the world would know him only as the heir of Thutmose III. The infant's eyes, still unfocused with the mystery of new birth, seemed to gaze directly into his soul.

Later, as he held the sleeping child while Meritamun recovered, the full weight of his sacrifice settled upon him like a mountain of stone. This boy would grow up calling him father, never knowing the truth of his parentage. The lineage would be preserved, the kingdom stabilised, but at the cost of erasing his existence from history.

"What shall we name him?" Meritamun asked weakly from her bed.

"Siamun," Menkheperre replied without hesitation. "Son of Amun. It is fitting."

She nodded, understanding the deeper meaning. Their son would bear a name that honored the god who had supposedly worked the miracle of his father's resurrection, another layer in the great deception that had become their lives.

In the days that followed, as Egypt celebrated the birth of the royal heir, Menkheperre began planning in earnest for his secret monument. Somewhere in the vast expanse of his kingdom, he would build a hidden chamber where the truth would wait like a seed in fertile soil, preserved for some distant future when it could finally take root and bloom.

The price of saving Egypt had been the murder of his own identity. But in that hidden place, Prince Menkheperre would live forever, waiting for someone, someday, to discover that he had once loved and sacrificed and ruled in all but name.

Two souls, one body, one throne. The deception was complete, the kingdom secure, and history forever changed. In the official records, only Thutmose III would be remembered. But in the secret chamber yet to be built, the true story would endure until the end of time itself.

Chapter 12 - The Divine Flame

October 1439 BC – Avaris Market

Joshua had spent weeks chasing rumors from caravan guards and desert traders, scouring every market stall and whispered tale. The legends of Moses—once a prince, now a ghost—haunted him. Each step he took in Avaris was driven by a gnawing sense that time was slipping through Israel's fingers like sand through a broken jar. Egypt was changing.

The marketplace of Avaris buzzed with activity as Joshua ben Nun approached the cluster of Midianite traders, his tall frame moving purposefully through the crowd. At forty-two, his weathered face betrayed little emotion, but his heart pounded against his ribs as he offered a small wooden carving to the merchant with the hennaed beard.

"I seek news of a man—one who fled Egypt many seasons ago. A Hebrew raised in Pharaoh's own house." Joshua's voice dropped to barely above a whisper. "His name is Moses."

The merchant's eyes widened before he beckoned Joshua deeper into the shadows of his tent. "This Moses tends the flocks of Jethro, priest of Midian, near the sacred mountain we call Horeb. He took Jethro's daughter to wife many years ago—they have sons, now grown." He stroked his beard thoughtfully. "He is not what you might expect. The years have turned him from prince to shepherd."

That night, Joshua found Aaron hunched over a small clay lamp, his fingers guiding a reed stylus across the final lines of a weathered parchment. He whispered the sacred words as he wrote them: *"And the Lord remembered His covenant with Abraham, with Isaac, and with Jacob..."*

The knock came like thunder. Aaron looked up, startled, the stylus slipping. Joshua entered before he could rise.

"Moses is alive." Joshua said, his voice barely above a breath but heavy as a trumpet blast.

The parchment slipped from Aaron's fingers. For a moment, the old man seemed frozen before a smile of vindication crossed his weathered face.

"All these years," Aaron murmured, "I have felt him in my spirit. When others declared him surely dead, I knew the God of our fathers would not have raised him from the Nile's waters only to let him perish without fulfilling his purpose."

He fixed Joshua with a penetrating look. "Our people cry out under the weight of bondage, each day more desperate. Yet more of them turn from the idols of Egypt and remember the God who made a covenant with Abraham." His voice strengthened. "And now we learn that Moses lives, near enough that we might reach him. This is no coincidence. This is the hand of the Most High, beginning to move."

"What would you have us do?" Joshua asked.

Aaron pushed himself to his feet with surprising vigor. "We will go to him. If Moses will not return to his people, then we shall bring the cry of his people to Moses."

By nightfall, three more had joined their conspiracy. As darkness enveloped the Hebrew settlement, the small party slipped away, five silhouettes moving toward the distant wilderness that separated Egypt from Midian.

Aaron stood for a moment, gazing toward the mountains that marked their destination. Somewhere beyond those peaks, his brother remained unaware that the currents of divine purpose were beginning to flow around him once more.

"Soon, my brother," Aaron whispered to the brightening sky. "Soon."

October 1439 BC – Midian

The merciless sun hung like burnished bronze in the cloudless sky, beating down upon the rugged landscape with desert fury. Heat shimmered in waves above the parched earth, distorting the horizon until it rippled like the Nile that Moses had left behind four decades earlier.

He wiped sweat from his weathered brow, his skin now dark as cedar and cracked from forty years under this unforgiving sun. His hands, once soft and adorned with gold rings in Pharaoh's palace, were now calloused and strong—the hands of a shepherd, not a prince. The desert had stripped away every vestige of his royal past, forging him anew like bronze in a smith's fire.

His sheep grazed among the sparse vegetation, their wool yellowed and dust-caked from desert life. Beyond them, Mount Horeb rose like a brooding giant, its jagged peaks scratching at the heavens. Local shepherds whispered of strange lights that danced among its crags at night, but Moses had dismissed such tales as superstition.

A sharp cry from one of the lambs broke the desert stillness. Moses counted heads with practiced efficiency—one missing. The troublesome ram with the crooked horn, always prone to wandering.

With fluid grace that belied his eighty years, Moses gripped his shepherd's staff and set off across the broken terrain. Desert life had kept him hard where palace luxury would have made him soft. His staff, worn smooth by four decades of use, had become an extension of his body.

The trail led upward over boulders the size of pharaoh's sarcophagi. It was as he crested a small ridge that the impossible presented itself.

An ancient acacia tree stood wreathed in flames that defied nature itself. The fire burned with pure intensity—white-hot at its core, edged with gold—yet the tree remained untouched. Not a leaf withered, not a fragment of bark charred. The sight struck Moses like a physical blow.

More unnerving was the absolute silence. No crackling filled the air, no smoke rose to mark the blaze. The very air seemed to hold its breath, as if creation itself had paused to witness this miracle. The light transformed the harsh landscape into something Moses could only understand as holy ground.

"I must turn aside and see this great sight," Moses said aloud, his voice sounding strangely hollow. "Why is it that the bush does not burn?"

As he drew near, the very atmosphere seemed to change, becoming dense with an overwhelming presence.

"Moses."

The voice came from within the flames, intimate and vast all at once.

"Moses."

Finding his voice at last, Moses answered, "Here I am."

"Come no closer. Remove the sandals from your feet, for the place on which you stand is holy ground."

With trembling fingers, Moses obeyed, his old sandals falling to the rocky soil.

"I am the God of your fathers," the voice continued, "the God of Abraham, the God of Isaac, and the God of Jacob."

Moses covered his face, primal fear seizing him.

"I have indeed seen the misery of my people in Egypt. I have heard them crying out because of their slave drivers, and I am concerned about their suffering. So I have come down to rescue them from the hand of the Egyptians and to bring them up out of that land into a good and spacious land, a land flowing with milk and honey."

The words awakened memories Moses had long suppressed—the cries of his people under the lash, the bitter tears of mothers separated from their children.

"And now the cry of the Israelites has reached me, and I have seen the way the Egyptians are oppressing them. So now, go. I am sending you to Pharaoh to bring my people the Israelites out of Egypt."

Moses felt as if the ground had fallen away beneath him. Return to Egypt? Face the Pharaoh whose predecessor had sought his life?

"Who am I," he protested, "that I should go to Pharaoh and bring the Israelites out of Egypt?"

"I will be with you," came the reply. "And this will be the sign to you that it is I who have sent you: When you have brought the people out of Egypt, you will worship God on this mountain."

"Suppose I go to the Israelites and say to them, 'The God of your fathers has sent me to you,' and they ask me, 'What is his name?' What shall I tell them?"

"I AM WHO I AM," declared the voice with such authority that the very rocks trembled. "This is what you are to say to the Israelites: 'I AM has sent me to you.' Say to the Israelites, 'The LORD, the God of your fathers—the God of Abraham, the God of Isaac and the God of Jacob—has sent me to you.' This is my name forever."

But Moses pressed further, his fear overwhelming even this divine revelation. "What if they do not believe me or listen to me and say, 'The LORD did not appear to you'?"

"What is that in your hand?" the voice asked.

Moses looked down at his shepherd's staff, worn smooth by decades of use. "A rod," he replied.

"Throw it on the ground."

With trembling hands, Moses cast the staff down. Instantly, it writhed and transformed, becoming a serpent that hissed and coiled upon the rocky ground. Moses leaped back in terror, his heart hammering against his ribs.

"Reach out and take it by the tail," commanded the voice.

Every instinct screamed against such folly, but Moses obeyed. The moment his fingers closed around the serpent's tail, it became rigid wood once more—his familiar staff, unchanged.

"Put your hand inside your cloak," came the next instruction.

Moses slipped his hand beneath his outer garment. When he withdrew it, he cried out in horror. His hand was leprous, white as snow with the dreaded disease that marked a man as unclean.

"Put it back into your cloak."

Again, Moses obeyed, though revulsion made his stomach churn. When he pulled his hand out a second time, it was restored—healthy flesh, weathered and strong as before.

"If they do not believe you or pay attention to the first sign," the voice explained, "they may believe the second. But if they do not believe these two signs or listen to you, take some water from the Nile and pour it on the dry ground. The water from the river will become blood on the ground."

Moses raised his objections one by one—his inadequacy, his fear that the people would not believe him. God answered each concern with demonstrations of power, turning Moses' staff into a serpent and back again, showing signs that would convince the doubters.

Then came the most startling revelation of all.

"What about your brother, Aaron the Levite? I know he can speak well. He is already on his way to meet you, and his heart will be glad when he sees you."

Moses staggered as if struck by an invisible fist. "Aaron?" The name escaped as barely a whisper yet seemed to echo in the supernatural stillness. "My brother Aaron—he lives?"

For forty crushing years, Moses had carried the weight of not knowing his brother's fate. In the darkest desert nights, he had tortured himself with visions of Aaron's death—his strong back broken under the overseer's lash, those gentle hands that had taught Moses the sacred stories crushed beneath Pharaoh's stones, that eloquent voice silenced forever by Egyptian brutality.

Hebrew slaves rarely survived to old age under such merciless toil. Aaron had been eighty-three when Moses fled—already ancient by any standard. How could he have endured another forty years of bondage?

"He lives," came the gentle confirmation. "And even now journeys to find you, his heart full of joy at the prospect of seeing his brother again."

Tears burst from Moses' eyes hot as blood, carving channels through the desert dust on his weathered cheeks. These were not gentle tears of joy, but the desperate weeping of a man whose heart had carried a wound for forty years.

"He lives," came the gentle confirmation from the voice that commanded wind and storm. "And even now journeys to find you, his heart overflowing with joy at the prospect of seeing his brother again."

Aaron—alive! Not merely surviving but actively seeking him. The knowledge struck like lightning, illuminating the vast loneliness that had defined his exile. For four decades he had lived with crushing guilt, believing his flight had been cowardice that left those he should have protected to face Pharaoh's wrath alone.

"But Lord," Moses continued, his voice trembling, "the Pharaoh who sought my life—surely he still rules. Surely his anger burns as hot as ever against the Hebrew who murdered one of his taskmasters."

"The king who sought your life is dead," the voice replied with quiet authority. "Think, Moses. Who was Pharaoh when you fled Egypt?"

Moses' mind raced backward through the years. Forty years ago... the ruler then had been young Thutmose III, barely more than a child of two summers, with his stepmother Hatshepsut serving as regent.

"Hatshepsut," he whispered, understanding flooding through him. "And young Thutmose."

"And all who sought your death for that deed have likewise perished," the voice continued. "The years have swept them away like dust before the wind. Return without fear of old enemies, for they exist no more."

Relief washed over Moses like cool water in the desert heat. The specific danger that had driven him to flee—the personal vendetta of a humiliated royal house—had died with those who held it.

The flames began to subside gradually, and Moses knew the encounter was drawing to its close. With a deep breath that seemed to draw the very presence of the Almighty into his lungs, he nodded his acceptance.

"Let it be as you have said, Lord."

The Return

The sun had descended considerably by the time Moses gathered his scattered flock and began the journey back to Jethro's encampment. His mind churned with all he had witnessed and heard, but one thought rose above all others—Aaron lived, and even now traveled to meet him.

When he reached the black goat-hair tents that had been his home for decades, Zipporah rushed to meet him, her dark eyes immediately reading the change in his demeanor.

"Moses, what has happened? You look as though you have seen..." She paused, searching for words.

"The face of God," Moses finished quietly.

That evening, as the cooking fires cast dancing shadows and the children played among the tent ropes, Moses gathered his family. Zipporah sat beside him, her weathered hands folded in her lap, while their two sons—Gershom, now a man of thirty-eight with children of his own, and Eliezer, barely twenty-five but already showing the wisdom of his father—listened with growing amazement as Moses recounted his encounter with the burning bush.

"The God of my fathers has called me to return to Egypt," Moses concluded. "To lead the Hebrew people out of bondage."

Gershom leaned forward, his brow furrowed with concern. "Father, you speak of returning to a land that sought your life. Surely this is madness."

"The Pharaoh who condemned me is dead," Moses replied. "As are all who knew of my crime. But more than that—God himself has commanded this thing. I cannot refuse."

Zipporah reached out and took her husband's weathered hand in both of hers. "If the God who has watched over us these forty years commands it, then we must trust in his protection." She paused, then smiled. "Besides, you said your brother comes to meet you. I would see this Aaron who shares your blood."

"You would come with me?" Moses asked, hardly daring to hope. He had prepared himself for the possibility that his family might choose to remain in the safety of Midian.

"Where you go, we go," Gershom declared firmly. "You are our father. Your people shall be our people, your God our God."

Eliezer nodded his agreement. "The children should know their heritage, should see the land from which their grandfather came."

And so it was decided. The next morning, they had loaded their possessions onto the sturdy donkeys that Jethro provided as a parting gift. The old priest blessed them with tears in his eyes, pressing upon Moses a staff of polished olive wood to replace the simple shepherd's rod that had been transformed at the burning bush.

"Go with the favor of the Most High," Jethro said, embracing his son-in-law. "You came to us a prince in exile. You leave as a deliverer of nations."

Moses lifted Zipporah onto her donkey, his heart heavy with the magnitude of what lay ahead yet light with the joy of reunion that awaited. Somewhere in the wilderness between Midian and Egypt, Aaron was traveling toward them—Aaron, alive and well, carrying in his heart the same divine calling that now burned in Moses' breast.

As they rode away from the only home his sons had ever known, Moses cast one last glance back toward Mount Horeb. The peak stood serene and majestic against the morning sky, giving no sign of the miracle that had transpired upon its slopes. But Moses would never forget. The mountain of God had become the place where his true life's work began.

"I am sending you," the voice had said. And now Moses rode forward into destiny, his family beside him, his brother somewhere ahead, and the power of I AM coursing through his veins like liquid fire.

The liberation of Israel had begun

Chapter 13 - Return to Avaris

November 1439 BC - The Meeting at Mount Horeb

The harsh, windswept slopes of Mount Horeb stood sentinel against the azure sky, their rugged contours carved by millennia of desert winds. Moses sat beneath the sparse shade of a gnarled acacia tree, his weathered hands gripping his shepherd's staff. Beside him, Zipporah kept watchful eyes on their two sons—Gershom and Eliezer—who played quietly with smooth stones in the dust. Forty years in Midian had sculpted his once-royal features into something more primal, more elemental—a face that had witnessed both the cruelty of men and the awesome power of God.

"Father, look!" Gershom pointed toward the shimmering distance where figures appeared, wavering in the heat haze like apparitions.

Moses narrowed his eyes, squinting against the relentless glare. Four men moved with purpose across the wasteland, each step raising small clouds of dust from the parched earth. At their head walked a figure whose gait struck a chord of recognition deep within Moses' soul.

"Aaron," Moses whispered, the name strange on his tongue after decades of silence.

Zipporah rose gracefully, gathering their sons to her side. "Your brother comes as Yahweh promised," she said softly.

As the distance closed between them, Moses stood to his feet, conflicting emotions warring within his chest. His older brother had aged—his beard now streaked with silver, his shoulders slightly stooped from years of labor—but the eyes remained the same, dark and intelligent beneath heavy brows. Behind Aaron walked three companions, their faces bearing the distinctive marks of Hebrew lineage and Egyptian hardship.

Aaron halted a few paces away, his three companions—Joshua and two weathered elders—flanking him respectfully. He studied the man before him, this shepherd-prince whose legend had grown in whispered tales throughout the slave quarters of Egypt.

"Moses?" Aaron asked, voice thick with disbelief. "Is it truly you, my brother?"

Moses nodded slowly, aware of Zipporah's steadying presence beside him, their boys pressed close to her robes. "Yahweh has spoken to me, Aaron. He sent me to find you, and you have found me."

Aaron fell to his knees, dust rising around him. His companions followed suit, recognizing the gravity of this moment. "All these years... we thought you dead."

"I might as well have been," Moses replied, helping his brother to his feet while Joshua and the elders rose. "But now Yahweh has awakened me from that slumber. He appeared to me in the burning bush upon this very mountain."

Aaron's eyes widened, and he glanced back at his companions before returning his gaze to Moses. "The God of our fathers spoke to you?"

"He did. And He has commanded us to return to Egypt, to free our people from Pharaoh's grasp."

The brothers embraced, an embrace forty years in the making—Moses, the prince-turned-shepherd, and Aaron, the slave who had never left Egypt's cruel embrace. Joshua stepped forward, his youthful face bearing wisdom beyond his years, while the two elders watched with reverent anticipation.

"My lord Moses," Joshua said, his voice carrying the respect of one who had heard the stories. "We have waited long for this day."

Moses studied the young man, sensing something of destiny about him. "And who are you, son of Israel?"

"I am Joshua, son of Nun, of the tribe of Ephraim. These are Hur and Caleb, elders among our people." The two men bowed deeply.

Zipporah moved closer, her sons still clinging to her garments. "Aaron," she said with quiet dignity, "I am Zipporah, daughter of Jethro, priest of Midian. These are my sons—Gershom and Eliezer."

Aaron's eyes softened as he knelt before the boys. "Sons of my brother," he murmured, touching their faces gently. "In you, the promise continues."

"Tell me everything," Aaron said, settling with his companions beside Moses and his family in the meager shade. "Leave nothing untold. Our people suffer greatly under the new Pharaoh. The taskmasters grow crueler with each passing season."

As the scorching day yielded to the cool embrace of evening, Moses revealed all that had transpired between himself and the Almighty. Zipporah prepared simple fare from their provisions while the boys listened wide-eyed to their father's words. Joshua hung on every syllable, his warrior's mind already calculating the challenges ahead, while Hur and Caleb nodded gravely at each divine commandment.

Above them, birds of prey circled in the deepening twilight, silent witnesses to the pact that would forever alter the course of nations. The die was cast—shepherd and slave, exile and elder, woman and child—all bound together by the inexorable will of the God who had heard His people's cry from the furnaces of Egypt.

December 1439 BC - Moses arrives at Avaris

The mud-brick sprawl of Avaris rose from the delta plains like a festering wound on Egypt's flawless skin. Once a small settlement, it had swollen grotesquely with the imprisoned Israelite population, its narrow streets choked with humanity and despair. The stench of too many bodies confined in too little space hung in the humid air.

Moses and Aaron navigated the labyrinthine alleyways, drawing curious stares from hollow-eyed children and suspicious glances from adults who quickly averted their gaze. These were people who had learned the bitter lesson that attention from anyone associated with Egypt's ruling class brought nothing but suffering.

"Your house still stands?" Moses asked, pulling his desert cloak tighter around his shoulders despite the heat, suddenly conscious of his Midianite garb among his own people.

Aaron's laugh was without humor. "If you can call it a house. But yes, it stands. Elisheba has kept it as well as can be expected under Pharaoh's heel."

They turned down a particularly narrow passage, the buildings pressing in on either side, blotting out the sun, before emerging into a small courtyard where a modest dwelling stood. Shabby but clean, it bore the unmistakable signs of a woman's careful attention—herbs growing in cracked pottery, a swept threshold, linen drying on cords stretched across one corner.

"Aaron!" A woman's voice called out, and Elisheba appeared in the doorway, her once-beautiful face now lined with care, but her movements still graceful. She froze when she saw Aaron's companion. "Who is this stranger you bring to our home?"

Before Aaron could answer, a cluster of men and women had gathered at the edges of the courtyard, drawn by the arrival of outsiders. An elderly man with a patriarchal beard pushed forward.

"Is it not enough that we endure the Egyptians' cruelty?" he demanded. "Now you bring their spies among us?"

"This is no spy," Aaron replied firmly. "This is Moses, son of Amram and Jochebed, my brother whom we thought lost."

A stunned silence fell over the gathering, broken only by the distant crack of an overseer's whip and the answering cry of pain.

"Moses is dead," someone called out. "Drowned in the Nile or slain in the desert."

"Yet I stand before you," Moses said, his voice carrying the authority that had once commanded Egyptian troops. "Not by my own strength, but by the hand of Yahweh, who appeared to me in the wilderness and commanded me to return."

"To what purpose?" The old man challenged. "To witness our misery? Our suffering has only deepened since the days of your youth."

Moses met the man's gaze unflinchingly. "To deliver you from bondage, as Yahweh has promised."

Laughter, bitter and disbelieving, rippled through the crowd.

"The Egyptians have broken stronger men than you," a woman called out, her arms bearing the scars of repeated floggings. "What can one man do against Pharaoh's armies?"

"I do not come in my own name," Moses replied, raising his staff. "I come in the name of Yahweh, the God of Abraham, Isaac, and Jacob, who has heard your cries and remembered His covenant."

As the sun began to set, casting long shadows across the courtyard, Moses demonstrated the signs Yahweh had given him—the staff that became a serpent, the hand stricken with leprosy and then restored. One by one, the doubtful faces in the crowd transformed, disbelief giving way to tentative hope, then to awe, and finally to reverence as they fell to their knees.

"Yahweh has visited His people," Aaron proclaimed, standing beside his brother. "And has remembered His covenant."

By nightfall, what had begun as rejection had transformed into cautious acceptance. Inside Aaron's modest home, the elders of Israel gathered, speaking in hushed tones of rebellion and freedom, of a promised land flowing with milk and honey. And at the center of it all stood Moses, no longer the desert wanderer but the instrument of divine deliverance, his eyes gleaming with purpose in the flickering lamplight.

January 1439 BC Pharaoh's Arrival

The Nile moved like molten glass beneath the royal barge, its surface burnished copper in the dying light of the African sun. Menkheperre stood at its prow, shrouded in a fine linen cloak edged with gold thread that caught the last rays of daylight. His tall, lean frame remained motionless against the gathering dusk, shoulders squared with the rigid posture of a man born to command. His eyes—dark and penetrating beneath heavy lids—fixed unblinking on the horizon where Avaris waited, a smudge of pale stone against the purpling sky.

After twenty grueling days on the river, days of heat that shimmered above the water's surface and nights filled with the eerie cries of jackals, and his wive and child in the cabin beneath, the sight of Avaris brought no comfort to him—only a dull tightening in his chest, like a serpent slowly constricting around his heart. Each league closer to the ancient city had tightened the knot of dread within him, inexplicable yet undeniable.

The city was vastly larger than he remembered, sprawling across the eastern bank like a ravenous beast that had devoured the surrounding countryside. Where once there had been modest settlements and stretches of fertile land, now stood a teeming metropolis of mud-brick dwellings and stone edifices, the stench of too many bodies pressed together rising like a miasma in the evening heat. The once-defined boundaries had been obliterated by decades of expansion, the outer districts a chaotic labyrinth of narrow streets and overcrowded hovels. But what gripped his attention were not the crumbling walls or weathered pylons that stood sentinel over the harbor—it was the people lining the eastern bank. Hundreds of them. Silent. Still. A living wall of humanity stretching as far as the curve of the river would allow his eye to follow.

He knew who they were.

The Israelites.

Their bodies, hardened by decades of labor beneath the Egyptian sun, stood like statues carved from dark wood. Many bore the visible marks of servitude—scarred shoulders, calloused hands hanging loosely at their sides. They made no sound as the royal barge passed, offering neither protest nor genuflection that was the birthright of his station. Only their stares, unbroken and unwavering, like a wall of memory made flesh. A collective gaze that seemed to penetrate the gilded finery of his royal vessel and pierce straight through to his core.

Menkheperre did not need to ask what they were doing there. They had heard Pharaoh was coming—*their* Pharaoh—and they had come to see the face of the man whose decrees shaped their existence. Perhaps to measure him, to gauge what manner of ruler now controlled their fate.

A warm breeze carried the scent of the marshes to him—fertile mud, lotus flowers, and beneath it all, the ever-present dust of Egypt. He inhaled deeply, tasting the familiar flavors of his homeland on his tongue.

Just nine moons ago, he had stood in the shadowed sanctuary of Pi-Ramesses, north of here, marble floors cool beneath his bare feet despite the season's heat. The air had been thick with incense as Vizier Rekhmire and the High Priest of Amun flanked him, their whispers echoing in the vast chamber. Together, they had forged the Continuity Clause, declaring the death of Thutmose III and the immediate ascension of his "eternal form." The papyrus had felt heavy in his hands as he pressed the royal seal into the clay.

But watching the Israelites, their eyes reflecting the dying sun like countless tiny mirrors, he wondered how long such a lie could hold. These people had lived under the yoke of his dynasty for generations. They knew the old Pharaoh. And they would know the difference.

A cold finger of doubt traced its way down his spine despite the evening's warmth.

The recognition

Then he saw them.

Three figures stood apart from the crowd, motionless among the tall reeds that swayed like dancers in the evening breeze. The wind stirred their rough-spun robes but not their stillness, which seemed rooted to the earth like ancient sycamores.

The first was elderly, white-bearded and solemn, his face a map of deep lines etched by sun and time. But it was his eyes that commanded attention—dark pools like a drought-scarred well, bottomless and knowing. They held neither hatred nor fear, but something far more unsettling: certainty.

Beside him stood another of similar age, heavier in build with powerful shoulders that spoke of a lifetime of labor never quite beaten from his frame. His stance was solid as bedrock, calm but sharp-eyed, watching the royal procession with the measured assessment of a man accustomed to weighing threats. A wooden staff clutched in his gnarled hand seemed less a support for his age than a weapon held in momentary peace.

The third, a younger man around forty years, stood slightly behind them with the quiet alertness of a guard dog—tense, observant, his hand never straying far from the dagger at his waist. His eyes constantly scanned the riverbank, the approaching vessel, the guards that lined its deck. A protector, ready to move at the slightest provocation.

Something in them unsettled Menkheperre, like the feeling of sand shifting beneath one's feet during a desert crossing. Especially the tall one at the center. The man did not posture or preen as most did in the presence of Pharaoh. He simply stood, as immovable as the mountains of Sinai, watching with those ancient eyes.

Menkheperre stepped forward unconsciously, as if pulled by an invisible cord. One foot, then another, until he stood at the very edge of the bow, the spray from the Nile occasionally misting his sandaled feet. The bearded man's presence radiated a kind of quiet gravity that seemed to bend the world around him. It wasn't fear he felt, nor challenge.

It was recognition.

"Hold," he said, voice low but firm, carrying across the water like a stone skipping across its surface.

The rowers ceased immediately, their oars suspended above the river like frozen wings of some great water bird. The sudden silence was profound, broken only by the gentle lapping of water against the hull and the distant cry of an ibis returning to roost.

Silence fell over the vessel. Even his personal guard, standing ever watchful at his back, seemed to hold their breath.

The two groups studied each other across the narrowing gap of water. A still stalemate, pregnant with unspoken significance. Menkheperre could feel the gaze of his guards behind him, tense and uncertain at this unplanned delay, but he paid them no mind.

He stared at the man, and the man stared back.

Something in that face—aged and furrowed by time and desert winds—brought back flashes of Thebes. Of stone corridors cooled by ingenious airshafts and scented gardens where fountains played beneath the moon. Of his father sitting in council, speaking with a low, confident voice that could command armies with a whisper. That man had long passed into the arms of Osiris, his body now wrapped in fine linen and sealed in the Valley of Kings, but standing now before this stranger, Menkheperre felt the weight of that same presence.

It was absurd. The resemblance was vague at best, a trick of the fading light perhaps. And yet it stirred something deep within his chest, a recognition that defied logic.

Had they met before? No. That much was certain. A man like this would have left an impression impossible to forget. And yet...

Moses.

The name flared in his mind like a sudden spark in darkness. He had heard it whispered in temple courts when priests thought him out of earshot, hissed in the chambers of advisors like a curse—an exile, a threat, a prophet of the desert gods. The Hebrew who was not Hebrew, the Egyptian who was not Egyptian. But no one had ever seen him clearly. No records existed in the royal archives, no portraits adorned warning scrolls. A ghost of rebellion, more rumor than man.

Could this man be him? This quiet figure who stood with such authority among the reeds?

Menkheperre clenched his jaw, feeling the muscles tighten beneath his close-cropped beard. He hated riddles. Had since childhood when the royal tutors had tried to sharpen his mind with them. But this one had rooted itself in him, unwelcome and demanding as a thorn.

He stepped back from the prow, eyes still fixed on the bank, unwilling to be the first to break this strange communion.

"Forward," he commanded at last, his voice carrying the full weight of royal authority.

The rowers obeyed instantly. The oars dipped in perfect unison, and the barge began to move again, gliding toward the southern bend where the great stone palace of Thutmose III stood like a sentinel over the river—*his* palace now. His inheritance and his burden.

But as the shoreline passed and the three figures faded into the gathering mist of evening, Menkheperre remained at the prow, unable to shake the feeling that he had not merely seen a man.

He had seen a reflection. A mirror image distorted by time and circumstance, but a reflection, nonetheless.

His royal palace stood just a kilometer to the north, its white limestone walls and towering obelisks appearing like ghostly sentinels in the deepening twilight. So close to where he had spotted those three figures—those three men who had stood apart from the masses with such unsettling confidence. The closest he had come to the Israelite quarter since his return.

The barge glided into the royal docking area, where torches had been lit against the encroaching darkness. The flames danced in the light breeze, casting elongated shadows across the polished stone of the quay. A welcoming party awaited him, officials in crisp white kilts with gold pectorals gleaming at their throats.

At their center stood Vizier Rekhmire, tall and austere, his shaved head reflecting the torchlight like polished ebony. The man's face remained carefully neutral, betraying nothing of the thoughts behind those calculating eyes.

"Welcome to Avaris, Divine One," the Vizier intoned, bowing with perfect precision—neither too deep to suggest familiarity nor too shallow to imply disrespect. "We trust your journey on the blessed Nile was favorable."

Menkheperre stepped onto the dock, feeling the solid stone beneath his feet with a relief he would never admit to anyone. Twenty days on water was enough to make even a god yearn for land.

"Vizier," he acknowledged with a slight nod. He dismissed the formalities with a sharp gesture of his hand. The officials behind Rekhmire stiffened almost imperceptibly. "Walk with me."

They moved away from the entourage, toward the private path that led to the palace. When they were beyond earshot, Menkheperre spoke again, his voice low but incisive.

"What news from Avaris? Particularly from the Israelite quarter?"

Rekhmire's step faltered for just an instant before he regained his measured stride. "Divine One?"

"I am not a patient man tonight, Rekhmire," Menkheperre said, the exhaustion of travel making his tone harsher than intended. "There are rumors of a man named Moses returning to his people. What do you know of this?"

The Vizier's face remained composed, but his eyes narrowed slightly. "There have been... whispers, yes. Nothing substantial enough to trouble the ears of Pharaoh."

"And yet they trouble mine now. Who is he?"

"A ghost story, my lord. An Israelite raised in the house of your divine father, then exiled for killing an overseer. Some say he has returned from Midian with strange powers and stranger demands." Rekhmire's tone suggested he found such tales beneath contempt.

Menkheperre stopped walking, turning to face the older man fully. "I saw him tonight. On the riverbank among his people."

Now, a genuine surprise flickered across the Vizier's features before he could master it. "You are certain?"

"No," Menkheperre admitted. "But I will bring this man to me, Rekhmire. This Moses. I wish to look upon his face in proper light."

"As you command, Divine One." The Vizier bowed again. "Though, may I advise caution? The Israelites have been... restless of late. To elevate one of their own with royal attention—"

"I did not ask for your counsel," Menkheperre cut him off. "I asked for this man. See it done."

As they resumed their walk toward the palace, the first stars appearing in the deepening blue above them, Menkheperre could not shake the image of those eyes. Ancient eyes that had seemed to look straight through the facade of godhood to the man beneath.

He would not sleep that night. The face would follow him into his dreams, those eyes watching from the darkness behind his closed lids. And deep in his heart, Pharaoh Menkheperre knew that this was only the beginning of a confrontation that would shake the very foundations of Egypt.

Chapter 14 - Menkheperre Meets Moses

January 1438 BC The Dawn Confrontation

The first light of dawn stretched across the heavens like molten gold, casting long purple shadows across the alabaster courtyard of Pi-Ramesses. The air hung heavy with the scent of lotus blossoms and burning incense, mingling with the distant musk of the great river. Menkheperre stood motionless upon the dais, his bronzed skin gleaming beneath the regalia of Thutmose III. The weight of the double crown—the red and white pschent that symbolized his dominion over Upper and Lower Egypt—pressed upon his brow, a constant reminder of the deception he now embodied.

His fingers tightened around the royal crook and flail, the ancient symbols of kingship that had passed through the hands of a hundred pharaohs before him. Within his chest, his heart thundered like war drums, though his face remained a mask of imperial serenity. The scouts' reports echoed in his mind—Moses had returned from exile. Not as the broken fugitive he had expected, but as an emissary claiming divine authority.

"My lord," Rekhmire whispered beside him, his vizier's voice barely disturbing the dawn stillness. "They approach."

Rekhmire's lean frame was tense with anticipation, his shaven head glistening with sweat despite the early hour. His eyes, rimmed with kohl, darted nervously toward the eastern gate.

Menkheperre straightened, adopting the posture his father had maintained head high, shoulders back, eyes forward. Though young, barely twenty, he had studied the portraits and statues of his predecessor with obsessive dedication. Every gesture, every expression had been memorized and practiced until they became second nature.

"Let them come," he commanded, his voice deepened to match the timbre of the man he impersonated. "Let us see what power this Hebrew god wields."

The massive cedar doors groaned open on bronze hinges, and two figures emerged from the shadows of the entrance colonnade. When Moses and Aaron entered the courtyard, Menkheperre's breath caught in his throat. The legendary Moses—once military commander, former prince of Egypt, rumored husband to royalty—now stood before him like a vision from antiquity itself.

Eighty years had carved deep furrows into Moses' face, each line a testament to decades spent under the merciless desert sun. His beard, white as the limestone cliffs of Thebes, cascaded down his chest, partially concealing the simple shepherd's garb that hung from his still-broad shoulders. Despite his humble attire, he moved with the measured confidence of one accustomed to command, his weathered hands bearing the calluses of both warrior and herdsman.

But it was his eyes that captured Menkheperre's attention—eyes the color of distant mountains, piercing and clear, reflecting the sharp intelligence that had once made him a formidable figure at court. Those eyes had witnessed the glory of Egypt's golden age, had commanded armies, had perhaps even gazed upon the face of Pharaoh as an equal rather than a subject.

Beside him stood Aaron, his elder brother, three years his senior yet somehow seeming the younger of the pair. Where Moses radiated quiet authority, Aaron exuded nervous energy, his fingers fidgeting with the hem of his robe. His beard, streaked with gray rather than white, was neatly trimmed in the manner of a man who had remained among civilization while his brother wandered the wilderness. His eyes darted about the courtyard, taking in the towering statues, the painted columns, the silent guards who stood like statues themselves along the perimeter.

The brothers bowed, though not as deeply as protocol demanded—a subtle defiance that did not go unnoticed by the courtiers who watched from the shadows of the surrounding columns.

"So," Menkheperre said, his voice carrying across the courtyard like distant thunder, "the exile returns to Egypt."

Moses met his gaze steadily, unflinching before the supposed power of the living god-king. "I come with a message from the God of the Hebrews."

"Before that," Menkheperre said, descending three steps from the dais and motioning the brothers to follow him to a more private area of the courtyard. They walked toward an alcove shaded by towering date palms, their fronds rustling gently in the morning breeze. A small reflecting pool glimmered at its center, the surface occasionally broken by the darting forms of red and gold fish imported from the distant lands of Punt.

"Before your message," Menkheperre continued when they were safely away from curious ears, "you will tell me who you truly are. The stories say you were once called prince."

Moses nodded slowly, his gaze drifting momentarily to the eastern horizon where the sun now burned away the last wisps of dawn mist. "I served Egypt faithfully for years. I led your army against the Nubians when they threatened your southern border."

"I remember the tales," Menkheperre said, though of course, he did not personally remember. The campaign had occurred before his birth. "They say you won a victory that secured Egypt's southern territories for decades. That you brought back gold enough to plate the altars of Amun-Ra."

"The victory was hard-won," Moses acknowledged, his voice taking on a distant quality as if he were seeing not the palatial gardens before him but the blood-soaked battlefields of Nubia. "We lost many good men to Nubian arrows and fever. The gold was paid for in Egyptian blood." He blinked, returning to the present. "I was a different man then, serving a different master."

"You were more than a commander," Menkheperre pressed, watching Moses carefully, noting the subtle tightening around the old man's mouth. "You were married into the royal family."

At this, Aaron turned sharply to look at his brother, surprise evident in the sudden widening of his eyes and parting of his lips. The revelation seemed to strike him like a physical blow.

Moses sighed, a deep exhalation that seemed to deflate him momentarily. "There are many things from my past that few know." He glanced at Aaron apologetically, the look between them speaking volumes of secrets kept even from blood. "Yes, I was married to Tharbus, a Nubian princess. It was part of securing peace with her people."

Aaron's expression betrayed his shock, the color draining from his face. "Brother, that's news to me..."

"There was no need," Moses replied quietly, placing a weathered hand briefly on Aaron's shoulder. "That life ended when I fled Egypt. Yahweh set me on a different path—a desert path of redemption."

Menkheperre observed the exchange with keen interest, his dark eyes missing nothing. So, Aaron did not know everything about his brother's past. The implications fascinated him. If Moses had kept his royal marriage secret even from his own brother, what other secrets might he be keeping? What other connections might exist between this Hebrew shepherd and the royal house of Egypt?

"The princess Tharbus," Menkheperre continued, his voice smooth as honey yet probing as a surgeon's knife, "she converted to Egyptian ways, did she not? Took an Egyptian name? Worshipped at the temples of Isis and Hathor?"

Moses hesitated, his fingers unconsciously moving to a spot beneath his simple robe, perhaps where some memento hung hidden from view. Then he nodded once, a barely perceptible movement. "She became known as Iset."

A flicker of satisfaction crossed Menkheperre's face, quickly masked behind the impassive facade of royal dignity. Another piece of the puzzle confirmed. He had studied the records extensively—those that remained after Hatshepsut's passing. The connections were becoming clearer, like stars emerging one by one in the evening sky to reveal a constellation previously unseen.

"And after your supposed death," Menkheperre continued, circling closer to Moses like a desert jackal around its prey, "what became of her and any children she might have borne?"

Moses' expression hardened, the weathered skin of his face seeming to transform from sand to stone. "I have not come to discuss ancient history, Pharaoh. I come with a message from the Lord: 'Let my people go, that they may hold a feast to our God in the wilderness.'"

Menkheperre waved his hand dismissively, the gold bands on his wrists catching the morning light. "Yes, yes. Your request will be considered in due time. The council will hear you speak." He stepped closer to Moses, near enough now to see the fine web of wrinkles around the old man's eyes, to smell the scent of the desert that clung to his robes. "But first, tell me—do you know who I am?"

"You are Pharaoh," Moses answered simply, though something in his tone suggested he sensed the deeper meaning behind the question.

"Am I?" Menkheperre's eyes narrowed, searching Moses' face for any flicker of recognition or knowledge. "Or am I the legacy of what you left behind? The continuation of a bloodline you abandoned decades ago?"

Moses remained impassive, though his shoulders straightened almost imperceptibly. "The God of Abraham, Isaac, and Jacob has sent me to lead His people out of bondage. That is all that matters now. The past is dust beneath my sandals."

Menkheperre nodded slowly, recognizing the stone wall he had encountered. "I will allow you to address the council when I return from Thebes." He turned away with the practiced grace of royalty, the gesture clearly signaling that the audience was concluded.

As Moses and Aaron bowed and departed, Menkheperre watched them go from the corner of his eye, his mind churning with possibilities like the great water wheels that irrigated the fields of the Delta. The pieces were falling into place. If Moses was indeed Tharbus's husband, and Tharbus had become Isis, and Isis had given birth to Thutmose... then perhaps the blood of Moses himself ran in Menkheperre's veins. But why had Moses said Iset rather than confirming the connection to Isis?

The thought both thrilled and disturbed him. To be descended from this man—this Hebrew who now claimed to speak for a foreign god—

was a secret that could shake the very foundations of Egypt's divine monarchy.

Pharaoh's Calculations

The midday sun blazed overhead like the eye of Ra himself, casting Egypt in golden light so intense it seemed to transform the world into living sculptures of amber. Menkheperre stood on the palace balcony, the smooth limestone warm beneath his feet. He had removed the heavy crown, allowing a servant to dab the sweat from his brow with a linen cloth soaked in lavender water. Beside him, Rekhmire stood rigid as a royal standard, his ceremonial staff gripped tightly in his slender fingers.

Together they gazed out over the glistening waters of the Nile toward Tanis, where the river split into its many fingers before emptying into the Great Green Sea. The rich fields of barley and corn stretched across the landscape like a verdant carpet, punctuated by the occasional date palm standing sentinel over the bounty of Egypt. Beyond them lay the pastures where Egyptian livestock—cattle with sweeping horns, fat-tailed sheep, and nimble goats—grazed contentedly under the watchful eyes of herdsmen whose families had served Egypt since the time of the pyramid builders.

"What do you make of him?" Menkheperre asked, not taking his eyes off the horizon where the shimmering heat haze blurred the distinction between earth and sky.

Rekhmire considered his words carefully, running a hand over his smooth scalp before speaking. "He speaks with authority beyond his station. The years have not bent his spine nor dulled his gaze." He paused, considering. "But he is old, my lord. Perhaps his mind wanders with age. Perhaps this god of his is merely a phantom born of desert heat and loneliness."

"No," Menkheperre said firmly, his fingers tightening on the balcony's balustrade. "His mind is sharp as a bronze blade. Did you see how he reacted when I mentioned his marriage? The momentary surprise on his brother's face? That man remembers everything—every battle, every alliance, every whispered secret in a royal bedchamber. Age has not diminished him; it has distilled him to his essence."

"Perhaps. But why would he return now, after all these years? What could drive an old man to challenge the might of Egypt?"

Menkheperre turned to face his vizier, his eyes narrowed against the brilliant light. "That is what troubles me. He claims his god has sent him, but I wonder if there isn't more to it." He gestured toward the distant horizon. "Out there, beyond our borders, powers shift like sand dunes in the wind. The Hittites grow stronger. The Babylonians watch our wealth with envious eyes. Perhaps Moses serves not just his god but some earthly master who seeks to weaken Egypt from within."

Rekhmire shifted uncomfortably, his sandals scraping against the limestone floor. The weight of state secrets pressed upon him like a physical burden. "There is news, my lord. The embalming of your father is complete." He glanced around, ensuring no servants were within earshot before continuing in a lower voice. "Thutmose I—" he paused, acknowledging the deception they maintained, "—has been moved to the new tomb I prepared for him in the Valley of Kings."

"And the annals?" Menkheperre's tone sharpened.

"The scribes are working day and night; their fingers stained with ink. Your father's great deeds are being recorded on the temple walls as we speak. His campaigns, his victories—all will be preserved for eternity. Not even the passage of a thousand years will erase his name."

Menkheperre nodded with satisfaction, a smile briefly softening his stern features. "Good. And my brother?"

"Prince Amenhotep remains safely at Memphis, my lord." Rekhmire's voice dropped further, barely audible above the distant cries of water birds on the river. "Extra guards have been assigned to his residence, as you ordered. Men whose loyalty to you is beyond question."

Menkheperre turned back to the view, his eyes tracking the slow movement of a trading vessel making its way upriver, its square sail billowing with the north wind. "Moses claims the god of the Hebrews demands we release his people. What do you think would happen to Egypt's prosperity if we suddenly lost thousands of workers?"

Rekhmire gestured to the fields below, where tiny figures moved among the crops, their labor a constant, vital heartbeat in the body of Egypt. "The harvests would suffer. Granaries would empty. Construction would halt—the temples to your glory would remain unfinished, their stones lying forsaken in the quarries." His hand swept across the landscape. "Egypt would weaken, and our enemies would descend upon us like vultures on a carcass."

"Precisely." Menkheperre's expression hardened, his jaw clenching beneath the ceremonial false beard that marked his divine kingship. "Send word to the taskmasters. Increase the Israelites' labor. They now must gather their own straw but still produce the same number of bricks. Let them feel the cost of their prophet's demands."

"As you command," Rekhmire bowed deeply, his forehead nearly touching his knees in submission. "It shall be done before sunset."

"Let us see how dedicated Moses remains to his cause when his people blame him for their increased suffering. Let us see if his god provides straw when the taskmasters withhold it."

As Rekhmire departed to deliver the orders, his footsteps fading on the polished stone corridor, Menkheperre remained on the balcony, his thoughts returning to Moses. The old man's bearing, his commanding presence despite his age... it reminded him of the portraits of Thutmose I he had studied obsessively since childhood. And if the rumors were true, if Moses had indeed also married Hatshepsut after returning from Nubia...

The pieces were there, tantalizingly close to forming a complete picture. Moses, the warrior who conquered Nubia. Moses, who married the Nubian princess Tharbus, who later became known as Iset—could this be the same woman who later became Isis, the mother of his father Thutmose III? Moses, who possibly fathered a child with Hatshepsut— a child who would have been Neferure.

If true, that would make Moses his grandfather. The thought was both thrilling and unsettling, like drinking wine mixed with gall—sweet at first taste but bitter in the throat.

Menkheperre gazed out at the empire that stretched before him, an empire built on the backs of slaves, an empire that reached toward eternity through monuments of stone. For now, he was its guardian, holding the throne in trust until young Amenhotep could claim his birthright as the true Thutmose III. But what would Moses say if he knew that the blood of Hebrew slaves flowed in the veins of Egypt's royal line? Would his god strike down his own descendant to free his chosen people?

The sun continued its relentless journey across the sky, casting Menkheperre's shadow long across the balcony floor. Like that shadow, the question stretched before him, dark and inescapable. He was a steward of power, not its permanent master—but until his brother came of age, he would defend Egypt with every breath in his body.

The Bitter Harvest of Desperation

The merciless Egyptian sun hung like a copper disk in a cloudless sky, beating down upon the mud brick fields where hundreds of Israelite slaves labored. Their backs were bent not in submission but in the backbreaking work of gathering scattered straw, their hands bleeding from the sharp edges of the dried stalks.

In the distance, the massive form of a half-constructed storage city rose like a mirage, its incomplete walls a testament to the ceaseless labor of generations of Hebrew slaves. The crack of whips cut through the air like thunder, followed by cries of pain and desperate pleas for mercy.

The Israelite foremen staggered from the palace; their shoulders slumped not from physical burden but from the crushing weight of despair. Their faces bore the marks of brutal treatment—welts raised by Egyptian rods when they had failed to meet the impossible quotas. Their eyes, once bright with the momentary hope that Moses' return had kindled, now reflected only defeat and bitter resentment.

The Pharaoh's decree had been merciless: gather your own straw but deliver the same quota of bricks. An impossible demand designed to break not just their bodies but their spirit—and their faith in Moses' god.

"Why have you treated your servants this way?" they had pleaded before the throne, their foreheads pressed to the cool marble floor in desperate supplication.

"Idle!" Menkheperre had thundered back, rising from his throne like a cobra preparing to strike. His voice echoed through the vast audience chamber, bouncing off pillars painted with images of Pharaoh smiting his enemies. "You are idle! That is why you say, 'Let us go and sacrifice to the Lord.' Now go and work; no straw will be given you, but you shall deliver the same number of bricks. Perhaps then you will remember who is god in Egypt!"

As the foremen departed, shuffling through streets lined with curious Egyptians who watched their misery with indifference or contempt, they encountered Moses. The old prophet and his brother stood beneath the shade of a sycamore tree, their expressions hopeful until they saw the defeat etched on the faces of their approaching kinsmen.

"May the Lord look upon you and judge," the lead foreman cried, his voice cracking with emotion as he confronted the brothers. Spittle flew from his lips as months of pent-up suffering found its target. "For you have made us a stench in the sight of Pharaoh and his servants and have put a sword in their hand to kill us!"

The other foremen joined in, their voices rising in a chorus of accusation. "Our children starve while gathering straw! Our elderly collapse in the fields! The taskmasters beat us when we fail, and we always fail because what you have asked is impossible!"

Moses, stricken by their words, turned away from their accusations. His weathered face contorted with anguish, and for the first time since his return to Egypt, tears welled in his ancient eyes. He raised his gnarled hands toward the heavens; his staff clutched so tightly his knuckles whitened.

"O Lord," he cried out, his voice breaking with emotion, "why have you done evil to this people? Why did you ever send me? For since I came to Pharaoh to speak in your name, he has done evil to this people, and you have not delivered your people at all."

The setting sun cast long shadows across the palace courtyard as the foremen dispersed, returning to deliver the bitter news to their people. Aaron placed a comforting hand on his brother's shoulder, but Moses shrugged it off, walking alone toward the river where he had once been found as an infant among the bulrushes. His solitary figure grew smaller in the distance, bent but not broken, a man caught between his people's suffering and his god's silence.

Chapter 15 - Power of the Royal KA

January 1438 BC Royal chambers

The sun had long since disappeared behind the western cliffs, plunging the Valley of the Kings into velvety darkness pierced only by the cold, distant fires of the stars. Within the royal palace, however, light and warmth abounded. Dozens of oil lamps cast a golden glow across walls decorated with hunting scenes and images of Pharaoh smiting Egypt's enemies. In the royal bedchamber, braziers of sweet-smelling cedar burned, their aromatic smoke curling toward the ceiling painted with images of the night sky goddess Nut stretching protectively across the heavens.

Menkheperre reclined upon a couch of ebony inlaid with ivory and gold, his ceremonial regalia replaced by a simple kilt of the finest linen. Beside him sat Meritamen, the wife of Amun, her slender form was draped in gossamer linen so fine it seemed to trap the lamplight within its folds. Her eyes, rimmed with kohl and malachite, were fixed upon the sleeping infant who lay in an ornate cradle nearby—a masterpiece of craftsmanship carved from a single piece of ebony and inlaid with gold and lapis lazuli.

The wet nurse, a stout woman chosen for her ample milk and healthy children, sat discreetly in a corner, ready to attend the royal infant at his first cry. For now, though, young Siamun slept the exhausted sleep of the newly born, his tiny chest rising and falling beneath coverings of the softest linen.

"You seem troubled, my husband," Meritamen observed, placing a delicate hand upon Menkheperre's forearm. Her voice was melodious, trained from childhood to please royal ears. Her fingers, adorned with rings of gold and lapis lazuli, traced small circles on his skin. "Even on this day of triumph, your brow is furrowed like the fields after ploughing."

Menkheperre sighed deeply, accepting a cup of wine from a silent servant who then melted back into the shadows of the chamber. The wine was rich and dark, imported at great expense from the hills of Canaan, its surface sheened with oil of roses. "The Hebrew, Moses. Something about him disturbs me still, even here, even now."

"The old man who claims his god demands our slaves?" Meritamen asked, her perfectly shaped eyebrows rising in surprise. "Surely such a threat is easily dismissed. What power could a shepherd's god have against the might of Egypt and the divine protection of Amun-Ra? Look at how the gods have blessed you—a healthy son when the physicians feared the worst."

"It's not his demands that trouble me," Menkheperre said quietly, swirling the wine in his cup, watching the way it caught the lamplight like liquid rubies. "It's who he is—or rather, who I believe him to be."

Meritamen set aside the lotus flower she had been twirling between her fingers, her expression growing serious. "Tell me, husband. What shadow has this Hebrew cast over your thoughts? Even on this day of days, he seems to haunt you like a restless ka."

"I have studied the histories, the records that survived Hatshepsut's purges. I've spoken with the oldest priests, those whose memories stretch back to the days before I was born." Menkheperre leaned forward, his voice dropping to ensure only his wife could hear. The walls of palaces had ears, and some secrets were too dangerous to be overheard. "Moses was no ordinary commander. The stories say he was found as a baby in the river by a princess—Mutnofret, daughter of Ahmose I."

"And this is significant because...?"

"Because Moses rose to become more than a prince. He became Pharaoh himself, if only briefly. The records hint at it, though many were destroyed. He married into the royal line twice. First, the Nubian princess Tharbus, who became known as Isis in Egypt."

Meritamen's eyes widened, the realization dawning on her beautiful face. "Isis... the mother of Thutmose III? Your grandmother?"

"Precisely." Menkheperre nodded, pleased with his wife's quick understanding. "And it's believed he later married Hatshepsut herself, before his supposed death and her rise to power. The temples of Deir el-

Bahari speak of a consort, a figure whose name was later chiseled away. I believe that was Moses."

"So you think..."

"Moses is my grandfather," Menkheperre said firmly, the words hanging in the air between them like an incantation. "Through Thutmose II, who is Moses, and my father. The blood of both Egypt and the Hebrews flows in my veins.

"But he never admitted this to you when you met?"

"No." Menkheperre shook his head, draining his wine cup in one swift motion. "He avoided my questions about his true place in our family. Maybe he did not want his brother to know who he was before. But his evasion tells me more than his words could. He knows the truth. He sees himself in my features, just as I recognized something of myself in him."

Meritamen glanced at their son, the infant Siamun whose peaceful breathing punctuated the heavy silence. "If what you believe is true, this child carries the blood of this Hebrew god's chosen people. He is the descendant of slaves as well as kings."

"Perhaps that is why Moses has returned now," Menkheperre mused, rising from his couch to pace the chamber. The gold beads in his elaborate collar clicked softly with each step. "Not just for his people, but for his legacy. For us. Perhaps his god has shown him a vision of his bloodline sitting upon the throne of Egypt."

He walked to the window, pulling aside the linen curtain to look out at the night sky above Egypt. The moon hung full and heavy, casting a silver light across the sleeping city. The distant torches of the guards patrolled the perimeter walls, small moving stars in the darkness.

Suddenly, Menkheperre's shoulders tensed. He turned back to his wife; his amber eyes filled with a new concern. "There is another matter that weighs upon me—one that strikes at the very heart of my legitimacy as Pharaoh."

Meritamen rose gracefully, moving to stand beside him. "What troubles you?"

"The royal Ka," Menkheperre said, his voice barely above a whisper. "The divine essence that passes from one Pharaoh to the next at the moment of death. When I ascended the throne, all believed Moses long dead. The royal Ka passed to my father, and then to me, as is the natural order."

Meritamen's delicate fingers tightened around his arm. "But if Moses lives and never truly died..."

"Exactly," Menkheperre nodded, the implications hanging heavy in the air between them. "If Moses never died, what became of his royal Ka? Did it remain with him in exile? Did it pass to my ancestors despite his continued existence? These are questions no priest has ever had to answer."

He moved to a small writing table in the corner of the chamber, where papyrus, ink, and reed pens awaited the royal command. With practiced movements, he began to write, his hieroglyphs flowing across the surface with elegant precision.

"*The royal Ka passes at death. Moses was believed dead when I ascended. Therefore, the Ka passed to me legitimately.*" He read aloud as he wrote, then paused, his pen hovering above the papyrus.

"*But if Moses lives and never truly died...*" His voice trailed off as a new possibility formed in his mind—one so radical that it bordered on heresy.

Meritamen watched him closely, sensing the weight of his thoughts. "What is it, my husband?"

Menkheperre's pen remained suspended, a drop of ink gathering at its tip. "*What if the Hebrew god is real?*" he finally continued, both writing and speaking the dangerous words. "*What if their deity took the royal Ka from Moses when he fled Egypt and passed it to my father? What if there are powers beyond our understanding that can transfer the divine essence from one vessel to another?*"

The drop of ink fell to the papyrus, spreading into a dark stain like an omen. Meritamen drew in a sharp breath, her eyes darting instinctively to the doorway to ensure they were truly alone.

"Such thoughts would be considered blasphemy by the priests," she whispered.

"Yet I cannot banish them from my mind," Menkheperre replied, setting down the pen and rising to his full height. "If true, it would mean that both Moses and I might be legitimate in our claims—each chosen by different gods for different purposes. It would mean that the cosmic order is more complex than the priests have ever taught, that the divine world operates according to laws that mortals have only begun to comprehend."

He returned to the window, gazing out at the vastness of his kingdom. "It would mean that what we face is not merely a contest between a king and a former prince, but a war between gods—Amun-Ra and the Hebrew deity—with Egypt itself as the prize."

"And the child?" Meritamen's eyes moved to the sleeping infant, her maternal instinct flaring at the thought of divine conflict. "Where does Siamun stand in this cosmic struggle?"

Menkheperre's gaze softened as it fell upon his newborn son. "Perhaps he is the bridge—or the battlefield. The blood of both worlds flows through his veins. In time, he may be called upon to reconcile what now seems irreconcilable."

The moon cast a silver light across the Nile, turning its surface to a ribbon of molten metal that wound through the sleeping land. And somewhere in the distance, Menkheperre knew, Moses was communing with his god, perhaps speaking of the very questions that now plagued the Pharaoh's mind.

The Divine Commission

The night air hung heavy with stillness as Moses knelt alone on the rocky ground, his shepherd's staff lying beside him. Stars scattered across the heavens like jewels on Pharaoh's robe—a memory from another life that seemed to belong to someone else. His calloused hands, now those of an eighty-year-old man, trembled slightly as he waited.

"I am old, Lord," Moses whispered into the darkness. "My strength fails. My voice falters. How can Menkheperre, who sits as Living Horus, listen to one who fled Egypt as a criminal?"

The voice came not as thunder, but as perfect clarity—resonating within Moses yet clearly not his thoughts.

"Moses, attend to My words," said the Lord. "See, I have made you like God to Pharaoh, and your brother Aaron will be your prophet."

Moses looked up sharply, uncertain he had understood correctly. "Like God to Pharaoh? But Lord, he believes himself divine."

Moses knew well what this meant. In his youth, raised in Pharaoh's household, he had been schooled in the sacred mysteries of Egypt. The royal Ka—the divine essence, the spiritual double that embodied kingship itself—was believed to pass from one Pharaoh to the next upon death. It was this divine force that transformed a mere mortal into the Living Horus, the embodiment of divine rule on earth. Without the royal Ka, one could not truly be Pharaoh; with it, one was no longer merely human but a vessel of divine power.

"Menkheperre believes he carries the royal Ka," Moses continued, his voice steady despite his inner turmoil. "In the eyes of Egypt, when my adopted father died, this divine royal soul passed to Menkheperre's father, and then to him. It is what makes him untouchable, unchallengeable. It is what makes his word divine law and his person sacred. How can such a man listen to me?"

"It is I who elevate and I who humble," came the reply. "When you stand before Menkheperre, he will see in you what he has never witnessed before—power that does not flow from his pantheon, authority that does not require his recognition. You will be as a god to him."

Moses pressed his forehead to the ground, overwhelmed. "The priests taught that the royal Ka is the most powerful spiritual force in existence—the essence of divine kingship itself. They taught that it cannot be divided or diminished, that it exists in fullness in Pharaoh alone."

"You are to speak all that I command you," continued the Lord, "and your brother Aaron is to tell Pharaoh to let the Israelites go out of his land. But I will harden Pharaoh's heart, and though I will multiply My signs and wonders in the land of Egypt, Pharaoh will not listen to you."

Moses considered these words carefully. "You will harden his heart, yet command me to demand Israel's freedom? Lord, if You have determined he will refuse, why must we go before him at all?"

"So that My power may be displayed," came the answer. "So that generations yet unborn will know that I am the Lord. Menkheperre believes he carries divinity within him—the royal Ka passed from father to son. He must learn that there is only one true God, and that even Pharaoh is merely a man."

Moses nodded slowly. "The royal Ka grants its bearer dominion over the Two Lands, power over life and death, and divine right to rule as intermediary between gods and men. It is what allows Pharaoh to maintain Ma'at—cosmic order—through his very existence. If Menkheperre sees divine authority in me..."

"What is this royal Ka but a shadow of true divinity?" The voice seemed to fill the night air now. "When you stand before him with My power flowing through you, he will recognize something his priests cannot explain. He will see in you divine authority that challenges everything he believes about himself and his gods."

"Then I will lay My hand on Egypt," the voice continued, "and by mighty acts of judgment I will bring the divisions of My people, the Israelites, out of the land of Egypt. And the Egyptians will know that I am the LORD, when I stretch out My hand against Egypt and bring the Israelites out from among them."

Moses ran his hand over his face, feeling the deep lines carved by desert sun and years of exile. "So, I am to be your instrument of judgment against the land that raised me. I am to stand before the man who believes himself to be the living embodiment of divine power on earth—who believes the royal Ka flows through his veins, granting him authority over all creation—and tell him that there is a greater power he must obey."

"You are to be My voice, My presence before Pharaoh. When Menkheperre looks upon your face, he will see not merely Moses the exile, but a manifestation of power beyond his understanding. The question of who possesses the royal Ka will pale before the reality of who I AM."

For a moment, Moses glimpsed what lay ahead: confrontation with Menkheperre, demonstrations of divine power that would shake Egypt to its foundations, the ultimate liberation of a people who had known nothing but bondage for generations.

"I will go," Moses said finally. "Not in my strength, but as your representative. If You have truly made me like God to Pharaoh, then let Your words be in my mouth and Your power in my hands."

"Remember this moment," said the Lord, "when doubt assails you in Pharaoh's court. Remember that it is not Moses who stands before the throne, but My appointed vessel. When Menkheperre sees you, he will know, though he may fight against this knowledge that his understanding of divinity has been too small."

Moses gripped his staff and rose unsteadily to his feet, feeling strength flow into his aged frame. Tomorrow, he would stand before Menkheperre not as a returning exile, but as one invested with divine authority that would challenge the very foundations of Egyptian theology.

Two men—possibly grandfather and grandson—now locked in a contest of wills that would determine the fate of not just a people but of a bloodline that spanned the chasm between slave and king. A contest that would shake the very foundations of Egypt and echo through history for thousands of years to come.

And perhaps, at its heart, a battle between gods for the soul of an empire and the future of a child who bore the blood of both.

Chapter 16 - Avaris Rebelling

February 1438 BC – Pelusaic Nile at Avaris

Menkheperre stood at the bow of his barge, his hands gripping the gilded rail, eyes narrowed against the harsh midday sun. The scepter of Osiris—a symbol of his divine authority—hung from his belt, its weight a constant reminder of the burden he carried.

"We approach Avaris, Divine One," Rekhmire announced, appearing at his side with the silent grace that had made him an indispensable vizier.

Menkheperre gave a curt nod, his gaze fixed on the approaching shoreline where the city of Avaris rose—a testament to Egyptian ingenuity built upon the backs of Hebrew labor. White limestone buildings gleamed in the sunlight, their reflections dancing across the water's surface. The great temple of Set dominated the skyline, its pylons reaching toward heaven like supplicant hands.

"And what of the mood of the city?" Pharaoh asked, his voice deliberately measured. "Speak plainly, Rekhmire."

The vizier's expression remained carefully neutral, but Menkheperre detected a slight tension in the man's shoulders. "Unrest continues, Divine One. The Hebrew quarters have become difficult to control. Their elders speak openly of this Moses and his demands. Some have abandoned their assigned tasks, claiming their god requires them to prepare for departure."

"Departure," Menkheperre repeated, the word like poison on his tongue. "As if Egypt were a tavern, one could simply walk away from after the meal is finished...as if Pharaoh's Ka no longer bound them, as if the divine thread had snapped."

He turned his attention to the eastern bank, where clusters of people had gathered to witness Pharaoh's return. In years past, such crowds would have prostrated themselves, faces pressed to the earth in reverence.

Now, he could see figures standing upright, their postures a silent rebellion against centuries of protocol.

"The royal guard reports have been... concerning," Rekhmire continued, lowering his voice despite the distance between them and the nearest attendants.

As the barge approached the royal dock, Menkheperre caught sight of something that made his blood run cold. A small group of Hebrew laborers stood at the water's edge, their faces neither lowered in submission nor twisted in fear. Instead, their eyes met his with unmistakable contempt. And then, as the royal vessel drew closer, one man bent down, picked up a stone, and hurled it toward the barge.

The stone fell short, creating ripples in the sacred waters of the Nile— waters that had cradled Moses' basket millennia ago, waters that had carried the dynasty's fortunes for generations. The symbolic violation was more devastating than any physical damage could have been.

"Arrest that man," Menkheperre ordered, his voice deadly calm.

Before his guard captain could respond, more stones flew from the gathering crowd. Most splashed harmlessly into the water, but one struck the hull with an audible crack.

"Nubian archers!" the captain shouted, and instantly a dozen tall, ebony-skinned warriors with leopard-skin cloaks stepped forward, nocking arrows to their bows.

"Hold," Menkheperre commanded, raising a hand. The archers froze; arrows aimed at the crowd but unfired. Pharaoh's eyes swept across the faces of the Hebrew laborers—men who had built his monuments, women who had carried water for his gardens, children who had been born into his service. In their expressions, he saw something that had never been directed at him before: hatred.

Their jeers rose above the lapping of the waves, words in their harsh Hebrew tongue mixed with broken Egyptian. "*Moshe! Moshe!*" they chanted, invoking the name of the man who challenged Pharaoh's authority—the man who might be his grandfather.

"Divine One," Rekhmire whispered urgently, "this is unprecedented. We should divert back to the Royal Palace. The royal guards can secure—"

As the barge docked, Egyptian soldiers formed a protective phalanx around the royal pavilion, their shields creating a wall of polished bronze between Pharaoh and his subjects. The prescribed rituals of arrival proceeded with mechanical precision.

But Menkheperre heard none of it. His mind was consumed by the jeering faces, the flying stones, the name of Moses chanted like an incantation against him. Throughout his father's reign, they fought against—Hittites, Nubians, Libyans—but never had the threat come from within the very fabric of Egypt itself.

As he stepped onto the dock, Menkheperre felt a profound shift within himself. The diplomatic calculations that had guided his initial handling of Moses and Aaron suddenly seemed naïve, even dangerous. The Hebrew god had not responded to reason or accommodation. Perhaps it was time for a more direct assertion of divine Egyptian power.

"Rekhmire," he said as they walked toward the waiting palanquin that would carry him to the palace, "arrange for the high priests of Amun, Ptah, and Set to attend me this evening. We must consult the oldest texts, the most powerful rituals."

"As you command, Divine One." Rekhmire bowed, but hesitation flickered across his face. "May I ask to what purpose?"

Menkheperre paused, turning to face his vizier fully. "The Hebrew Moses claims his god is the only true deity—that our gods are mere inventions of stone and wood. Such blasphemy cannot go unanswered. If his god can perform wonders, then the gods of Egypt shall respond with such force that none will doubt where true divine power resides."

He glanced back at the water, where the surface once again is smooth and untroubled. "The divine Ka flows through me, Rekhmire." It is time to demonstrate what that truly means."

As the palanquin bearers lifted him onto their shoulders, Menkheperre gazed out at his city—the city his ancestors had rebuilt, a city that now seemed to tremble with unseen forces of change. For a moment, he thought of his newborn son in the royal palace, safely distant from this unfolding conflict Siamun, whose mixed blood might one day bridge the chasm that was rapidly forming between two peoples, two faiths, two visions of the world.

But bridges could only be built after battles had been fought and won. And Menkheperre intended to win.

4 February 1438 BC - Palace of Thutmose III

The throne room of Thutmose III's palace blazed with the light of a hundred oil lamps, their golden glow reflecting off polished granite floors and columns painted in vibrant blues and reds. Menkheperre sat rigid upon the symbolic seat of Egypt, his back straight as a spear, his hands gripping the carved lion heads that formed the throne's armrests. The crook and flail—symbols of his authority to both nurture and punish— lay across his lap.

Now, as the afternoon sun began its descent toward the western horizon, Menkheperre prepared to face the Hebrew prophet once again. But this time, he had taken precautions. Flanking his throne stood the most powerful priests in Egypt: Usermontu, High Priest of Amun; Paherypedjet, High Priest of Ptah; and Neferkheperure, High Priest of Set. Each wore the ceremonial garb of his office, each carried the sacred implements of his god's power.

Behind them stood a line of court magicians, men who had spent lifetimes mastering the secret arts of transformation and illusion. They were Egypt's defense against supernatural threats—and Menkheperre intended to use them.

"They approach, Divine One," announced the chamberlain, his voice echoing in the vast hall.

Menkheperre gave a barely perceptible nod. "Let them enter. And let all present remember that they stand in the presence of a living god."

The massive cedar doors swung open, revealing the unlikely pair who had brought such disruption to the ordered world of Egypt. Moses, his white beard flowing over his chest, leaned heavily upon a staff of acacia wood—a shepherd's staff, simple and unadorned save for its unusually smooth surface, as if years of handling had polished it like precious stone. Beside him walked Aaron, older and more vigorous, his eyes alert as a hawk's as they swept the assembled court.

Neither man prostrated himself before Pharaoh. Neither even bowed. They just walked forward until they stood at the prescribed distance from the throne, their postures suggesting equals meeting for negotiation rather than subjects approaching their sovereign.

"You have requested this audience," Menkheperre said, deliberately choosing a word that undermined their presumption of demanding. "Speak your purpose quickly. Pharaoh's time is not to be wasted with repetition of what has already been decided."

Moses lifted his head, meeting Menkheperre's gaze directly—an act that caused several courtiers to gasp audibly. "Thus says the Lord, the God of Israel: 'Let My people go, that they may hold a feast to Him in the wilderness.'"

The same words. The same demand. But now delivered with a confidence that bordered on certainty, as if the outcome were already determined.

Menkheperre leaned forward slightly, studying the old man's face. Was there anything of himself in those weathered features? Any sign of the royal blood they might share? He could see nothing definitive—just an old Hebrew with an extraordinary presence, a man who should have been broken by age but instead seemed to draw strength from some unseen source.

"I have considered your previous request," Menkheperre said, his voice carrying to every corner of the hall. "And my answer remains: I do not know this God of yours, nor will I let Israel go. Egypt's greatness was built by the labor of many peoples over many generations. To release an entire population on the word of an old man would be the act of a fool, not a divine king."

He paused, letting his gaze shift to Aaron. "However, I am not unreasonable. If your god is real—if he has sent you as you claim—surely, he has provided you with some proof of his power. Some sign that would distinguish him from the countless desert deities that rise and fall like dust storms beyond our borders."

Aaron stepped forward, his posture suggesting he had anticipated this challenge. "Indeed, Pharaoh speaks wisely in asking for a sign. The Lord our God has prepared us for this very question."

With deliberate slowness, Aaron raised the staff he carried—identical to Moses' in all but age—and then, with a dramatic gesture, cast it upon the polished floor before the throne.

For a heartbeat, nothing happened. The staff lay inert, a simple piece of wood against the gleaming stone. Then, with a movement that defied nature itself, the wood began to writhe, its form elongating, its surface transforming from dull brown to glistening scales.

Where the staff had fallen, a serpent now coiled—massive and sinuous, its diamond-patterned back rising and falling with each breath. Its jaws opened to reveal curved fangs, and a hiss echoed through the suddenly silent throne room.

Menkheperre did not flinch, though every instinct screamed for him to recoil from the creature. Instead, he allowed a cold smile to cross his lips. "An impressive trick," he said, his voice betraying none of the shock he felt. "But hardly evidence of divine power."

He turned to the line of court magicians who stood rigid with anticipation. "Show these Hebrews the true nature of Egyptian magic— magic blessed by gods who have protected this land since before time itself was measured."

The chief magician stepped forward, a lean man with a shaved head and eyes lined with kohl that enhanced their penetrating quality. Without a word, all the magicians, the wise men and the sorcerers of Egypt raised their staffs—slender rods of tamarisk wood inscribed with hieroglyphs of power—and cast them to the floor with practiced precision.

The transformation was instantaneous. Where six staffs had fallen, six serpents now coiled, each as large and menacing as the one Aaron had produced. The court erupted in exclamations of awe and approval. This was familiar magic, Egyptian magic, a reassuring display of their culture's superiority over foreign influences.

"You see," Menkheperre said, settling back into his throne, "what your Hebrew god can do, the gods of Egypt can replicate tenfold. This is no miracle, Moses. It is merely manipulation of the natural world—a skill our priests mastered while your ancestors still wandered the deserts in ignorance."

But even as the words left his mouth, something extraordinary happened. Aaron's serpent, which had remained coiled in place during the Egyptian display, suddenly lunged forward with impossible speed. Before anyone could react, it had seized one of the Egyptian serpents in its jaws. Then another. And another.

One by one, with methodical precision, Aaron's serpent devoured all six of the Egyptian conjurations, growing visibly larger with each consumption. The court magicians backed away in horror, their faces ashen, their confidence shattered.

When the last Egyptian serpent had disappeared down the throat of the Hebrew creation, a profound silence fell over the throne room. The remaining serpent turned its head toward Menkheperre, its unblinking eyes fixing on him with what seemed like deliberate challenge before it sluggishly reverted to its original form—a simple wooden staff lying on the floor.

Aaron stepped forward and retrieved it, his expression carefully neutral. But in his eyes, Menkheperre could see the unmistakable light of triumph.

"Thus says the Lord," Moses intoned into the silence, "By this you shall know that I am the Lord." He pointed one gnarled finger toward Menkheperre. "The Hebrew god does not merely duplicate the works of other deities. He consumes them. He is not one god among many—he is the One God above all."

Menkheperre's knuckles whitened as he gripped the armrests of his throne. The display had shaken him more deeply than he dared admit. This was no mere illusion or sleight of hand. Something profound had occurred—something that challenged the very foundations of Egyptian cosmology.

But Pharaoh could not show weakness. Not before his court. Not before his priests. And certainly not before the man who might share his blood.

"An entertaining display," he said, forcing his voice to remain steady. "But Egypt is not governed by parlor tricks or carnival performances. The fate of a nation—the cosmic order itself—rests upon traditions older than your Hebrew tribes can comprehend."

He rose from his throne, drawing himself to his full height, the ritual beard of office jutting forward like a symbol of his defiance. "I do not recognize your god's authority over my kingdom or my people—including those Hebrews who have benefited from Egypt's bounty for generations. Your request is denied. More than that, it is rejected as the foreign interference it clearly represents."

Moses did not appear surprised by the refusal. If anything, a strange look of sad recognition crossed his face, as if he had known exactly how this encounter would unfold.

"Then hear the words of the Lord," Moses said, his voice suddenly stronger, filling the chamber with surprising power for one so advanced in years. "Since you refuse to acknowledge the God of Israel, you shall come to know Him through His judgments. Tomorrow, the Nile—the lifeblood of your kingdom, the river you worship as a god—shall be the first to bear witness to His power; it shall turn into blood for seven days."

Menkheperre felt a chill run through his body, despite the warm air of the throne room. He remembered all too clearly the stories of how the infant Moses had been found in that very river, how the waters had delivered him to a destiny that now seemed to be circling back upon itself like a serpent devouring its tail.

"Get out," he commanded, his voice tight with suppressed rage.

"As Pharaoh commands," Moses replied with formal politeness that bordered on mockery. "But remember, when the waters turn to blood and the creatures of the Nile die in their multitudes, it is not Moses who has done this thing, but the God you have refused to acknowledge."

With that, Moses and Aaron turned and walked from the throne room, their backs straight, their steps unhurried, as if they departed not as dismissed supplicants but as emissaries who had delivered their message and now returned to report to a higher authority.

As the doors swung closed behind them, Menkheperre sank back onto his throne, his mind racing. The serpent had consumed the Egyptian magic, not merely matched it but devoured it. What did that portend for Egypt itself? What power could cause the Nile to turn to blood?

And most troubling of all: if Moses truly was his grandfather, what did that make Menkheperre himself in the eyes of this Hebrew god? Was he a potential ally being offered one last chance at reconciliation? Or was he already marked as an enemy to be broken, regardless of the blood they might share?

"Divine One," Usermontu, the High Priest of Amun, approached the throne cautiously. "We must perform purification rituals immediately. The foreign magic has contaminated the sacred space."

Menkheperre nodded absently, but his thoughts were elsewhere. The confrontation had clarified something important. Moses did not approach him as a long-lost relative seeking reconciliation or even acknowledgment. He came as a representative of a rival power—a power that claimed authority not just over a tribe of slaves but over the natural world itself.

This was not a family dispute. It was a war of gods, with Egypt as the battlefield.

"Prepare the royal barge," he ordered suddenly, rising once more to his feet. "I will go to the Nile at dawn. If this Hebrew god threatens our sacred river, then Pharaoh himself will stand against him, in the name of Hapi and all the gods who have blessed Egypt's waters since the beginning of time."

As his courtiers hurried to carry out his commands, Menkheperre gazed at the spot where the serpent had performed its impossible feast.

In his mind's eye, he saw not staffs transforming into snakes, but the very foundations of his world shifting beneath him like sand in a desert storm.

His son Siamun's face appeared in his thoughts—the infant who carried both Egyptian and Hebrew blood in his veins. What world would that child inherit? Would he rule a united Egypt at peace with its gods? Or would he preside over the ruins of a kingdom torn apart by forces beyond mortal comprehension?

Menkheperre's hand moved to the ceremonial dagger at his belt, his fingers closing around its jeweled hilt. Whatever power Moses wielded, whatever god stood behind him, Pharaoh would not yield. The divine Ka flowed through his veins—the essence of kingship passed down through generations. If this were to be a battle between gods, then Pharaoh himself, the living embodiment of divine power on earth, would stand against the Hebrew deity.

Let the waters turn to blood if they must. Egypt had endured for thousands of years

It would endure this challenge as well, no matter the cost.

Chapter 17 - Blood and Fear

5 February 1438 BC - Pelusaic Branch of the Nile

Darkness still clung to the eastern horizon as Menkheperre emerged from his palace onto the grand terrace overlooking the Nile. The massive stone structure, built by his grandfather Thutmose I, commanded the western bank of the river—a deliberate statement of Pharaoh's dominion over Egypt's lifeblood. The air hung heavy with moisture, promising another sweltering summer day, but for now, the pre-dawn chill raised gooseflesh on the arms of the priests who accompanied their king to the riverside.

Menkheperre had risen before his attendants, an unusual occurrence that had sent his chamber servants into a panic. He had dressed in minimal ceremony, selecting a simple gold pectoral rather than the elaborate ceremonial breastplate that protocol demanded for public appearances. Speed, not pageantry, was his priority this morning.

As the royal procession made its way down the broad stone steps that led from the palace to the private harbor, Menkheperre's mind raced with thoughts of the serpent demonstration in his throne room. He had spent a sleepless night analyzing every detail, searching for evidence of trickery. He had found none. The magic Moses and Aaron had performed was real—as real as anything Egypt's priests could produce, and perhaps more powerful.

But today would be different. Today, Menkheperre would meet Moses not in the artificial confines of the palace but at the very heart of Egypt's power: the Nile itself. The river was more than a waterway; it was a deity, the manifestation of the god Hapi, the source of Egypt's fertility and wealth. No foreign god could challenge its divine might.

The royal barge—a magnificent vessel inlaid with gold and precious stones—awaited at the private dock. Around it, smaller boats carried priests representing every major temple in Avaris. They brought sacred implements of their office: censers trailing ribbons of fragrant smoke, alabaster jars of holy water, golden bowls filled with offering grains.

As Menkheperre boarded the barge, his gaze swept across the river to the western shore. There, moving figures caught his attention—walking steadily along the bank, heading north towards a position directly opposite the palace.

Menkheperre saw them clearly: Moses and Aaron, their aged frames upright and purposeful as they walked along the eastern shore. With them were four others—elders of the Hebrews, their beards white against their simple garments.

"They come to witness their god's power," Menkheperre said flatly. "Good. They shall instead see the might of Egypt."

As the first sliver of the sun's disk appeared above the eastern horizon, turning the sky from indigo to flame, Menkheperre raised his arms in the ritual gesture of supplication. His voice, trained from childhood to project authority, carried across the water.

Usermontu, High Priest of Amun, approached with head bowed. "Divine One, all is prepared. The offerings to Hapi await your command. We have brought the sacred waters from the temple spring, mixed with the essence of lotus and papyrus as tradition demands."

Menkheperre nodded, his eyes never leaving the distant figures now positioned directly across from the palace. "Begin the rituals. Let Moses see that Egypt has protected this river since before his ancestors left their sheep-herding tents."

The High Priest of Hapi stepped forward, a ceremonial libation vessel of pure gold gleaming in the strengthening sunlight. He raised it high above his head, filled with a mixture of wine, honey and the morning's first-drawn Nile water – ingredients that symbolized the river's life-giving properties.

The priests moved with practiced efficiency, arranging themselves around the ceremonial braziers that had been secured to the barge's deck. Golden vessels containing sacred oils and incense were placed in precise positions, representing the cardinal points of creation.

"Mighty Hapi, son of Osiris, who brings the fertile waters to nourish the Black Land, hear your son and servant. I stand before you as Horus stands before Osiris, as the living embodiment of divine order upon the earth. Accept our offerings and shield your sacred waters from foreign corruption."

Across the water, Menkheperre could see movement. Aaron had raised his staff—that simple shepherd's crook that had transformed into a devouring serpent. The old man's lips moved, though the distance prevented his words from reaching the Egyptian shore.

"Now," Menkheperre commanded. "Complete the offering before..."

The High Priest began to pour the sacred mixture into the Nile, the golden liquid catching the morning sunlight as it streamed from the vessel. Simultaneously, other priests cast fragrant herbs and precious resins into the braziers, sending clouds of sweet-smelling smoke into the air. The High Priest turned toward the river to complete the libation ceremony.

But as he approached the edge of the barge, a collective gasp rose from the assembled priests and oarsmen. Menkheperre felt his heart stutter in his chest.

The clear waters around their vessel were changing before their eyes. A crimson stain appeared first near the western shore where Moses stood, then spread with unnatural speed toward the royal barge.

The transformation moved like a living thing—a scarlet serpent racing through the water, encircling the royal vessel and its accompanying boats.

"Menkheperre watched the red tide coil along the banks like a living thing. He didn't speak. Not to his guards. Not to the priests. Not even to the gods. The crook and flail at his sides suddenly felt heavier, not symbols of divine order but props in a pageant where the script no longer mattered. The people cried, the priests bled themselves, but the Nile ran red just the same."

Was this what it meant to lose the Ka—not in battle, but in silence? Not in death, but in disbelief? Menkheperre had ruled with symbols, with legacy, with fear. But now even fear had a rival, and the gods had offered no answer.

Within moments, the Nile—the sacred, life-giving Nile—was transformed completely. Where cool, green-brown water had flowed moments before, a thick, crimson substance now churned beneath their hulls. Its metallic scent rose to fill the morning air, causing oarsmen to gag and cover their mouths.

"Blood," whispered the High Priest of Hapi, the libation vessel slipping from his nerveless fingers to splash into the transformed river. "The river is blood."

Usermontu rushed to the edge, dipping his fingers into the red liquid and bringing them to his nose. "It has the scent of blood, Divine One. The texture, the color..." His voice trailed off, his expression one of horrified disbelief.

Menkheperre moved forward, shoving aside the priests who tried to maintain the ceremonial barrier around him. Standing at the very edge of the barge, he stared into the transformed river. His reflection gazed back at him from a mirror of blood—Pharaoh's face distorted by ripples of crimson.

The royal barge, once gleaming white and gold against the natural waters of the Nile, now appeared to float upon a sea of slaughter, the contrast between the vessel's opulence and the horrific transformation beneath it stark and jarring.

A silver flash broke the crimson surface—a fish thrashing in its death throes before floating belly-up in the unnatural tide. Then another appeared, and another, until the surface was dotted with dead and dying creatures, their bodies bumping gently against the hull of the royal barge.

Across the water, Aaron lowered his staff while Moses stepped forward to the very edge of the riverbank. Cupping his hands around his mouth, Moses shouted with practiced projection that carried across the water, now perhaps only eighty meters wide at this stretch of the river.

"LET MY PEOPLE GO!" The words boomed over the water's surface, clear enough for all on the royal barge to hear. Then, as the water began to transform, Aaron continued with a raised voice: "Thus says the Lord: 'By this you shall know that I am the Lord. The fish in the river shall die, the river shall stink, and the Egyptians will be unable to drink water from the Nile!'"

Menkheperre's face darkened at the audacity of the direct command. Even at this distance, he could see the determination on the old spokesman's face as he delivered his god's ultimatum.

"Impossible," Menkheperre breathed, though the evidence lay before him. "No magic can transform an entire river."

The chief magician, who had been so confident during the serpent demonstration, fell to his knees on the deck. "This is beyond our arts, Divine One. The foreign god possesses power we cannot match."

"Nonsense!" Menkheperre rounded on him, fury rising to replace his momentary shock. "This is a trick—an illusion meant to frighten us into surrender. Find the mechanism. Discover how they have contaminated the water!"

As if in answer to his denial, a wave of crimson water splashed over the side of the barge, staining Pharaoh's ceremonial sandals with blood. An ill omen that sent whispers of dread through the assembled priests.

From their position on the western shore, Moses and his companions watched in silence. Even at this distance, Menkheperre could feel the weight of the old man's gaze. Not triumphant, not gloating, but somehow sorrowful—as if he took no pleasure in this demonstration of his god's power.

"Return to the palace," Menkheperre commanded, his voice tight with suppressed rage. "Now!"

The oarsmen hesitated, their faces pale with fear as they looked at the blood they would have to navigate through.

"NOW!" Pharaoh bellowed, and the men lowered their oars into the crimson tide, their expressions twisted in revulsion as they began to row back toward the western shore.

As they approached the palace dock, Menkheperre could see that crowds had gathered along the riverbank—drawn by news of the royal ceremony and now witnessing its disastrous conclusion. Their cries rose into the morning air:

"Great Pharaoh! What has happened to our river?" "How shall we drink? How shall we water our crops?" "The gods have abandoned us!"

The last cry cut Menkheperre more deeply than the others. The gods had not abandoned Egypt—they could not. He was their living embodiment, their chosen instrument on earth. This was a challenge, not a defeat.

When the barge bumped against the royal dock, Menkheperre disembarked with as much dignity as he could muster, ignoring the bloody footprints his sandals left on the white stone path.

"Perform the counterspell," he commanded the assembled priests following behind him. "All of you, combining your powers. Surely the collected might of Egypt's priesthood can overcome this Hebrew sorcery."

For three hours, as the sun climbed higher in the sky and sweat soaked through their ceremonial robes, the priests of every major and minor deity in the Egyptian pantheon performed their most powerful rituals on the palace terrace overlooking the blood-red Nile. They burned sacred herbs, chanted ancient spells, sacrificed additional animals, and mixed potions of rare ingredients. Some even cut their flesh, offering their blood to counteract the blood that now flowed where water should be.

Nothing changed. The Nile remained thick and red, its surface increasingly dotted with dead fish and frogs that could not survive in the transformed environment. The stench grew worse with each passing hour, a metallic, putrid odor that caused even the most stoic priests to cover their noses with scented cloths.

Across the water, Moses and his companions had departed, leaving Egypt to confront the consequences of Pharaoh's defiance.

By afternoon, reports arrived from up and down the Nile Valley. The transformation was not limited to the palace section of the river. From Bubastis in the south to Tanis in the north, every canal, every pond and pool that connected to the river had turned to blood. Even water stored in vessels drawn from the Nile before the plague began had been affected.

Standing on his palace balcony, watching columns of smoke rise from districts where panic had turned to violence, Menkheperre's hands tightened on the stone railing until his knuckles whitened.

"This is not finished," he whispered to the blood-red river that had been Egypt's lifeblood for millennia. "This is only the beginning."

Menkheperre paced the length of his private audience chamber, the bloody footprints from his sandals now dried to a rust-brown against the polished limestone floor. The room had been cleared of all but his most trusted advisors—men who had witnessed the morning's catastrophe and whose faces still carried the shock of what they had seen.

"Seven days," Menkheperre said, breaking the tense silence. "The Hebrew claimed this curse would last seven days." He spat the words as if they carried a bitter taste, his eyes fixed on the eastern horizon where Moses and his delegation had stood only hours before.

Menkheperre turned sharply, his eyes narrowing. "And how is it that any wells remain pure? If this Hebrew god is as powerful as Moses claims, should not all the water in Egypt be affected?"

Rekhmire stepped forward from the shadows, his face composed despite the gravity of their situation. As Vizier of Upper and Lower Egypt, he alone could speak frankly to the Living Horus without fear of immediate reprisal.

"Only water connected to the Nile has changed, Divine One. The desert wells and those few spring-fed cisterns remain clear. It is... peculiar." Rekhmire hesitated before adding, "Some might see it as a message. That their god controls our river but spares the water sources the Hebrews themselves rely upon in Avaris."

"Send word to all taskmasters throughout the kingdom," Menkheperre commanded, his voice taking on a sharp edge. "The Hebrew slaves are to be assigned new duties immediately - they will carry water from their untainted sources to wherever it is needed. Their wells, their springs, whatever sources remain pure. If their god protects their water, then their backs will serve Egypt's needs. Double their quotas if necessary to ensure adequate supply."

Menkheperre's hand shot out, seizing a delicate alabaster figurine from a nearby table and hurling it against the wall where it shattered into countless fragments.

"I will not be threatened by shepherds and slaves!" he roared. "This is a challenge to the very foundations of Egypt." He drew a deep breath, visibly composing himself as he turned back to Rekhmire. "What of our army? How quickly can we assemble our forces?"

Rekhmire blinked, momentarily thrown by the change in direction. "The army, Divine One? To what purpose would we deploy soldiers against blood?"

"Not against blood," Menkheperre said, his voice dropping to a dangerous whisper. "Against rebellion. This magic emboldens the Hebrews. Already, they speak openly of departure. What happens when their courage grows further, when they begin stealing weapons, when they unite with our enemies to the east? We must be prepared."

Understanding dawned on Rekhmire's face. "You believe this is merely the prelude to armed insurrection."

"I believe we must be ready for all possibilities." Menkheperre moved to a large map table at the center of the room, its surface depicting the full extent of Egypt's territories. With a sweep of his arm, he indicated the major garrison cities. "How quickly can we recall the regiments stationed at Thebes, Cusae, Memphis, and Heliopolis?"

Rekhmire approached the map, professional assessment replacing his earlier dismay. "The Theban regiments would require at least fifteen days to march north, assuming they depart immediately. Cusae, perhaps twelve days. Memphis and Heliopolis could reinforce us within seven days, though moving large forces requires considerable supplies." He paused, his finger hovering over the Delta region. "And there is the matter of water. Our troops cannot march without it, and if the Nile remains as it is..."

"They will bring their own supplies," Menkheperre declared. "Send messengers immediately. Every garrison commander is to assemble his full complement and prepare to march to Avaris. Tell them—" He hesitated, unwilling to admit the true nature of their crisis even to his most distant commanders. "

Rekhmire bowed. "As you command, Divine One. I shall dispatch the fastest messengers within the hour." He hesitated before adding, "And what of the immediate crisis? The people grow restless without water."

Menkheperre turned to the balcony where the setting sun cast long shadows across the blood-red Nile. "The priests will continue their counterspells. The people will dig along the riverbank for seepage. We will survive seven days of inconvenience."

"And if the Hebrew returns with further demands? Further demonstrations of his god's power?"

A cold smile touched Menkheperre's lips. "By then, my armies will have begun to gather. Let Moses threaten us again when twenty thousand Egyptian spears gleam in the sunlight." He turned fully to Rekhmire, his expression hardening.

Alone in the audience chamber, Menkheperre returned to the balcony. From this height, he could see fires burning in the distance—riots in the city's poorer quarters where water had grown scarce fastest. The blood-red Nile reflected the flames, creating an illusion that the very river burned beneath the darkening sky.

He had faced rebellions before, putting down insurrections along the southern borders, crushing bandits who dared disrupt the trade routes. But this was different. This invisible enemy struck not at Egypt's borders but at its very heart. For the first time in his reign, Menkheperre felt a cold tendril of doubt curl through his chest.

"No," he whispered to himself, banishing the unwelcome sensation. "I am Pharaoh. I am divine. No foreign god holds power in my land."

Six days passed in increasing desperation. The wells not connected to the Nile—few and scattered throughout the region—became precious resources guarded by soldiers. Fights broke out daily despite the military presence. Wealthier citizens sent slaves with silver to bribe the guards, while the poor formed long queues that stretched through narrow streets, waiting hours for a single jar of clean water.

Reports from Avaris added to Menkheperre's fury. The Hebrew quarter suffered far less than the Egyptian districts. Their wells, always considered inferior because they were not fed by the sacred Nile, now provided clean water while Egyptians thirsted. Some Egyptians even sneaked into Avaris at night, begging or stealing water from the very slaves they had dominated for generations.

On the morning of the eight day, Menkheperre rose before dawn as he had on that first terrible morning. No elaborate ceremony awaited him now—only a small contingent of haggard priests whose continuous rituals had failed to break the Hebrew spell.

He stood on the same balcony where he had watched the river transform, his eyes scanning the eastern horizon for any sign of Moses. The old man had not returned, had made no further demands. His silence was more unnerving than any threat could have been.

As the first rays of sunlight touched the eastern shore, Menkheperre noticed something strange. The reflection seemed wrong—brighter, clearer than it had been for the past seven days. He leaned forward, his hands gripping the balcony's edge.

Below him, the Nile flowed clean and clear, its natural green-brown color restored as if the blood had never been. Fish once again darted beneath its surface, their scales catching the morning light. Along the banks, ibises had returned to wade in the shallows, spearing small creatures with their curved beaks.

A priest noticed the change and cried out, falling to his knees in prayer. The word spread quickly through the palace, then into the city beyond. By midmorning, thousands of Egyptians lined the riverbanks, filling jars and drinking deeply of the restored waters.

Menkheperre watched it all in silence, his face betraying nothing of his thoughts. The Hebrew god had done exactly as Moses had proclaimed—contaminated the river for seven days, no more and no less.

Not because Egyptian magic had prevailed, but because this had been the plan from the beginning.

When Rekhmire approached shortly before noon, he found Pharaoh still at his post, watching the river with an unreadable expression.

"The first messengers have returned, Divine One," Rekhmire announced. "The garrisons at Memphis and Heliopolis are already preparing to march.

Menkheperre nodded without turning. "Good. The Nile has returned to us, but I have not forgotten."

Rekhmire bowed deeply and backed from the royal presence, leaving Pharaoh alone with the restored river and his darkening thoughts. As the vizier's footsteps faded down the corridor, Menkheperre spoke softly to the empty air.

"This is not victory, Moses. This is merely the first encounter in our war."

Chapter 18 - The Stench of the Gods

19 February 1438 BC– Frogs! Frogs!

The royal barge cut through the green waters of the Nile, now restored to its natural state after seven days of blood. Menkheperre stood at the prow, his face set in grim determination as he surveyed the western bank. His eyes narrowed against the morning sun, searching for any sign of the Hebrew delegation.

"There," Rekhmire said quietly, pointing to a small gathering of figures near a stand of papyrus reeds. "Moses approaches with his brother and the elders."

Menkheperre nodded, his jaw tight. Five days had passed since the waters had returned to normal, five days during which he had received reports of troops gathering at Memphis and Heliopolis, preparing to march to the capital. The memory of blood-red waters still haunted his dreams, but in daylight, his resolve hardened like clay in the kiln.

As the barge neared the western shore, Menkheperre could make out Moses clearly—that weathered face beneath a crown of white hair, the simple shepherd's staff that had somehow commanded the Nile itself. Beside him stood Aaron, his spokesman, and the one who is called Joshua.

"Maintain your distance," Menkheperre commanded the oarsmen when they were still twenty paces from shore. "Close enough to speak, far enough to retreat if necessary."

The oarsmen complied, adjusting their strokes to hold the royal vessel steady against the current. Menkheperre stepped forward, adorned in full regalia—the double crown of Upper and Lower Egypt, the ceremonial flail and crook crossed over his chest, the gold and lapis lazuli pectoral depicting the judgment of souls. He had dressed deliberately to invoke the full authority of his divine office.

"Moses!" he called across the water. "You have demonstrated your magic. The Nile suffered your spell for seven days, as you promised. Now it flows clean again. Is this not proof that Egypt's gods have overcome your foreign deity?"

Moses stepped to the water's edge, his posture straight despite his advanced years. When he spoke, his voice carried a quiet authority that somehow matched Pharaoh's royal projection.

"Thus says the Lord, the God of the Hebrews," Moses began, the formal opening that Menkheperre had come to expect. "Let My people go, so that they may worship Me. If you refuse to let us go, my God will plague your whole country with frogs."

A ripple of nervous laughter passed through the Egyptian priests who accompanied Pharaoh. Frogs? After the terror of blood, the threat seemed almost comical.

Menkheperre smiled coldly. "Your god bargains poorly, Moses. From blood to frogs? Even children catch frogs for sport along the riverbank."

Moses did not respond to the taunt. Instead, he turned to Aaron and nodded. The elder brother raised his staff over the river.

"So be it," Menkheperre said. "Let us see the power of this... Hebrew god." He motioned for the barge to withdraw, maintaining his dignity even in retreat.

At first, nothing happened. The river remained calm, reflecting the morning sunlight in gentle ripples. Then, almost imperceptibly, the water began to churn.

Bubbles rose to the surface—first dozens, then hundreds, then thousands. The water boiled with movement, as if some massive creature stirred beneath the depths. The priests on the barge moved closer to one another, their eyes wide with growing alarm.

Then the first frogs emerged—small, green-gray bodies glistening like wet jade as they leapt from the water onto the muddy banks. One, then three, then dozens, then hundreds. Their movements were quick and erratic, legs splaying in unnatural bursts of energy. The reeds rustled and parted as more poured forth, slick and unblinking, their throats pulsing with the beginnings of a low, croaking cacophony. They seemed to come from every direction—not only from the Nile, but from the marshes, the canals, the very soil itself, as if the land were vomiting them up in revolt.

Menkheperre's soldiers stumbled back, expressions twisted with revulsion, some gagging, others drawing their weapons uselessly. A priest dropped to his knees, muttering frantic prayers. It was not just unnatural—it was wrong, as though the gods had withdrawn from Maat and left chaos in their wake.

"Return to the palace," Menkheperre commanded, his voice a brittle shard of control against the rising tide of madness. His tone was level, yet beneath it lurked a tremor, a barely restrained fury, or was it fear?

"Immediately," he repeated, louder now, each syllable a whipcrack. The guards snapped to attention, grateful for an order to obey. Menkheperre turned on his heel, his cloak brushing against the slick earth already smeared with crushed bodies. He could feel them squelch beneath his sandals. But he would not flinch. Let the others see only the mask of Pharaoh. Let them believe he was still the master of this land, and not a man who had just glimpsed the breath of a god he could neither control nor command,

By midday, the scale of the plague had become clear. What had begun as scattered clusters of amphibians along the river's edge had spread like a living carpet across Avaris. The palace courtyards, once pristine expanses of polished stone, now writhed with countless green and brown bodies. They filled the grain stores, clogged the sacred pools, and pressed against the temple doors in heaving, croaking masses.

Menkheperre watched from his private balcony as servants scrambled below with baskets and shovels, their faces wrapped in linen against the overwhelming chorus of sound. The noise was maddening—a constant, rhythmic din that seemed to pulse with the very heartbeat of the Nile itself. Even here, above the chaos, he could not escape it.

"The kitchens are overrun, Divine One," reported the chief steward, his usual composure cracked like a dropped pot. "The cooks cannot prepare the evening meal. The creatures leap from every vessel, every storage jar. The bread ovens..." He gestured helplessly.

The Pharaoh said nothing, but his knuckles whitened as he gripped the balcony's edge. In the distance, smoke rose from the Israelites quarters of the city where they are burning the creatures in great pyres. The acrid smell mixed with the humid air, creating a nauseating haze that hung over the capital like a funeral shroud.

23 February 1438 BC– Stench of the Frogs

The mountainous heaps of rotting frogs had begun to collapse under their own fetid weight, spilling across courtyards and streets in rivers of blackened flesh that bred clouds of flies so thick they darkened doorways. Rekhmire pressed a perfumed cloth to his nose as he entered the royal bedchamber, but even the strongest myrrh could not mask the stench that had transformed the once-glorious capital into a charnel house. He found Menkheperre standing at his window, motionless as a statue carved from despair, his face gaunt and hollow-eyed from three sleepless nights of breathing death itself.

"Divine One," the vizier began, his voice thin with exhaustion, "the removal continues, but the stench—"

"It is unbearable," Menkheperre finished for him. "I have a nose, Rekhmire."

Throughout the city, slaves and citizens alike worked to gather the millions of dead frogs. Great piles rose outside the palace walls, dark mounds that grew higher with each passing hour. The priests had forbidden burning them, insisting the creatures be offered to Hapi, the frog-headed god of fertility. The rotting flesh had begun to attract small insects, and nobody dared approach the foul-smelling heaps. The stench pervaded everything—clothing, food, even the sacred oils used in temple rituals.

"What would you have me tell the Hebrew overseers, Divine One? The people have heard of your promise to Moses. Many believe you will allow the slaves a three-day festival in the wilderness as requested."

Silently, a thought surfaced: Where once the Ka bound Egypt to its gods, now even the sacred ones rot in the streets. Pharaoh still wore the crown, but it no longer fit the soul beneath it.

Menkheperre stared out at the city where massive heaps of dead frogs sat festering in the heat. Even from a distance, he could see the occasional swirl of small insects around the mounds, harbingers of decay. The palace guards stood at attention, their discomfort evident despite their rigid posture, each man positioned as far from the nearest heap as his post would allow.

"Tell them nothing has changed," he said finally. "The removal of the frogs fulfils my obligation. There will be no festival, no journey into the wilderness. The building projects continue as scheduled."

"But Divine One, you promised—"

"I promised consideration in exchange for relief," Menkheperre snapped. "I have considered. My answer is no." He turned from the window, striding back into the cool interior of his chamber. "Double the guards outside Avaris. No Hebrew is to leave their assigned post. If any speak of this 'god' of theirs, have them flogged."

When Rekhmire had gone, Menkheperre returned to the window. The afternoon sun beat down on the heaps of frogs, intensifying the putrid smell that wafted upward. In the distance, he could see citizens giving the piles a wide berth, their faces covered with cloths.

"Your frogs are dead, Moses," he whispered into the hot afternoon air. "And now your god falls silent."

He scratched absently at his hand, his skin irritated by the heat and stress of the past days. Soon, the frogs would decompose, the smell would fade, and life would return to normal. Six days, perhaps less, and this plague would be nothing but a fading memory.

The question that troubled him most was not what plague would come next, but whether his show of strength had been sufficient. Would the Hebrew slaves understand now that their god was no match for Pharaoh? Or would Moses return with more demands?

Outside, a priest waved censers of incense near one of the piles, attempting to mask the stench with sacred smoke. It was a futile gesture. Menkheperre turned away from the window, seeking refuge in the cooler interior of his chamber.

Let them pile their frogs as offerings to Hapi. Let them perform their rituals and prayers. In the end, it was not gods but men who determined the fate of nations, and Menkheperre was determined to remain the master of his.

And that final question—"What plague shall come next?"—assumed there would be more. Horemheb, it seemed, already believed in the power of the Hebrew god to deliver further punishment.

A knock on the door interrupted his thoughts. "Enter," he commanded.

Rekhmire stepped into the chamber, bowing low." The priests of Heket are distraught. They say we have angered the frog goddess by allowing her sacred creatures to be destroyed in such numbers."

"The frog goddess," Menkheperre repeated flatly. "Where was Heket's protection when these creatures invaded our bedchambers and food stores? The gods of Egypt stand silent while a foreign deity plays sports with us."

Rekhmire's eyes widened slightly at the unprecedented criticism. "Divine One, you yourself are divine. Surely—"

"Surely what, Rekhmire? Surely, I should have prevented this? Surely, I should release a valuable workforce because an old shepherd threatens me with amphibians?" Menkheperre stood, pacing the length of the room.

"The Hebrew quarter was... less affected," Rekhmire admitted. "Their wells remained clear of frogs, while ours—"

"While ours were infested," Menkheperre finished. "A curious coincidence, wouldn't you say? Moses can predict exactly which waters will be plagued and which will be spared?"

"It is... troubling," Rekhmire conceded.

Menkheperre picked up Horemheb's scroll again. "My chief scribe in Memphis believes more plagues will come. He writes of his fear openly. He questions my judgment."

"Shall I have him disciplined, Divine One?"

Menkheperre considered the question, then shook his head. "No. I need honest reports now more than courtly flattery. Besides..." He handed the scroll to Rekhmire. "He makes valid observations. Our magicians made the situation worse. The frogs died exactly when Moses predicted—not before, not after. The timing was too precise to be a coincidence."

"What will you do, Divine One?"

Menkheperre moved to the window, looking out over his city where pillars of smoke still rose from the burning piles of dead frogs. "Has there been any word from the Hebrew quarter? Any new demands from Moses?"

"None, Divine One. He appears to be waiting."

"Waiting for what? My surrender? Or..." Menkheperre's eyes narrowed. "Or for his next demonstration."

"The troops from Heliopolis arrived at sunset," Rekhmire reported. "Three thousand spearmen and two hundred chariots. Memphis reports their forces will arrive within two days."

Menkheperre nodded, a grim smile touching his lips. "Good. Post additional guards around Avaris. No one is to leave their assigned work area without direct permission. Any gathering of more than three Hebrews is to be dispersed immediately."

"And if Moses appears again?" Rekhmire asked cautiously.

Menkheperre turned from the window, his expression hardening. "Bring him to me. I wish to see what threat he brings next."

Left alone again, Menkheperre returned to the table where several more scrolls awaited his attention. He hesitated, then reached for Horemheb's journal once more. The scribe's final question haunted him: *What plague shall come next?*

As if in answer, a strange itch began between his fingers. He glanced down to see a tiny black speck moving across his skin, so small he had to squint to make it out.

A louse.

He crushed it between his fingernails, leaving a smear of blood no larger than a grain of sand.

Beyond the palace walls, in the mud-brick structures of Avaris where the Hebrews dwelled, a different approach to the frog problem had emerged. Unlike the Egyptians, who piled the creatures as offerings to their gods, the Israelites burned them in great pyres at the edges of their settlement.

"They are unclean," explained an elder to the younger men who gathered the remains. "They must be consumed by fire, not left to rot and corrupt our dwellings."

Smoke rose from multiple points around Avaris, thick columns that carried the acrid smell of burning amphibian flesh. The Egyptians watched with barely concealed disgust at what they perceived as disrespect for the sacred creatures of Heket.

Aaron, standing atop a small rise overlooking the smoldering remains, spoke quietly to his brother Moses. "The burning will be complete by nightfall. Already, the smallest ones have turned to ash."

Moses nodded, his eyes on the distant palace where Menkheperre had retreated. "And Pharaoh's heart?"

"Hardened again," Aaron replied. "Word comes from the royal scribe that Pharaoh has doubled the guards around our quarters and increased the work quotas."

Moses leaned heavily on his staff, the burden of his responsibility evident in the set of his shoulders. "Then we must prepare for what comes next. The Lord has spoken. There will be no respite for Egypt until Pharaoh relents."

Aaron studied his brother's weathered face. "When shall I raise the staff again?"

"When the frogs are gone completely," Moses answered. "Give them time to believe they have triumphed. Let Pharaoh convince himself that our God has finished His work."

28 February 1438 BC Plaque of Gnats

Nine days passed. The piles of frogs the Egyptians had gathered had finally been cleared away, though their memory lingered in the lingering stench that clung to the city. In Avaris, no trace remained of the creatures the Israelites had burned. The ashes had been scattered by the east wind that now blew steadily across the delta.

At dawn, Aaron stood alone at the edge of Avaris, facing the rising sun. He carried his shepherd's staff, polished smooth by years of use. No Egyptians were present to witness what happened next. No royal barge floated on the nearby canal. No guards watched from their posts; all had been drawn to the center of Pi-Ramesses, where Menkheperre was holding court.

Aaron raised his staff and then struck it downward, driving its end into the dusty earth. The impact sent a small cloud of dust billowing upward around his feet. He spoke the words Moses had taught him, the divine command that would bring the next plague upon Egypt.

As the dust settled, Aaron turned and walked back toward the settlement, never looking back to see the subtle change that had begun in the very particles of earth disturbed by his staff. The dust itself seemed to quiver, to take on life, to transform into something else entirely.

Menkheperre was presiding over a dispute between two noblemen when he first noticed the itch. It began as a slight irritation behind his ear, then spread to his neck and hands. He resisted the urge to scratch, maintaining the dignity expected of a god-king, but he could not help noticing that others in the great hall were experiencing similar discomfort.

The nobleman speaking faltered mid-sentence, raising a hand to his throat where tiny black specks could be seen moving against his skin. A priest standing nearby let out an involuntary gasp, staring at his arms where the same specks swarmed.

"Divine One," Rekhmire whispered urgently, leaning close to Pharaoh's ear, "they are everywhere."

Menkheperre looked down to see his own hands covered with the tiny creatures—gnats, barely visible to the naked eye, crawling across his skin by the hundreds. When he breathed, he could feel them in his nostrils. They clung to his eyelashes, gathered at the corners of his mouth.

A panicked murmur spread through the hall as everyone realized what was happening. Men and women alike began swatting at themselves, trying vainly to rid themselves of the minuscule invaders.

"Summon the priests of Geb," Menkheperre commanded, his voice steady despite his growing revulsion. "And find out if this affliction extends beyond this hall."

But the priests of Geb, god of the earth, had no remedy. The gnats had appeared simultaneously throughout Pi-Ramesses, an infestation so sudden and complete that no one had been spared. They were in the food stores, the bed chambers, the temples, the stables. They covered animals and humans alike, a living dust that could neither be washed away nor driven out.

Three days later, the situation had only worsened. The gnats had multiplied, their numbers seemingly endless. People walked with cloths pressed over their mouths and noses, but nothing truly kept the creatures at bay. They found their way into every crevice, every fold of clothing, every corner of every room.

Menkheperre stood in his private chamber, surrounded by priests waving burned herbs whose smoke was supposed to drive away the pests. It did little good. The gnats just rode the smoke currents, swirling in the air before settling once more on skin and surfaces.

"The magicians," Menkheperre said, turning to his chief priest. "What do they say?"

The priest bowed low, though the gesture lacked its usual grace as he simultaneously tried to brush gnats from his forehead. "Divine One, they have tried. They have cast their enchantments, performed the sacred rituals of Geb and Khepri, but..." he hesitated.

"But?"

"They cannot replicate this plague. They say..." Another hesitation. "They say this is the finger of a god."

Menkheperre's face darkened. "A god? Or Moses' god?"

"They did not specify, Divine One."

"And Avaris? What of the Hebrew quarter?" The priest exchanged glances with Rekhmire, who stepped forward. "There are reports, Divine One, that Avaris is... untouched. The gnats do not cross their boundaries."

Menkheperre clenched his jaw so tightly that a muscle twitched beneath his skin. "Bring me Moses and Aaron. I would hear their demands again."

1 March 1438 BC– Plaque of Flies

When Menkheperre saw Moses and Aaron for the first time since the plague of gnats had begun, he was standing at the great southern gate of Pi-Ramesses. He had come to witness with his own eyes what his officials had reported—that the gnats plaguing his city stopped at an invisible line that marked the border of his power.

And there it was, as if drawn by a divine hand: on the Egyptian side, the air itself seemed thick with the swarming creatures, while the air over Avaris remained clear. Between them stood Aaron, staff in hand, waiting as if he had known Pharaoh would come.

As Menkheperre approached, flanked by guards whose discipline was tested by the constant onslaught of gnats, he saw Aaron deliberately raise his staff again, this time pointing it eastward, directly at the heart of Pi-Ramesses.

"What now, Hebrew?" Menkheperre demanded, using a linen cloth that shields his mouth from the gnats. "What further torment does your god command?"

"Thus says the Lord," Moses replied, "Let My people go, so that they may worship Me. If you refuse to let them go, I will send swarms of flies upon you, your officials, your people, and your houses. The houses of the Egyptians shall be filled with swarms of flies; even the ground will be covered with them."

"More insects?" Menkheperre laughed bitterly, "Is that the best your god can do?"

Moses did not respond to the taunt. Instead, he turned and began walking back toward Avaris, his staff leaving a trail in the dust that separated the plagued land from the untouched.

The next day, Menkheperre stood on the balcony of his eastern chamber, watching in mute horror as a dark cloud appeared on the horizon. Unlike the morning mists that sometimes rose from the delta marshes, this cloud was dense, moving with purpose directly toward Pi-Ramesses from the east.

"What is it?" asked Rekhmire, who had come to deliver the morning reports.

"Flies," Menkheperre said softly. "He warned of flies."

As they watched, the cloud drew closer, resolving into billions of individual insects—not the tiny gnats that still plagued them, but larger flies with metallic bodies that caught the morning light in flashes of green and blue. They came in a great swarm, a moving wall that devoured the distance between the eastern lands and the capital.

"Divine One," Rekhmire said urgently, "perhaps we should retreat to the inner chambers."

But Menkheperre did not move. He stood transfixed as the swarm descended upon his city. Unlike the gnats, which had appeared suddenly and simultaneously throughout Pi-Ramesses, these flies came as an advancing army, overwhelming each district they encountered before moving on to the next.

People ran for shelter, closing doors and shutters, draping cloth over windows, but the flies found ways inside. They gathered in such numbers that they darkened rooms, their collective buzzing drowning out human voices.

"Avaris," Menkheperre said suddenly, turning to Rekhmire. "What news from Avaris?"

"Nothing unusual reported from Avaris, Divine One. The city functions normally, and there is no mention of flies." Rekhmire replied.

As if to confirm his observation, a small contingent of flies broke away from the main swarm, heading directly for the palace balcony where he stood. Menkheperre stood his ground, watching as they approached, then veered away at the last moment, rejoining the main body that continued its inexorable progress through the city.

"A message," Menkheperre said quietly. "They could have attacked me directly. They chose not to."

"Divine One?"

"Moses controls them," Pharaoh said, his voice oddly calm. "Just as he controlled the frogs. Just as his brother controlled the gnats. Directing these plagues with precision. Avaris remains untouched. Avaris is spared. The flies come from the east, not from all directions."

Rekhmire stared at his king, uncertain how to respond.

"Send for Moses," Menkheperre said finally. "Tell him I will speak with him. Perhaps... perhaps there is room for compromise."

Chapter 19 - Dead of the Stock

2 March 1438 BC – Flies will be gone Tomorrow

Menkheperre sat alone in his private chamber, the windows sealed against the swarms outside with wet clothes that servants refreshed hourly. The flies gathered on the outside of the fabrics, their bodies creating shifting patterns of shadow when lamps were lit inside.

He had met with Moses earlier, agreeing under duress to allow the Hebrews to sacrifice to their god, but within Egypt's borders, not in the wilderness as Moses demanded. Moses had refused the compromise, insisting that the sacrifices the Hebrews must make would be abominable to the Egyptians, requiring instead a three-day journey into the desert.

In the end, Menkheperre had relented, if only to end the plague of flies. Moses had promised the swarms would depart the next day, and Menkheperre had promised freedom for their religious festival.

Now, in the privacy of his chamber, Pharaoh pondered what had happened. The precision of the plagues troubled him deeply. Blood that contaminated Egyptian water sources but left Hebrew wells untouched. Frogs that invaded Egyptian homes but spared Avaris. Gnats that stopped at an invisible boundary. Flies that came only from the east, leaving Avaris to the south unaffected.

He traced a pattern on a papyrus before him—a circle divided by a line. On one side, he had written "*Moses' God.*" On the other hand, "*Egypt's Gods.*" Under the first, he had listed "*Blood. Frogs. Gnats. Flies.*" Under the second, nothing.

Where were Egypt's gods in all this? Where was Hapi when the Nile turned to blood? Where was Heket when her sacred frogs died by the millions? Where was Geb when the dust of the earth transformed into biting gnats? Where was Khepri when the flies descended?

More disturbing still was the escalating nature of the plagues. Each built upon the last, each more intolerable than its predecessor. If he should break his promise again—and the thought had already crossed his mind—what would come next?

Menkheperre rose and crossed to the window, lifting a corner of the damp cloth to peer out into the night. The buzzing of flies was omnipresent, a reminder of his city's suffering. In the distance, he could make out the dim lights of Avaris, peaceful and untouched.

"This is war," he whispered to himself, letting the cloth fall back into place.

He returned to his papyrus and stared at it with new understanding. This was not merely a negotiation between a ruler and his subjects. This was a divine conflict—a war between gods, with Egypt as the battlefield. Moses had made it clear from the beginning: "Thus says the Lord, the God of the Hebrews." Every plague was a declaration, every demand a challenge to Pharaoh's divine authority.

Menkheperre pressed his hands against his temples, feeling the weight of the double crown he had removed hours earlier but still carried spiritually. The royal Ka—the divine essence that passed from one Pharaoh to the next, the very power that made him a living god—was under attack. Was it possible that Moses, once a prince of Egypt himself, believed he was the rightful bearer of that power? Or did this Hebrew god seek to strip the Ka from him entirely, transferring divine authority to Moses and his people?

The thought was blasphemous, yet he could not dismiss it. Each plague struck at the heart of Egypt's divine order. The Nile—the lifeblood of his kingdom—had been the first target. Then Heket's sacred frogs had been corrupted, turned from blessing to curse. The earth itself had risen against them as gnats. And now these flies, directed like an army, attacking where commanded, sparing what was forbidden. "Who truly possesses the divine right to rule this land?" Menkheperre murmured. "Me, crowned by the gods of Egypt? Or Moses, guided by his invisible deity?"

He took up his stylus again and added beneath his list: "Royal Ka — disputed."

It was this, he realized, that lay at the heart of their conflict. Moses did not merely want freedom for his people. His god demanded recognition, supremacy. Each plague was a demonstration that the power of life and death in Egypt belonged not to Pharaoh but to this foreign deity.

And yet, the royal Ka had been passed to him through an unbroken line of Pharaohs stretching back more generations than could be counted. The gods of Egypt had placed him on this throne. How could he surrender to the god of former slaves? How could he acknowledge that some unseen force wielded more power in his kingdom than he did?

No, he decided, reaching for his stylus. He would not keep his promise. The flies would depart, as Moses had assured him, and then all would return to normal. The Hebrews would remain where they belonged, building our city, subject to his divine will.

And if their god sent another plague? Well, Egypt had endured blood and frogs, gnats and flies. Whatever came next, they would endure that as well. This war between divinities would not be surrendered so easily.

Menkheperre wrote a single word in the space beneath "Egypt's Gods": "Pharaoh." He was the living god of Egypt, the bearer of the royal Ka. He would not bow to the god of slaves, nor surrender his divine birthright to Moses. The battlefield might be littered with frogs and flies today, but tomorrow would bring a new confrontation—and this time, he would be prepared.

Outside, the flies continued their relentless assault on his city, waiting for the morning when Moses would command them to depart—a respite that would prove all too brief in the greater struggle that lay ahead.

14 March 1438 BC– Warning, Stock will die

Dawn broke over the eastern horizon in a blaze of crimson and gold, as if the sun itself was dipped in blood before rising to command the heavens. Moses stood at the edge of Avaris, watching as the first rays illuminated the massive royal palace of Pi-Ramesses in the distance. The plague of flies had lifted as promised, swept away by an eastern wind that had come as suddenly as the insects themselves. Now the air was clean again, almost sweet with the scent of morning dew upon the reeds.

Aaron approached, his staff in hand, eyes still heavy with sleep. "You did not rest, brother?"

Moses shook his head, his beard now fully white despite being only eighty summers old. The weight of God's mission had aged him visibly since that first encounter at the burning bush. His eyes, however, remained clear and piercing, filled with a fire that matched the desert flame where God had first spoken his name.

"There is no time for rest," Moses replied. "Pharaoh will break his word. I have seen it in his eyes."

"So soon?" Aaron asked, disbelief edging his voice. "The flies have barely departed."

"Power does not surrender easily, brother. Especially divine power." Moses turned to face Aaron fully, his weathered face solemn in the growing light. "Menkheperre believes himself a god. Every concession to Yahweh diminishes his own divinity in the eyes of Egypt. He cannot allow that."

"Then we must go to him again."

"Yes," Moses nodded. "And this time, the Lord will strike at something more precious than water or comfort. This time, He will strike at wealth itself."

The brothers set out immediately, their sandaled feet raising small clouds of dust as they made their way from Avaris toward the palace. Well before they reached the outer gates, the Egyptian guards recognized them, their approach noted and reported well before they reached the outer gates. No longer were they common Hebrew elders seeking audience; they were emissaries of a power that had turned the Nile to blood and commanded the creatures of earth and air.

Surprisingly, they were admitted without delay. Menkheperre was already seated upon his morning throne, a smaller, less ostentatious seat than the great throne of public audiences. He wore no ceremonial crown, only a simple circlet of gold around his head. His eyes were sunken, dark circles beneath them betraying a night without sleep.

"The flies are gone, Moses," Pharaoh said, his voice carrying across the chamber. "As you promised. You see that I keep my word—the Hebrew laborers have been released from their tasks to prepare for your... festival." He emphasized the last word with thinly veiled skepticism.

Moses stepped forward, his staff striking the polished floor with each measured step. "I come not to thank you, Pharaoh, but to warn you. For the Lord God of the Hebrews says this: 'Let My people go, that they may serve Me.' Three days' journey into the wilderness, as was agreed."

Menkheperre's jaw tightened. "I have given you leave to sacrifice, but within Egypt's borders. I cannot allow my entire labor force to vanish into the desert. Who knows if you would return?"

"This is what the Lord says," Moses continued, his voice deepening with divine authority. "'If you continue to restrain them and refuse to let them go, then the hand of the Lord will bring a severe plague on your livestock in the field—on your horses, donkeys, camels, herds, and flocks.'"

The chamber grew deathly quiet. Livestock were not merely animals in Egypt; they were wealth, power, military strength, and agricultural capability. Horses pulled war chariots, oxen ploughed fields, cattle and sheep provided meat, milk and wool. A nation's might could be measured in its herds.

"Another threat?" Menkheperre laughed, but the sound was hollow. "Your god seems fond of these demonstrations, Moses. Yet I note that each plague, while inconvenient, has passed quickly enough."

"The Lord will make a distinction," Moses replied, unmoved by the pharaoh's false bravado. "Between the livestock of Israel and the livestock of Egypt, so that no animal belonging to the Israelites will die."

Menkheperre rose suddenly from his seat, his fists clenched at his sides. "First, you claim dominion over Egypt's waters, then its creatures, and now its herds. Where does your god's authority end, Moses? At the threshold of my bedchamber? Or does he claim my very crown as well?"

"All authority is His," Moses answered. "The earth and everything in it belong to the Lord."

The pharaoh's face darkened. "Get out," he snarled. "Before I forget the power your god has shown, and have you both thrown to the crocodiles."

But Moses stood his ground, his eyes locked with Menkheperre's. "Tomorrow," he said firmly. "The Lord has set a time. Tomorrow the Lord will do this in the land."

With that, Moses turned and departed, Aaron at his side. As they walked away, Menkheperre called after them.

"Moses! When will you understand? I am Egypt! Its people are mine to command, its beasts mine to sacrifice, its land mine to rule. Your Hebrews have been mine for two hundred years. No god—not yours or any other—can change what has been ordained by divine right!"

Moses did not look back, but his words carried clearly through the still morning air. "Tomorrow, you will know whose divine right truly governs this land."

Menkheperre wasted no time. No sooner had Moses departed than he summoned his chief steward, a thin, efficient man named Paser who had served the royal household since Menkheperre was a boy.

"Bring me reports of all royal livestock," the pharaoh commanded. "Every beast in every field. I want them moved—today."

Paser bowed low. "Moved, Divine One? All of them? Where shall they go?"

"Into the city. Into covered shelters. Every beast that can be brought within walls, bring them. Those that cannot be moved, sell immediately to merchants from Canaan or Libya—any foreigners in our markets today."

"But Divine One," Paser protested, "there are thousands of animals. The royal herds alone would fill every available—"

"Then empty the granaries! Use the temple enclosures! Requisition private stables if you must! I want every beast of value protected before nightfall." Menkheperre's voice rose with each command, his face flushed with urgency.

"It shall be done," Paser bowed again, deeper this time, before hurrying away.

Menkheperre turned to the window, gazing out across his city toward the fields beyond. Already, he could see dust rising from the roads as messengers raced to carry his commands throughout the region. Would it be enough? Could the destruction Moses predicted be averted by simple precaution?

What troubled him most was the distinction—that invisible boundary that separated Avaris down to Goshen from the rest of the Delta, protecting the Hebrews while his people suffered. Such precision spoke of a power beyond normal understanding, a deity who could distinguish between ownership and allegiance with supernatural accuracy.

Throughout that day, the capital was thrown into chaos. Royal herds were driven through the streets, bellowing and bleating as they were forced into spaces never designed to hold them. The smell of dung and sweat filled the air as thousands of animals were crowded into makeshift pens. Tempers flared as private citizens found their courtyards commandeered for royal stock. The markets overflowed with panicked sellers trying to offload animals at any price, even as buyers grew suspicious of the sudden surplus.

By sunset, Menkheperre stood on his balcony, watching as the last of the visible herds were driven through the city gates. Paser approached, exhausted, his linen kilt stained with dust and sweat.

"It is done, Divine One," he reported. "All royal livestock have been relocated or sold. The temple herds likewise. Many noble households have followed your example, though some refused to believe the danger."

"And the fields?" Menkheperre asked, his eyes scanning the darkening landscape.

"Not empty, my Pharaoh. Many commoners cannot move their animals, having nowhere to put them."

Menkheperre nodded grimly. "So, we have saved what we could. We shall see tomorrow if Moses' god can distinguish between a cow in a field and a cow in a stable."

That night, an unnatural silence fell over Egypt. No jackal howled in the distance; no night birds called from the marshes. Even the insects seemed hushed, as if all creation held its breath, waiting for divine judgment to fall.

15 March 1438 BC – Animals in the field died

The sun was barely above the horizon when the reports began to arrive. Paser burst into Menkheperre's private chambers without ceremony, his face ashen.

"Divine One! The animals—they're dying. Every beast left in the fields."

Menkheperre had slept poorly, if at all, and was already dressed. "How many?" he demanded.

"All of them, my Pharaoh. Every report says the same. Horses collapse in their traces. Oxen fell while ploughing. Sheep and goats drop where they graze. No sickness, no warning—they fall and die." Paser's voice trembled. "And there's more. The animals we brought within the city... they live. Not one has perished."

Menkheperre moved to the window and looked out over his city. In the distance, he could see columns of smoke rising where farmers burned the carcasses of their dead livestock. The economic devastation would be incalculable. War chariots without horses were useless. Fields without oxen would go unplowed. The loss of milk and meat would bring hunger, if not famine.

"Bring me my scribes," he ordered. "I want a full accounting of what remains. Every beast that is alive, every beast that has died. Measure the extent of this... plague."

As Paser hurried to obey, Menkheperre returned to his private writing table. The papyrus from the previous night still lay there, with its divided circle. On one side, *"Moses' God"*—now with *"Blood, Frogs, Gnats, Flies,*

Livestock" listed beneath. On the other hand, "*Egypt's Gods*" with only "*Pharaoh*" written in defiance.

He stared at it for a long moment before dipping his brush in ink. Beneath "*Livestock,*" he added a new word: "*Wealth.*"

That was what this plague had struck—not merely animals, but the foundation of Egypt's economic power. A nation's strength measured in hooves and horns, now rotting in the fields. Yet his foresight had saved much. The royal herds, safely sheltered in the city, remained alive. The armies would still have chariots; the royal table would not want for meat. He had outwitted Moses' god, at least partially.

The thought gave him strength. This war between divinities was escalating, but he had proven that precaution could blunt divine wrath. Perhaps the Hebrew god was not omnipotent after all, merely powerful in specific ways that could be anticipated and countered.

"And Goshen?" Menkheperre asked, already knowing the answer.

"Untouched, Divine One. We have reports. Not a single animal belonging to the Hebrews has died. Their flocks graze peacefully, their oxen plow, their donkeys carry loads—all while ours lie dead in the fields."

Menkheperre received the news in silence. The distinction remained perfect—an invisible line drawn between his people and Moses', between his divine authority and the Hebrew god's.

Later that afternoon, Moses and Aaron appeared again at the palace gates, requesting audience. Menkheperre considered refusing them entry but decided against it. Better to face this challenge directly than hide behind palace walls.

"Has your god proven his point, Moses?" Pharaoh asked when the brothers stood before his throne. He decided to wear his full regalia, the double crown heavy upon his head, the crook and flail crossed over his chest.

"The Lord asks again," Moses replied, "let my people go, that they may serve me."

"I have lost cattle and horses, sheep and camels," Menkheperre acknowledged. "But not all, many were protected by my command. Your god is powerful, Moses, but not all-powerful. Not within my kingdom."

"Those animals lived because the Lord permitted it," Moses countered. "To show you that His hand directs both life and death in this land. Had he wished it, no stable or city wall could have protected them."

"Perhaps," Menkheperre smiled thinly. "Or perhaps we have learned to anticipate your god's methods. What would he strike next, I wonder? Our crops? Our firstborn? Our very breath? Whatever it is, Egypt will endure, as it has endured for three thousand years."

Moses studied the pharaoh's face, seeing the calculation behind his eyes. "Your heart remains hardened," he said at last. "You seek to bargain with the unbargainable, to measure divine will against human defiance. This cannot end well for Egypt."

"Yet it is not Egypt that suffers most in these exchanges," Menkheperre replied. "Your people still build my city. Your god may kill my livestock, but your backs still bear the weight of my stone. If this is a victory for your deity, it is a hollow one."

"The Lord is not finished," Moses warned. "This is but one step on a path that leads either to freedom or to greater suffering than Egypt has ever known."

"Then we shall walk that path together, Moses," Menkheperre declared. "Your god and mine, in contest for this land and its people. But remember this—Egypt was ancient when your ancestor Abraham first set foot on its soil. Our gods have ruled here since time immemorial. This land knows its true master."

Moses shook his head sadly. "No, Pharaoh. This land, like all lands, belongs to the Lord alone. You are but a tenant, and an ungrateful one at that."

With those words, Moses and Aaron departed once more, leaving Menkheperre alone with his thoughts and the growing fear that despite his precautions, despite his divine bloodline, he might be fighting a war he could not win.

Outside the palace walls, the smell of burning carcasses filled the air, a grim harbinger of plagues yet to come. In Goshen, the Hebrews tended their healthy flocks and whispered among themselves that perhaps, after four centuries of bondage, deliverance was finally at hand.

Chapter 20 - Boils

17 March 1438 BC – Itching, Swelling, Boils

When the plague struck at dawn two days ago, it was with merciless precision. Every beast left in the open fields—every ox, donkey, horse, camel, sheep, and goat—collapsed and died where it stood. The animals belonged to commoners who couldn't move them quickly enough, to distant estates whose owners hadn't received warning in time, to skeptics who had dismissed Moses' threat. Yet every animal Pharaoh had ordered moved under roof or shed—and there were thousands—survived untouched. The royal stables remained full, the requisitioned granaries still echoed with the snorts and bleats of healthy beasts, and the temple enclosures protected their sacred bulls.

Menkheperre's foresight had saved Egypt's military might and much of its wealth, though the countryside now reeked with the stench of death as farmers burned or buried countless carcasses."

By midday, the palace guards announced the arrival of the two Hebrews. Moses and Aaron. Always Moses and Aaron, like vultures circling a dying beast, waiting for Egypt to fall.

The audience chamber fell silent as they entered. Moses carried a small leather pouch, his eyes dark and knowing. Aaron's face betrayed nothing, but his knuckles were white where they gripped his staff.

"Thus says the Lord, the God of the Hebrews," Moses began, his voice cutting through the silence like a bronze knife. "How long will you refuse to humble yourself before me? Let my people go, that they may serve me."

Menkheperre forced a laugh, though it sounded hollow even to his ears. "First blood, then frogs, then gnats and flies. Your god enjoys his little spectacles, doesn't he? Next, he'll be conjuring dancing girls and trained monkeys."

Without warning, Moses thrust his hand into the pouch and withdrew a fistful of fine ash. He nodded to Aaron, and both men cast the ash skyward, directly before Pharaoh's throne.

The ash hung suspended, defying gravity, swirling like desert sand in a khamsin wind. Then it flowed—not fell, but flowed—toward the open windows, drawn by some invisible current, dispersing into the sky above the city.

"This soot from the furnace," Moses intoned, "will become fine dust over all the land of Egypt and will cause boils that break out in sores on man and beast throughout all the land."

Moses stared directly into Pharaoh's eyes, unblinking. "The Lord God could have crushed Egypt with a single blow. Instead, He sends warnings, that you might know His power and release His people from bondage."

The words hung in the air like the ash had, then Moses and Aaron turned as one and departed, their sandaled feet making no sound on the polished floor.

The high priest of Sekhmet approached the throne, his face grave beneath his leopard-skin headdress. "My lord, perhaps we should consider—"

"We consider nothing," Menkheperre spat, his voice cracking like a whip. "Return to your temple. Prepare your medicines. If this plague comes—if—we shall need every remedy in Egypt."

The first itch came as he prepared for the day's affairs, a small irritation on his forearm where the gnats had feasted days before. The skin burned hot as desert sand at noon. He scratched it with one long, manicured nail, leaving white furrows in his flesh that quickly turned angry red.

Night fell like a shroud over the palace. Menkheperre sat on the edge of his vast cedar bed, staring at his arms in the lamplight. What had begun as a single irritation had multiplied a hundredfold. His skin erupted with angry red welts that throbbed with each heartbeat. When he touched one, it burst beneath his finger, weeping clear fluid that burned like fire.

His personal physician knelt before him, his own face mottled with similar eruptions. The man's hands trembled as he opened his medicine box.

"What curse is this?" Menkheperre demanded, his voice thick with pain and fury.

The physician's eyes were red-rimmed, his voice raw. "It appears to be the beginning of what Moses warned of, Divine One. Reports come from every quarter of the city. First the itching, then the swelling, then—" he gestured helplessly at his face, where several boils had already burst, leaving glistening trails of fluid down his cheek.

"And treatments?"

"My assistants prepare salves of honey, animal fat, and herbs. But..." The physician hesitated, his gaze dropping to the floor.

"Speak!" Menkheperre commanded, then gasped as the effort of shouting caused a boil on his neck to rupture, sending liquid fire down his chest.

"The sores resist our remedies, my lord. They spread like..."

"Like a curse," Menkheperre finished. "Like the curse of a god."

By dawn, Egypt howled with pain. From the foulest slum to the most splendid palace, no Egyptian was spared. Men, women, children—all clawed at their skin like animals, desperate for relief from the maddening itch that preceded each eruption. When the boils burst, the agony only intensified, the exposed flesh burning as though touched by hot metal.

The temples were filled with supplicants, but the priests themselves could barely perform the rituals, their ceremonial purity shattered by the weeping sores that covered their bodies. In the streets, people collapsed, their skin a battlefield of swollen red welts and open, oozing wounds.

Menkheperre refused to cancel the morning council. Though each movement was torture, he had servants dress him in his lightest robes, forgoing the heavy crown for a simple gold band. He would not hide. He would not show weakness. He was Pharaoh, and Pharaoh did not bow to pain.

His officials gathered, each man's face a mask of suffering. Some had bound cloths over the worst of their sores, but nothing could hide their misery.

"Avaris?" Menkheperre asked, the single word all he could manage through clenched teeth.

His spymaster, a thin man whose skill at gathering secrets was matched only by his current agony, shook his head. "Untouched, Divine One. Not a single Hebrew shows signs of this affliction. They go about their business as though nothing has happened."

"Of course they do," Menkheperre growled. The unfairness of it burned hotter than the boils. "Their god protects them while punishing us."

The high priest of Sekhmet, his face barely recognizable beneath the eruptions, whispered, "My lord, our magic fails. Our medicines bring no relief. This plague..." He swallowed hard. "It is beyond our power to counter."

"Nothing is beyond the power of Pharaoh!" Menkheperre roared, rising from his throne. Pain exploded across his body, but he embraced it, used it to fuel his rage. "I am the living god of Egypt! The royal Ka flows through me! Not through Moses, not through his invisible god!"

He stalked the chamber, each step an exercise in agony. "Five plagues now have struck at what is sacred to Egypt—our water, our land, our homes, our peace, our health. Each targeting something protected by our gods. This is no random punishment. This is a challenge. A gauntlet thrown at the feet of Egypt's pantheon."

His oldest advisor, a man who had served Menkheperre's father, spoke softly. "And our gods have failed to answer the challenge, Divine One. Five times the Hebrew god has struck. Five times our deities have remained silent."

Menkheperre rounded on him, eyes blazing. "The gods speak through Pharaoh! I am their voice, their hand, their will made flesh! If they seem silent, it is because they wait for me to act!"

Later, alone in his chamber, Menkheperre slumped before his papyrus. With a trembling hand, he added "*Boils*" beneath "*Moses' God.*" The column under "*Egypt's Gods*" remained empty save for the word "*Pharaoh.*"

He saw it now, the pattern laid bare before him. Each plague had targeted a specific Egyptian deity—Hapi, god of the Nile; Heket, goddess of fertility; Geb, god of earth; Khepri, god of creation; Sekhmet, goddess of healing. One by one, the Hebrew god was challenging—and defeating—Egypt's divine protectors.

Night descended, bringing no relief from the torment. Menkheperre stood at his window, scratching unconsciously at sores that would not heal. Beyond the palace walls, Egypt whimpered in darkness, while Avaris' lights burned bright and undimmed.

For a single, terrible moment, doubt crept into Menkheperre's heart. What if this Hebrew god were real? What if he truly was more powerful than all of Egypt's pantheon combined?

The thought vanished as quickly as it had formed, burned away by pride hotter than the desert sun. He was Pharaoh. The living god of Egypt. He would not bow to the god of slaves, no matter what afflictions were visited upon his land.

He would endure. Egypt would endure. And when this war between gods was over, the Hebrews would know the true meaning of suffering.

The Gathering of Forces

They came from the south, a river of bronze and leather flowing toward Pi-Ramesses beneath a merciless sun. The troops from Memphis, two thousand strong, marched in formation.

From his balcony, Menkheperre watched their approach, his face impassive despite the fire that still raged beneath his skin. The boils had begun to dry and crack, forming crusts that split with each movement, but he stood straight-backed and regal, refusing to acknowledge his suffering.

"How many?" he asked the commander of his guard, a burly man whose face bore the pitted scars of recently healed sores.

"Two thousand from Memphis, Divine One. The garrison from Heliopolis sends one thousand. They report another two thousand marches from the southern provinces."

"When will they arrive?"

"Two weeks, if the gods are kind." The commander hesitated.

Menkheperre nodded, his eyes never leaving the approaching column. Not ideal, but it was something. A show of strength. A demonstration that despite five—no, six—demonstrations of the Hebrew god's power, Egypt still stood. Pharaoh still ruled.

The past days had been a nightmare. As the boils spread, so too had the whispers. In taverns and marketplaces, in the shadow of temples where priests struggled to maintain age-old rituals despite their afflictions, people spoke in hushed voices of the God of the Hebrews. Some had even been seen at the edges of Avaris, leaving offerings, begging protection from future plagues.

Treason. Blasphemy. Betrayal of Egypt's gods, of Pharaoh himself.

"Establish camps around Avaris," Menkheperre ordered, his voice like iron. "No Hebrew leaves without permission. Double their work quotas. I want them too exhausted to plan, too broken to hope."

The commander's face darkened. "Divine One, is it wise to provoke them further? The plagues—"

"The plagues will end," Menkheperre cut him off, his voice deadly soft. "No god, foreign or otherwise, can sustain this assault forever. We need only outlast them."

As the commander departed, Ptahhotep, High Priest of Ra, entered the chamber. Once, his face had been smooth as polished alabaster. Now it bore the marks of the Hebrew god's wrath—pockmarked, scarred, a living testament to Egypt's humiliation.

"You summoned me, Great House," he said, using the formal title for Pharaoh.

Menkheperre gestured toward the balcony, where the troops continued their relentless advance into the city.

"What do you see, Ptahhotep?"

The priest watched for a moment, his eyes narrowing against the glare. "I see the might of Egypt returning, Divine One."

"I see endurance," Menkheperre said, his voice hard as granite. "I see men who have suffered as we have suffered, felt the same pain, endured the same humiliation. Yet they march. Their flesh may be weak, but their spirits remain unbroken."

He turned to face the priest. "Where is Ra in all this? Where is the sun god's protection when his children burn with sores?"

Ptahhotep bowed his head. "The ways of the gods are mysterious, Great House. Perhaps this is a test of our faith."

"A test?" Menkheperre laughed, the sound like stones grinding together. "Six plagues later, and you still believe this is merely a test of faith?"

He stalked to the table where his papyrus lay, the evidence of his defeat recorded in his hand. "No, Ptahhotep. This is war. A war between gods, and currently, we are losing."

The priest approached cautiously. "Then perhaps, Divine One, a tactical retreat would be wise. Allow the Hebrews their three days of worship in the wilderness—"

"And admit defeat?" Menkheperre's voice cracked like thunder. "Never! The arrival of these troops marks a turning point. We will establish control. We will demonstrate that Pharaoh still rules Egypt, not some invisible deity who speaks through the mouth of a murderer and a shepherd!"

"And if another plague comes?"

Menkheperre's jaw clenched tight enough to crack stone. "We will endure it, as we have endured the others. Blood, frogs, gnats, flies, boils— what could come next that we cannot survive?"

Later, as the sun plunged toward the western horizon, setting the desert ablaze with crimson light, Menkheperre stood upon the city walls with his commanders, watching as the troops from Memphis and Heliopolis established their camps. Their discipline remained impeccable, even in suffering. Tents rose in perfect rows, sentries took their positions, and fires blazed into life.

Beyond the military encampment lay Avaris, its mud-brick houses glowing golden in the sunset. Even from this distance, Menkheperre could see figures moving freely, untouched by the misery that had befallen Egypt. Children played in the streets. Women gathered at wells. Men returned from their day's labor, their backs unbowed, their skin unmarked by the curse that had ravaged the Egyptians.

Chapter 21 - The Fields are Wasted

15 March 1438 BC–Prediction of a Hailstorm

Menkheperre stood on the high balcony of the palace at Tanis, his hands gripping the smooth stone balustrade until his knuckles whitened beneath his copper skin. Beside him, Rekhmire's normally placid face was taut with concern. They had summoned the Hebrew once more, this time without the theatrics of the throne room. Menkheperre had thought a more intimate setting might yield different results.

"How long will you continue this obstinacy?" Menkheperre asked, his voice quiet yet tense as a drawn bowstring. "Your people have suffered enough. I have suffered enough. Egypt bleeds because of your stubbornness."

The old Hebrew, Moses, stood before them with his staff planted firmly on the polished floor. His brother Aaron remained silent at his side, but it was Moses whose eyes held Menkheperre's gaze without wavering.

"It is not I who prolongs Egypt's suffering, Great House," Moses replied, using Menkheperre's royal title with neither mockery nor deference. "The Lord God of the Hebrews has spoken: 'Let my people go.'"

Menkheperre felt the familiar surge of rage rise in his chest. How many times had he heard those words? How many times had this commoner, this exiled murderer, stood before him making demands as though he were the one wearing the Double Crown?

"Your god has no dominion here," Menkheperre said, his voice dropping to a dangerous whisper. "I am Egypt. I am the Morning and Evening Star. The Nile flows because I command it."

Moses merely shook his head, his eyes reflecting something Menkheperre found infuriating—pity.

"Thus says the Lord God of the Hebrews," Moses intoned, raising his staff slightly. "'Let my people go, that they may serve me. For if you refuse to let them go, behold, tomorrow about this time I will cause very heavy hail to fall, such as has not been in Egypt from the day it was founded until now. Therefore, send now and gather your livestock and all that you have in the field, for the hail shall come down on every man and beast that is found in the field and is not brought home; and they shall die.'"

Rekhmire stepped forward, his scholarly demeanor struggling against his obvious frustration. "Enough of these threats! Have we not endured blood and frogs and lice? Did not flies swarm our homes and disease claim our livestock? Your tricks grow tiresome, Hebrew."

But Menkheperre held up a hand, silencing his vizier. A cold, hollow sensation had formed in the pit of his stomach. The Hebrew had mentioned hail, yet no hail had fallen. Not yet.

"What hail do you speak of?" Menkheperre asked, struggling to keep his voice level.

Moses' weathered face remained impassive. "The Lord will send hail upon Egypt, such as has never been seen since its founding. Every man and beast found in the field and not brought home will die when the hail falls on them."

"More threats," spat Rekhmire. "More trickery and illusion."

Menkheperre said nothing. He had seen too much already to dismiss the Hebrew's words entirely. Six times now, the old man had stood before him making proclamations, and six times disaster had followed. Blood had fouled the sacred Nile. Frogs had infested the land in numbers beyond counting. Lice had tormented man and beast alike. Flies had swarmed the royal palace itself, sparing only the Hebrew settlements and Goshen. A mysterious plague had decimated Egypt's precious livestock. And boils—Menkheperre unconsciously rubbed his arm, remembering the painful eruptions that had afflicted even his divine flesh.

"You have until tomorrow to release the Hebrews," Moses continued, seemingly unaffected by the tension crackling in the air. "After that, the Lord's hand will fall upon Egypt once more."

"Get out," Menkheperre said softly, dangerously. When Moses did not immediately move, he roared, "GET OUT!"

The guards moved forward, spears at the ready, but Moses and Aaron turned and walked out with unhurried dignity.

After they had gone, Rekhmire approached cautiously. "My Pharaoh, these are but the desperate threats of a troublemaker. The man is skilled in certain magics, yes, but he is not—"

"Silence," Menkheperre commanded, his eyes fixed on the eastern horizon. "Look there."

Rekhmire followed his gaze. In the distance, beyond the gleaming waters of the Nile, dark clouds were gathering, unlike any storm clouds they had ever seen. They boiled and churned against the sky like the smoky breath of Apophis himself.

"Summon the priests of Nut," Menkheperre ordered, referring to the sky goddess. "Have them make offerings immediately. And send word to the fields—all workers and animals to return to shelters."

"My Pharaoh?" Rekhmire questioned, his scholarly mind struggling with the implications.

"Do it!" Menkheperre snapped, his eyes never leaving the approaching darkness.

16 March 1438 BC A Severe Hailstorm

The next day, early morning, an unnatural gloom had descended over Tanis, north of Pi-Ramesses. The storm clouds had swallowed the sun, plunging the royal city into a twilight that made the lamps necessary even at noon. Menkheperre paced the royal chambers, his ceremonial crook and flail discarded on a gilded table. Outside, an eerie silence had fallen— even the birds had gone quiet.

Then it reached Pi-Ramesses

The first thunderclap shook the very foundations of the palace. Menkheperre froze mid-stride, his heart pounding against his ribs. The sound was not the familiar roll of thunder from the rare Delta storms.

This was the sound of the sky cracking open, as though Set himself were tearing the heavens apart in his rage.

Then came the rain—not the gentle life-giving waters that occasionally blessed the Delta, but stinging sheets that lashed horizontally across the landscape, driven by winds so fierce they bent the date palms nearly double.

"My Pharaoh!" A guard burst into the chamber, water streaming from his armor. "You must see—it is—" Words failed him.

Menkheperre followed the man to a sheltered portion of the balcony. What he saw made his blood run cold. Mingled with the rain were stones of ice—some as small as pomegranate seeds, others as large as a man's fist—falling from the sky with deadly force. Where they struck, they shattered roof tiles, splintered wooden structures, and tore through the tender green shoots in the fields surrounding the city.

"The flax," Menkheperre whispered, watching as the carefully cultivated crops were pummeled into the mud. "The barley."

The plants had been nearly a foot high, promising a bountiful harvest. Now they were being systematically destroyed before his eyes. Only the wheat fields, where the shoots had not yet broken ground, remained protected beneath the soil.

Lightning split the sky in jagged white forks, striking the ground with terrible accuracy. Where it touched, fire erupted, only to be quenched almost immediately by the torrential downpour. The contradictory elements—fire and ice falling together from the sky—filled Menkheperre with a superstitious dread that no amount of royal training could suppress.

A massive hailstone crashed through the wooden lattice protecting the balcony, shattering on the floor at Menkheperre's feet with a sound like breaking pottery. Frozen water splashed against his ankles, the cold shocking against his skin. He stared at the chunks of ice, feeling as though he were staring at his own heart, suddenly external and vulnerable.

The wind howled like a thousand mourners, driving sheets of water horizontally across what had been, only hours before, a clear blue sky.

Lightning split the darkness, illuminating the devastation below—trees stripped bare, crops flattened, livestock lying motionless in the fields. The air smelled of wet earth and smoke from fires the storm had somehow both started and extinguished.

"My Pharaoh," Rekhmire appeared at his side, voice raised against the howling tempest. His advisor's linen robe clung to his body, soaked through despite the protection of the palace walls. He turned south, gesturing toward Goshen, his arm trembling—whether from cold or fear, Menkheperre could not tell. "The Hebrew settlements in Goshen, it looks like they are untouched by the storm. The sun shines in that direction as though it were an ordinary day."

Menkheperre felt something break within him. Not his resolve—that remained as immovable as granite—but something else, some fundamental certainty about the nature of the world and his place in it. His fingers tightened around the balcony's stone railing until his knuckles whitened. The gods themselves seemed to have chosen sides, and it was not his.

"Bring me the Hebrew," he commanded, his voice eerily calm beneath the storm's cacophony.

The soldiers departed, hunched against the onslaught of medium-sized hail that drummed against their shields. Their sandals splashed through puddles that had formed in the palace corridors, water seeping in from every crack and crevice as though the very stones wept.

When Moses arrived, he came alone. The storm had mysteriously eased in the stretch between Avaris and Pi-Ramesses, as though creating a corridor for his passage. His robes were completely dry, as though he had walked through sunlight rather than the apocalyptic storm that continued to ravage Tanis. Not a single drop of rain glistened in his beard. The staff in his hand seemed to hum with an energy that made the hairs on Menkheperre's arms rise.

The old Hebrew's eyes held neither triumph nor pity—only certainty, a terrible knowledge of what was yet to come if Pharaoh's heart remained hardened. Around them, the palace creaked and groaned under the assault of the unnatural storm, a sound like the gods themselves shifting restlessly in their celestial seats.

As soon as Moses stepped fully into the chamber, the unnatural calm that had accompanied his journey shattered. The hail returned with miraculous suddenness, as though it had been held at bay by invisible hands now withdrawn. A volley of ice hammered against the palace roof with renewed fury, the sound like war drums announcing divine judgment. Water began streaming through new leaks in the ceiling, forming puddles at the edges of the room, yet not a single drop touched the Hebrew prophet who stood dry in the center of the deluge.

"I have sinned this time," Menkheperre said, the words bitter as unripe fruit on his tongue. Never had he admitted wrongdoing to another living soul. "The Lord is righteous, and my people and I are wicked."

The words were ash in his mouth, but necessity drove him to continue.

"Entreat the Lord that there be no more mighty thundering and hail, and I will let you go. You shall stay no longer."

Moses regarded him steadily. "As soon as I have gone out of your palace, I will spread out my hands to the Lord. The thunder will cease, and there will be no more hail, that you may know that the earth is the Lord's. But as for you and your servants, I know that you do not yet fear the Lord God."

The old man's presumption rekindled Menkheperre's rage, but he held his tongue. Let the Hebrew think what he would. Once the danger had passed, Menkheperre would reassert his divine authority. The gods of Egypt would not be mocked forever.

Moses departed the city as promised. As he left, the hail ceased. The thunder fell silent. The dark clouds parted, allowing Ra's light to shine once more upon the battered landscape.

3:30 pm– Menkheperre inspecting the Damages

Menkheperre surveyed the devastation from his chariot, Rekhmire at his side. The fields lay in ruin, green shoots beaten into the mud. Trees stood broken and stripped of leaves. Dead cattle and sheep dotted the landscape where they had been caught unprotected in the open.

"The damage is extensive, my Pharaoh," Rekhmire said quietly. "But we have grain stores enough to see us through until the next planting. And the wheat crop remains safe beneath the soil."

Menkheperre nodded absently, his thoughts elsewhere. Something the Hebrew had said troubled him deeply. *That you may know that the earth is the Lord's.* Not Geb's, not Nut's, not under the dominion of any of Egypt's ancient deities—and certainly not under Menkheperre's divine authority.

"Send word to the border garrisons," he said finally. "The Hebrews are to remain where they are."

Rekhmire's eyes widened. "But my Pharaoh, you promised—"

"I know what I promised," Menkheperre snapped. "And I know what Egypt requires. Would you have me release a workforce of hundreds of thousands because of a storm? Because of coincidence and clever trickery? I am Pharaoh. I do not bend to the winds of foreign gods."

The vizier fell silent, but Menkheperre could read the doubt in his eyes—the same doubt that had begun to gnaw at his certainty.

5 April 1438 BC– Swarms of Locust

Twenty days passed. The damage from the hailstorm had been assessed, the dead buried, and damaged structures repaired. Life in Tanis had begun to return to its normal rhythm, though food prices had risen sharply with the destruction of the flax and barley crops.

Menkheperre sat in his private garden, a rare moment of solitude in the ceaseless demands of rulership. The lotus pool before him reflected the clear blue sky overhead. Birds chirped in the sycamore trees—life continuing as it should.

A shadow fell across him. He did not need to look up to know who it was.

"The Hebrew has returned, hasn't he?" Menkheperre asked, still gazing at the tranquil water.

"Yes, my Pharaoh," Rekhmire confirmed. "He and his brother wait in the antechamber."

Menkheperre sighed deeply. "What does he want now? Has his god not taken enough from Egypt?"

"He speaks of locusts, my Pharaoh. As he warned before."

A cold dread settled in Menkheperre's stomach. He had hoped—foolishly, he now realized—that the worst was behind them. That perhaps the Hebrew's god had made his point and would now relent.

"Bring him."

When Moses and Aaron appeared before him, Menkheperre did not rise from his seat by the pool. Let them come to him, in his garden, surrounded by the symbols of Egyptian permanence and power.

"How long will you refuse to humble yourself before my God?" Moses asked without preamble. The old man's directness still had the power to shock, even after all these confrontations.

"I have endured your god's tantrums," Menkheperre replied coldly. "I have watched my people suffer. And yet Egypt stands, as she has stood for thousands of years, as she will stand long after your tribes are dust in the desert."

Moses shook his head sadly. "Thus says the Lord God of the Hebrews: 'If you refuse to let my people go, behold, tomorrow I will bring locusts into your territory. And they shall cover the face of the earth, so that no one will be able to see the earth; and they shall eat the residue of what is left, which remains to you from the hail, and they shall eat every tree which grows up for you out of the field.'"

Before Menkheperre could respond, Rekhmire stepped forward, his scholarly restraint finally breaking.

"Have you not brought enough destruction upon us?" the vizier demanded. "Our fields lie ruined, our livestock decimated. And for what? Because you and your people would rather wander the desert than contribute to the glory of Egypt that has fed and housed you for generations?"

Moses remained impassive, but Menkheperre noted how his brother Aaron's eyes flashed with indignation.

"How long shall this man be a snare to us?" Rekhmire continued, turning to Menkheperre. "Let the men go, that they may serve their god in the wilderness. Do you not yet understand that Egypt is being destroyed?"

Menkheperre's head snapped up, eyes blazing. "You overstep, Rekhmire."

"My Pharaoh, I speak only out of concern for Egypt," the vizier replied, dropping to one knee. "Perhaps a compromise—let the Hebrew men go to worship as they wish, but keep their women and children as surety for their return."

Menkheperre considered this, then turned to Moses. "Go, serve your god. But who exactly will be going?"

"We will go with our young and our old, with our sons and our daughters, with our flocks and our herds," Moses replied without hesitation. "For we must hold a feast to the Lord."

Menkheperre laughed bitterly. "The Lord look upon you and judges! You intend evil. No! Only the men may go and serve your god, for that is what you requested." He waved his hand dismissively. "Now get out of my sight!"

Moses and Aaron were escorted from the garden. As they departed, Menkheperre caught the old Hebrew glancing at the eastern horizon, where the sky remained clear and blue. The look on his face—one of absolute certainty—sent a chill through the Pharaoh's body.

That night, a hot wind began to blow from the east—a khamsin, but earlier in the season than any Menkheperre could remember. It continued through the night, dry and relentless, sucking moisture from the land.

By morning, Menkheperre stood once again on his balcony, watching the approaching doom with a sick fascination. On the eastern horizon, a dark cloud had appeared—not the black thunderheads of the hailstorm, but a seething, roiling mass that blotted out the rising sun.

"What is it?" he whispered, though he already knew.

"Locusts, my Pharaoh," Rekhmire answered, his voice hollow with dread. "More than has ever been seen before."

The swarm advanced with terrible speed, carried on the eastern wind. As it approached, Menkheperre could hear it—a sound like rushing water, like the roar of a distant conflagration. Then they were upon the city, blotting out the sky so completely that lamps had to be lit at midday.

Menkheperre watched in horror as they descended on what remained of Egypt's crops. The wheat, which had been spared the hail by remaining underground, had sprouted in the intervening weeks. Now the tender green shoots disappeared beneath the living carpet of insects. Where the locusts lifted, nothing remained but bare earth.

They covered every surface—buildings, statues, even people who were not quick enough to seek shelter. They flew into open mouths, tangled in hair, and crunched underfoot with every step. The air filled with their stench—a cloyingly sweet, rotten odor that turned the stomach.

"My Egypt," Menkheperre whispered, watching as the divine land was devoured before his eyes. For the first time in his reign, he felt not just anger or frustration, but genuine fear. Not for himself—a Pharaoh did not indulge in personal terror—but for his kingdom, for the cosmic order that he was sworn to uphold.

"Find the Hebrew," he commanded, his voice cracking. "Bring him immediately."

This time, Menkheperre did not wait for Moses to be brought to him. He strode through the locust-infested corridors of his palace, guards frantically clearing a path before him, until he reached the antechamber where the brothers waited.

"I have sinned against the Lord your God and you," Menkheperre said without preamble, the words bitter on his tongue. "Now therefore, please forgive my sin only this once, and entreat the Lord your God that He may take away from me this death only."

Moses regarded him with that same infuriating compassion that made Menkheperre want to strike him. "It will be as you ask."

The Hebrew left the palace, and within hours, a strong west wind began to blow. It gathered the locusts as a broom sweeps dust, driving them eastward, back toward the Red Sea. Not a single locust remained in all the territory of Egypt.

But as the skies cleared and the damage was assessed—not a green thing remaining on tree or plant throughout the land—Menkheperre felt his heart harden once more. The humiliation of begging, not once but twice, burned in his breast like a coal. He was Pharaoh, son of Ra, the living god of Egypt. He would not be broken by these displays, no matter how devastating.

"The Hebrews remain where they are," he informed Rekhmire that evening, as they stood surveying the stripped landscape from the palace walls. "Egypt has endured for thousands of years. We have weathered famines before. We will rebuild."

Rekhmire opened his mouth as if to protest, then closed it again. The doubt in his eyes was now unmistakable, but Menkheperre ignored it.

"The gods of Egypt will prevail," Menkheperre said, as much to convince himself as his vizier. "They must."

But as night fell over the devastated kingdom, Menkheperre stood alone in his chambers, the weight of the Double Crown heavier than it had ever been. He thought of Moses' god—invisible, without statue or temple, yet wielding power that had brought mighty Egypt to its knees.

For the first time in his life, Menkheperre wondered if he might be wrong. The thought was so alien, so contrary to everything he had been raised to believe about his divine nature and authority, that he physically recoiled from it.

No. He was Pharaoh. He was Egypt. And Egypt would endure this trial as it had endured all others throughout its glorious history.

But as he gazed out at his ravaged kingdom, a small voice whispered from the darkest corner of his soul: *What comes next?*

Chapter 22 - Darkness

10 April 1438 BC – Egyptian New Year Dawn

Menkheperre awoke to golden sunlight streaming through the high windows of his bedchamber, painting the alabaster walls with patterns of light and shadow. He stretched languidly, muscles relaxed beneath sheets of fine linen, and smiled. Today was Wepet Renpet—the Opening of the Year—the first day of the Egyptian calendar, marked by the new moon that had passed in darkness the night before.

It was a day of renewal, of fresh beginnings. The priests would offer prayers to Thoth, god of wisdom and time. The people would celebrate with feasts. And he, Menkheperre, would attend the ceremonies with his wife and son, basking in the glory of Egypt's eternal power.

He rose from his ornate bed, its ebony frame adorned with ivory inlays of hunting lions, and strode to the balcony. The great city of Pi-Ramesses stretched before him in the morning light, its temples and palaces gleaming like jewels scattered across the landscape. The Nile flowed serenely, its life-giving waters reflecting the cloudless sky.

"A perfect day," he murmured, breathing in the air scented with lotus blossoms and incense from the nearby temples.

But as the morning progressed and the sun climbed higher, approaching the ninth hour, something changed. The light began to dim—not gradually like the approach of evening, but with an unnatural suddenness that sent a chill down Menkheperre's spine.

He had been in council with his advisors when the first servant burst into the chamber, eyes wide with terror.

"My lord! The sun—something is wrong with the sun!"

Menkheperre rushed to the balcony, his heart pounding. High above, the blazing disk of Ra was being devoured. A dark shadow crept across its face like some celestial serpent swallowing the god himself. The courtyard below erupted in chaos as people poured from buildings, pointing upward, their voices rising in a cacophony of fear and confusion.

"An eclipse," one of the priests gasped, falling to his knees. "But this was not predicted! The astronomers saw no sign—"

The darkness deepened. What began as a partial obscuring of the sun continued beyond natural limits. Even as the moon should have passed on, the shadow remained, deepened, became absolute. Within an hour and a half, the world had plunged into a blackness more complete than any night Menkheperre had ever known.

This was not the gentle darkness of evening, which still held the silver light of stars and moon. This was a suffocating void, thick and oppressive, that seemed to press against the skin like a physical thing. Servants scrambled in panic, colliding with furniture and each other as they sought to light lamps. But even when flames were kindled, they provided only feeble circles of light, as if the darkness itself consumed the glow.

"Moses," Menkheperre breathed, gripping the stone balustrade until his knuckles whitened. A memory stirred—that morning, he had received reports of the Hebrew prophet standing by the western bank of the Nile at dawn, staff raised toward the heavens.

"He has done this," Pharaoh's voice came from behind him, trembling with rage. "The Hebrew sorcerer has stolen Ra himself!"

The palace descended into chaos. No one dared move beyond arm's reach in the impenetrable blackness. Food was consumed where it lay within immediate grasp. Children whimpered in their mothers' arms.

Three Days of Darkness

The darkness persisted through that entire day and into night—though how could one tell the difference? Time became meaningless in the absolute void. Menkheperre remained in his chambers, servants pressed close around him with their trembling lamps, their small flames seeming to make the darkness more oppressive by contrast.

The second day brought no relief. The darkness continued, thick and suffocating. Throughout the city, no one ventured from their homes. The once-vibrant streets of Pi-Ramesses lay silent and empty, as if the entire civilization had been swallowed by the underworld.

Menkheperre stood at his balcony—pointless in the darkness, but habit drew him there. He strained his eyes, searching for any hint of light, any sign that this nightmare would end. Nothing. Only the oppressive weight of shadow upon shadow.

His mind raced with memories. Stories told by the oldest priests, whispered tales of a darkness that had fallen on Egypt nearly two hundred years before, during the reign of a long-dead pharaoh. But those had been only stories, myths to frighten children. This was real. This was now.

"The Hebrew god is stronger than ours," someone whispered in the darkness nearby—a servant, perhaps, or a guard. The words hung in the void like a curse.

"Silence!" Menkheperre commanded, but his voice lacked conviction. How could he deny what his own eyes—or lack thereof—confirmed?

On the third day, as time dragged on in the endless night, something miraculous happened. Those brave enough to venture near windows began to see pinpricks of light appearing in the black vault above. Stars. One by one, they emerged like diamonds scattered across black velvet.

"Is it over?" whispered an advisor who had not left Pharaoh's side since the darkness began.

Menkheperre pressed his face to the window, hardly daring to breathe. The stars grew brighter, more numerous. After three days of absolute darkness, their light seemed brilliant beyond measure. And then, on the eastern horizon, the faintest hint of gray began to appear.

"Dawn," he breathed. "Dawn is coming."

12 April 1438 BC – Light Returns

The sunrise that morning was unlike any Menkheperre had ever witnessed. As the first rays broke over the horizon, the entire city seemed to exhale as one. People emerged from their homes like spirits returning from the dead, faces pale and drawn, eyes blinking painfully in the sudden brilliance.

Menkheperre stood on his balcony, drinking in the sight of his city reborn in golden light. The Nile sparkled. The temples gleamed. Life had returned to Egypt. The three days of darkness had ended.

But his relief was short-lived. Around noon, the light began to fade again—not into absolute darkness as before, but into an unsettling twilight. The sun, which should have been high and bright, dimmed as if veiled by invisible hands. Noon became dusk.

"Not again," Menkheperre growled, fists clenched. "Send for Moses. Bring the Hebrew to me now!"

Moses Before Pharaoh

When Moses stood before the throne, the chamber was lit by dozens of lamps, their light holding back the unnatural twilight that pressed against the windows. The prophet's face, illuminated from below, appeared otherworldly, his eyes reflecting the lamplight like polished copper.

"You see what your god has done," Pharaoh said, his voice tight with controlled fury. "Three days of darkness, and now this. He makes war on Ra himself, the very source of life."

Moses stood unmoved, his staff planted firmly on the polished floor. "The Lord God of the Hebrews says: 'Let my people go, that they may serve me.'"

Pharaoh leaned forward on his throne, jaw clenched. The past three days had taken their toll—dark circles shadowed his eyes, and his hands trembled slightly as they gripped the armrests. "Go, serve your god," he finally conceded, the words scraping his throat like desert sand. "But tell me this—who exactly will be going?"

"We will go with our young and our old," Moses replied, his voice resonant and clear. "With our sons and our daughters, with our flocks and our herds. For we must hold a feast to the Lord."

Pharaoh's laugh was bitter, echoing against the columns. "The Lord be with you indeed, if I ever let your little ones go with you! Look, you have some evil purpose in mind. No! Only the men may go and serve the Lord, for that is what you asked for."

"Our livestock also must go with us," Moses continued, unmoved as desert stone before wind. "Not a hoof shall be left behind, for we must take of them to serve the Lord our God. And we do not know with what we must serve the Lord until we arrive there."

Pharaoh's face contorted with fury. His patience, worn thin by plagues and humiliation, finally snapped. "Get away from me!" he shouted, rising from his throne with such force that his crown tilted. "Take care never to see my face again, for on the day you see my face, you shall die!"

The Final Warning

Moses' eyes took on a mysterious light, as if reflecting fires not yet kindled. When he spoke, his voice filled the chamber with quiet authority that somehow carried more weight than Pharaoh's rage.

"Thus says the Lord: At midnight, when the moon is full, I will go out amid Egypt, and every firstborn in the land of Egypt shall die, from the firstborn of Pharaoh who sits on his throne, even to the firstborn of the slave girl who is behind the hand mill, and all the firstborn of the livestock. There shall be a great cry throughout all the land of Egypt, such as there has never been, nor ever will be again."

He paused, letting the terrible prophecy settle over the now-silent court. The lamps flickered as if they too trembled at his words.

"But not a dog shall growl against any of the people of Israel, either man or beast, that you may know that the Lord makes a distinction between Egypt and Israel. And all these your servants shall come down to me and bow down to me, saying, 'Get out, you and all the people who follow you.' And after that I will go out."

Pharaoh's face had drained of color, but his expression remained hard as stone. Menkheperre, standing to the side, felt his heart constrict. The firstborn. His son was a firstborn.

Moses turned to leave, his silhouette sharp against the lamplight. "As you say," he called back. "I will never see your face again."

As soon as Moses departed, the full brilliance of the sun burst forth once more. Sunlight flooded through the high windows, illuminating dust motes that danced in the air. The familiar warmth touched skin that had been chilled despite the season.

But for Menkheperre, the return of light brought no comfort. Moses had spoken his final warning, and the words echoed in his mind like a death sentence: "Every firstborn in the land of Egypt shall die."

The First Crescent

That evening, as the sun set in a blaze of crimson and gold, word came to Moses from the watchers he had posted. The first sliver of the new moon had been sighted in the western sky—a thin blade of silver light appearing just after sunset.

Moses stood among the elders of Israel, his face solemn. "Gather the elders," he commanded. "The time has come."

Within hours, the assembly was complete. Families, tribal leaders, elders—they stood in the cooling evening air, faces turned toward their prophet.

"This night," Moses declared, his voice carrying across the crowd, "marks the beginning of the first month. This shall be for you the beginning of months. It shall be the first month of the year for you— the month of Nisan."

A murmur ran through the assembly. While the Egyptians had their new year three days ago, marking it by the invisible new moon, the Hebrews now declared their own new year, marked by the visible crescent that signaled the month's beginning.

"Tonight begins Nisan 1," Moses continued. "And on the fourteenth day of this month, at twilight, you shall prepare the Passover lamb. For at midnight on that night, the Lord will pass through Egypt."

The people listened, their faces a mixture of hope and dread. Freedom was coming—but at a terrible price for Egypt.

Meritamun Returns

From his high balcony later that same evening, Menkheperre observed the crowd that had gathered outside the palace walls. Nine plagues now, each more devastating than the last. And now Moses had promised one final plague, one that made his heart constrict within his chest.

"All firstborns will die when the moon is full."

Those words echoed in his mind as he gripped the balcony's stone railing. Below, approaching the royal dock, a modest barge made its way with the current. His breath caught when he recognized the royal insignia. Meritamun had returned against his explicit orders.

Two months ago, as the plagues intensified, he'd sent his wife and their son, Siamun, to the safety of Bubastis. The sacred city dedicated to Bastet, the protective cat goddess, had seemed the safest refuge. And now they had returned, precisely when Moses had declared the most terrible judgment yet.

"My lord," a servant ventured, "the royal barge approaches. It appears to be the queen."

"I can see that," Menkheperre snapped, eyes never leaving the vessel. There she stood at the bow with their nine-month-old son bundled in her arms.

Without waiting for ceremony, Menkheperre strode toward the stairs. Court officials flattened themselves against walls as he passed, eyes wide with surprise at this breach of decorum. By the time he reached the dock, servants were already securing the mooring ropes.

Menkheperre didn't wait for the gangplank. He leapt onto the gently rocking deck, ignoring gasps from the royal guard.

"What have you done?" he demanded, voice low but intense. "Why have you returned?"

Meritamun lifted her chin, dark eyes unwavering. "I've come to you. Where else should I be when Egypt faces its greatest trial?"

"You should be far from here," he hissed, stepping closer to examine his son. The child's chest rose and fell with steady breaths, his little fists curled beside his round face. "I sent you to Bubastis for safety—for Siamun's safety."

"And what safety is there in Egypt now?" she countered, shifting Siamun to her hip as the child stirred. "The plagues follow us everywhere. Even in Bubastis, the waters turned to blood. The darkness fell there too."

"But Moses—" Menkheperre began, then lowered his voice. "He has declared a final plague. The firstborn, Meritamun. Every firstborn in Egypt will die. Our son."

Her eyes filled with tears, but her voice remained steady. "Then I will not spend our final hours together on some distant barge, wondering if you still draw breath. I will not let fear rob us of whatever time remains."

She reached out with her free hand, touching his face gently. "If we're to lose everything, let us lose it together. And if by some miracle we survive, let our son know that his parents faced Egypt's greatest trial side by side."

Siamun chose that moment to wake, his dark eyes blinking up at them both. He smiled, revealing two tiny teeth, and reached a chubby hand toward his father's face.

Menkheperre's resolve crumbled. "Come," he said, extending his arms to take the child. "Let us go inside."

The Royal Chambers

Night had fallen over Thebes, the darkness unusually complete despite the return of the stars. No moon would rise tonight—it was still too new, too close to the sun. Menkheperre stood over the small ornate cradle where Siamun now slept, the child's peaceful breathing contrasting sharply with the turmoil in his father's mind.

"What comes for you, little one?" he whispered, gently touching the soft black curls on his son's head. "And how am I to stop it?"

Nine plagues now—blood, frogs, gnats, flies, livestock, boils, hail, locusts, and that terrible darkness. Each had come exactly as Moses predicted. And the prophet had never been wrong.

"Not this one," he whispered fiercely. "Not my son."

Decision crystallized within him. He would speak to the Hebrew again. Perhaps there was still time to negotiate, to find some compromise. And if not—if not, then he would find some way to protect his child, even if it meant defying Pharaoh himself.

Siamun stirred in his sleep, tiny fingers twitching. Menkheperre reached down and carefully adjusted the linen blanket.

"Sleep well, my son," he murmured. "Your father will find a way."

Chapter 23 - New Year, New Beginning

13 April 1438 BC

Menkheperre was jolted from sleep by the sound of ram's horns echoing across the still morning air. First one, then more, their sonorous calls rippling outward from Goshen like waves across water. The sound was unmistakable—shofars, the curved horns the Hebrews used in their religious ceremonies.

He sat upright in bed, heart pounding, as the calls continued. This was not the usual Hebrew worship he had occasionally heard from a distance. This was deliberate, coordinated, triumphant. The blasts carried across the city from Avaris to Pi-Ramesses, announcing something significant.

"What is that sound?" Meritamun whispered beside him, pulling Siamun closer in her arms. The boy had awakened too, his dark eyes wide but unafraid.

Menkheperre rose and strode to the balcony, the morning breeze cool against his skin. The sun was just cresting the horizon, painting the sky in shades of gold and crimson. From his vantage point, he could see toward the Hebrew settlement. Even at this distance, he could make out groups of people gathered, their faces turned eastward toward the rising sun, the shofars continuing their proclamation.

"They're celebrating," he said, jaw tightening. "The Hebrews are celebrating."

He knew what it meant. During his years overseeing the Hebrew labor, he had learned their ways. Last night, after the darkness lifted and the sun had set, their watchers had sighted the first thin crescent of the new moon—a blade of silver light appearing just after sunset in the western sky. According to their reckoning, that sighting marked the beginning of the month of Nisan, their first month, their sacred new year.

While Egypt had celebrated Wepet Renpet three days ago, before the terrible darkness descended, the Hebrews were now declaring their own new beginning. Their priesthood was announcing it with shofar blasts that echoed through the city, impossible to ignore.

"It's their new year," Menkheperre muttered, fingers gripping the balustrade. "Moses has declared it."

As if summoned by the thought, a memory surfaced—Moses standing before Pharaoh just yesterday, his final warning still ringing in Menkheperre's ears: "At midnight, when the moon is full, I will go out amid Egypt, and every firstborn in the land of Egypt shall die."

The shofar blasts continued, each note seeming to carry a message: Your time is running out. The countdown has begun. In twelve days, when the moon reaches its fullness, judgment will fall.

Menkheperre watched the sun climb higher, the golden light that should have brought comfort after three days of darkness now feeling ominous. Below in the palace courtyard, servants were beginning to stir, looking toward Goshen with worried faces. The Hebrew celebration was loud, bold, defiant—slaves acting as though they had already won their freedom.

"Twelve days," he whispered, his eyes finding his son. Siamun had fallen back asleep in his mother's arms, his chest rising and falling with peaceful breaths, unaware that a death sentence hung over him.

The shofars finally fell silent, but their echo seemed to linger in the air, in Menkheperre's mind. The morning sun filtered through the alabaster screens of his chamber, casting honeyed patterns across the polished limestone floor. For the first time in days, the light felt normal, steady, reliable. The darkness had truly passed.

But the shadow that hung over Egypt's firstborn remained, growing darker with each passing day, each waxing phase of the moon.

"I must do something," Menkheperre muttered, turning from the window. "I cannot simply wait for this to happen."

"And what can you do?" Meritamun asked gently. "Nine plagues have come exactly as the Hebrew predicted. Nine times his god has demonstrated power over all Egypt. What makes you think the tenth will be different?"

"Because this one threatens my son!" The words burst from him with raw emotion. "I will not stand idle while death stalks our child."

Meritamun rose, carrying Siamun to his father. The boy reached for Menkheperre with chubby arms, babbling happily. "Then find Moses," she said quietly. "If there is any way to protect our son, the Hebrew will know it."twelve

Avaris – The Passover Preparations

While Menkheperre wrestled with his fears, the Hebrew settlement of Goshen hummed with purposeful activity. The sighting of the new moon's crescent two nights ago had set in motion a series of carefully orchestrated preparations.

On the tenth day of Nisan—nine days from now—each family would select a lamb. Not just any lamb, but one without blemish, perfect and pure. It would be kept for four days, examined daily to ensure its perfection, before being slaughtered at twilight on the fourteenth day.

Moses had given explicit instructions. The lamb's blood would be painted on the doorposts and lintels of their homes. When the Lord passed through Egypt at midnight, He would see the blood and pass over those houses, sparing the firstborn within.

"Do you truly believe it will work?" Aaron asked his brother as they walked through the settlement. Around them, families were already discussing which lamb they would choose, making preparations for the feast that would follow.

"The Lord has said it," Moses replied simply. "And the Lord has never failed in His word."

Miriam joined them, her weathered face grave. "The Egyptians are beginning to hear of our preparations. Their spies report back to Pharaoh. Soon they will understand what we plan."

"Let them understand," Moses said. "Let them see that the Lord makes a distinction between Egypt and Israel. Perhaps some among them will have the wisdom to seek shelter under the blood."

But even as he spoke, Moses knew that few Egyptians would humble themselves to follow Hebrew instructions. Pride would be their downfall, as it had been Pharaoh's throughout the plagues.

18 April 1438 BC – Growing Tension

As the days passed and the moon waxed toward fullness, tension mounted throughout Egypt. Word of the Hebrew preparations had spread, carried by servants and spies, by merchants and travelers. The story was always the same: the Hebrews were preparing for something they called "Passover," marking their doors with lamb's blood to protect their firstborn from a coming plague.

In the markets of Pi-Ramesses, Egyptian mothers clutched their sons closer, fear written across their faces. Some laughed nervously, dismissing the Hebrew prophecy as superstition. But many had lived through the previous plagues and knew better than to mock the power of the Hebrew god.

Menkheperre summoned his spy Nehesi daily, demanding every detail of the Hebrew preparations. "Tell me again," he insisted. "Exactly what does Moses say will protect them?"

"The blood of a lamb, my lord," Nehesi repeated, his thin face troubled. "Applied to the doorposts and lintel. When their god sees the blood, He will 'pass over' that house."

"And if an Egyptian were to do the same?" Menkheperre pressed. "If we were to mark our doors with blood?"

The spy shifted uncomfortably. "Moses has not forbidden it, my lord. But he has not offered it either. His instructions are for the children of Israel."

Menkheperre turned away, jaw clenched. His pride warred with his fear for his son. To follow Hebrew instructions would be to admit the superiority of their god over Egypt's deities. It would be to humble himself before slaves. But if it would save Siamun...

The Royal Council

"Absolutely not!" Menkheperre's voice rang through the council chamber. "I will not have it said that Egypt's royal house cowered before Hebrew sorcery!"

Rekhmire had brought his concerns before Pharaoh and the high council, hoping to find some solution, some protection for Egypt's children. Instead, he found only stubborn pride.

"My lord," he pressed, choosing his words carefully, "nine plagues have come exactly as Moses predicted. The Hebrew god has proven His power again and again. Is it not wisdom to take precautions?"

"Precautions?" Menkheperre's eyes flashed. "You mean to mark our doors with blood like frightened slaves? To perform their barbaric rituals? Never!"

The high priest of Ra stepped forward, his ceremonial robes rustling. "The gods of Egypt are supreme," he intoned. "We have prepared powerful amulets and spells of protection. These will shield our firstborn from any harm."

Rekhmire looked at the priest's confident face and felt no reassurance. Where had these powerful spells been when the Nile turned to blood? When darkness covered the land for three days? The priests' magic had failed time and again against the Hebrew god's power.

"And if the spells fail?" he asked quietly.

"They will not fail," the priest insisted. But Rekhmire saw the flicker of doubt in his eyes.

He left the council chamber with a heavy heart. Pharaoh would do nothing to protect Egypt's children. The priests offered only empty assurances. If his son was to be saved, he would have to find another way.

21 April 1438 BC – Four Days Until the Full Moon

The moon was growing, night by night, toward its full phase. Throughout Goshen, Hebrew families had selected their lambs on the tenth day of Nisan as commanded. Now those perfect animals lived among them, tethered in courtyards, playing with children, becoming part of the household.

This was deliberate, Moses had explained. They needed to know the lamb, to bond with it, before the sacrifice. The cost of redemption must be real, the loss keenly felt.

In the Egyptian quarters, mothers watched the waxing moon with dread. Some had begun marking their own doorways with various symbols and amulets, hoping to ward off the coming plague. But deep down, most knew it was futile. The Hebrew god had proven immune to Egyptian magic.

Menkheperre spent every spare moment with his son. He watched Siamun take his first independent steps, laughed at the boy's delighted squeals, memorized every detail of his perfect face. If these were to be their last days together, he would not waste them.

"What will you do?" Meritamun asked on the evening of the eighteenth day, as they watched Siamun sleep.

"I don't know," he admitted. "Pharaoh forbids following the Hebrew ritual. The priests offer spells I don't trust. And Moses..." He trailed off, shaking his head.

"Moses knows how to save him," Meritamun said softly. "You know he does."

"Yes," Menkheperre agreed, the word bitter on his tongue. "The Hebrew knows. But he has offered no help to Egyptians, only warnings of death."

They stood in silence, watching their son's peaceful breathing, counting down the days until the full moon rose.

24 April 1438 BC – The Day Before

The moon was nearly full, just one day from its perfect roundness. Throughout Goshen, Hebrew families made their final preparations. Tomorrow at twilight, they would slaughter their lambs. Tomorrow night at midnight, the Lord would pass through Egypt.

Moses gathered the elders one final time to review the instructions. Every detail mattered. The way the lamb was to be roasted. The manner of eating—with belts fastened, sandals on feet, staffs in hand, ready to depart at a moment's notice. The bitter herbs to remind them of slavery's bitterness. The unleavened bread prepared in haste.

"Remember," Moses said, his aged voice still strong and clear, "you must not leave your houses until you hear the shofars. When the Lord passes through to strike Egypt, He will see the blood on the lintel and the two doorposts, and the Lord will pass over that door and will not allow the destroyer to enter your houses to strike you."

The elders nodded gravely, then dispersed to their families to make final preparations. The air thrummed with anticipation and dread. Liberation was coming—but at a terrible price for Egypt.

The moon rose nearly full over Egypt, beautiful and terrible, counting down the hours until midnight of the next day.

Until Passover.

Until liberation.

Until death walked through Egypt's streets.

Chapter 24 - The Ingathering

25 April 1438 BC – The Day of the Passover

6 am - Palace at Avaris

The question hung in the still air of his chamber, unanswered. Outside, the sky above Pi-Ramesses was still pale with dawn when the messenger arrived. Dust clung to his sandals. His tunic was damp with Nile mist. He bowed low before Menkheperre, who stood alone in the granite court, facing east as the sun began its slow rise over the marshes.

"My lord," the messenger said, voice hoarse with urgency. "The Hebrews are packing their tents."

Menkheperre's shoulders stiffened beneath his linen robe. He turned slowly, his profile sharp against the growing light. "All of them?"

"Yes, Majesty. From the Store-Cities to the brickyards—every family, every slave. They are gathering their flocks. They say the time has come."

A long silence fell. The only sound was the distant thud of a palace gate closing behind the runner who had delivered the news. The courtyard birds had not yet begun their morning chatter, as if they too sensed the weight of this moment.

Menkheperre said nothing at first. His eyes drifted toward the western horizon, where the Nile split into threads and the land of Avaris stirred in shadow. Nine plagues had befallen Egypt. Nine times the Hebrew prophet had stood before the throne, staff in hand, speaking words of power and doom. Nine times, Pharaoh had refused. Menkheperre had waited for this moment—dreaded it, prepared for it, hoped against it.

"They move as if they already know," he said quietly, "what has not yet been decreed."

He descended the steps into the court, the stone cold beneath his bare feet. The scent of lotus still clung to his robes from the purification rites the night before. He had not slept. The priests had chanted until the moon set, burning incense to Ra, to Isis, to Seth—to any god who might shield Egypt from what was coming.

"Summon the commanders," he ordered, his voice cutting through the morning stillness. "I want the entire army ready for inspection by mid-morning."

"Yes, Majesty." The courier bowed deeply, then turned to carry out the command.

He whispered to himself—not in fear, but in acknowledgment.

"So, it has come."

8 am – Pi Ramesses Army Base

Menkheperre rode out into the parade grounds of Pi-Ramesses, where the full might of his northern army stood in gleaming formation. The Sun God's rays caught on polished bronze and beaten gold, transforming the field into a sea of light. Arrayed beneath banners snapping in the morning breeze, over twenty thousand men stood ready—six hundred elite war chariots, each manned by seasoned archers and drivers clad in bronze and leather, formed the vanguard. Behind them, rows upon rows of standard chariotry, numbering in the thousands, stretched toward the horizon. Infantry battalions, hardened from campaigns in Canaan and Kush, stood in silent ranks—archers with composite bows, spearmen with ox-hide shields, and axe men from the Delta regiments, each cohort marked by its sigil and plume.

Overhead, the sun climbed past the pylons of the Temple of Seth, glinting off helmets and chariot yokes. Menkheperre moved along the lines atop his chariot, its sides inlaid with electrum and lapis lazuli. The blue-dyed ostrich plumes that marked him as supreme commander nodded with each step of his matched white stallions. Flanked by his captains and the High Steward of War, he surveyed the army that had conquered nations and brought tribute from lands beyond the cataracts.

He stopped often, inspecting reins, examining arrow quivers, calling officers by name. "General Khaemwaset," he called to a weathered soldier with the scars of many campaigns etched into his face. "Your men from the Nubian campaign? They are recovered?"

"Ready for your command, Divine One," the general replied, touching his heart in salute. "Each man has six arrows in his quiver and rage in his heart for any who would challenge Egypt."

Menkheperre nodded, satisfied. He moved on, the leather reins loose in his hands as his charioteer guided the horses through the formations. Every chariot was oiled and armed. Shields were polished to mirror brightness, spear points freshly sharpened.

The morning sun climbed higher as they completed their circuit of the camp. At the final formation, Menkheperre raised his hand, and the bronze horns sounded across the field. Five thousand men struck their shields in unison—a thunder that rolled across the delta and sent birds wheeling from the marshes.

"They are ready," he murmured to his charioteer, watching the perfect ranks hold their salute. The man nodded, already turning the horses toward the palace road.

Noon - Palace at Avaris

Menkheperre dismounted in the courtyard, dust still on his sandals from the camp. His army was at its peak—disciplined, swift, and lethal. And he would need every sword it offered. That evening, the Hebrews would slaughter their lambs. The moon would rise red. And Egypt would be tested once more.

Menkheperre was preparing to re-enter the palace after his inspection when he paused, startled by a sound carried on the wind. At first it was a murmur, then a ripple, then a rising roar like the tide rushing in.

Cheering.

It echoed faintly across the Nile delta, rolling in from the south like a chant. A crowd's voice. Joyful. Fierce.

He narrowed his eyes and turned to the officer nearest him, a captain of the royal guard. "What is that sound?"

The commander cupped his ear, brow furrowing beneath his polished helmet. Another runner was already sprinting across the sunlit courtyard, sandaled feet slapping the stone, sweat glistening on his shaven head.

"Majesty!" the runner cried, breathless, dropping to one knee. "The Hebrews—they are marching!"

Menkheperre stepped forward, the gold beads in his ceremonial beard catching the light. "Where?"

"From Goshen, my lord. Hundreds, no, thousands are moving toward Avaris. Whole families, with livestock, singing as they go. They wear traveling cloaks though the day is warm."

A tremor of disbelief passed over Menkheperre's face. He had thought they would wait for night, for darkness, for secrecy. This bold procession in daylight was a declaration.

The officer at his side added, his voice low with concern, "And that is not all, Divine One. We have reports from Thebes, slaves fled three weeks ago, Majesty. Vanishing from the great construction sites."

"Gone?" Menkheperre repeated, voice cold as a desert night.

"As if pushed by a wind none of us can see," the runner said, glancing skyward. "As if something has compelled them to rise in a single breath and move. The overseers could not hold them. Some tried to bar the gates—" He hesitated.

"Speak," commanded Menkheperre.

"The men who tried to block their path fell ill, Majesty. Clutching their throats. Some... died where they stood."

The cheers grew louder, like thunder scattered across the reed beds. The rhythmic sound of feet, of staffs striking dust, of ancient songs rising after centuries of silence.

Avaris, the fortified hub of Pharaoh's rule in the delta, was being flooded—not with soldiers, but with singing slaves.

Menkheperre stood frozen, shoulders rigid beneath his gold-trimmed cloak. He could feel it—some force older than Egypt moving through the land, rousing the dust of the road, whispering in the ears of slaves, driving them forward. Not with spears. Not with swords. But with a purpose.

He looked south, toward Thebes, toward the heart of the empire. And for the first time, he saw the whole kingdom shifting under his feet. The Hebrew god was gathering his people, in the full light of Ra's gaze, not in darkness

"Send word to the garrisons," he said, his voice low, nearly drowned out by the distant cries of jubilation, "Seal the river crossings. Post riders on the canal routes. No one leaves Egypt without my command."

His commanders exchanged glances, their eyes dark with unspoken thoughts.

He did not say what both he and his captains already knew.

It was already too late.

2 pm -Avaris Central

Dust filled the air as sandals scuffed the dry earth. Israelite families moved quickly, efficiently—no shouting, no panic, just quiet purpose. There were no wagons, no oxcarts groaning with possessions. They packed light: rolled mats, bread dough wrapped in cloth, skin water flasks, and staffs in hand.

Along the roads leading into Avaris, families streamed like tributaries joining a mighty river. An old woman with henna-stained hands clutched a small bundle of hyssop, already dried and tied for the night's ritual. Two young boys carried a lamb between them, its legs bound, its eyes wide but calm. A mother adjusted the sling that held her infant, whispering ancient promises into the child's ear.

Children clung to their parents, wide-eyed. The elderly leaned on the arms of younger kin. Newcomers from Goshen streamed in—hundreds by the hour, their faces sunburnt and stunned with the sudden freedom of movement. And still, they were welcomed. Doors opened. Bitter herbs and basins were shared without question.

In the courtyards and alleys of Avaris, small fires were being prepared, stacked in hearths of brick and stone. Lambs were tethered outside homes, calm for now, but the air was thick with the knowledge of what would come before nightfall.

A young woman paused in her work of grinding herbs, looking up at the cloudless sky. "Do you think they will try to stop us?" she asked her mother, her voice barely above a whisper.

The older woman kept kneading her dough, knuckles white with effort. "Not tonight," she said. "Tonight, even Egypt will bow to a greater power."

Above it all, a strange hush hung, as if time itself were holding its breath. The normal sounds of an Egyptian afternoon—merchants calling their wares, children playing in the streets, the distant shouts of taskmasters—were absent. In their place, the sounds of preparation: the soft scrape of knives being sharpened, the bleating of lambs, the low murmur of ancient prayers being taught to children who had never known anything but Egypt.

Moses and Aaron moved among the people, their staffs marking their path through the crowded streets. They did not need to shout instructions. Every family already knew what must be done. The word had spread like fire through dry brush—from mouth to ear, from house to house, from village to village.

"Be ready," Moses told them, his eyes alight with something beyond mere human certainty. "When morning comes, we walk free."

3 pm - Avaris Central

The procession appeared first as a distant shimmer in the afternoon heat. It drew closer, the sound preceded the sight—the deep, resonant call of ram's horn shofars echoing across the settlement like the voice of ancient promises finally fulfilled.

Children scrambled onto rooftops and pressed against courtyard walls as the bearers came into view, carrying between them the carefully wrapped sarcophagus that had rested at Bubastis for a hundred and forty years.

"Joseph! Joseph!" The name rippled through the crowd of Ephraim's descendants, passed from lip to lip like a sacred flame. These were his people—bone of his bone, blood of his blood—and as the ornate coffin was set down in their midst, weathered hands reached out to touch the bindings that held their forefather's remains.

The shofars sang again, their wild, triumphant notes rising above the cheers, and old women wept openly while young men raised their fists to the sky. Here was the man who had saved them from famine, who had brought them into Egypt as honored guests, and now, after two hundred and twenty years, he would lead them out again—not in life, but in the keeping of his final oath. The very air seemed to thicken with the weight of fulfilled prophecy, and even the Egyptian taskmasters who had followed the procession stood silent, sensing something far beyond their understanding moving through the streets of Avaris.

4 pm – All over Avaris

The shadows lengthened across Avaris, stretching toward the east, toward the promised journey.

Then, one by one, the fires were lit.

Outside his modest dwelling, Esais, a man whose ancestors entered Egypt with Jacob himself, gathered his family. With practiced movements, he slaughtered the lamb, collecting its blood in an earthenware basin. The animal was then hung from a low tree branch to drain fully, its lifeless eyes staring vacantly at the gathering dusk.

Throughout Avaris, this scene repeated hundreds of times. Flint knives—not metal, as Moses had specified—quickly ended the lives of unblemished lambs. Blood was carefully collected, not a drop wasted.

With the lambs slaughtered, the next step of the ritual began. In Esais' household, the eldest son dipped a bunch of hyssops into the basin of blood. With deliberate strokes, he marked the wooden lintel above the door and the two doorposts on either side. The crimson stain stood out starkly against the pale wood, a vivid declaration of faith in the God of Moses.

For the first time, the Israelites did not care if their blood ritual was visible to Egyptian eyes. For generations, they had kept their customs private and their worship discreet. But tonight, they displayed their allegiance to their God without fear or shame.

Inside the homes, women worked quickly to prepare the Passover meal. The lambs were roasted whole over fire, not boiled, not eaten raw, but roasted with fire as Moses had instructed. Bitter herbs were arranged on platters, reminders of the bitterness of slavery. Unleavened bread, mixed and baked in haste, completed the meal.

As darkness fell completely, families gathered around low tables. Unlike other feasts, they did not recline in comfort. Instead, they ate with sandals on their feet, staffs nearby, loins girded—dressed for immediate departure.

7 pm - Palace at Avaris

In the upper chambers of his palace, Menkheperre dined in near silence with his queen. The oil lamps flickered against the gold-painted walls, casting moving shadows across scenes of royal triumph—Pharaoh smiting enemies, Pharaoh offering to the gods, Pharaoh eternal and divine.

The table was set with delicacies from across the empire—dates from Nubia, wine from Memphis, fish from the marshes—but he barely touched the food. His eyes kept moving to the window, to the darkness gathering over his kingdom.

The queen, serene in a linen dress embroidered with blue lotus, studied him. Her dark eyes, lined with kohl, reflected the dancing lamplight. "You have done all you can," she said, her voice gentle yet firm. "The army is ready. The priests have made offerings."

Menkheperre's hand tightened around his golden cup. Three times he had nearly yielded to the Hebrew demands. Three times, his advisors had stiffened his resolve. Now, they whispered that the worst was over—that the god of slaves had spent his power in plagues of frogs and lice, of darkness and boils.

"They say the slaves burn their meals in the street," the queen said softly, breaking a piece of bread with jeweled fingers. "And smear blood on their doors."

Menkheperre didn't look at her. "They act like men preparing for war," he said. "Or judgment."

A court official appeared at the doorway, bowing low. "Divine One, the High Priest of Amun requests audience."

Menkheperre waved him in. The priest entered, his leopard skin cape marking his sacred office, his shaven head gleaming in the lamplight.

What do the omens say?" Menkheperre asked without preamble.

The priest's eyes flickered. "The stars are... strange tonight, Divine One. The astrologers speak of patterns not seen in living memory." He hesitated." There is a stillness in the sacred precincts. The temple cats will not eat. The ibises have flown from their roosts."

Outside, the air was still. No wind. No cries. No frogs, no gnats, no locusts. Just an unnatural quiet, as if the world itself had stepped back, waiting.

Menkheperre raised a cup of wine to his lips and drank, but it tasted of ash. Nine plagues had struck Egypt. Nine times the land had bled and suffered. Nine times he had hardened his heart.

Tonight, would be different. Tonight, the gods would answer.

As darkness settled fully over Pi-Ramesses, Menkheperre rose from his meal, leaving his plate nearly untouched. He walked to the balcony and looked out over his sleeping city, toward the distant glow of fires in Avaris.

"Post double guards on the royal chambers," he ordered quietly. "No one enters until dawn."

The night stretched before him, vast and unknown. Somewhere in its depths, a death was coming. He only prayed it would pass him by.

Chapter 25 - Death of the Firstborn

25 April 1438 BC

10:30 pm - Palace at Avaris

Menkheperre stood at his chamber window overlooking Pi-Ramesses, knuckles white against the limestone sill. The full moon bathed the city in cold light, while in the distance, the fires of the Israelite quarters had dwindled to orange pinpricks.

An unnatural silence had fallen over Egypt—the breathless hush of approaching calamity.

Drawn by paternal instinct, Menkheperre turned to where his infant son lay sleeping. The royal prince, barely eleven months old, slumbered peacefully in his ornate cedar cradle. His tiny chest rose and fell beneath a covering of the finest delta linen, dark lashes resting against rounded cheeks. A single gold amulet gleamed at his throat, catching the lamplight as the child remained blissfully unaware of the dread that consumed his father.

The Pharaoh reached down with a hesitant hand, brushing his fingers lightly across his son's forehead. The skin felt cool and smooth beneath his touch. How fragile he seemed in sleep, this child upon whose slender shoulders rested the future of the mightiest empire on earth.

Menkheperre's mind echoed with Moses' words, spoken with such terrible certainty in the great hall three days prior: "At midnight the Lord will pass through Egypt and strike down every firstborn son, from the firstborn of Pharaoh who sits on the throne to the firstborn of the slave girl at her grinding stone, and all the firstborn of the cattle as well."

He had laughed then, surrounded by his court, secure in his divinity. He had scoffed at the God of slaves who dared challenge the gods of Egypt. But now, alone in the night save for his sleeping child, doubt gnawed at him like a desert scavenger stripping a carcass.

Nine times the Hebrew prophet had come before him. Nine times he had issued his warnings. And nine times the warnings had manifested into horrors that still haunted Menkheperre's dreams—water turned to blood, darkness so absolute it could be felt, hail mixed with fire that scarred the very earth. Nine times, the God of the Hebrews had humbled mighty Egypt. Nine times, Menkheperre had hardened his heart afterwards, pride and rage overriding his reason.

A soft knock at the chamber door interrupted his thoughts. Rekhmire, his most trusted vizier, entered and bowed low, his usually composed features taut with poorly concealed anxiety.

"Great One, Live Forever," he began, the ritual greeting sounding hollow in the strained atmosphere." General Khaemwaset reports that the armies are assembled as commanded. Five thousand of your finest soldiers stand ready to move against the Israelites come dawn, should this... prediction... prove false."

Menkheperre nodded, acknowledging the report while finding no comfort in it. What use were bronze swords and cedar chariots against a force that could turn the Nile to blood and call darkness down from the sky?

"And what of the people?" he asked, his voice low so as not to wake his son. "What mood prevails in the city?"

Rekhmire hesitated, then spoke with careful deliberation. "Fear walks the streets like a physical presence, Divine One. Many Egyptians have barricaded themselves inside their homes. Others have marked their doorposts with lamb's blood, imitating the Hebrews. The temples are overflowing with supplicants. The priests of Anubis cannot keep pace with the offerings."

"And what of our gods?" Menkheperre asked bitterly. "What do they say to this Hebrew challenge?"

"The oracle at the temple of Ptah remains silent," Rekhmire admitted. "The sacred Apis bull refuses food and water, and the temple cats have fled the sanctuary of Bastet."

Menkheperre dismissed him with a curt gesture. When the door closed behind Rekhmire, he returned to the window, watching as the minutes crawled past with excruciating slowness. His fingers curled into fists at his sides, the royal signet ring cutting into his flesh. He barely noticed the pain.

It was an hour before midnight.

11 pm – Home of Aaron

The home of Aaron stood at the western edge of Avaris, indistinguishable from the other humble dwellings save for the unusually thick smears of blood that marked its doorframe. Inside, the air was close and warm, heavy with the lingering scent of roasted lamb and bitter herbs. A single oil lamp cast wavering shadows across the walls of packed mud, illuminating the solemn faces of those who had gathered for this momentous night.

Moses sat cross-legged on a reed mat in the center of the small main room, his weathered hands resting lightly on his knees. At eighty years old, his beard flowed white against the rough homespun of his robe, but his eyes burned with the intensity of a much younger man—the fire of absolute conviction. The decades spent in Pharaoh's palace and later in the wilderness of Midian had carved deep lines into his face, creating a map of harsh experience and hard-won wisdom.

Around him sat his family: Aaron, three years his senior but looking a decade older, his stooped shoulders bearing the weight of years spent in bondage; Miriam, her once-beautiful face now a web of wrinkles, yet her eyes still sharp and alert.

The silence was broken only by Moses' low, resonant voice as he repeated the Lord's instructions to those present.

"When the Lord goes through the land to strike down the Egyptians," he intoned, each word deliberated and weighted with divine authority, "he will see the blood on the top and sides of the doorframe and will pass over that doorway. He will not permit the destroyer to enter your houses and strike you down."

The moonlight slipped through narrow gaps in the dwelling's mud-brick walls, casting silver ribbons across the room that seemed to move and breathe with each subtle draft. Moses' eyes were closed in prayer now, his lips moving in silent supplication to the God who had spoken to him from the burning bush. Aaron's gnarled hand rested on his brother's shoulder, his prayers joining those of Moses in a wordless communion.

Around them sat twelve families who had sought refuge in Moses' home for this fateful night, their faces a tableau of emotions—fear mingled with hope, anxiety with anticipation. Children clutched at their mothers' robes, quieted by the gravity of the adults' demeanor. The remains of their hasty meal lay scattered on woven mats—fragments of roasted lamb, piles of bitter herbs, and the flat, unleavened bread they had prepared with such urgency.

Every person was dressed for travel—sandals bound to their feet, walking staffs within reach, outer garments fastened. Bulging sacks of provisions and hastily gathered possessions crowded the corners of the room. They had been told to be ready, and they were.

Joshua ben Nun, middle-aged man of forty-three with the broad shoulders of one who had hauled Egyptian stone since childhood, paced the cramped space like a caged desert lion. Unlike most of the others, whose faces reflected generations of servitude, Joshua carried himself with the natural grace of a warrior. His dark eyes constantly swept the room, assessing, calculating, as though preparing for battle rather than deliverance.

He paused in his pacing to approach Moses, crouching down beside the older man with a deference that softened his otherwise formidable presence.

"How will we know when it is time?" he asked, his voice barely above a whisper yet carrying the sharp edge of restrained energy. "How will we know when it is safe to leave?"

Moses opened his eyes with calm assurance that seemed to emanate from some deep internal wellspring.

"We will know," he answered quietly. The weathered lines of his face softened momentarily. "The Lord has not brought us this far to abandon us now, Joshua. Trust in His timing as you trust in His power."

Joshua nodded, not entirely satisfied but accepting the elder's wisdom. He returned to his post near the door, one hand resting on the curved ram's horn that hung at his waist—the shofar he had been instructed to sound when the moment came.

As the night grew deeper, the air in the small dwelling seemed to thicken with anticipation. No one spoke above a whisper. No child cried. Even the usual night sounds of Avaris—the barking of dogs, the occasional shout of guards, the braying of donkeys—had fallen silent, as though all creation awaited what was to come.

And still, Moses prayed, his communion with the unseen God an anchor in this sea of uncertainty.

The midnight hour approached.

26 April 1438 BC

Midnight - Palace at Avaris

The palace timekeeper's measured voice echoed through the corridors of the royal residence, announcing the midnight hour with ritual precision. The sound had barely faded when Menkheperre felt it—not a sound, not a wind, but a presence that made the hairs on the back of his neck rise in primordial alarm.

The very air seemed to congeal around him, becoming difficult to draw into his lungs. The torches in the chamber sputtered and dimmed without cause, their flames shrinking to mere pinpoints of struggling light. Beyond his window, the brilliant moon veiled itself behind a thin cloud that had materialized from nowhere, casting the world into deeper shadow.

Menkheperre's mouth went dry. He felt a cold sweat break out across his skin, chilling him despite the warm night air. Some primitive instinct, older than civilization itself, screamed a warning in his mind—danger, death, flee! But he was Pharaoh, Living Horus, Son of Ra. He stood frozen, caught between his mortal fear and divine pride.

A small sound broke the spell—a faint cough from his son's bed.

His heart leapt to his throat as he rushed to the bedside, royal dignity forgotten in paternal terror. The infant was stirring, his small body restless beneath the fine linen sheets, his breathing suddenly labored and uneven. Another cough escaped his lips, this one deeper, more troubling.

"No," Menkheperre whispered, gathering the child into his arms with desperate tenderness. "No! Not this. Not him."

The cough deepened into a choking sound, the infant's body stiffening in his father's embrace. His eyes flew open, but there was no recognition in them—only confusion rapidly transforming into terror as he struggled for breath. In the dim light streaming through the window, Menkheperre could see his son's face with horrifying clarity—the perfect features contorting in pain, the small mouth gasping desperately like a fish pulled from the sacred Nile, the dark eyes bulging with panic.

Menkheperre pressed the boy to his chest, feeling the rapid, erratic beating of the small heart against his own. His son's body began to tremble, the tremors growing into violent convulsions that shook his entire frame. The golden arm bands that had adorned the infants since birth clattered against each other, a terrible percussion accompanying his struggle.

"Help!" Menkheperre's voice thundered through the palace chambers, all pretense of godhood abandoned in his desperation. "The physicians! Bring them now!"

His command reverberated through marble halls and alabaster pillars, carried by servants who ran with faces white with fear. But even as the echo of his cry faded, another sound rose in its place—a sound that chilled his blood more thoroughly than his son's distress.

From beyond the palace walls, it began—a single wail at first, high and terrible in its grief. Then another joined it, and another, until a chorus of anguish swelled through the night air. Like a wave of sound, it spread through the city—house after house, family after family, as the firstborn of Egypt began to fall.

Menkheperre barely registered the growing cacophony of despair. His entire being was focused on the child in his arms, whose breathing had become increasingly tortured. The boy's lips were turning blue even as Menkheperre watched in helpless horror, his small hands clawing weakly at his throat, his eyes locked with his fathers in a mute plea for help that the most powerful man in the world could not provide.

"My son," Menkheperre whispered, tears streaming unchecked down his face, splashing onto the boy's contorted features. "My son, my son..."

The door to the royal chamber burst open with such force that it slammed against the wall, dislodging a piece of gilt decoration that clattered to the floor. Meritamun rushed in, her usual grace abandoned, her face ashen in the moonlight. Her night robes of fine linen billowed behind her like the wings of some night bird, her black hair unbound and streaming down her back. The queen's eyes, wide with maternal terror, fixed immediately on the scene before her.

"My baby!" she cried, her voice breaking on the words as she fell to her knees beside them. "What is happening to him? "She reached for her son with trembling hands, her jeweled fingers touching his face with desperate gentleness. The boy's eyes found hers briefly, a flicker of recognition surfacing through the pain before another spasm wracked his small body, arching his back in Menkheperre's arms.

Moses," Menkheperre choked out, the name like poison on his tongue. "It is Moses' God. The Hebrew curse."

The child's body convulsed one final time, a terrible tension passing through him like lightning before he went suddenly, completely limp in his father's embrace. His small head lolled back, arms hanging loose at his sides. The golden arm bands slipped down to his wrists, too large now that the tension had fled his muscles. His eyes, still open, stared sightlessly at the ceiling, reflecting the dim light of the sputtering torches but seeing nothing of this world.

"No!" Meritamun's scream pierced the night, a sound so primal and agonized that the servants and guards who had gathered at the door stepped back in visceral fear. She tore at her hair; her face contorted with grief beyond reason. "No, no, no!"

She gathered her son's lifeless body from Menkheperre's unresisting arms, rocking him back and forth against her breast, her keening wail joining the chorus of grief that rose from the city beyond. She pressed her lips to his forehead, his cheeks, his hands, as if her desperate love could somehow call him back from the shadows.

Menkheperre staggered to his feet, his legs barely supporting him. The weight of his failure crushed down upon him like a physical force, bending his spine and drawing his shoulders forward in a posture of total defeat. He had been warned. Nine times he had been warned, and nine times he had hardened his heart. And now his son, his only son, his heir, the future of the Two Lands, the continuation of his divine bloodline, lay dead in his mother's arms.

The royal physicians arrived at last, led by Pentu, the venerable chief healer whose skills were renowned throughout the kingdom. But even Pentu stopped at the threshold, his medicine bag hanging useless at his side, his aged face crumpling with sorrow at the scene before him. What herbs could combat the wrath of a god? What incantations could call back a soul that had been claimed by a power greater than Egypt's pantheon?

"Leave me," Menkheperre commanded, his voice hollow, a shell of its usual authority. The physicians and servants bowed and retreated, their own eyes averted from the naked grief of their divine ruler.

Meritamun remained, clutching her dead son to her breast, her body rocking rhythmically as she crooned a lullaby between sobs—the same melody she had sung to him since infancy. The sound of it now, in this chamber of death, was almost more than Menkheperre could bear.

He crossed to the window once more, staring out at his city bathed in moonlight. His Egypt. His legacy. Broken by an invisible hand in a single night. The wailing throughout Pi-Ramesses had grown to a deafening roar as more families discovered their losses. Palace guards ran through the corridors, their faces stricken with grief as reports flowed in from every quarter of the city.

Below in the courtyard, Menkheperre could see one of his elite charioteers—a man who had fought fearlessly in battle against the fierce Hittites—kneeling in the dust, cradling what appeared to be the body of a teenage boy. The man's mouth was open in a silent howl of anguish that needed no sound to convey its intensity.

"Are you satisfied?" Menkheperre whispered to the unseen God whose power had laid Egypt low. "Have you proven your might now? Is this vengeance sweet to you?"

Only silence answered him. The God of Moses offered no explanation, no comfort, no mercy—only the terrible evidence of His wrath made manifest in the lifeless bodies of Egypt's firstborn sons.

The sound of approaching footsteps drew Menkheperre's attention from the window. Rekhmire appeared at the door, his usually immaculate appearance in disarray. His councilor's badge of office hung crooked on his chest, and there were dark stains on his kilt where he had wiped his hands. Something in the older man's eyes told Menkheperre that he had suffered a loss this night.

"My lord Pharaoh," Rekhmire said, his voice breaking. He did not complete the customary honorifics—the reference to Menkheperre's divinity seemed a bitter mockery in this moment. "Reports are coming from every quarter. There is not a house in Egypt where someone has not died. From the highest noble to the lowest slave girl, the firstborn... they are all gone."

Rekhmire's voice caught on the last word. Menkheperre saw the man's throat work convulsively as he fought for composure.

"Your son?" Menkheperre asked softly, already knowing the answer.

"My Amenhotep. Eleven years old today." Rekhmire's voice was a bare whisper now. "He died in my arms not half an hour past."

Menkheperre closed his eyes briefly, absorbing yet another blow in a night of unending sorrows.

Now both were gone, along with uncounted thousands across the land of Egypt.

Menkheperre turned back from the window, his shoulders slumped in defeat. The God of Moses had indeed proven himself mightier than all the gods of Egypt combined. Nine plagues he had endured, nine times he had stood firm. But this—the death of his son, the death of Egypt's future—this he could not withstand.

"Enough," he whispered, the word barely audible. Then, straightening slightly, he repeated it with the last vestige of his royal command. "Enough. They have won."

He drew himself up, summoning the remnants of his dignity. His decision crystallized in his mind with sudden clarity. There could be no further resistance, not after this demonstration of power. Egypt needed to heal, to bury its dead, to rebuild what could be rebuilt. And that could not happen while the Hebrews remained within their borders, under the protection of their terrible, invisible God.

"Go to Moses at once. Tell him that he and all the Israelites must leave. All of them. With their flocks, their herds, their possessions. They may go and worship their God as they have asked."

Rekhmire bowed deeply. "I will do it at once, my lord."

As the man turned to leave, Menkheperre added, "And tell Moses... tell him to bless me also." The words tasted bitter in his mouth, but he forced them out, nonetheless. Defeat must be acknowledged if Egypt is to survive.

As Rekhmire departed, Menkheperre knelt beside Meritamun, placing a gentle hand on her shoulder. She flinched at his touch but did not pull away.

"He will be given the finest burial," Menkheperre said softly. "All the honors due a prince of Egypt."

"What good are honors to the dead?" Meritamun whispered, her voice hollow. "What good are all the treasures of Egypt now?"

Menkheperre had no answer. Together, they kept vigil over their son as the night wore on, listening to the sounds of grief that echoed through the city.

1:30 am – House of Aaron

Rekhmire led a small delegation through the devastated streets of Pi-Ramesses toward Avaris, accompanied by two high officials and a contingent of soldiers. The men moved with leaden steps, their faces slack with shock and grief. More than one soldier had tear tracks visible on his cheeks, and none made any attempt to hide their sorrow. Discipline had crumbled in the face of such overwhelming tragedy.

The wailing from Egyptian homes pierced the night air—a constant, undulating sound of communal grief unlike anything Rekhmire had ever heard. From every taskmaster's house they passed came the unmistakable sounds of mourning—the high, thin keening of women, the deeper groans of men driven beyond the bounds of stoicism.

The contrast could not have been starker. The homes of the Israelites stood silent in the moonlight, their doorposts marked with now-dried blood, the lives within preserved by an invisible covenant. Light spilled from beneath doors and through shuttered windows, indicating that none slept within, but no sounds of distress emanated from these dwellings.

Rekhmire felt a surge of bitter resentment. His son's body lay cooling on his bed, attended by the boy's mother and sisters. The house of his neighbor, an overseer of granaries, echoed with the man's howls of anguish over his dead firstborn. Yet here, among these slaves, life continued untouched by the devastation that had swept through Egypt like a desert wind.

When they reached Moses' dwelling, Rekhmire found his hand trembling as he raised it to pound on the wooden door. The force of his knock surprised even him, the sound echoing in the unnatural quiet of the Israelite quarter.

After a moment, the door opened slowly. Moses himself stood in the doorway, his tall frame silhouetted against the warm light from within. His face was solemn but unsurprised, his eyes steady as they met

Rekhmire's grief-ravaged gaze. Behind him, Rekhmire could see others—Aaron with his white beard, several younger men with the lean, muscled bodies of laborers despite their finery, women dressed for travel with infants held close to their breasts.

"Pharaoh commands that you and your people leave Egypt this very night," Rekhmire announced, his voice cracking despite his effort to maintain dignity. The formal language of court pronouncements seemed absurd now, in this night of death, but he forced himself to continue. "Take your flocks, your herds, everything that is yours. Go and worship your God as you have requested."

Moses nodded once, a gesture neither triumphant nor apologetic—merely acknowledging what he had known would come. He said nothing, which somehow infuriated Rekhmire more than any gloating might have done.

"And," Rekhmire added, forcing the words past the lump in his throat, swallowing the last remnants of his pride as he delivered his master's final message, "Pharaoh asks for your blessing."

Something flickered in Moses' eyes then—not satisfaction, but perhaps a momentary compassion that Rekhmire found almost unbearable.

"May the Lord judge between us," Moses replied quietly. "Tell your master we will depart before dawn."

His gaze softened slightly as he looked at Rekhmire's face, seeming to recognize the personal grief written there. "You have lost someone," he said, not a question but a statement of fact.

"My son," Rekhmire answered, surprised by his candor. "My firstborn. As has every Egyptian house this night."

Moses bowed his head briefly. "It was not by my choice that it came to this," he said, his voice heavy with the weight of divine agency. "I brought only the message, not the judgment itself."

"Yet you are spared," Rekhmire said bitterly, gesturing to the blood-marked doorpost. "All of you."

"Not spared," Moses corrected him gently. "Passed over. There is a difference that perhaps someday you will understand."

There seemed to be nothing more to say. Rekhmire turned away, his mission completed, eager to return to his own house of mourning.

"It is time," Moses said to Joshua. "The Lord has fulfilled His promise. We are free."

Moses nodded to Joshua. "Sound the shofar."

The middle-aged man lifted the ram's horn to his lips and blew a long, piercing note. The sound echoed through the night, soon joined by other shofars throughout Avaris as the signal spread.

The eerie chorus of ram's horns overwhelmed the sounds of Egyptian mourning. Across Avaris, Israelites emerged from their homes, faces set with determination as they began gathering possessions packed earlier in anticipation of this moment.

Four hundred and thirty years had passed since the Almighty first called Abraham from Ur of the Chaldeans, promising to make of him a great nation. Through all the generations of sojourning—from Abraham's wanderings in Canaan, to Isaac and Jacob walking the same promised land as strangers, to the seventy souls who descended into Egypt in the days of plenty—the children of Israel had multiplied and grown strong. Now, as the shofar's call pierced the Egyptian darkness, that long season of exile was drawing to its close. The God who had spoken to their father Abraham beneath the stars, who had wrestled with Jacob by the Jabbok, who had appeared to Moses in the burning bush, was about to fulfil His ancient covenant and lead His people home.

The Egyptian neighbors, still reeling from their losses, came out as well. Some stood frozen in their doorways, cradling the bodies of lifeless children, their tear-streaked faces watching in numb incomprehension. Others, driven by a fear bordering on superstition, thrust jewelry and valuable items at the departing Israelites.

"Take it, take everything, only go!" they cried, their voices ragged with grief and terror. "Leave us and take your God with you!"

Necklaces of gold and lapis lazuli, silver bracelets, fine linen garments, vessels of bronze and precious oils—the wealth of Egypt was pressed into Israelite hands with desperate urgency. Those who had been slaves only hours before found themselves laden with treasures, the spoils of their long suffering paid out in a single night of divine reckoning.

Moses watched this fulfilment of yet another promise—that his people would not leave Egypt empty-handed—with solemn acknowledgment. There would be time to reflect on the justice and mercy of what had transpired this night. For now, there was the urgent business of departure.

2:00 am – South Edge of Avaris

In the cold, clear light of the full moon, the first families began to leave Avaris by two in the morning. They knew their destination—Succoth, some thirty kilometers away, the first staging point in a journey whose duration and difficulty none could yet fully comprehend. The full moon illuminated their path as they filed out of the city that had been their prison for generations, its silver light catching on jeweled adornments that had graced Egyptian necks and wrists.

Moses stood at the edge of Avaris, watching as the stream of people grew into a river—hundreds, then thousands, then tens of thousands moving as one great tide of humanity. Women carried infants swaddled against their breasts. Children clutched treasured possessions. Men drove livestock or shouldered heavy burdens. The elderly were supported by the young. The sick were borne on makeshift litters. None were left behind.

Beside him, Aaron placed a gnarled hand on his shoulder, his aged eyes wide with wonder at the sight before them.

"Six hundred thousand men, plus women and children," Aaron murmured in awe, his voice barely audible above the sounds of the massive procession forming before them. "Just as the Lord promised to our father Abraham."

Moses nodded, his eyes scanning the massive procession forming before him. Four hundred and thirty years in Egypt, generations born and dying in bondage, and now, in a single night, deliverance had come. The weight of responsibility settled on his shoulders like a tangible thing. These people were now his to lead, his to protect, his to bring to the land that had been promised so long ago.

"Come," he said to Aaron and Miriam, lifting his walking staff. "The Lord goes before us."

As they took their places at the head of their people, Moses felt a profound mixture of emotions wash over him—gratitude, humility, and a kind of solemn joy. Behind them, the sounds of Egypt's mourning gradually faded. Ahead lay the wilderness and beyond it, the promise of a new beginning.

The exodus had begun.

Chapter 26 - Firstborn Buried and Raised

27 April 1438 BC

6 am – Palace at Avaris

The sky above Pi-Ramesses hung like tarnished bronze, the light filtering through a veil of dust and despair. Dawn crept across the great city, but it brought no relief—only revealed the horror the night had delivered. The sound that rose from every quarter was primal, a keening that clawed at the very foundations of the empire. Egypt wept with a thousand voices, each throat raw with grief.

Death had stalked the streets with terrible precision—all firstborn, all claimed in a single, devastating stroke. The wailing had begun just after midnight and had not ceased, a terrible chorus that ebbed and flowed like the Nile in flood season but carried only sorrow in its current.

Pharaoh Menkheperre stood as if carved from the same stone as his monuments, barefoot in the palace courtyard, dust clinging to his ankles. His royal robes were stained and rumpled—the linen he'd worn when he felt his son's final breath against his chest. The boy lay before him now on a cedar bier, his small form wrapped in white, his face—mercifully—covered.

General Khaemwaset approached from the shadows of the colonnade, his own face haggard, the skin beneath his eyes bruised with exhaustion and sorrow. He had buried his son as the sun arose like a blood-red eye over Pi-Ramesses, indifferent to the agony of mortal men. He moved with the careful precision of a man holding himself together by will alone.

"Great Pharaoh," he said, voice rough as desert sand. "We must act now. The dead cannot wait. Before Ra completes his journey, they must begin theirs."

When Menkheperre failed to respond, General Khaemwaset turned to the commanders gathered in the courtyard. Their ranks had been hastily assembled men dragged from scenes of personal tragedy to attend to national calamity. Some wore their grief openly, tears carving tracks through the dust on their cheeks. Others had retreated behind masks of duty, though their eyes betrayed them, wild with incomprehension and rage.

"Divide the city," General Khaemwaset commanded, his voice finding strength in necessity. "Assign your men by district. Every household to tend its own. Those with no one left must be carried by those who remain."

Officers departed with heavy steps, dispatched to quarters military and civil, to embalmers' compounds already overwhelmed, to the homes of taskmasters and the cramped confines of laborers' quarters.

For most of Egypt's sons, there would be no seventy days of purification, no canopic jars, no spells from the Book of the Dead. Beyond the city walls, soldiers carved trenches into the unforgiving earth. Taskmasters, their whips hanging useless at their sides, directed lines of slaves who worked in strange silence, digging graves for the sons of their oppressors.

Brothers lowered their brothers into the ground. Fathers placed amulets they could ill afford into cold hands. Sons became the bearers of sons. And all the while, Egypt's heart broke beneath the weight of firstborn claimed before their time.

8 am - Arrivals at Succoth

As the mighty empire bent to bury its seed, just twenty-five kilometers to the south, a different harvest was being gathered.

The plains of Succoth, empty for generations, now teemed with humanity as more Israelite families arrived with each passing hour. They came in columns, in family groups, in tribes—some stumbling with exhaustion, others walking with the straight-backed pride of the newly liberated, all with eyes that darted backward toward the road from Egypt.

At the perimeter of the sprawling camp, men stood with tribal standards held high. Ancient symbols, preserved through centuries of bondage, now flew freely in the desert wind—the lion of Judah, the ship of Zebulun, the serpent of Dan. As each family arrived, they were greeted and directed to their ancestral tribes, reuniting bloodlines that slavery had severed.

Some collapsed into the arms of relatives long thought lost. Others sank to their knees and pressed their foreheads to the earth, whispering prayers of thanks to the God who had remembered His promise. After the first shock of arrival passed, cook fires bloomed across the plain like earthbound stars, and the aroma of unleavened bread and parched grain rose to compete with the dust. Families gathered, passing water skins and sharing the sparse provisions they had carried from bondage. Children, sensing the relief in their parents' manner, began to play—their laughter an alien sound after so many generations of silence.

11 am – Plains of Succoth

As the morning lengthened, a ram's horn sounded from the center of the camp—a long, wavering note that carried across the multitude. The elders passed among the tribes, calling them to assembly. Each tribe gathered on the nearest rise of ground, forming concentric circles around their leaders, their faces turned eastward toward the distant mountains.

Moses had instructed the elders in the words that must be spoken, and now they rang out across the assembly, carried from group to group in voices strong with conviction.

"The Lord has delivered us from the hand of Pharaoh," they proclaimed. "But He has claimed what is His by right."

The elders raised their arms, weathered hands outstretched toward the people.

"Every firstborn son belongs to the Lord. Every firstborn male animal. They are not yours to keep, but to dedicate in service. Not with death, but with life."

Across the vast camp, fathers lifted their firstborn sons high, their hands beneath the small arms of children or gripping the shoulders of young men. The sun glinted off tear-streaked faces—not tears of sorrow, but of wild, disbelieving joy.

"You must teach your sons, and their sons after them," the elders continued, "that it was not by sword or bow that we were freed, but by the mighty hand of the Lord. And this shall be a sign upon your hand and a reminder between your eyes for all generations."

Women began to sing, their voices rising in harmonies preserved through centuries of kitchen whispers and lullabies. Men stamped their feet, raising clouds of dust that caught the sunlight. The firstborn stood bewildered but proud—suddenly the focus of attention, marked for a destiny greater than the mud pits and brick yards.

Moses stood near the heart of the camp, his staff planted firmly in the soil, watching it all with eyes that saw both past and future. As the sun climbed and the voices rose, he said nothing—but his silence was filled with purpose.

When the sun reaches its merciless peak at midday, the Israelites seek refuge beneath the makeshift shelters of Succoth. Their bodies ache with exhaustion, bones heavy from a sleepless night spent in the solemn rituals of Passover—the hurried preparations, the blood upon doorposts, the anxious waiting as death's angel passed through Egypt's streets.

Now, with the desert heat pressing down like a furnace, they huddle in whatever shade they can find, their eyes burning with fatigue and the brightness of freedom's first day. The shelters offer blessed respite from the sun's assault, temporary havens where mothers cradle sleeping infants and fathers close their eyes against the glare.

5 pm -Avaris and Pi-Ramesses

The sun hung low over Avaris, the light bleeding across the western sky in shades of crimson and gold that matched the blood still staining doorposts and lintels. The streets, which should have been alive with the evening's commerce, lay deserted. The foreign quarter, once packed with the bodies and voices of Israelite slaves, now stood empty as a tomb.

A handful of taskmasters wandered the abandoned dwellings, their faces tight with disbelief and growing anger. They found only emptiness within—cold hearths, scattered belongings, the detritus of lives suddenly abandoned. Yet they dared not cross the thresholds where blood still darkened the lintels, as if some invisible force held them back from those doorways marked by death's own hand. Their authority had vanished with their charges. Their purpose, like their whips, hung limp and useless at their sides.

In the royal palace, Pharaoh Menkheperre and Vizier Rekhmire stood on the high terrace overlooking the city. The braziers between them released thin tendrils of incense, but the perfumed smoke could not mask the lingering scent of death that clung to everything like a shroud.

Menkheperre's eyes were sunken, his cheekbones sharp beneath skin stretched too tight. When he spoke, his voice carried none of the divine authority that had once made men tremble.

"Look at what remains, Rekhmire," he said, gesturing toward the silent city below. "The fields lie untended. The brickyards are empty. The great works were abandoned. All of them—gone."

Rekhmire's gaze narrowed as he surveyed the hollow shell of what had been the empire's industrial heart. "They fled while we mourned," he said, the words bitter as unripe fruit. "While we buried our own, they stole away like thieves."

Menkheperre's hands gripped the stone balustrade until his knuckles shone white in the fading light. "We gave them leave to go," he said, each word drawn from him like a barbed arrow from flesh.

The silence that settled between them was heavy with recrimination, with shame, with the dawning realization of consequences that would echo through generations.

Their contemplation was interrupted by the arrival of General Khaemwaset, his back bent low in deference, a papyrus scroll clutched in his fist.

"Divine One," he murmured, "I bring the accounting you commanded."

General Khaemwaset took the scroll and unrolled it with practiced fingers. He read aloud, his voice flat, each number a fresh wound in Pharaoh's heart:

"Three thousand died in the cities, Great One, including one hundred from our elite chariot corps."

Menkheperre flinched as though struck.

"We will still have six hundred elite chariots, fully armed and provisioned for desert travel," General Khaemwaset continued. "I've already drawn replacements from our reserves and promoted the best cavalry officers. They've completed accelerated training."

He scanned further down the document. "The remaining gaps in our ranks—five hundred men across all divisions—will be filled with taskmasters and foot soldiers who've received secondary charioteer training."

Menkheperre looked up, his eyes meeting the general. "Taskmasters?"

"They have volunteered to a man, my lord," the general replied. "Bowmen, spearmen, riders—they offer their service freely."

"For what purpose?" Menkheperre asked, his attention caught.

"Vengeance, Divine One," the general answered, unable to keep a note of satisfaction from his voice. "They blame the Hebrews for the death of their sons. They wish to pursue them. To bring them back—or to end them."

Something stirred in Menkheperre's dead eyes—not quite life, but purpose. The paralyzing grip of grief loosened just enough to allow room for anger, cold and clarifying as winter rain.

"Then we shall give them their chance," he said, turning away from the darkening view of his diminished kingdom. "We shall give them the blood they thirst for."

Menkheperre strode toward the war hall, his steps gathering strength with each footfall. "Ready the six hundred chariots," he commanded.

"Prepare the columns for march. Let the standards of Egypt fly again. Let the desert learn to fear the approach of Pharaoh's justice."

6 pm – Succoth and the flame of fire

The sun slipped behind the jagged teeth of the western hills, taking with it the last of the day's punishing heat. Across the vast encampment at Succoth, a strange stillness descended, as if the very air held its breath. The silence was unlike anything they had known in Egypt—not the fearful quiet of slaves awaiting a taskmaster's whip, but the reverent hush of freedom still too new to be trusted.

Fires blossomed across the plain like fallen stars—their glow soft against the deepening indigo of twilight. Families huddled close, breaking their unleavened bread, speaking in murmurs as if afraid louder voices might shatter the fragile peace. In every circle, elders recounted stories passed down through generations of bondage—tales of Abraham under desert stars, of Isaac bound and released, of Jacob's ladder reaching to heaven. Stories that had once seemed distant as myths now felt immediate, fulfilled.

On the horizon, the moon rises, nearly full—the same moon that had watched over their desperate flight from Pi-Ramesses.

Then it happened.

Heads turned. Conversations faltered. Food forgotten in their hands suddenly slackened with shock.

At the eastern edge of the camp, where the darkening sky met the black lip of the desert, a column of fire erupted into being. It rose twenty cubits high, perhaps more, brilliant as lightning yet steady as a tree. The flame did not flicker or waver but stood like a blade thrust into the earth by some celestial hand. Its light outshone the moon, casting long shadows across stunned faces. The cry that followed was not terror but awe—a sound that began as scattered gasps and swelled into a wave of exclamation.

The fire should have scorched the ground beneath it, blackened the sand, consumed the sparse desert scrub. Yet nothing burned. The flame blazed with holy intensity, yet the air remained cool, carrying no scent of smoke. Most strange of all, the pillar pulsed with a rhythm like a vast heartbeat, alive with purpose and intent.

Aaron stumbled backward, his feet scrabbling against stone, his eyes wide as a child's. His voice, when it came, was barely a whisper, stripped of all authority.

"What manner of thing is this?"

Moses stood beside his brother, his weathered face transformed by the light. Gone was the hesitation that had marked him in Pharaoh's court, gone the doubt that had plagued him through the plagues. In its place was something like recognition—as if he gazed upon the face of a long-lost friend.

"The presence of the Lord," he said, the words vibrating with reverence. "He has come to lead us Himself."

The camp erupted into motion. People poured from beneath makeshift shelters, abandoning meals and conversations. They moved like sleepwalkers, drawn by a force stronger than fear.

There were no screams, no panic, no prostration. Instead, a profound silence settled—the silence of awe, more eloquent than any prayer.

Mothers held their sons close, especially the firstborn, now dedicated to God's service. They whispered blessings, promises of a future without Egyptian whips. Old men sank to their knees; hands lifted in wordless gratitude. Some pressed their palms to the cool sand, confirming they were awake. Children reached upward with innocent wonder.

Moses strode forward, his staff raised high, the firelight catching on its polished surface. When he spoke, his voice carried with the authority that had once commanded the Nile to turn to blood.

"Prepare yourselves!" he cried. "The Lord goes before us! We will follow wherever He leads!"

The command rippled outward. Stunned immobility gave way to deliberate purpose. People returned to their fires, not to rest, but to gather possessions. Water skins were filled. Donkeys were roused. Elders gave orders while young men secured bundles.

But through it all, no one turned their back on the pillar. Even as they worked, their eyes returned again and again to the miracle that stood immovable yet urged them forward.

The pillar marked more than direction. It was the visible proof of Moses' promise from the beginning—that the God of their fathers had heard, had remembered, and would not let them walk alone.

And so began the true Exodus—not the panicked flight from death, but a deliberate march toward destiny, led by the very presence of their God.

Chapter 27 - The Chase Begins

27 April 1438 BC

The General's Decision

The lone runner staggered through the palace gates of Pharaoh Menkheperre just before the midnight hour, his legs faltering beneath him like those of a newborn gazelle. In the shadow of the great stone columns that rose like sentinels against the star-strewn Egyptian sky, he collapsed to one knee, his chest heaving as though a demon's hands were squeezing the very breath from his lungs.

The torches flared along the alabaster causeway; the light caught the frantic gleam in the runner's eyes—eyes that had seen something terrible upon the eastern road.

"They've turned east," he rasped, each word scraping from his throat like stone against stone. His lips were cracked and bleeding, his tongue swollen with thirst. "Beyond Succoth. Toward the wilderness."

General Khaemwaset stepped from the shadows beneath the great colonnade. He is wearing the leather battle garb of an Egyptian general, and a short sword hangs at his hip, its pommel worn smooth from decades of use

He studied the messenger with cold, calculating eyes, his face carved from granite, betraying nothing of the fury that roiled within. With a dismissive nod, he released the man to the care of the palace servants, then stood in contemplative silence as the words rolled through his mind like distant thunder.

Above, the palace was shrouded in an unnatural quiet. Pharaoh Menkheperre slept in the royal chambers, his body sprawled across sheets of the finest linen, now stained with the tears of a broken god-king. The royal physicians had administered a sleeping draft, desperate to give their ruler respite from the howling grief that had consumed him since the death of his firstborn that morning.

General Khaemwaset stood beneath the stars, torn between duty and compassion. Pharaoh needed to know of this development immediately. Instead, he turned to the captain of the guard, a battle-scarred veteran who had served three Pharaohs.

"Do not wake him," he ordered, his voice low but carrying the weight of royal command. "Let him rest. Tomorrow, he must lead with the strength of Ra himself."

The captain saluted, fist to heart, and vanished into the shadows of the palace portal.

During the early hours of the morning, before dawn, General Khaemwaset had gathered the surviving commanders in the war room beneath the eastern wing of the palace. The chamber was austere by royal standards—walls of plain limestone instead of painted scenes of victory, floors of polished granite rather than precious tiles. A massive table of Lebanese cedar dominated the center, its surface inlaid with a map of Egypt and her territories.

"The final count?" he asked the chief scribe, a wizened man whose fingers were permanently stained with the black ink of his profession.

Five hundred soldiers lost," the man replied, his voice steady despite the enormity of the number. "All were firstborn sons."

General Khaemwaset nodded, his eyes sweeping the chamber, noting the set jaws and hardened gazes of the men around him. Their grief had curdled into something darker—a poison that would fuel their pursuit as surely as grain beer fueled the building of monuments.

"We will move at first light," he declared, his finger stabbing at the map. "The scouts report they travel slowly, burdened by children, the elderly, and their stolen treasures. We shall catch them before they reach the eastern wilderness."

"And when we do?" asked a young commander, his face still bearing the bruise of recent mourning rituals.

General Khaemwaset's lips thinned to a bloodless line. "Then we take back what is ours. Egypt's honor demands no less."

Edge of Etham

In the hushed moments before dawn's first blush colored the eastern sky, the vast multitude of Israelites reached the edge of Etham. Behind them lay the fertile black lands of Egypt—the only home most had ever known. Before them stretched the wilderness, a savage vastness of sand and stone that seemed to breathe with malevolent life in the pre-dawn gloom.

The stars overhead hung impossibly close in the desert air, shimmering like polished silver scattered across the deepest obsidian. Among the twelve tribes, men whispered that these were the watching eyes of their ancestors, bearing witness to the exodus long promised.

The pillar of fire that had guided them through the night blazed like a torch thrust into the vault of heaven itself. It stood sentinel as the last weary families shuffled into the makeshift camp, its light casting long shadows across the packed earth.

With the first tentative light of dawn seeping across the horizon, the pillar of fire began to change. The assembly watched in hushed awe as it coiled inward upon itself, the flames retreating into a core of intense brilliance. Then, as if God himself had breathed out a great sigh, it transformed, expanding and whitening into a thick column of cloud that towered over the camp like a mountain born from mist.

Joshua—Moses' lieutenant and the commander of what fighting men they had—stood beside the prophet, his weathered hand resting on the hilt of his bronze sword. Unlike Moses, whose eyes were ever fixed on the divine, Joshua's gaze constantly swept the horizon, searching for signs of pursuit.

"They're settling quickly," he observed, nodding toward the orderly rows of families arranging themselves by tribal affiliation. "We've covered more ground than I thought possible. Even with the old ones and the little ones."

Moses nodded, his eyes never leaving the cloud. A strange light played across his features—not merely the reflection of the divine manifestation, but something that seemed to emanate from within his very skin.

"We rest now," he said, his deep voice carrying the resonance of absolute certainty. "The Lord gives us breath before the next command."

Throughout the sprawling camp, fires sprang to life, fed by the precious little fuel they had carried from Egypt. Unleavened bread—hastily prepared during their flight—was warmed on hot stones. The aroma of baking dough mingled with the sharp tang of desert herbs crushed underfoot.

Menkheperre pursues the Israelites

The pre-dawn darkness cloaked the royal palace in shadow when the sound of hurried footsteps echoed through the corridors. In his chamber, Pharaoh Menkheperre stirred fitfully in his sleep, his dreams troubled by visions of fleeing slaves and empty treasuries.

The chamber doors burst open with a crash that sent the pharaoh's eyes flying wide. Rekhmire, his vizier, stood silhouetted in the doorway, an oil lamp flickering in his trembling hand, casting dancing shadows across the painted walls.

"My lord! Great Pharaoh, you must wake!" Rekhmire's voice carried an urgency that cut through the lingering haze of sleep.

Menkheperre sat up slowly, his eyes adjusting to the lamplight. "Rekhmire? The sun has not yet broken the horizon. What brings you to disturb the peace of night?"

The vizier moved closer, his breathing labored as if he had run the length of the palace. "My pharaoh, General Khaemwaset has taken matters into his own hands. Even as you slept, he roused the army. They march now in pursuit of the Hebrew slaves—without your command, without your presence!"

The words struck Menkheperre like a physical blow. His eyes flashed with an anger that would have made lesser men flee. He sprang from his bed, the fine linen sheets falling away as he stood in his sleeping garments.

"Without my command?" His voice was low, dangerous. "How dare he presume to lead Egypt's might without his pharaoh!"

Rekhmire remained kneeling, his head bowed. "He said the trail grows cold with each passing hour, that we cannot afford to wait. But my lord, an army without its pharaoh is like a body without its soul."

Menkheperre strode to his armor stand, his jaw set with grim determination. The bronze and gold pieces gleamed in the lamplight, waiting to transform him from man to god-king. "Prepare my war chariot," he commanded, his voice carrying the authority of one who had never known refusal. "Alert my guards. If Khaemwaset thinks he can claim glory that belongs to the throne of Egypt, he is gravely mistaken."

Within moments, the palace courtyard erupted into controlled chaos. Soldiers scrambled to prepare the pharaoh's golden chariot while grooms readied his finest horses. The thunder of hooves and wheels soon filled the air as Menkheperre, now clad in his war regalia, raced across the desert landscape like a vengeful deity.

The sun crested the horizon as his chariot bounded over the dunes, painting the sand in shades of gold and crimson. In the distance, a great dust cloud marked the passage of the Egyptian army. As Menkheperre's chariot crested a particular dune, the soldiers turned in amazement to see their pharaoh approaching like a god of war himself.

"The pharaoh comes!" General Khaemwaset shouted over the noise, his face betraying a mixture of surprise and apprehension. "Make way for the son of Ra!"

Menkheperre's chariot thundered past the ranks of soldiers, the golden wheels sending up sprays of sand as he claimed his rightful place at the head of the army. Without a word, he raised his hand and signaled forward. The great host, now complete with its divine commander, resumed its march toward Succoth.

The Abandoned Camp

The dust hung like a copper-colored veil across the sun as Pharaoh Menkheperre's chariots thundered into the abandoned camp at Succoth. The ground bore the unmistakable scars of the Israelites' passing—the crushed circles where tents had stood, fire pits still holding the gray ghosts of ash.

Menkheperre stood tall in his war chariot, the gold-leafed wood gleaming despite the dust. The blue war-crown of Egypt sat upon his head, its polished surface catching the harsh light. His eyes, rimmed with kohl not for decoration but to cut the desert glare—scanned the eastern horizon with the intensity of a hunting falcon.

"East," confirmed one of the Bedouin scouts, a wiry man whose loyalty had been purchased with gold and the promise of Egyptian women.

"Then we ride!" Pharaoh declared, raising his hand in command, the muscles of his forearm corded like twisted rope. Gone was the soft flesh of palace luxury; grief had stripped him to sinew and bone and raw purpose.

But a grumble stirred through the ranks behind him—not of dissent, for such would mean instant death, but of physical distress. The desert sun pressed down upon the army like a smith's hammer on hot bronze, relentless and merciless. Many of the soldiers, especially those newly conscripted to replace the firstborn sons lost in the plague, stumbled in their heavy leather armor. Their tongues lolled from parched mouths; their eyes glazed with the first dangerous signs of heat sickness.

General Khaemwaset guided his chariot alongside Pharaoh's chariot, the horses' flanks nearly touching.

"Majesty," he said, his voice pitched low for Menkheperre's ears alone. "They cannot march in this heat. Not yet. The men from Lower Egypt are not desert-bred. Let the sun fall. Then we can push through the night without rest."

"Very well," he growled, the words extracted like thorns from his throat. "But at sunset, we ride until our sandals fall apart. Until our horses drop. Until every last Hebrew child feels the shadow of Egypt fall across their face once more."

He dismounted with fluid grace, the mark of a man born to command. His bare feet touched the scorching sand, but he showed no sign of discomfort as he paced the edge of the abandoned camp.

Behind him, the army began to make camp with practiced efficiency. Tents arose like mushrooms after rain. Water was distributed in carefully measured rations. Scouts were dispatched in widening circles to secure the perimeter and search for forgotten Hebrew treasures.

Israelites Leaving Etham

The great encampment at Etham had settled into a rhythm of rest and cautious hope as the afternoon lengthened into evening. The sound of children's laughter fluttered across the air like birdsong—a sound so long absent from Hebrew gatherings that many of the elders paused in their tasks, heads cocked, momentarily confused by the unfamiliar music of joy.

At the edge of the camp, the great cloud—their divine guide and protector—stood immobile, a celestial sentinel bathed in the gold of the sinking sun. Its base was anchored to the earth while its crown seemed to brush the very firmament itself.

Then, with the deliberation of a conscious being, it moved.

At first, the movement was so subtle that only those specifically watching for it noticed. A gentle glide toward the northeast, aligning itself with the old trade route—the Way of the Philistines that led eventually to Canaan. A murmur passed through the tribes as awareness spread like ripples in a pool. Hope, which had been a cautious ember, flared suddenly into flame.

"It's leading us to the Philistine Road!" cried a man from the tribe of Asher, his voice cracking with excitement. He pointed with a trembling finger. "The easy way! We'll be in Canaan by the next new moon!"

Cheers rippled through the camp like a wave, gathering strength as they spread. Women clasped hands. Men embraced. Children were lifted high on shoulders to witness the divine guidance that would lead them to the promised land of milk and honey.

Joshua pushed through the growing crowd, his face set in lines of wary optimism as he caught up to Moses at the edge of the gathering. Unlike the celebrating masses, Moses stood apart, his ancient eyes fixed on the moving cloud with an expression caught between wonder and apprehension.

"It's the smart route," Joshua said, his voice taut with barely suppressed excitement. His hand rested on the hilt of his sword. "Straight to the Promised Land. Safer. Shorter. We could avoid the deep desert entirely."

Moses said nothing. His staff was planted firmly in the sand; his gnarled hands wrapped around its weathered surface as if drawing strength from the wood that had brought Egypt to her knees.

But then—like a dancer pausing mid-step—the cloud stopped.

As if a hand from heaven had gripped its very substance and anchored it mid-sky.

The wind died, as though the breath of the world itself had been suddenly stilled. Even the goats ceased their perpetual bleating, lifting their heads to the sky with the uncanny awareness animals often display before earthquakes or great storms.

A heartbeat of perfect silence. Two. Then, slowly, with the inevitable deliberation of fate itself, the cloud began to move.

South.

Into the maw of the deeper wilderness.

"No..." someone whispered, the single syllable falling into the silence like a stone into a well.

The cheers that had swept through the camp moments before collapsed into a stunned silence. Confusion rippled through the crowd. South led away from Canaan, away from settled lands, away from the ancient road that would carry them to freedom.

A woman clutched her young son's shoulder, her fingers digging into his flesh until he squirmed. "There's nothing south but sand and cliffs," she hissed, her voice tight with renewed fear.

"The sea lies that way," muttered an older man, a former fisherman from the Egyptian delta. He shook his head, bewilderment etched in the deep lines of his face. "There's no passage—only water and death."

Yet the cloud advanced—slow and deliberate, its movement undeniable, its purpose inscrutably divine.

Then, as the first stars began to prick the darkening eastern sky, the transformation began. Fire bled through the white vapors, a molten core igniting from within like a coal breathed to life. Flames coiled upward like a living thing, serpentine and mesmerizing. Within seconds, the entire column had transmuted from cloud to fire, a pillar of divine flame that towered twenty meters into the darkening sky, its heart pulsing with the rhythm of creation itself.

Aaron—Moses' brother and high priest to the newly liberated nation—stumbled backward, his ceremonial robes swirling around his ankles. "It's alive," he breathed, his voice carrying in the unnatural stillness. "The very presence of God, moving among us."

Moses alone seemed unsurprised by the transformation. He stepped forward into the glow, the light catching on his white hair and beard, surrounding him with a halo of fire that made him appear more than human. For a moment, he stood motionless, as if engaged in silent communion with the flame.

Then he turned to face the stunned multitude, his silhouette stark black against the supernatural brilliance behind him.

"He goes before us," he proclaimed, his voice rising with the authority that had challenged Pharaoh himself. "Not to the land of ease, but the path of purpose. Not the road of kings, but the way of the Almighty!"

"Now! We follow where He leads!" he commanded, the words thundering across the gathering with supernatural force.

The hesitation lasted only moments—a brief, collective indrawn breath. Then the dam of uncertainty broke. Men doused fires with sand. Women strapped infants to their backs with practiced movements. Elders leaned on staffs and blinked into the blaze, faces set with the stubborn determination of those who had survived generations of slavery.

Packs were shouldered. Tents collapsed. Animals were gathered. The sound of movement—the rustle of obedience—rose like a drumbeat, growing stronger with each passing moment.

And south they went.

Toward Pi-hahiroth. Toward the sea. Toward the great hill of Baal Zephon, where a storm god watched in silence from his lonely perch, witness to the inexorable approach of enemies locked in a chase that would reshape the very foundations of the world.

Pharaoh is Closing in

Menkheperre marched at the head of his forces, disdaining the comfort of his chariot. His cloak—woven of the finest linen and edged with gold thread—was drawn tight around his powerful shoulders. His breath plumed in the moonlight, spectral evidence of mortal frailty in a man claimed to be divine.

The fires of the Hebrews were gone, doused and abandoned. Only footprints and scattered ashes remained, still warm to the touch, betraying how narrowly they had missed their quarry.

"They were here," said the commander of the chariots, dismounting beside his king. Unlike most of the army, who staggered with exhaustion after the forced march, he moved with the fluid energy of a man half his age. "But they have turned from their course."

"Where?" Pharaoh asked, his voice rough with dust and disuse.

The Bedouin scout approached, prostrating himself briefly before rising to point into the darkness. "South, divine one. Into the deeper wilderness. Toward the sea."

A murmur rose from the gathered commanders. South made no sense. East lay Canaan—the logical destination for a people seeking to escape Egyptian rule. South led only to the narrow wedge of land caught between the Red Sea and insurmountable mountains—a natural trap from which there was no escape.

Menkheperre's eyes gleamed in the torchlight, a predatory satisfaction spreading across his face. "The mouse runs into the cat's paw," he said, a grim smile touching his lips for the first time since his son's death. He turned to his army, raising his voice so it carried to the farthest ranks.

"Rest now," he commanded. "Drink. Eat. When the moon rises, we ride without pause. The gods themselves have delivered our enemies into our hands."

He stared into the southern horizon, where the faintest smudge of moving dust was still visible. In his mind's eye, he could already see the slaughter to come—the righteous vengeance of Egypt visited upon those who had dared challenge her supremacy.

"They think they are free," he said, his voice pitched low, meant for himself and the gods alone. "But they will see the shadow of Egypt fall across them once more. And this time, there will be no escape. This time, there will be no mercy."

Behind him, six hundred chariots stood in precise rows, their bronze fittings gleaming coldly in the starlight. Six hundred instruments of death, poised to descend upon the fleeing slaves and their upstart god.

And somewhere in the vastness ahead, a pillar of fire moved through the night, leading the children of Israel toward a confrontation that would echo through the ages—a meeting of divine power and human might whose outcome would reshape the world.

Chapter 28 - Cornered by the Sea

29 April 1438 BC - Menkheperre follows the pillar of fire

Menkheperre rode at the head of his forces, disdaining the comfort of his chariot. His breath plumed in the moonlight, spectral evidence of mortal frailty in a man claimed to be divine. In the distance, mocking him, the pillar of fire blazed like a torch set in the heavens—a beacon announcing the location of the slaves who had humiliated him, who had escaped when he had ordered them to stay.

He sneered, and the firelight caught the gleam of gold at his throat and wrists. "Fools," he spat, turning to his commander, who drove his chariot alongside. "They might as well light our path for us."

Behind him stretched the might of Egypt's army, a dark serpent winding across the desert floor. The rumble of chariot wheels, the clink of bronze spearheads, the creak of leather armor—these sounds formed a grim symphony of approaching vengeance. These men were veterans of campaigns against the Nubians and the Mitanni; they had crushed rebellions and extended Egypt's borders. Now they marched to reclaim their honor against mere slaves.

They had lost kin in the terrible plagues. They had lost honor when the Israelites departed laden with Egypt's wealth. But they had not lost purpose. In their hearts burned a fire as fierce as the column that guided their quarry—a fire of hatred, of wounded pride, of determination to restore the natural order of the world.

Menkheperre's eyes narrowed, calculating distances, measuring the strength that remained in his tired horses. "We will catch them soon," he growled, his voice rough from shouting commands and breathing dust. A cruel smile played at the corners of his thin lips. "And when we do, we will end this farce."

He raised his hand, signaling to General Khaemwaset behind him. The order rippled down the line: no rest, no pause. Only forward, toward vengeance.

The army pressed on, weary but unrelenting. The dust of thousands of feet drifted like smoke behind the host, obscuring the stars at their back. In that cloud of dust hung the ghosts of their certainties—the belief in their invulnerability and the impotence of the Hebrew god. Certainties shattered by plagues and death. But pride remained, and the hot desire for retribution.

30 April 1438 BC - Israelites Rest at Baal-Zephon

The pillar of fire moved with unwavering pace through the desert night, a celestial beacon that blazed against the star-speckled heavens. Its light cast long, dancing shadows across the ragged procession of Israelites as they trudged southward, their faces etched with the mingled lines of exhaustion and hope. Thousands upon thousands, they moved as one great organism, guided by this divine flame that seemed to breathe and pulse with otherworldly life.

Their path wove through a shallow basin of the dried Bitter Lake, once a sea finger now reduced to a cracked wasteland. The ground beneath their sandaled feet was rough and fractured, a long, jagged scar in the earth carved by ancient waters that had long since retreated. With each footfall, clouds of white alkaline dust rose like ghostly apparitions around their ankles, coating their skin and clothes in a fine, chalky residue. Yet none complained—not with that blazing fire lighting the way ahead, its fierce glow a constant reminder of the power that had delivered them from bondage.

The light of morning revealed they had passed Pi-Hahiroth, that last outpost of Egyptian influence. Directly ahead, rising from a lone hill in the middle of the vast open plain, loomed the statue of Baal-Zephon. It stood unnaturally tall, a monument to pagan worship that seemed to mock their passing. Carved from dark stone that had weathered to a mottled gray brown, its face was worn smooth by centuries of desert winds, yet its carved eyes remained intact, fixed eternally eastward as if anticipating their arrival. The statue cast a long shadow across the barren ground, a finger of darkness pointing toward the coming host.

By midday, with the sun burning at its zenith, the great cloud moved past the statue of Baal-Zephon. Then, with a finality that sent a ripple of murmurs through the crowd, it stopped.

Moses, watching with solemn eyes that seemed to hold the weight of ages, raised his gnarled hand. The lines on his face deepened as he spoke, his voice rough as desert sand yet carrying the authority of one who communed with the divine.

"We will rest here," he commanded, his gaze sweeping over the masses of people who had followed him into this desolation. "The Lord has chosen this place."

They made no tents. There was no time. After two days of walking, broken only by brief, fitful sleep, they collapsed onto the dusty plain. Parents cradled children in their laps; elders sat with backs bent, massaging swollen feet; young men stood guard with improvised weapons, their eyes scanning the horizon for signs of pursuit.

To the west, the Red Sea shimmered in the sun, its waters stretching to the horizon like a wall of molten bronze. The high ridge of Migdol towered behind them, its rocky flanks seemingly impassable, cutting off retreat. To the south, far in the distance, the craggy outline of Mount Ataka loomed like a sleeping giant, indifferent to their plight.

Israelites: From Rest to Crisis

The camp had settled into an uneasy quiet. Children played in the dust between the tents while their mothers prepared what little food remained. Men sat in circles, speaking in low voices of the journey ahead, their eyes distant with exhaustion and uncertainty. The afternoon sun beat down mercilessly, but there was a strange comfort in this moment of stillness— the first true rest they had known since fleeing Egypt.

Some had begun to doze in whatever shade they could find. Others mended torn sandals or tended to blistered feet. The elderly sat with their backs against the few scraggly trees, watching their grandchildren with weary but loving eyes. It was the kind of peaceful interlude that comes after great upheaval, when the body finally allows itself to believe that safety might be possible.

But peace, they were learning, was a luxury the freed could ill afford.

It began with a single figure—a young shepherd who had climbed partway up the ridge to search for strays from his small flock. He stood silhouetted against the sky, his hand shading his eyes as he gazed northward. Something in his posture changed. His shoulders tensed. His head tilted forward with sudden, sharp attention.

Others noticed his stillness. A few called out to him, asking what he saw. But the shepherd didn't answer. Instead, he began scrambling down the rocky slope with desperate haste, his feet sliding on loose stones, his voice cracking as he finally found his tongue.

"Look north!" he shouted, his words carrying across the camp like wildfire. "Look north!"

Then came the murmur.

First, a few voices, uncertain and questioning. Then shouts, sharp with alarm. Then a silence so complete it seemed to swallow the very breath from their lungs.

A line of dust moved across the northern horizon, a brown smudge against the pale blue sky. It grew as they watched, spreading like a stain, resolving into shapes that could not be mistaken.

Israelites Trapped

"Egyptians!" a man shouted, his voice cracking. The cry was taken up, passed from mouth to mouth, until it filled the air like the beating of terrified wings.

From the ridge to the north, Pharaoh's army descended—a sea of bronze and red and dust. They moved with practiced precision, the chariots taking the lead, flanked by runners and followed by the main body of spearmen. They rode past the outer edges of the camp, not rushing, not attacking—yet—but moving to block any possible escape route.

Sandaled feet and chariot wheels turned the plain into thunder. The sound filled the air, a physical presence that pressed against the ears and chest, that made children cry and women clutch their amulets.

They didn't attack.

They stopped.

Between the Israelites and the low hills behind them, the Egyptian army formed a wall of men and weapons and cold intent.

The message was clear, even without words: There would be no mercy. There would be no negotiation. There would be only death or a return to chains, heavier than before.

The only way left was into the sea.

The sea, whose waters lapped at the shore with quiet indifference, as if unaware of the drama unfolding on its banks.

The Line of War

Menkheperre stood in his chariot, his body taut as a drawn bow as he surveyed the frightened mass before him. The desert wind tugged at his blue war crown and the pleated linen of his royal kilt, bringing him the scent of fear that rose from the Israelite camp. It was a sweet perfume to his nostrils, a balm to his wounded pride.

His charioteers lined up behind him, columns crisp and gleaming despite the dust of their march. Six hundred of Egypt's finest, each vehicle a testament to the craftsmanship of the empire, each driver and archer selected from the elite of the military caste. Behind them, foot soldiers with drawn bows stood like statues, unmoving, arrows nocked but not yet raised.

Menkheperre's lips pulled back from his teeth in a smile that held no mirth. The slaves were cornered, trapped between his army and the impassable sea. Like game driven into a hunter's net, they huddled together, bleating their fear to a god who had led them into this trap.

"Let me strike!" he barked, his hand going to the khopesh sword at his belt. The curved blade rasped against its sheath, eager for blood. "Now, while they are confused. While they are afraid."

General Khaemwaset stepped forward, his sandals leaving prints in the soft sand. The face was lined with fatigue, but his eyes were clear, calculating.

"Majesty," he said, his voice pitched low so that only Pharaoh could hear, "the men need rest. Two days of pursuit without pause have taken their toll. Let them eat, drink, and breathe. Let them prepare properly for battle."

Menkheperre scowled, his face darkening like the sky before a storm. His fingers curled tightly around the reins, causing his horses to shift nervously, sensing their master's mood. His eyes never left the mass of Israelites, searching for one figure in particular—the old man who had stood before his throne and demanded freedom in the name of an invisible god.

The memory of those encounters burned in his gut like acid. The plagues that followed, the death, the humiliation of capitulation. All because of one old shepherd who claimed to speak for a god more powerful than all the deities of Egypt.

For a moment, it seemed he would ignore his commander's counsel. His body tensed, leaning forward as if to urge his chariot into motion, to begin the slaughter immediately.

Then, abruptly, he gave a short nod. "Two hours," he conceded, his voice thick with restrained violence. "Then we crush them."

The commander bowed and withdrew, relief hidden beneath his impassive exterior. Two hours might make little difference to the outcome of the battle, but it would give him time—time to prepare the proper offerings to the gods, time to ensure that whatever happened here would have divine favor.

As he walked among the troops, giving orders for a brief rest, he cast a glance toward the sea. Something about this place, this moment, disturbed him. The statue of Baal-Zephon watched over them, its stone eyes fixed on the drama unfolding at its feet. But would the foreign god protect them, or the slaves?

For the first time in many years of service to Pharaoh, the commander of his army felt the cold touch of uncertainty.

The Cry of the People

Panic rippled through the Israelite camp like a sudden storm, transforming the exhausted resignation of moments before into a cacophony of terror. Men pointed at the horizon, at the lines of soldiers and chariots that blocked their escape; women clutched their children to their breasts, as if their bodies alone could shield the little ones from the Egyptian spears; voices rose in fear and anger, a discordant chorus that filled the air.

In the center of the camp, Moses stood with his brother Aaron and sister Miriam, surrounded by the elders of the tribes. The old prophet's face remained impassive, his eyes fixed on the pillar of cloud that had led them to this place. But all around him, the fear was transforming into something uglier.

"Were there no graves in Egypt?" shouted Dathan, a burly man with a face creased by years of labor in the quarries. He pushed his way to the front of the gathering, jabbing an accusing finger at Moses. "That you brought us here to die in the desert. Is this what your god promised—a quicker death than slavery could give us?"

His words found fertile ground in the hearts of the frightened. A chorus of angry assent rose around him.

Korah, once a man of standing in Avaris, now just another fugitive in the wilderness, stepped forward. His face was gaunt with hunger and worry, his eyes wild. "We told you!" he cried, spittle flying from his lips. "We begged you in Egypt—leave us be! Better to serve the Pharaoh than to die here, our bodies left for jackals and vultures!"

Others took up the cry, their fear finding outlet in rage directed at the man who had led them. "Our children!" wailed a woman, her face streaked with tears and dust. "What have you done to our children?"

Through it all, Moses remained silent, communing with the presence that dwelt in the cloud. In his mind, he saw again the burning bush, heard again the voice that had called him from obscurity into this impossible task. Was this, then, the culmination—to lead his people to death between the sea and the sword?

No, something whispered in his heart. No, this is not the end. This is the beginning.

The Cloud Defends

As the clamor of fear and accusation reached its peak, a change came over the pillar of cloud that had guided them. Those nearest to it fell silent first, their words dying on their lips as they stared upward in wonder.

The pillar began to move.

It rose, seeming to stretch toward the heavens, lengthening and shifting westward between the Israelites and the waiting army. It settled like a living wall, thick and high, a barrier of vapor and mystery that separated the hunters from their prey.

From the Egyptian side, the cloud appeared as a dark fog, impenetrable and ominous. No light penetrated its depths; no sound escaped from beyond its curtain. It brought with it a chill that cut through armor and linen alike, making seasoned soldiers shiver and horses stamp nervously. It seemed alive, watching, waiting—a sentinel from another world.

From the Israelite side, the cloud presented a different aspect. It glowed faintly from within, like moonlight diffused through water, casting a gentle radiance over the camp. Its presence brought an unexpected calm, a sense that they were sheltered, protected by the very force that had led them to this place.

Menkheperre watched the transformation with growing unease, his earlier confidence giving way to a creeping dread. This was not natural. This was not something his priests had prepared him for.

The afternoon waned. The sun began its descent toward the western horizon, casting long shadows across the plain. The Egyptian army maintained its position, weapons ready but unused, their purpose thwarted by the mysterious fog that denied them sight of their quarry.

Night approached. The stars began to blink awake, appearing first as faint pinpricks against the deepening blue, then brightening as darkness claimed the sky. Within the Egyptian camp, torches were lit, their flames dancing in the wind that blew from the sea.

Menkheperre stood at the edge of his camp, staring at the wall of cloud that had not dissipated with nightfall. His advisors waited at a respectful distance, sensing his mood, fearing his wrath.

"At dawn," Pharaoh said at last, his voice low but carrying to those who needed to hear. "We attack. Cloud or no cloud, god or no god. At dawn, we end this."

"They will not escape us," growled General Khaemwaset, his face partially wrapped against the storm. "Dawn will find them trapped between our spears and the water."

In his tent, Menkhperre lay awake, listening to the distant sound of the sea. Sleep eluded him, driven away by memories of plagues, of water turned to blood, of darkness that could be felt. Of his son's face, still and cold in death.

No, he would not be denied again. Whatever power protected the slaves, he would break it. He was Pharaoh, son of Ra, the living god of Egypt. His will would be done.

Multitude along the Sea

The camp was quiet now; the earlier panic subsided into an uneasy sleep. Only the sentries remained awake, their eyes fixed on the glowing cloud that still separated them from their pursuers.

Moses stood, his aged frame straight and unbowed by the weight of responsibility he carried. The staff in his hand—once a simple shepherd's tool, now an instrument of divine power—seemed to pulse with inner light. His face, lined by years and weathered by desert winds, held a serenity that belied the desperate circumstances.

He lifted his staff and turned toward the water.

Behind him, thousands stirred. First the elders, then the people—roused not by sound but by some instinct that told them the moment had come.

They gathered their meager possessions, helped the elderly to their feet, and lifted their children onto their shoulders. No words were needed; they had followed this man through plagues and wilderness. They would follow him now, even if it meant walking into the embrace of the sea.

The people stretched along the Red Sea's shore; a vast stream of humanity poised at the edge of the impossible. From Pharaoh's vantage point, had he been able to see through the cloud, they would have appeared as countless ants trapped against the water's edge.

Moses walked forward, step by measured step, his staff extended before him like a talisman. The first waves lapped at his sandals, cool against his skin.

As Moses reached the water's edge, the wind began to blow.

Chapter 29 - Red Sea Crossing

6 pm, 29 April 1438 BC – The Sea divides

Moses stood at the water's edge, his weathered feet sinking slightly into the damp sand. The Red Sea before him was calm, like a vast mirror of obsidian stretched to the distant horizon, reflecting the first stars of evening. His beard, streaked with silver, fluttered against his chest as he gazed across the glistening blackness. The weight of six hundred thousand souls pressed upon his shoulders, heavier than the staff he now slowly raised, as though saluting a distant army only he could see.

"Lord," he whispered, his voice carried away by the gentle lapping of waves, "show us Your deliverance."

A breeze began to stir. At first, it was gentle, whispering through the Israelite ranks like the breath of a sleeping giant. Women paused in their anxious conversations, and children looked up from their games, feeling the cool touch against their cheeks.

Then it grew. Within the hour, the wind strengthened, transforming from gentle whisper to urgent command, howling down from the northeast with supernatural intensity. Sand and salt danced in the air, stinging exposed skin and forcing eyes shut.

The Israelites, weary from their desperate flight from Egypt, confused by the sudden change in weather, huddled along the banks where the sheltering dunes offered some respite. Mothers pulled children close, wrapping threadbare blankets around trembling shoulders. Men secured tents and belongings against the rising gale.

Moses stepped back onto the shore, one hand shielding his face from the assault of sand, the other clutching his staff with whitened knuckles. Aaron, his brother and spokesman, joined him, gray hair whipping wildly about his face.

"It's going to be a long night," Moses said grimly, pulling his woolen cloak tighter against the supernatural wind. His eyes, dark and knowing beneath heavy brows, gazed toward the heavens. "But by dawn, the Lord will have made a way."

Aaron nodded, his faith a quiet thing beside his brother's thunderous certainty. Together they crouched nearby, sheltered in the hollow of the dunes, watching as the impossible storm grew to a shrieking fury above the increasingly turbulent sea.

The Israelites had moved even closer to the sea, stretching in a vast, vulnerable line of over ten kilometers against the shoreline. Men, women, children, elders – a nation on foot, with flocks and herds and the spoils of Egypt.

The Sea Opens

The wind grew stronger still, a force beyond nature, hurling itself at the high ridge of Shalouf rock with focused purpose. Above, the moon hung nearly full in the midnight sky—only four days past its peak—casting silver light across the darkened waters. Here, twenty kilometers north of modern Suez, lay the shallow overflow channels where Red Sea waters spilled during high tide into the small bitter lakes beyond. What appeared as sea was merely the overflow—barely more than marshland when the tide was low—and beneath the surface lay ground that had been dry land countless times before, waiting to be revealed once more.

The overflow waters obeyed the wind as a slave obeys its master. Before the eyes of those near Shalouf, the tide began to peel away, defying all-natural law. First to the sides, rippling and churning like a living thing, then backward, pushed relentlessly toward Pi-Hahiroth and draining into the small bitter lakes beyond. The moon's light followed the retreating waters, illuminating the impossible sight.

Small fish and crustaceans, caught in the retreating overflow, flapped and skittered across the newly exposed ground. Seaweed and marsh grass glistened on the muddy bottom that had been dry land at low tide countless times before, made luminous by moonbeams. The smell was primordial – salt and brine and marsh mud suddenly exposed to the night air that grew colder as the hours passed.

2 am, 1 May 1438 BC – The Red Sea Crossing

The Israelites, drawn to the shoreline by the roaring wind and the strange light, stared in stunned silence. Hands reached for one another in the darkness. Breaths were held. Children pressed close to their mothers, eyes wide in the pale moonlight.

By two in the morning, with the night at its deepest point and the nearly full moon directly overhead, the path through the overflow lay bare – a highway through what had been, hours before, impassable marsh waters. Moses stood again, his tall figure silhouetted against the impossible sight, his shadow long and dark on the exposed mudflats. Aaron, Joshua, and Miriam gathered beside him, their faces etched in silver and shadow.

Wordlessly, they packed their few belongings in the pre-dawn darkness. Moses looked back at the people, his people, huddled in fear and wonder under the waning moon, and nodded once – a gesture both command and permission – then stepped onto the exposed marsh bottom.

The ground was muddy but firm underfoot, not the sucking quicksand many had feared. Strings of seaweed clung to his ankles as he walked forward, staff extended, each step a declaration of faith. Aaron followed, then Miriam, her eyes wide with awe. Then hundreds more, then thousands, moving hesitantly at first, then with growing confidence.

From horizon to horizon, the Israelites began to walk between walls of water, their shadows stretching long across the seabed. Elders wept silently, understanding the magnitude of the miracle. The livestock, sensing neither danger nor safety but only the urging of their masters, followed reluctantly, hooves clicking on exposed shells and stone.

By early dawn, the Israelites had nearly completed the crossing. The seabed, now exposed and dry, stretched wide—so wide that the multitude of men, women, children, and herds could move steadily in broad columns. Ten kilometers of open ground lay between the parted seas, the passage made possible by a relentless wind that had blown all night, pushing the sea aside in both directions.

The walls of water on each side rose no higher than the waist of a man, perhaps half a meter tall. Yet they held their shape like a force restrained. The water trembled at the edges, tugging restlessly as if yearning to reclaim what had been borrowed. The further the people walked, the more uneasy the air grew. A hush fell over them, not from fear, but from awe.

Pursuing without command

An hour before dawn, when night is at its deepest and men's spirits at their lowest, Pharaoh Menkheperre was shaken awake. His commander's face was wild with urgency, sweat cutting clean lines through the dust on his forehead.

"My lord," he gasped, protocol forgotten in his haste, "they are walking into the sea."

Menkheperre blinked sleep from his eyes, then laughed – a short, harsh sound. "Into the sea? Have they chosen drowning over the sword?" He rose from his portable couch, reaching for his ceremonial breastplate, doubt creeping into his voice. "What madness is this?"

They marched forward to where the camp of the Israelites had been, now abandoned save for scattered belongings deemed too burdensome for the flight.

Menkheperre stood atop the hill near Baal-Zephon as the supernatural cloud began to lift, revealing what lay beyond.

What he saw was no mirage, no trick of the pre-dawn light. The sea was gone, and in its place, a path stretched far into the horizon like a god's causeway. The walls of water gleamed in the early light, impossibly vertical, impossibly still. He saw no Israelites, only evidence of their passing – wandering lost luggage, the occasional bleating sheep or lowing cattle separated from their flock along the route. They had crossed during the night, while his army slept in darkness.

For the first time since ordering the pursuit, Menkheperre hesitated. He considered ordering a flanking maneuver around the Bitter Lake, a more prudent approach, but the rage in the army had long overtaken discipline. The death of their firstborn sons demanded blood payment, and the supernatural sight before them only inflamed their desire for vengeance.

Without waiting for his command, General Khaemwaset ordered the charge with wild shouts and upraised swords. The disciplined rows of Egyptian military dissolve into a frenzied mob, united only in bloodlust. Rows of chariots—hundreds wide—raced into the sea path, wheels throwing up splashes of brine and mud. The thundering of hooves and the screech of chariot wheels echoed against the water walls as Egypt's finest warriors pursued Israel into the heart of the miracle.

The Wind Stopped

Moses walked at the center of the crossing, staff in hand, watching as the last tribe passed him, oxen bellowing as they pressed forward across the hardened seabed. He turned once to glance behind—and saw a storm of dust rising at the edge of the western shore.

Pharaoh Menkheperre, so he taught, had come.

The Egyptian chariots swept down the slope and poured into the seabed path, wheels slicing into the moist clay. Their armor caught the morning light, but their eyes were fixed on vengeance. The soldiers knew the land, but not the warning in the wind.

And the wind had stopped.

Where once a steady east wind had held the waters at bay, now there was only stillness. That stillness became a whisper. That whisper became a shift.

Menkheperre did not move. Something in him – perhaps the wisdom that comes with kingship, or was it fear that kept him rooted on the hilltop? From his vantage point, he watched the army vanish into the horizon where the sea once was, their dust cloud diminishing with distance.

Twenty minutes passed, marked only by the gradual lightening of the eastern sky. Then he saw them. Shapes in the distance, chariots returning at full gallop, riders screaming words lost to the wind and distance. Their organized formation had collapsed into panicked flight.

Behind them, walls of water began to tremble and bow inward, no longer held back by divine command. The miracle was ending.

He thought they might make it. Some always do, he told himself, even in the greatest defeats. The charioteers with the strongest horses might outrun disaster.

But then the sea in front of Menkheperre collapsed with terrible suddenness. A roar thundered across the plain, primitive and final. Water surged forward, cutting off the retreat like a gigantic blade. Behind and before, the waters crashed together, blue green becoming white foam becoming churning death.

In stunned silence, he watched them drown. He watched the pride of Egypt disappear beneath waves that should never have parted. He watched chariots splinter like toys and horses thrash in their final moments. He watched men who had called him god that morning discover the limits of his protection.

Not one survived.

Lonely Road Home

The wind had ceased as suddenly as it had begun. The water was still once more, glinting innocently under the rising sun, as if nothing had ever happened. No evidence remained of the miracle or the massacre, only the eternal rhythm of small waves against the shore.

Menkheperre stood with his four remaining bodyguards and his chariot driver. None of them spoke. What words could address what they had witnessed?

He watched the sea, his face a mask of stone. The weight of his double crown seemed suddenly unbearable, though he wore only a simple war helmet.

There was no sign of his army. No Israel. No screams. No survivors. No bodies washing to shore – the sea had claimed them all. Perhaps all had drowned, he thought briefly. Possibly the sea had swallowed pursuer and pursued alike in some cosmic balancing of scales.

Or perhaps – and this thought brought a chill that had nothing to do with the morning breeze – possibly they had made it across. Possibly they now stood on the opposite shore, watching as he watched, understanding as he was beginning to understand, that something had changed in the order of the world.

Menkheperre turned slowly, his movements those of a much older man. He did not speak for hours as they rode north, back toward the green ribbon of the Nile, toward what remained at Pi-Ramesses.

His mind replayed what he had seen – the impossible parting, the equally impossible return of the waters. No magic of Egypt's priests could account for it. No god in Egypt's pantheon had ever demonstrated such power.

He returned to Pi-Ramesses, alone in thought, leaving the silence of the Red Sea behind him. But in truth, that silence would follow him to his grave.

As the small procession gradually returned from the killing waters, the sun climbed higher, beating down on their backs with merciless intensity. Menkheperre's skin felt raw beneath his armor, salt-scoured and burning. The chariot wheels ground against the sand with a sound like the moaning of ghosts. Five of them, all that remained of Egypt's mighty host, kept their faces averted from their king, afraid to witness whatever emotion might crack through his bronze mask of stoicism.

Fear coiled in his belly like a cobra – not the quick, sharp fear of battle, but something deeper and more insidious. He had been stripped naked before the universe, his power revealed as the childish pretense it truly was. The sensation was so alien, so utterly at odds with everything he had known since birth, that for long moments he could not name it. The realization came to him between one heartbeat and the next: for the first time in his life, Menkheperre, Lord of the Two Lands, Beloved of Amun, felt mortal.

Then suddenly, as they crested a dune that revealed the thin green ribbon of the Wadi-Tumalit Valley stretching toward the western horizon, understanding crashed into him with the force of revelation.

The gods had spared him. They had taken Moses, taken the slaves, his army – a blood sacrifice of unprecedented magnitude – but preserved their chosen vessel. The royal Ka, that divine essence passed from pharaoh to pharaoh, had been fully transferred to him at last, tested in the crucible of catastrophe and found worthy.

He straightened his shoulders, feeling the weight of the invisible double crown settling more comfortably upon his brow. The gold of his pectoral caught the sunlight and flashed like divine fire across the rolling sands. A hawk screamed overhead, circling in the burning blue – Horus himself, watching his son.

"Make way," he commanded, his voice stronger now, and the drivers snapped their whips over the tired horses with renewed vigor. The road back to Pi-Ramesses stretched before him like a promise. He had lost an army and a nation of slaves, yes – but what were these compared to divine confirmation of his rule? He had been baptized in destruction and emerged anew.

He was Pharaoh Menkheperre, Thutmose III, and his legend was beginning.

Chapter 30 - Leprosy at Avaris

Arrival at Tjaru Fortress

The morning sun crested the eastern desert like a disc of molten copper, painting the limestone walls of Tjaru fortress with bands of amber light. Menkheperre's war chariot rattled through the imposing gates, its gilded panels and royal insignia gleaming in the dawn. The fortress that traditionally housed five thousand of Egypt's finest warriors—men who had carried the standard of the Divine Pharaoh across the burning sands of Sinai and into the fertile valleys of Canaan— stood eerily subdued. Only a few dozen soldiers were visible on the ramparts, their bronze armor catching the early light, their eyes haunted by something they dared not speak aloud.

Their posture stiffened at the sight of the small procession approaching, recognizing their Pharaoh, their royal shoulders pulled back, spears snapping to attention.

"Halt," Menkheperre commanded his driver, his voice cutting through the morning stillness like a well-honed blade. He stepped down from the chariot with the fluid grace that decades of royal bearing had ingrained in him. Despite three days of hard travel, his linen kilt remained pristine, his dark eyes alert beneath the royal uraeus that adorned his brow.

The commander of Tjaru rushed forward, his sandaled feet slapping against the packed earth. He prostrated himself; forehead pressed to the ground; arms extended in supplication before his god-king. Dust clung to the sweat on his brow as he trembled before the living embodiment of Horus.

"Great One, Life, Prosperity, Health," the commander intoned, his voice slightly muffled against the earth, "we did not expect your divine presence so soon."

"Rise," Menkheperre ordered, his eyes sweeping the emptied barracks where only ghosts of routine and discipline remained. A muscle twitched beneath his left eye—the only outward sign of the fury and calculation churning behind his impassive features. "Where are my soldiers?"

The commander rose to his knees, keeping his gaze respectfully lowered. Menkheperre noticed the man's fingers trembling slightly, the way his throat worked to swallow before speaking. The scent of fear rose from him like heat from sunbaked stone.

"Deployed as you commanded, Divine One," the commander replied, his voice struggling to maintain its steadiness. "Five hundred at the border post. The remainder stand guard at the crossroads to Avaris, allowing none to pass toward the city unless on urgent business."

"Why the crossroads to Avaris?" Menkheperre asked, his tone measured and flat, betraying nothing of the tension coiled within him.

The commander's eyes widened slightly, then darted away. Here came the news that Menkheperre had not expected yet would seize upon with the opportunistic instinct of a desert jackal.

"We divert people who enter Egypt to bypass Avaris through the Wadi-Tumilat," the commander explained, hesitation evident in his voice, "because leprosy has broken out at Avaris."

"Leprosy?" Menkheperre repeated, allowing a hint of concern to crease his brow while his mind raced ahead, calculating the advantages this unexpected development offered.

He fixed his gaze on the commander. "You've done well to bring me this news so swiftly. Your vigilance honors the crown."

The man bowed low, visibly bolstered by the praise.

"I will go myself to see if that is true," he declared, the decision made instantly. He turned, his royal cloak swirling around him, the scent of precious myrrh and cedar wafting from the fabric. Without another word, he returned to his chariot, and the procession continued toward the cities of Pi-Ramesses and Avaris.

As the wheels of his chariot churned up the dust of the road, Menkheperre's thoughts ran deeper than the Nile in flood season. "The god has made it easy for him," he thought, his lips curling into the faintest smile. It would have been difficult to convince the old men, women, and children to abandon Avaris, to march west to Heliopolis and Memphis without raising suspicions. But now? Now he had the perfect pretext.

He could tell them that the army was pursuing the Israelites who had fled into the desert. None would question why husbands and fathers didn't return, not immediately. And by the time questions arose, a new truth would have been established—one that preserved the divine infallibility of Pharaoh and the might of Egypt.

More importantly, he realized with cold clarity that he had to eliminate the four witnesses who witnessed what happened three days ago. The river of time would wash away all evidence, and history would remember only what he decreed should be remembered.

As Menkheperre approached the eastern gate of Avaris, the evidence of evacuation was unmistakable. Long lines of people streamed southward under the merciless sun; their backs bent under the weight of hastily gathered possessions. The royal road was choked with carts and litters, with families driving their livestock before them—goats bleating in confusion, cattle lowing mournfully as they were forced from familiar pastures. The dust kicked up by thousands of feet hung in the air like a shroud, turning the blue sky to hazy amber.

The faces of the refugees told their own story—wide-eyed terror mixed with the stoic resignation that centuries of living under the whims of gods and kings had bred into the Egyptian peasantry. Children whimpered, old men grumbled, and mothers clutched infants to their breasts and whispered prayers to Taweret for protection.

Though countless eyes turned toward Menkheperre as his chariot passed, no one dared raise a voice to question him. It was not protocol to address the Pharaoh directly, even in times of crisis. The people's questions—about the fate of the army, the sudden return of the royal procession, and the absence of familiar commanders—burned behind silent stares. But tradition demanded patience. The official report would be issued by the scribes in due time, delivered through temple proclamations or shouted by town criers at the gates. Until then, even grief had to wait.

Within the city gates, a different scene awaited. The streets of Avaris, usually teeming with merchants and craftsmen, were largely deserted save for small groups of women gathering final belongings, young men loading carts with family treasures, and children clinging to their mothers' skirts, their eyes wide with confusion and fear. Soldiers stood at key intersections, their faces partially covered with linen cloths to protect them from the rumored contagion, spears held ready to maintain order among the dwindling population.

The smell of abandonment already permeated the air—food left to spoil in the heat, animals not yet collected roaming freely, the acrid scent of lamp oil spilled in haste. Beneath it all lay the deeper odor of fear, as palpable as the heat radiating from the mud-brick buildings.

A woman's cry pierced the unnatural quiet of the marketplace, cutting through the distant rumble of cartwheels and shuffling feet. Menkheperre turned to see her collapsing against a stone wall, her wails echoing between the empty stalls where dates and figs and freshly caught fish had been sold only days before.

"My home," she sobbed as her companions tried to comfort her, their own faces streaked with tears and dust. "Three generations we have lived here. The shop my husband built with his own hands—the garden where my children learned to walk—all to be abandoned."

An older woman wrapped weathered arms around her shoulders. "Better to lose a home than a life, daughter. The gods will provide elsewhere."

Menkheperre watched impassively, his face betraying nothing of the calculation behind his eyes. The hawk-like set of his features remained unchanged, as if carved from the same desert stone as the great sphinx. Let them mourn their homes and businesses; better that than mourning their husbands and sons, whose bodies would never return for proper burial.

When Menkheperre reached the eastern gate of his Royal palace, the massive cedar doors swung open to reveal Rekhmire waiting in the courtyard. The Vizier's lean frame seemed to have grown even thinner since Menkheperre had last seen him, and new lines had etched themselves around his eyes—the marks of sleepless nights spent managing the unfolding catastrophe.

Before Menkheperre could ask any question, Rekhmire prostrated himself briefly, then rose to report with the efficiency that had made him indispensable. "I did send your wife back to Thebes the day after you left to pursue the Israelites, Divine One," he said, his voice carefully neutral. "As you had ordered."

The Vizier paused, his weathered hands clasped behind his back, waiting for permission to continue. What he did not know—what Menkheperre could never tell him—was that there had been no pursuit worthy of the name.

Now he stood before his most trusted advisor, bearing the weight of a lie that felt heavier than his golden crown. Let Rekhmire believe the army still rode in the desert, chasing shadows and Hebrew dust. Let him believe there was still an Egypt capable of pursuit, of vengeance, of anything beyond the hollow ceremony of retreat. The truth—that Pharaoh's army lay beneath the waters, that the God of the Hebrews had proven mightier than all the gods of Egypt—was a burden Menkheperre would carry alone.

But Rekhmire's keen eyes had already noted the small size of the Pharaoh's return party. "Divine One," the Vizier ventured carefully, "I see only four guards returned with you. Where rides the great host that departed to bring back the Hebrew slaves?"

Menkheperre's jaw tightened, but his voice remained steady. "General Khaemwaset," he said, letting controlled anger color his words. "You remember how he had grown... erratic in the final days of the plagues? His behavior became increasingly unstable, his judgment clouded by rage." He paused, as if the memory pained him. "When we reached the edge of the desert, I ordered the army to make camp and wait for proper reconnaissance. But Khaemwaset," Menkheperre shook his head in apparent disgust. "He defied my direct command. Claimed the gods were whispering strategies in his ears. He rallied the charioteers and infantry, convinced them that glory awaited if they pressed forward immediately."

The Pharaoh's voice dropped to a bitter whisper. "He took my army into the deep desert against my express orders, chasing after the Hebrews like a madman. I returned with my personal guard to report this... treachery... and to decide whether to send reinforcements or let his foolishness teach him—and them—a lesson they'll not soon forget."

Rekhmire's face relaxed slightly, the explanation fitting with what he had observed of Khaemwaset's increasingly volatile demeanor. A rogue general was a problem he could understand and manage—far better than the alternatives his mind had been conjuring.

Menkheperre descended from his chariot, the gold ankh in his right hand catching the light. "We must make this evacuation complete," he declared, his voice carrying the weight of divine decree. "Abandon these cities."

He cast a long, grim look over the fortified town, its streets half-empty, its temples silent, its statues smeared with dust. "The land groans under judgment. The Nile no longer flows with blessing but with blood. There is no sanctuary here—not in Avaris, not in Pi-Ramesses, not in any house where the breath of the gods has turned against us. The shadow of death has passed through this land, and it will return. No shrine or stronghold will be spared."

He turned to Rekhmire, his tone iron. "Send word to all loyal households: dismantle what can be carried, burn what cannot. The gods have withdrawn from these cities—so must we. Let the dust bury what remains."

He strode through the columned entrance of the palace, Rekhmire falling into step beside him. Servants scattered before them like quail before a hunting cat, their eyes downcast, their movements hurried. The usual elaborate protocols of the royal court had been abandoned in the crisis; only the barest essentials of deference remained.

Menkheperre's gaze swept across the palace courtyard, then beyond, to where the massive monuments and temples that had been the pride of Egypt's northern reach pierced the sky. The obelisks of Ra, the colonnaded temples of Ptah and Amun, the sprawling storehouses that had once held the tribute of Asia—all stood as testaments to Pharaonic power. Power that had been humbled by a god he did not recognize, wielded by a prince of Egypt, turned shepherd of slaves.

As evening fell like a purple veil over the dying city, the only five survivors of the Red Sea disaster made camp in the gardens of the palace, away from the remaining inhabitants of Avaris. The scent of lotus blossoms mixed with the smoke from cooking fires as Menkheperre stood alone on a balcony overlooking the scene, his silhouette stark against the blood-red sunset.

He listened to the diminishing sounds of departure—the distant bleating of goats, the creaking of cart wheels, the muffled weeping of women—his attention was fixed on the darker work being carried out in the shadows of the royal compound. The palace guards moved with grim efficiency among the tents where the witnesses rested, their curved bronze blades catching the last light of day.

There were no screams, no calls for mercy—only the swift, silent work of men who understood that their survival depended on absolute obedience and absolute discretion.

A few minutes later, a captain approached the balcony, keeping his eyes fixed on the ground before Menkheperre's feet. "The evacuation proceeds as ordered," he reported, his voice deliberately flat. Then, more softly: "We also did as you commanded, Divine One."

Menkheperre nodded once, dismissing the man with a gesture. Now he alone remained as witness to Egypt's humiliation. All others who had seen the waters' part and then crash down upon the flower of Egypt's army slept the sleep of eternity. The truth would die with them, replaced by the story he would craft—a tale of leprosy and prudent retreat, of strategic redeployment rather than devastating defeat.

As night embraced the emptying city, Menkheperre's eyes reflected the cold light of distant stars. History, he knew, was written by those who survived to tell the tale. And he would ensure that Egypt's tale remained one of divine glory, unblemished by the intervention of foreign gods.

Dead of the Cities

Dawn revealed a city in the final stages of abandonment; its streets were emptied of life like a carcass picked clean by desert scavengers. What had once been the jewel of the Nile Delta—home to merchants and artisans, priests and scholars, foreign envoys and domestic nobility—now stood like a massive tomb awaiting its occupants.

The rising sun cast long shadows through deserted alleys where herons and ibises now wandered freely, pecking at discarded food and garbage. The morning market, which should have been alive with the cries of vendors and the haggling of customers, lay silent. Doors swung open on empty homes, precious possessions left behind in the rush to leave the city—pottery too heavy to carry, furniture too bulky to load onto carts, wall paintings lovingly created over generations now abandoned to the mercy of the elements.

The air hung heavy with absence, as if the very soul of the city had fled with its inhabitants, leaving behind only stone and mud-brick shells where life had once flourished. Even the usual chorus of songbirds seemed subdued, as though they too sensed the unnatural emptiness of the human hive.

Menkheperre rode slowly through the streets, his small procession the only movement in the ghostly landscape. The hooves of his chariot horses echoed against the walls, a hollow sound that emphasized the void around them. He had exchanged his war chariot for a lighter, more ornate vehicle, its panels inlaid with ivory and gold, drawn by two white Arabian stallions whose coats gleamed like polished alabaster in the morning light.

At the Temple of Amun-Ra, priests were loading the last of the sacred objects onto carts, their movements hurried despite the weight of the golden vessels they carried. The normally meticulous rituals of handling divine objects had been abbreviated in the urgency of departure. Young acolytes stumbled under the weight of shrine equipment, while elder priests supervised the careful wrapping of statues and ritual implements.

"Great One," the High Priest bowed deeply as Menkheperre approached, his ancient frame bent like a reed in a strong wind. His head had been freshly shaved that morning, the ritual oils making his scalp gleam in the sunlight. After sixty years of service to Amun, Menkheperraseneb had seen kings come and go, had witnessed floods and famines, victories and defeats—but never had he overseen the abandonment of a temple while its walls still stood strong. "The gods travel with us to Thebes, as you have commanded."

Menkheperre nodded, watching as the priests wrapped a magnificent statue of Amun in layers of fine linen, their hands reverent despite their haste. The god's features—normally stern and powerful beneath the double-plumed crown—disappeared beneath the protective wrappings, as if Amun himself turned his face from the humiliation of retreat.

"And what do the gods say of this evacuation?" Menkheperre asked, his voice carrying just the right blend of authority and pious inquiry. He knew well how to play the game of theological politics, how to remind the priests that while they might interpret the will of the gods, he alone embodied divine power on earth.

The old priest hesitated, his rheumy eyes studying Pharaoh's face, seeking the safe path through this dangerous conversation. He chose his words with the care of a man stepping through a field of cobras.

"The gods speak through Pharaoh's lips, Great Horus," he said finally, inclining his head in deference. "If you command that these cities must be abandoned, then surely it is the will of Amun-Ra himself. Perhaps the divine one sends this leprosy as a sign that the seat of royal power should return to ancient Thebes, where the gods first blessed Egypt with divine kingship."

A convenient theology, Menkheperre thought, but useful, nonetheless. The priests were already constructing the narrative that would preserve both their power and his, wrapping defeat in the mantle of divine decree. He gestured for the priests to continue their work and moved on, his entourage falling in behind him like the tail of a comet.

The chariot climbed the rising ground toward the royal citadel, the horses' muscles straining against the incline. From this highest point in the city, the pinnacle from which he had once watched military parades and religious processions with the arrogant certainty of unassailable power, Menkheperre could now see the slow exodus stretching across the landscape like an army in retreat.

Women and children, the elderly and the infirm, all making their way southward toward Heliopolis and eventually Thebes. The line of humanity stretched like a great serpent along the riverside road; their possessions balanced on their heads or loaded onto beasts of burden. Donkeys brayed under excessive loads, children whimpered with exhaustion, old men leaned on sticks as they shuffled forward, leaving behind everything they had known.

"How many?" he asked Rekhmire, who stood at his side, the Vizier's tall form bent slightly as if the weight of the disaster had physically pressed down upon his shoulders.

"Perhaps twenty thousand from Pi-Ramesses alone," the vizier replied, his voice pitched low though there was no one to overhear them. The morning breeze carried the scent of the river to them, along with the more pungent smell of thousands on the move—dust and sweat and fear mingling in the hot air. "More from Avaris and the surrounding settlements. The road to Thebes will be crowded for weeks."

Below them, the last organized groups were departing the city—artisans from the royal workshops with their specialized tools bundled on their backs, scribes from the House of Life carrying precious scrolls of knowledge, servants from the palace itself herding the last of the royal cattle and fowl. Among them walked the skilled builders who had raised the monuments of Pi-Ramesses, the engineers who had designed its waterworks, the artists who had decorated its temples with scenes of Pharaoh's victories.

All that human ingenuity, all that accumulated knowledge, now trudging southward with bundles on their backs, their faces turned from the city they had made great. Children born within these walls looked back over their shoulders, confused and frightened by the sudden upheaval, unable to understand why they must leave the only home they had ever known.

"The cycle turns," Rekhmire murmured, his eyes distant as if seeing beyond the immediate crisis to the great wheel of history that had raised and toppled dynasties since time immemorial. "As it has always done. Great cities rise and fall like the inundation of the Nile."

Menkheperre's eyes narrowed, the lines around his mouth deepening into furrows carved by decades of absolute power. "This is not the natural turning of cycles, old friend," he said, his voice carrying the edge of a blade. "This is my will being enacted. The Hebrew slaves escaped, my forces hot on their heels. They will return—they have not defeated Egypt."

He knew it was a lie. They had drowned. They would never return. Only he knew the truth.

"From the highest to the lowest," Rekhmire observed, his sandaled feet stirring the dust of a street that had been swept clean every morning since the city's founding. "None are spared when the gods decree a city must die."

"Not the gods," Menkheperre corrected sharply, whirling to face his vizier, his eyes flashing with sudden anger. "Pharaoh. Remember that Rekhmire. What happens here is by my command, not the whim of deities."

He strode ahead, his back rigid with the pride that even catastrophic defeat had not diminished. The royal retinue hurried to keep pace with him, servants exchanging worried glances behind their master's back.

Yet as they rode toward the royal barge that would carry them southward, following the human tide of refugees, even Menkheperre could not suppress a shiver of disquiet. Cities were not meant to die this way—not abandoned in their prime, not emptied of life while their walls still stood strong. There was something unnatural about it, something that defied the order of creation that Pharaoh himself was sworn to uphold.

Menkheperre thought as he stepped onto the barge, feeling the subtle shift of the deck beneath his feet, this too was part of the eternal pattern—the rise and fall of cities, the ebb and flow of Egypt's power. Pi-

Ramesses had been built to project Egypt's strength northward, toward the lands of Canaan and beyond. Now that strength was being pulled back, concentrated in the ancient southern capital of Thebes where the gods had first crowned the kings of a unified Egypt.

As the barge slipped away from the dock, the oarsmen dipping their blades into the sacred waters of the Nile with practiced precision, Menkheperre did not look back at the dying city. His eyes were fixed southward; toward the future he would shape from the wreckage of his defeat.

Behind him, Pi-Ramesses and Avaris stood silent in the midday heat, their emptied streets and abandoned temples monuments to a humiliation that history would never record. In the sacred precinct of Ra, a lone priest—too old to make the journey south—shuffled through his final rituals, his prayers unheard by gods who had turned their faces from the Delta.

The living god of Egypt, the divine Pharaoh Menkheperre, sailed away from the evidence of his mortality, his mind already crafting the story that future generations would believe. Not a story of defeat at the hands of a shepherd and his foreign god, but a tale of strategic withdrawal, of divine wisdom in the face of natural calamity.

And as the royal barge rounded a bend in the river, the abandoned cities disappeared, swallowed by distance and already fading into myth.

Chapter 31 - Scapegoat Hatshepsut

June 1438 BC - Thebes

The Great Hall of Thebes blazed with light, hundreds of oil lamps reflecting off polished stone and beaten gold. Their flames danced in the evening air, casting long, undulating shadows across the imposing columns that rose like ancient trees to support the painted ceiling. The assembled nobility of Egypt stood in perfect formation, arrayed in their finest linen, adorned with intricate jewelry that glimmered in the golden light. Their faces, painted with kohl and malachite, were carefully composed to mask their confusion and fear. For weeks, they had watched as refugees poured into the city, bringing with them tales of a mysterious plague that had forced the abandonment of Pi-Ramesses and Avaris.

The air hung heavy with incense and anticipation, the usual court whispers silenced as they awaited Pharaoh's first public address since his return from the north. Servants stood motionless against the walls, their eyes downcast, aware of the palpable tension that filled the chamber like a physical presence.

Now they awaited Pharaoh's first public address since his return from the north. His absence had spawned a thousand rumors, each more alarming than the last. Had Egypt's invincible armies truly been defeated? Had the Hebrew slaves truly escaped? No one dared speak such thoughts aloud, but they lingered like specters in the minds of all present.

Menkheperre Thutmose had prepared carefully for this moment. His royal chambers had been a hive of activity behind closed doors, scribes working through the night to perfect the proclamations that would reshape Egypt's understanding of recent events. He had spent days in seclusion, ostensibly in prayer and purification, but in truth finalizing the story that would become Egypt's official history. The drowning of his army, the humiliation at the Red Sea, the escape of the Hebrew slaves—none of these would be acknowledged. Instead, a new narrative had been crafted, one that maintained Egypt's dignity and Pharaoh's infallibility.

He stood alone now in his private antechamber, examining his reflection in a polished copper mirror. The marks of his ordeal—sleepless nights, gnawing rage, consuming shame—had been carefully concealed beneath layers of cosmetics applied by the skilled hands of his body servants. His eyes, haunted by the memory of waters crashing down upon his finest charioteers, now projected only regal authority. He adjusted the double crown of Upper and Lower Egypt that sat upon his head, its weight a constant reminder of the burden he carried.

"It is time, Divine One," murmured a chamberlain, bowing so low his forehead nearly touched the alabaster floor.

Menkheperre drew a deep breath, steadying himself. With one final glance at his reflection, he adopted the mask of the living god, the undefeated ruler of the most powerful empire the world had ever known. He strode forward as drums began to pound, announcing his arrival.

The High Priest of Amun stepped forward as Menkheperre entered the Great Hall, ready to perform the traditional rituals that preceded royal pronouncements. His elaborate headdress caught the lamplight, casting strange patterns across his ritual garments. The scent of sacred oils wafted from his person as he raised his arms, mouth opening to begin the invocation. But Menkheperre raised his hand, stopping the man in mid-stride. The priest's eyes widened almost imperceptibly—the only sign of his shock at this breach of sacred protocol.

"Today I stand before all Egypt," Menkheperre declared, his voice carrying to every corner of the vast chamber, rich and powerful like the annual flooding of the Nile. "Not before the gods alone, but before my people. The gods know my heart and my purpose. Now you shall know it too."

A ripple of surprise moved through the assembly. For Pharaoh to speak directly to his subjects, bypassing the priestly intermediaries, was unprecedented. The nobles exchanged quick, nervous glances, wondering what could have prompted such a radical departure from thousands of years of tradition. Some of the older courtiers, veterans of three reigns, muttered prayers under their breath, fearing that such disregard for proper ritual might anger the very deities Pharaoh claimed to represent.

"You have heard of the calamity that has befallen our northern cities," Menkheperre continued, his eyes sweeping the crowd like a falcon surveying the reeds for prey. His gaze lingered briefly on those he suspected might harbor doubts, those whose loyalty might waver in troubled times. "You have seen the refugees arriving at our gates, their possessions piled high on carts, their children dusty from the road. You have heard whispers of disease and abandonment."

He paused, allowing the tension to build before delivering the official version of events. The silence grew thick enough to cut with a bronze dagger, broken only by the occasional crackle of a lamp flame or the stifled cough of an anxious courtier.

"I tell you now that Pi-Ramesses and Avaris have indeed been stricken—not by natural disease, but by divine retribution." His fingers tightened around the royal crook and flail, ancient symbols of his authority. "The gods have shown me a vision of the corruption that had taken root in those cities. Foreign influences had polluted the purity of Egyptian ways. The worship of strange gods had been tolerated in shadowed corners and hidden shrines. The sacred order—the very Ma'at upon which our empire stands—had been undermined by those who forgot their place, who reached beyond their station."

Murmurs swept through the crowd as nobles exchanged glances. Many had homes and business interests in the northern cities; none had suspected such spiritual corruption. Several paled visibly, wondering if their dealings with foreign merchants might now be viewed with suspicion. One elderly nobleman, whose wealth had been built on trade with Canaan and Punt, swayed slightly, steadied only by the quick hand of his son.

"Most grievous of all," Menkheperre's voice rose, echoing off the stone walls with the force of thunder rolling across the desert, "the gods of Egypt have punished us. During this ordeal with the Israelites, they kept quiet; they did not listen to us because of the one who defied the divine order decades ago." His face contorted with calculated outrage. "Hatshepsut! She who dared to claim the throne that belongs only to the true sons of Amun, who wore the false beard and usurped the privileges of Pharaoh!"

The High Priest shifted uncomfortably, his jeweled collar catching the light as he moved. His eyes, lined with ceremonial kohl, narrowed slightly. Hatshepsut's reign had ended decades ago, and while unusual, few now living remembered it as particularly offensive to the gods. Indeed, many of the most beautiful temples in Thebes had been commissioned during her prosperous rule. The priest's mind raced, trying to anticipate where Pharaoh's unprecedented pronouncement was leading.

"The gods have spoken," Menkheperre declared, bringing his fist down upon the arm of his golden throne with such force that several nearby attendants jumped. "Hatshepsut's monuments corrupt the very soil of Egypt. Her name, inscribed in sacred places, is an offense to Ma'at, the divine order. While she lived, she conducted forbidden rituals in the darkest hours of night, inviting the wrath of the gods upon any place that honors her memory."

The lie hung in the air, bold and terrible, like a vulture circling over dying prey. Yet who would dare contradict the word of Pharaoh? Who would claim greater knowledge of divine will than the living Horus himself? Across the hall, faces that had moments before shown only confusion now displayed the dawning realization of what was happening. An elderly scribe, one of the few present who had served in Hatshepsut's court as a young man, bit his lip until a trickle of blood ran down his chin, but he remained silent.

"To cleanse Egypt of this taint, I have ordered the northern cities abandoned." Menkheperre rose from his throne, the gold of his pectoral gleaming in the lamplight, his shadow stretching enormous across the polished floor. "Their wealth and people have been relocated to Bubastis, Heliopolis, Memphis and here, to Thebes, the true heart of Egypt. And I have commanded that wherever she proclaimed herself king, an abomination to our gods, her name shall be struck from every monument, every temple, every record throughout the land. Her face shall be chiselled away, her cartouches obliterated until it is as if she never existed."

The pronouncement fell upon the assembly like a stone dropped into still water, sending ripples of shock outward. Such a systematic erasure was unprecedented, even in a land where pharaohs had occasionally attempted to remove their predecessors from history. The scale of what Menkheperre proposed would require thousands of workers, years of effort, and would fundamentally alter some of Egypt's most sacred spaces.

The High Priest hesitated only a moment before bowing deeply, his ornate headdress catching the light. His mind whirled with the implications, both religious and political, but his survival instinct won out over his theological concerns. "As Pharaoh commands, so shall it be done," he intoned, his voice carrying the weight of religious authority that would sanctify the king's decree.

One by one, the nobles and officials followed suit, bowing their acknowledgment of the royal decree. Whether they believed the accusation was immaterial, survival depended on compliance. Some bent with the eager enthusiasm of opportunists, already calculating how they might benefit from this new order. Others lowered themselves stiffly, their faces masks of neutrality that concealed their private doubts.

"Egypt enters a new age," Menkheperre declared, his arms spread wide as if embracing the future he envisioned. "An age of purity and strength. The northern experiment has ended. Power returns to its rightful place, here in Thebes, where the gods first blessed our ancestors." His eyes, dark and penetrating, swept across the assembly once more. "Those who embrace this new direction will prosper. Those who cling to corrupt foreign ways..." His eyes narrowed, and his voice dropped to a deadly whisper that nonetheless carried to every ear in the hushed chamber. "They will find no place in the Egypt that is to come."

The threat was unmistakable. Already, Menkheperre had positioned his most loyal commanders at strategic points throughout the hall, their hands resting casually on the hilts of their swords. The message was clear: accept this new truth or join the ranks of the erased.

As the assembly digested these pronouncements, Menkheperre raised his arms, signaling the end of his address. Servants rushed forward with offerings and incense, resuming the rituals that tradition demanded. The familiar scents of myrrh and frankincense filled the air, providing a comforting return to normalcy after the shocking disruption of established order.

But the Pharaoh's mind was already elsewhere, planning the Egypt that would rise from his carefully constructed deception. An Egypt that would never know how close it had come to collapse, how thoroughly its army had been destroyed, how completely its god-king had been humiliated by a tribe of former slaves and their invisible deity. His fingers, heavy with gold rings, drummed restlessly against his throne as he watched the performance of rituals he no longer truly believed in, having seen their impotence in the face of the Hebrew god's power.

The crowd dispersed slowly, nobles clustering in small groups to whisper their concerns. None dared speak openly against Pharaoh's words, but confusion shadowed many faces. The older courtiers, who remembered Hatshepsut's reign with its prosperity and monumental building projects, exchanged particularly troubled glances; they were careful to maintain expressions of solemn agreement whenever a royal guard passed nearby.

Rekhmire, the Grand Vizier who had faithfully served Menkheperre for this past year, approached the throne after the hall had emptied, bowing deeply. His face, lined with the wisdom of fifty years, betrayed nothing of his inner thoughts.

"Ensure that the stonemasons begin immediately with Hatshepsut's monuments," he commanded, his voice lower now, meant only for his vizier's ears. "I want her memory obliterated before the next full moon. No trace must remain."

Rekhmire bowed again, his face betraying nothing of the sadness he felt at the thought of defacing the beautiful works that stood as testament to one of Egypt's most accomplished rulers. "It shall be as you command, Divine One. The crews await only your word."

Menkheperre thought to himself that after a while, the wives, old people, children of the soldiers that died in the Red Sea would believe that their husbands and sons were merely reclaimed by the desert, posted to distant garrisons, or absorbed into the royal bodyguard. The truth would fade like footprints in sand, washed away by the careful construction of an alternative history.

"Let it be known throughout Egypt," he said aloud, his voice hardening with renewed resolve, "that Egypt's glory now lies in Thebes, and here it shall remain until I decree otherwise."

As he rose from the throne, the double crown heavy upon his brow, Menkheperre knew that the battle for his legacy had just begun. Maybe the Hebrews had escaped him, but history would not. On the walls and pillars of Thebes, his craftsmen would carve a different story—one of divine punishment and purification rather than military defeat, of a pharaoh's wisdom rather than his stubborn pride.

And in that story, there would be no mention of a parted sea, no acknowledgment of a god more powerful than Egypt's pantheon. That truth would be washed away, just as surely as the waves had swept away his chariots, leaving nothing but the lie that would preserve his power. He strode from the hall, his sandals slapping against the stone floor, each step taken with the deliberate purpose of a man who understood that perception was more important than reality, that myths outlived men, and that history belonged to those who survived to write it.

The sun beat down mercilessly upon the vast sea of humanity that snaked across the desert floor, sweat-drenched bodies trudging forward in a relentless march toward destiny. Heat rose in shimmering waves from the scorched sand, distorting the distant horizon into a rippling mirage that seemed to mock their progress. The procession stretched back as far as the eye could see—thousands upon thousands of souls.

July 1438 BC - Mount Horeb

Moses, his face weathered by the elements and etched with the responsibility of leading these thousands, stood at a rise in the sand, his eyes fixed upon the jagged silhouette of Mount Horeb that loomed against the horizon. The wooden staff in his hand—the same staff that had turned to a serpent before Pharaoh, that had parted the waters of the Red Sea—now served as a support for his increasingly weary bones.

Two moons had waxed and waned since they had fled the mud-brick hovels of Avaris, leaving behind the whips of their Egyptian masters and the only life many had ever known. Two moons of uncertainty and hardship of miracles and murmurings, of deaths and births beneath the vast canopy of desert stars. The old had died along the way, their bones marking the trail behind them like milestone markers on a Roman road. Infants had been born into freedom, taking their first breaths in a world where they would never know the sting of an overseer's lash.

The desert had tested them with thirst and hunger, with scorching days and bitter nights, yet still they pressed on, bound together by something greater than their suffering. Behind Moses, Aaron and Miriam moved among the people, their voices raised in encouragement, their presence a reminder of the divine purpose that had set them on this extraordinary journey.

"Moses!" The voice belonged to Joshua, a young warrior who had emerged as Moses' most trusted lieutenant. He approached now, his muscular frame glistening with sweat, his eyes gleaming with a faith that had only been strengthened by each miraculous deliverance. "The scouts have returned from the western approach. They report no sign of Egyptian pursuit."

Moses nodded, his eyes never leaving the distant mountain. "They will not follow," he said, his voice deep and resonant, carrying the quiet certainty of one who had witnessed the impossible. "The sea has taken Pharaoh's army, and his pride with it. Egypt will turn inward now, nursing its wounds and rewriting its history to erase the shame of defeat."

Joshua followed Moses' gaze toward Mount Horeb, understanding dawning in his eyes. "That is where He will speak to us again."

A rare smile crossed Moses' weathered face. "Yes. There on the mountain, where I first heard His voice from the burning bush, God will show us the way forward, where we shall become a nation."

As if in acknowledgment of his words, a cooling breeze suddenly swept across the desert, bringing momentary relief from the punishing heat. The people sighed collectively, lifting their faces to the wind, taking it as a sign of divine favor. Their journey had only just begun, but already they were being transformed, forged in the crucible of freedom into something new and unprecedented—a people bound not by shared territory or kings, but by covenant with the unseen God who had broken the power of the mightiest empire on earth.

Moses descended from his vantage point, moving among his people with the quiet authority that had grown within him since that first reluctant encounter at the burning bush. Children reached out to touch his robes as he passed, women offered him water from precious skins, and men straightened their backs in his presence. They had been slaves for four hundred years, their spirits nearly broken by generations of oppression. Now they walked upright, their eyes fixed on a future none of them could fully imagine, but all could feel drawing them forward.

The desert stretched before them, vast and unforgiving. But somewhere beyond its trials lay the land promised to their ancestors, flowing with milk and honey. And it was toward this promise that they marched, one footstep at a time, leaving behind them the false gods and buried treasures of Egypt, carrying with them only what truly mattered: faith in the God who had heard their cries, and the courage to follow Him into the unknown.

Chapter 32 - All is Lost

February 2011 AD – Luxor

The harsh beam of Arthur Maddisson's torch slashed through the darkness of the ancient chamber, illuminating hieroglyphs unseen by human eyes for millennia. Dust particles danced in the light, stirred by his quickened breath as he moved along the weathered limestone walls. Sweat trickled down his temples despite the cool underground air, the salty droplets stinging his eyes, but he dared not wipe them away—not when he was so close to the discovery that would turn conventional Egyptology on its head.

"By God," he breathed, the words escaping in a rush of exhilaration as his calloused fingers traced the distinct cartouche, feeling the ancient chisel marks beneath his touch. "Regnal year forty-eight."

He stepped back, running a hand through his salt-and-pepper hair, its former auburn now faded from years under the merciless Egyptian sun. His weathered face, lined from decades of desert expeditions and academic battles, broke into a rare smile that crinkled the corners of his eyes. After twenty years of being dismissed by his colleagues at Oxford as an eccentric dreamer, vindication was finally within his grasp.

The historical records confirmed the pharaoh's reign continued until his fifty-fourth year, and inscriptions beyond the forty-third year were exceedingly rare. The walls before him held evidence of activities and campaigns from years forty-two through forty-eight—a crucial missing piece of the historical record that the establishment had claimed did not exist. For reasons unknown, the pharaoh never returned to add more inscriptions after this point, though he ruled for six more years. That mystery alone had consumed Arthur's thoughts since his days as a young doctoral student.

Arthur's pencil barrel along across the pages of his field notebook as he meticulously sketched the wall section from multiple angles, his experienced hand capturing every detail of the ancient carvings. The beam of his torch revealed cobwebs in the corners, disturbed for the first time in millennia. The musty scent of enclosed earth mingled with the acrid tang of bat droppings from higher chambers, creating that distinctive aroma Arthur had come to associate with discovery.

Over the past four weeks, working in secrecy beneath the monastery with only Farouk's assistance, he had methodically documented a treasure trove of historical corrections: the references to Hatshepsut from regnal year forty-two, clearly noting "Djeser Akhet next to Hatshepsut's mortuary." This single inscription proved his long-held theory that the famous temple had been constructed with serious architectural flaws—not the masterpiece of engineering that tour guides boasted about and his colleagues defended with religious fervor.

"Philips would choke on his cognac if he saw this," Arthur muttered with grim satisfaction, thinking of his most vocal critic at Cambridge who had once publicly called his theories "the desperate fabrications of a man who peaked too early."

Even more significant was the detailed account of a previously unknown Nubian war from regnal year forty-seven. The hieroglyphs described a massive campaign that historians had somehow missed—or deliberately obscured. The wall depicted the pharaoh himself, standing tall in his chariot, bow drawn as he faced an army of Nubian warriors. Arthur's skilled drawings captured every nuance of the carved figures, the accompanying text speaking of villages burned, thousands captured, and tributes of gold and ivory flowing back to Egypt. This wasn't merely a footnote to history; it was an entire chapter that had been erased.

"They'll have to listen now," Arthur murmured, his voice echoing against the limestone walls, carrying the weight of decades of ridicule and dismissal. The establishment had ridiculed his theories for years, but stone doesn't lie. Those pompous bastards in their comfortable university offices would have to acknowledge him now. Once he presented these detailed sketches and translations...

The sudden thunder of footsteps above jolted him from his thoughts, the vibrations sending fine particles of dust raining down into the shaft onto the lift. Something was happening—something violent and urgent. Arthur's heart slammed against his ribs as he hastily gathered his equipment, shoving notebooks and sketching materials into his weathered leather satchel.

He quickly jumped into the lift, more dust raining down. The winding mechanism protested as the platform began its slow ascent, carrying him from the depths of history back to the uncertain present.

As he ascended to the top, Farouk's anxious face appeared at the opening, the Egyptian's normally composed features twisted with fear. His dark eyes, usually alight with intellectual curiosity, now flashed with panic as he helped Arthur out of the lift.

"We must hide everything inside the lift, Professor," Farouk urged, his English precise despite his agitation. "The Egyptian Antiquities Society is at the entrance gate. They believe there are illegal digging happening, treasure hunting. They are performing an inspection!"

Arthur felt the blood drain from his face as he realized the potential consequences. Not just academic disgrace, but imprisonment—Egyptian authorities dealt harshly with those who disturbed archaeological sites without proper permits. His connection to the monastery had allowed him to bypass the usual channels, but that protection would evaporate the moment officials discovered what lay beneath the guest quarters.

"How did they find out?" Arthur demanded, already moving with surprising agility for a man of sixty-two, gathering the remaining equipment.

Farouk shook his head, the worry lines between his brows deepening. "Perhaps someone talked. The village has many eyes, Professor, and many ears eager for reward money."

As quickly as they could, they placed everything into the lift— sketching supplies, tools, notes—and closed the door that led to the hidden passage. The room now looked like a normal guest house again, with no evidence of their clandestine activities beneath.

Arthur's heart still hammered in his chest as he surveyed the room, looking for any telltale signs they might have missed. The bed was neatly made; books arranged casually on the small table—nothing to suggest anything beyond a visiting scholar's temporary residence. Only the fine layer of limestone dust on his boots might betray them, and he hurriedly wiped them clean with a cloth he then stuffed into his pocket.

Bishop Christos burst through the front door, his black robes billowing behind him like the wings of a great raven, face flushed with exertion and fear. The elderly cleric's silver beard trembled with each labored breath, his normally serene features distorted by an emotion Arthur had never seen in the man before—pure terror.

"Farouk!" he shouted, his voice sharp with urgency. "They're attacking the church! We must get out—now!"

Arthur's head snapped up from his final inspection of the room. "Who's attacking?"

"Muslim Brotherhood," Christos panted, already moving toward the passage that led to the rear of the monastery complex. "They've stormed past the Antiquities inspectors. A mob has gathered—they're setting fire to the outer buildings!"

Arthur felt a cold knot form in his stomach. Political tensions had been simmering throughout the region for months. The distant roar of an angry mob filtered down from the gate, punctuated by the crash of breaking glass and what sounded horribly like gun shots. Arthur cursed savagely, grabbing his bag and passport from beneath the thin mattress where he always kept them. He hesitated, looking toward the concealed lift entrance, thinking of all they were leaving behind—not just his equipment, but the evidence. Four weeks of pain staking documentation, the detailed drawings that would prove his theories correct.

Farouk saw the direction of his gaze and gripped his arm with surprising strength. "Professor, no," he said firmly. "The evidence means nothing if you are dead."

Arthur looked at the door, and it was as if Farouk could read his intentions through the tension in his muscles, the stubborn set of his jaw that had earned him the nickname "The Bull" among his graduate students.

"No time!" the bishop hissed, pulling him toward the narrow escape corridor, his gnarled fingers digging into Arthur's sleeve. "They've already breached the front entrance! They are calling for Christian blood!"

The old scholar in Arthur wanted to resist, to retrieve just one notebook from the supplies below, but the survivalist in him—the man who had weathered sandstorms in the Western Desert and flash floods in the Valley of the Kings—knew better. With a last, agonized glance at the hidden panel, he allowed himself to be pulled away.

They followed Bishop Christos through the church to the back of the monastery through a hidden door disguised as a confessional booth—a relic from more dangerous times that had, sadly, become necessary once again. The narrow passage smelled of mold and ancient incense, forcing them to move sideways at points where the walls closed in. Arthur's shoulders scraped against rough stone as they hurried through, the sounds of destruction growing louder behind them.

They emerged blinking into the blinding Egyptian sunlight, the intensity of it momentarily stunning after the dim interior of the monastery. A Land Rover waited, engine running, partially hidden behind a stand of date palms. Richard Blackwood sat behind the wheel, his lean frame tense, knuckles white where they gripped the steering wheel. Beside him, Amara Khalil's dark eyes widened with relief as she spotted them emerging from the hidden doorway.

"Thank God," Richard called out, his clipped British accent tight with stress. "We've been trying to reach you for days, Arthur! The whole region's gone up like a powder keg!"

Amara turned in her seat, her olive complexion pale with concern. "The borders are closing, Professor. We need to get to Cairo immediately."

The vehicle lurched forward, tires spinning on the dusty ground as Richard navigated the narrow track that wound down from the monastery plateau.

Arthur twisted in his seat at the sound of a tremendous explosion, looking back just in time to see the guest house in which he had been staying collapse with a thunderous roar as a bomb went off inside its ancient walls. A column of black smoke rose against the piercing blue sky, carrying with it the ashes of his evidence.

The shock wave rocked the Land Rover, sending small stones pattering against its sides like deadly hail. Richard swore colorfully as he fought to keep the vehicle on the narrow track, the tires sliding dangerously close to the edge where a steep drop awaited them.

"They had explosives," Arthur murmured in disbelief, watching flames engulf what remained of the monastery's eastern wing. The fire spread quickly, devouring the dry wooden fixtures inside the stone buildings. "Dear God, they came prepared for destruction."

"It's happening all over," Amara said grimly, her fingers flying over her satellite phone. "Coordinated attacks on Christian sites across three governorates. Someone's stirring the pot deliberately."

As they sped away, Arthur's mind raced through calculations—how quickly the fire would spread, whether the underground chamber would survive, how long it would take for the authorities to secure the area. But deep down, he knew. The site would be buried under tons of debris, the entrance to the chamber crushed beyond recognition. His discovery was lost.

Farouk seemed to read his thoughts. "Perhaps when things calm down," he offered, though his tone held little conviction. "Perhaps we could return..."

Arthur shook his head, watching the monastery recede in the distance, the pillar of smoke now visible for miles across the desert plain. The evidence that would have filled a critical gap in Egyptian history was gone, trapped beneath stone and ashes, waiting once more for the slow march of centuries to pass.

The Land Rover bounced mercilessly over the rough desert track, each jolt a physical reminder of Arthur's failure to secure his discovery. In the distance, the silver ribbon of the Nile gleamed under the afternoon sun, indifferent to the human dramas playing out along its ancient banks, just as it had been for thousands of years.

Cairo International Airport

The Cairo International Airport seethed with humanity—businessmen clutching briefcases, families corralling children, tourists laden with souvenirs of pyramids and sphinxes. The air was thick with a babel of languages, announcements echoing unintelligibly through the vast terminal. Armed guards patrolled in pairs, their eyes constantly scanning the crowds, fingers resting near triggers—a subtle but unmistakable sign of the tensions gripping the country.

Arthur sat apart from the bustle, his salvaged notebook open before him on the cracked plastic seat. Every detail of his lost discoveries was recorded in his precise handwriting on these pages, accompanied by detailed sketches that captured every hieroglyph and carving he had found. But pencil drawings on paper were a poor substitute for the firsthand examination now buried beneath tons of rubble.

Farouk dropped into the seat beside him, two paper cups of strong, sweet coffee in hand. The young man had refused to leave Arthur's side despite the professor's insistence that he would be safer with his family in Alexandria.

"What now?" Farouk asked, his dark eyes studying Arthur's face with intensity. Arthur accepted the coffee with a nod of thanks, the aromatic steam rising between them. He took a sip, the bitter liquid scalding his tongue, but he welcomed the pain—anything to distract from the hollow ache in his chest.

"Nobody will believe me," he said at last, his voice rough with frustration and the lingering effects of smoke inhalation. "All the proof is gone. We'd have to dig through ten meters of dirt and rubble to recover anything, and that's assuming the chamber itself wasn't completely destroyed in the blast."

"Your drawings—" Farouk began, leaning forward earnestly.

"Drawings aren't enough," Arthur cut in, tapping his notebook with a sharp gesture. "Not for something this revolutionary. The academic vultures will tear me apart without being able to examine the inscriptions firsthand. You know how it works, Farouk. Extraordinary claims require extraordinary evidence. All I have now are my sketches and my word—neither of which will satisfy the establishment."

Arthur stared into his coffee, the dark liquid reflecting his haggard face. The lines around his eyes had deepened dramatically in just twenty-four hours, the weight of his lost discovery etching itself into his features.

"I had it, Farouk," he continued, his voice dropping to nearly a whisper. "Right there in front of me. Proof that would have transformed our understanding of Ancient Egypt. The Nubian war campaign completely missing from historical records—an entire military expedition with thousands of soldiers that somehow never made it into the official accounts. And those inscriptions from years forty-four through forty-eight..." He trailed off, the magnitude of the loss settling on his shoulders like physical weight.

Farouk placed a hand on Arthur's arm, the gesture conveying a depth of understanding that words could not. The young Egyptian had invested his own dreams in their shared discovery, risking his promising career for a chance at historical truth.

"At least I know what I saw, what I discovered," Arthur conceded after a moment, straightening slightly. "But without access to those walls, the academic world will dismiss it as speculation—or worse, fabrication. Philips will have a field day. He's been waiting for years to discredit me completely."

The overhead speakers crackled to life, announcing his flight to London. As he rose to board, gathering their meagre belongings, Farouk clasped Arthur's shoulder firmly, his grip conveying both strength and solidarity.

"Maybe someone will find something else," he said, his eyes bright with stubborn hope. "Something that proves what you saw on those walls. The truth has a way of emerging, Professor." Arthur nodded grimly, wanting to believe the man's optimism. "Maybe. But I won't hold my breath. For now, I need to get safely to London."

As he joined the queue for boarding, Arthur noticed Amara and Richard already at the gate, deep in conversation with a man who looked distinctly like a British embassy official. Richard caught his eye and gave a slight nod—they had secured safe passage. At least something had gone right today.

The Boeing 747 climbed steadily into the cloudless Egyptian sky, the roar of its engines drowning out the chaotic thoughts swirling through Arthur's mind. From his window seat, he gazed down as the sprawling chaos of Cairo gave way to the geometric precision of irrigated fields along the Nile—neat green squares bordered by the relentless tan of desert, an ancient pattern unchanged since pharaonic times.

He pressed his forehead against the cool glass, exhaustion finally catching up with him now that the immediate danger had passed.

The aircraft banked slightly, turning towards the Mediterranean Sea. Soon Egypt would be behind him, physically if not mentally. London awaited with its gray skies and academic politics, the familiar battlegrounds where Arthur had fought and lost so many times before.

Arthur's thoughts turned to Moses and the ancient Israelites who had supposedly fled this land thousands of years ago, crossing the same desert he now viewed from 10,000 meters. Another story that blended myth and history, accepted or rejected based on evidence—or the lack thereof. How many true stories had been lost to time simply because proof did not survive? How many discoveries buried forever beneath sand or stone or water?

Below him lay the land of pharaohs and prophets, of mysteries buried in sand and stone. Somewhere down there, beneath the rubble of a blown-up monastery, lay the truth he had briefly held before his eyes. The truth about the missing years of a pharaoh's reign, about a construction that defied conventional wisdom, about a war that history had forgotten.

Why had the pharaoh stopped visiting this place after his forty-eighth year? What had happened in those final six years of his reign that had kept him away? Another mystery to add to the countless others that Egypt still held, another question that might have been answered if only his access to the chamber had survived.

Perhaps one day, someone would uncover it again. Perhaps one day, the establishment would be forced to acknowledge what he alone now knew. Until then, the ancient secrets remained buried, just as they had been for thousands of years before his brief intrusion.

The Red Sea stretched out beneath the aircraft, an endless blue expanse separating continent from continent, its waters reflecting the harsh sunlight in dazzling patterns that hurt the eyes. Arthur leaned back in his seat, finally allowing his burning eyelids to close. He had crossed his own Red Sea of sorts—from certainty to doubt, from triumph to loss. But he carried the knowledge with him, even if he couldn't prove it to the world.

Not yet anyway.

The airplane continued eastward, leaving Egypt behind, carrying Arthur and his unverifiable truth toward an uncertain future. In his breast pocket, pressed close to his heart, lay his notebook—sixty pages of detailed observations and careful sketches that now represented the only remaining record of what might have been the discovery of his lifetime.

As he drifted toward exhausted sleep, Arthur wondered if this was how it felt to be Moses—to have glimpsed the promised land, only to know that you would never set foot there. To carry a truth that others would question, to face the wilderness knowing that vindication might come only after your time had passed. His last conscious thought before sleep claimed him was of those hieroglyphs, perfectly preserved for thousands of years, now lost once more to the darkness of time, waiting for another discoverer, another moment when their ancient messages might finally be heard.

To be continued…

Author Commentary & Notes

Understanding the Real People and Events Behind the Story

This novel is a work of historical fiction — but every fictional thread has been carefully woven through the fabric of real history.

What you've just read is not merely a tale for entertainment. It is a narrative built on extensive research into the Bible, Egyptian history, and ancient Near Eastern cultures. Wherever possible, I used the real names of historical figures, their actual timelines, and the locations, inscriptions, and the Egyptian records and the scriptural references that support or hint at their existence.

But history often leaves gaps — and it is in these gaps that storytelling begins.

— *Mechiel Pentz*

Rolf Krauss Chronology

The historical framework follows the Bible as a primary reference, synchronized with the Egyptian chronology as outlined by Rolf Krauss.

Kamose	1542-1539
Ahmose I	1539-1514
Amenhotep I	1514-1493
Thutmose I	1493-1482
Thutmose II	1482-1479
Hatshepsut	1479-1458
Thutmose III	1479-1426

The works of the ancient historian Josephus have also been considered, offering valuable insights into how later traditions preserved key historical moments.

Ancient Egypt Map

This map shows the cities, landmarks, and cataracts mentioned in the book, at the end of the 17th dynasty, for the reader's reference, spanning from Tjaru in the Nile Delta of Lower Egypt in the north to Meroe in the southern region of Nubia."

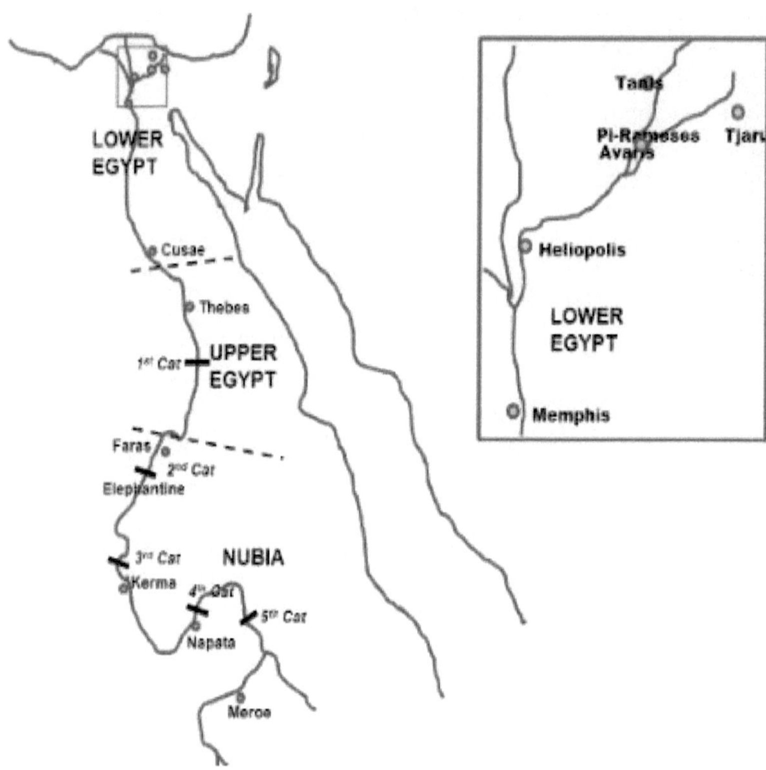

Pi-Ramesses and Avaris

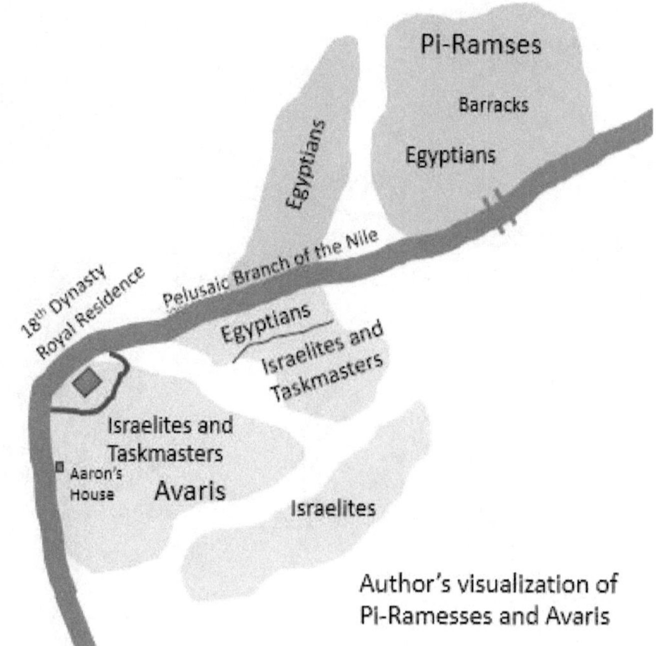

Author's visualization of Pi-Ramesses and Avaris

Exodus Route and Red Sea Crossing

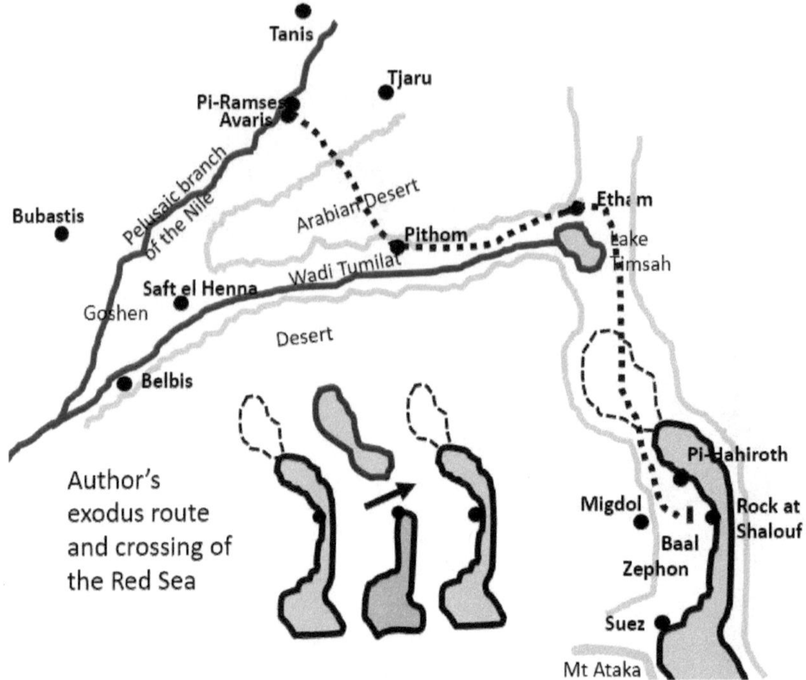

Author's Exodus route and Crossing of the Red Sea

9 781764 162579